COME BACK
TO ME

Kevin McGann

COME BACK
TO ME

Hometown Publishers

Hometown Publishers
www.hometownpublishers.com

First Published by Hometown Publishers April 2022.

ISBN: 978-1-7777725-4-3 (Paperback)
ISBN: 978-1-7777725-5-0 (E-book)

Library and Archives Canada (LAC) national library collection.

Cover Design by Kevin McGann.
Front Cover Photograph by Marina Pechnikova/Pexels.

Dedication

To Mathew, Jessica,

Daphne, and Brendan

To my parents,

Maria and Charles

Acknowledgements

To my family and friends,
for their invaluable contribution
and on-going support.
Thank you.

Chapter 1

Sunday, December 20, 2009

Thomas hung up the phone and put on his jacket before returning to the kitchen to pick up the piece of paper that he had written the information on. He glanced at his watch; it was almost twelve. He could catch her for lunch and tell her the exciting news, he thought, as he closed the door behind him.

Outside the wind was brisk, so he did up his jacket then looked up at the cloudy sky. They were calling for snow over the next few days, and he smiled at the likelihood of there being a white Christmas, before sauntering down the path to the sidewalk.

As he strolled down the street, he recalled how much fun they had putting up the Christmas tree and decorating the room, and how excited they were when they talked about going shopping for presents this afternoon. While Thomas contemplated their holiday plans, he smiled happily at the people passing by with their bags filled with gifts. There was definitely a feeling of Christmas in the air and Thomas was looking forward to spending his first with fiancée.

"My little girl!" screamed a woman standing to Thomas's far left. He turned to watch her drop her bags, point over his shoulder, and start in his direction. Thomas turned around to see a young girl on the road picking something off the ground. He looked at the approaching car, and at the driver talking on his cell phone, not paying attention to the road. Thomas realized he wouldn't see the girl till it was too late. Maybe he could shove her out of the way, but he would be pushing her into on-coming traffic from the other direction, and they would both be hit. He could grab her, throw her off the road onto the sidewalk, but there was no guarantee she would make it. Definitely not, if the car tried to swerve out of the way. As these options ran through his head, Thomas was already moving toward the girl and picking her up. He wrapped himself around her, pulled her close to his body and protected her head with his hands, then waited for the impact. The driver slammed on the brakes, but it was too late, he hit Thomas with the full force of the car.

Thomas felt a tremendous pain in his legs as he was lifted off the ground and into the air. He held the girl tightly as his right shoulder and right side of his back hit the windshield, and along with the sound of the glass shattering, he heard the distinct cracking of his bones. He bounced off the windshield, turned in the air, then landed on the trunk on his back with a loud thump, it was followed by his head whiplashing off the metal with a sickening thud. He rolled off the car and onto the road still cradling the girl's head and body as blood poured out onto the street. Thomas saw a bright light, then everything went black.

Chapter 2

Three Months Earlier

Thomas Carlyle quickly walked through the revolving door of the luxurious, downtown hotel. He quickly glanced over the foyer, spotted the escalator, and went in its direction. While descending he removed his overcoat and looked in the mirror, I'm glad I bought this suit, he thought. Thomas noticed his dirty blond hair was wind-blown and calmed it down with his right hand before walking off, stopping at the coat check, and proceeding to the Grand Ballroom. He stopped at the closed doors and read the sign to the left of the entrance, 'First National Ballet Fundraiser.' Inside, he could hear someone speaking, and realized that he was something he didn't want to be, late. "I hope these doors are at the back," he whispered nervously as he slowly clasped his hand around the door handle and turned it. Thomas stopped for a moment, wishing now he hadn't come, and thought about leaving. When he faintly heard the speaker saying thank you, and the audience starting to clap, he knew it was now or never. He took a deep breath, opened the door, and walked in.

All the tables were to the right and spread out in a half-moon shape around the hall. To his left was a raised platform with a podium on it, and a DJ's stereo system and speakers. The space in between the tables and the podium was the dance floor, which is where he now anxiously stood, and somewhere amongst the three hundred and forty-nine guests and thirty-five tables was his empty seat. He didn't want to continue to stand where he was, nor did he want to go from table to table. How will I ever find it? he thought. As Thomas was contemplating what to do next, he hadn't noticed a lady walking onto the podium until she introduced the new Artistic Director of the First National Ballet, Alfred 'Alfie' Smythe. Then watched as a man in his late fifties, sporting a traditional black tuxedo, crossed the dance floor to the loud applause of the audience. Alfie thanked the lady at the podium, shuffled some papers, and surveyed the tables from right to left. Thomas started to retreat to the back of the room unnoticed, but it was too late.

"Young fellow…young fellow," called Alfie in his English accent.

Thomas was so busy trying to make it to the back, behind the tables, that he didn't hear him.

"Young fellow," he said again and conceded Thomas was oblivious to his summons. "Please, can someone…" he said pointing toward Thomas.

Thomas suddenly noticed people at the table closest to him were trying to get his attention and pointing, as he followed their fingers to the podium, he realized everyone was staring at him.

"Hello, young man, can I help you find your seat?"

Thomas wanted to say no and crawl under the table but replied in a shaky voice. "Uh…yes, please." Someone at a far table slowly stood and waved him over. Thank God, he was rescued, he thought, and started towards them.

Alfie hadn't noticed the girl standing. "Why don't you come up to the podium and we will get this sorted out?"

Rather than make a scene, Thomas changed direction. There's the door, he thought, I should bolt. Instead, with everyone watching, he shyly climbed onto the podium.

Alfie stood away from the microphone. "Welcome young man," he said with an outstretched hand.

Thomas shook his hand and felt a little more at ease.

"What's your name?"

"Thomas Carlyle," he replied quietly.

Alfie motioned toward the microphone to inquire about his seat, but abruptly stopped, and glanced at Thomas. "Maggie Carlyle?" he questioned.

"She's my grandmother."

To Thomas's surprise, Alfie hugged him. "Maggie was a very dear friend, and I'm sorry to hear of her passing," he whispered. Alfie stood back and was fighting back tears as he turned around to the audience and spoke. "Please excuse me for one more moment ladies and gentlemen." Alfie moved away from the microphone and gazed at Thomas. "I want to apologize to you and your family, I was on vacation in Europe and didn't hear about her passing and funeral till it was too late," he said sincerely. "She was a lovely lady and I'm truly sorry for your loss."

"I understand, thank you," replied Thomas detecting the sadness in his eyes. "She always spoke very highly of you, Alfie," he said leaning over, "or should I say, Alfred the Great."

Alfie laughed out loud, and recalled how Margaret used to call him Alfred the Great when he was being arrogant. It was her polite way of telling him to stop, and she was right to do so, he was egotistical back then.

After a while, Maggie stopped calling him that, and one day he asked her why? "Alfie, there isn't a need to anymore," she replied, "because now you are truly a dancer and a gentleman." Over the years, he never forgot how her kindness and patience not only molded him into a dancer and a gentleman, but also as an artistic director. He affectionately squeezed Thomas's arm, gathered his thoughts, and turned to the audience. "Five minutes ago, I was going to read from these," he said picking up sheets of paper, crumpling them up, and throwing them to the floor. "But I've decided not to, instead, I am going to tell you this story," he revealed glancing at Thomas. "This young fellow is the grandson of the greatest ballerina this company, the world, has ever seen, Margaret Carlyle…Her presence electrified the stage, and her commitment was unprecedented and second to none…When talking with this young man just now, a lifetime of fond memories flashed through my mind." He paused momentarily. "Some of the information I am going to share with you is second hand, so I am going to ask…" Alfie surveyed the crowd. "Where's Hank Lewis?" A seventy-eight-year-old raised his hand. "There you are! Hank, if I say something incorrect, please speak out and make sure you put me on the right track." Hank responded by putting his thumb up. "Fifty years ago, Hank was the stage manager, musical director, and accountant for the company, not at different times, all at the same time!" stated Alfie to the laughter of the guests. "Back then, the company performed at a playhouse down by the waterfront, and it was also where our local dance academy held their recitals, competitions, and so on…It was at one of these competitions that Margaret was noticed by the American Ballet School of Dance and was asked to take the examination and accepted. During this time, the company and playhouse helped her with her tuition, and let me tell you, it was money well spent," acknowledged Alfie. "Years later, when she started dancing professionally, Margaret would send a portion of her salary to the company and playhouse and did so till the day she retired. And she was one of the reasons why the company and playhouse was able to grow and become what you all know fondly know today as the First National Ballet…But it wasn't just the money," clarified Alfie. "It was also about the time she took out of her busy schedule to participate in fundraisers or volunteer her time to teach classes…Let's not forget, she was doing this when she was one of the best in the world…At forty, she retired from dancing professionally, and taught ballet for twenty-five years at the First National Ballet School. Each year, giving one student a scholarship to help pay for their tuition costs…Maggie was a kind, generous, loving lady, who never forgot where it was, she came from," he said reflecting for a moment. "And it's her kind, generous spirit that I would like us to capture this evening at our fundraiser, thank you." There was a loud applause as Alfie left the microphone. He stopped in front of Thomas, squeezed his shoulder, and smiled. 'Thank you," he whispered, then climbed down the three steps back to his table unaware that he had left Thomas alone on the platform.

Chapter 3

A girl in her late twenties strolled across the dance floor toward Thomas. She was wearing an elegant black evening gown that clung tightly to her perfect figure, and her blonde hair was pulled back into a French braid, and when she stopped to look up at him her emerald, green eyes sparkled. "Thomas Carlyle," she said.

"Yes," he replied walking down the steps.

"I believe you are sitting at our table," she said opening up her arm. "My name is Rachel Carter, please, let me escort you to your seat."

"Thank you, Rachel," he said putting his arm through hers.

She led him to their table and introduced him to the eight people sitting around it: there was Dr. Victor Gordon and Dr. Geoffrey Mann, and their wives, Joanne and Mary; Mr. Barry Levinson and Ms. Beverly Cross, who were lawyers; Mr. Jack Collins, who was a very close friend of the Carter's; and Jessica Carter, Rachel's mother, who was just as stunning and could have been mistaken for Rachel's older sister.

"Hello, Thomas, nice to meet you," said Jessica with a kind smile.

"Nice to meet you, Mrs. Carter."

"Oh please, Jessica."

"Okay, Jessica," confirmed Thomas timidly, and waited for Rachel to sit before taking the vacant spot between her and Mr. Collins.

"Dom Pérignon?" asked Mr. Collins picking up the bottle.

"Please."

"At fifteen hundred dollars a head we should be getting a bottle each," suggested Mr. Collins. "What do you think?" he asked glancing at Thomas as he poured.

"I'll wait first and see if they break out the Glenfiddich and cigars after dessert," replied Thomas with a nervous grin.

Mr. Collins laughed loudly, gave an approving nod, then filled Jessica's flute.

Thomas turned to Rachel. "Are you a ballerina?" he asked hypnotized by her eyes.

"No, one of my closest friends became a principal dancer this year, and my parents are patrons," she explained with a smile before taking a sip of her champagne. "When I was younger, girls my age wanted to dance, sing, or do gymnastics, I preferred dressing up, putting on makeup, and pretending to be on the catwalk, and trust me, my mother has pictures and videos to prove it and embarrass me for the rest of my life," she said with a chuckle. "So, I started off appearing in catalogues, flyers, that sort of stuff, and luckily, when I was at university, I was able to continue to do it part-time. Today, I just model whenever I can."

"Are you kept busy?"

"Somewhat," she replied, holding back a smile.

"Well, I hope it picks up," he said sincerely. "I take it you enjoy it?"

"I love it! I really do! But going forward I would like to do something involving children, maybe run a daycare center or a children's camp. That's my dream. In fact, that's what I went to university for," she said glancing up at him. "What about you?"

As soon as she asked, the conversations others were having around them suddenly stopped, either by coincidence or on purpose, and they all listened in. "I work during the day and write in my spare time."

"Really, who do you work for?" inquired Mr. Collins.

"I work for QTech."

"Computers," he said with an air of approval. "Management?"

"No, distribution specialist," answered Thomas feeling uncomfortable, not with what he did, but with all the attention he was receiving.

"Many great men have started on the lower rung and worked their way up the ladder of success, some have even gone on to start their own companies and are multimillionaires today," said Jessica genuinely.

"I've heard they make great laptops," said Mr. Levinson.

"The best on the market," replied Thomas honestly.

"I've had mine for a few years now and I've been looking around for a new one," revealed Mr. Levinson. "I've done some research and QTech comes highly recommended."

"If you decide to buy one, I can put you in touch with someone who can offer you top of the line with a good discount," offered Thomas. "If you like, I can give you my phone?"

"Thank you, I'd appreciate that," replied Mr. Levinson.

Throughout the four courses Mr. Collins made negative comments about the meal: the soup was cold, there was not enough salad, the steak was the size of a meatball, and the dessert was too rich. His only approval went to the French red wine. Surprisingly to Thomas, all the comments he made were in his direction, and he wasn't sure why.

"Ladies and gentlemen, your attention please," instructed the MC. "I hope everyone enjoyed their meal?" he asked, prompting Thomas to quickly glance at Mr. Collins, who gave the MC a disapproving look, and hold back his laughter. "As is tradition, in a couple of minutes we will be presenting the Margaret Carlyle Scholarship Award to an up-and-coming dancer who has excelled in the areas of ballet, scholastics, and volunteer work. The same fine qualities that our beloved Margaret Carlyle possessed. This year's recipient will also receive a personalized crystal award, and have her name added to the past winners' plaque that resides at the First National Ballet School. After the presentation, the DJ will take over and the bar will be open, and throughout the evening, I will be stopping the music for special fundraiser events and activities, so please give generously," she said warmly. "So, on behalf of Margaret Carlyle, I ask her grandson, Thomas Carlyle, to join me and present the Margaret Carlyle Scholarship Award. Thomas, if you can please come to the podium, thank you."

Thomas had forgotten all about the presentation. He felt inside his pockets and quickly realized he'd left his notes in his overcoat. He slowly rose and headed to the podium thinking about what he was going to say as the audience clapped. He climbed the steps, positioned the microphone, and took a deep breath. "It looks as if I am standing between you and the bar," he joked followed by laughter. As he waited for it to subside, he fondly remembered his grandmother, and spoke from his heart. "Each of you knew Margaret Carlyle either as a ballerina, a colleague, a teacher, a friend, or perhaps if you were lucky enough, a combination of all four. Unfortunately, I was too young to ever see my grandmother dance professionally but was fortunate enough to meet many of her colleagues and friends who would visit her often and reminisce about the old days. Most of you are here tonight, and I would like to thank you all for spending that time with her, and creating those fond memories for me…As many of you know, Margaret Carlyle lived and breathed ballet, and her devotion and passion were contagious to those fortunate enough to be around her or watch her perform on stage…She was without a doubt, a ballerina in the truest sense of the word, and her renowned performances lifted her to the elite status as one of the greatest ballerinas of all time…Today, Margaret Carlyle is regarded as the most influential role model for professional and aspiring dancers," stated Thomas pausing momentarily. "After her career ended, her happiest days were filled getting up in the morning to teach her students ballet, then coming home in the evening and excitedly talking about each and every one of them…And every year, with youth-full enthusiasm and child-like excitement, she looked forward to presenting her scholarship award, which she cherished dearly." Thomas stopped and held up the envelope. "In here, is this year's recipient of the Margaret

Carlyle Scholarship Award, and unless there are any objections, I find it only fitting that I ask Ms. Penelope Daily, a teacher of twenty-five years, a respected member of the First National Ballet, and a very dear and close friend of my grandmother to come up to the podium to present this award on her behalf, not only this year, but every year."

There was a loud standing applause as Penelope Daily, a slight woman with long silvery hair, walked onto the platform, stopped in front of Thomas, gave him a hug and a kiss on the cheek, then continued to the podium. "Thank you, Tommy, for this honor," she said with a slight Dutch accent and tears in her eyes.

Thomas stood back and off to the right and listened as Penelope presented the award, he then moved forward to shake the recipient's hand before following them off the stage. As he walked toward his table, someone from behind grabbed his arm, and he turned to face a watery-eyed Penelope. "Tommy, thank you, you've made me so very happy," she said with a smile and admiring him. "You remind me so much of your grandmother, so kind and generous, and always giving without a second thought." She affectionately caressed his cheek before kissing it and merrily sauntering away.

Thomas returned to an empty table, looked around, and saw a crowd of men at the bar and noticed Mr. Collins was one of them. He then spotted Jessica and Rachel with a group of women heading out to the foyer and decided to take this opportunity to go outside onto the patio.

Chapter 4

The late summer air was cool and refreshing on Thomas's face as he walked off the patio onto a path that led him into a quaint garden. The lights of the old-fashioned lampposts gave off a romantic glow as he stopped, looked up at them, then beyond to the multitude of stars in the sky. He continued down the path, and off to his left, nestled in amongst bushes, was a gazebo that was too small for a band to play on but large enough for several people to sit in, and it was the centerpiece of the garden. He climbed up the two steps, sat down, and stared at the ground and thought about Kate. Law school consumed a lot of her free time, and it was expensive, but she was happy and doing well. Still, he wished she could have been here tonight.

"May I sit down?"

Thomas hadn't noticed the figure standing in front of him and glanced up at Rachel. "Of course."

"Are you sure? It looked like you were deep in thought," she said. "Maybe you want to be alone?"

"No, please sit, I would enjoy the company."

Thomas glimpsed at her body as she turned to sit next to him. She had a perfect figure, full rounded breasts, and he wondered what she modeled.

"It's a beautiful night," she said turning to face him. "Late summer and fall are my favorite times of the year. The bright sunny skies, all that color, the cool air, and star-filled nights"

"Mine too," agreed Thomas with slow nod.

She studied him curiously. "Do you ever go horseback riding?"

"Well, I've tried it once, no, twice."

"Did you like it?"

Thomas laughed. "It was fun, although I was a bit sore afterwards," confessed Thomas remembering the experience. "When you're on the horse, eh, the place where you put your feet?"

"Stirrups," said Rachel helping him out.

"Thank you, stirrups. They were either too high or too low, or something like that, so my body wasn't centered when I was riding, and I kept bouncing up and down in my saddle. Afterwards, I couldn't walk upright for a few days."

"That would be painful!" acknowledged Rachel giggling.

"Do you go horseback riding a lot?"

"Almost every weekend," she replied then looked up at the sky. "Tonight, would have been perfect, the stars are so beautiful and bright." She leaned back and let out a sigh. "I'm glad we're alone. It finally gives us some time to talk without my mother and Mr. Collins listening in."

"Your mom seems very nice."

"Oh, she is, and we're very close," she said glancing over at him. "So, what should we talk about?"

"How about you tell me about your modeling, and if you know any famous models?"

"I would rather talk about your writing," suggested Rachel moving closer to him.

He was about to reply when a couple approached them.

"Hello, Rachel."

"Hello, Mr. and Mrs. Cartwright."

"How's your father?" asked Mr. Cartwright.

"He's doing well."

"Shame he's missing tonight," said Mrs. Cartwright.

"It is. He was supposed to be here but was delayed in Atlanta so he's flying back tomorrow morning."

"Oh, poor dear," she replied.

"Thomas, is it?" queried Mr. Cartwright.

"Yes," he replied standing and shaking his hand.

"This is my wife Agnus, and I'm Fred, it's nice to meet you."

"You too," he said shaking Agnus's hand.

"It was a lovely speech, and a nice touch with Penelope, you made her night. There aren't many young, chivalrous gentlemen left these days," commented Fred. "We never knew your grandmother personally, but we saw her dance many, many times, she was—"

"So graceful and elegant," finished Agnus.

"Thank you both, you're very kind."

Rachel, realizing that the Cartwright's weren't in any hurry to leave, stood and motioned to Thomas. "Can we go for that walk now, before it gets too cold?"

"Sure," he replied a little puzzled as he got up, "it was nice meeting you."

"You too, young man," said Fred.

"Say hello to your father, Rachel," said Agnes.

"I will," she confirmed as she put her arm through Thomas's.

They left the gazebo and leisurely strolled in the opposite direction of the patio. At the end of the garden, close to the stone wall, there were spruce trees, bushes, and in the middle, a two-seated bench. They sat silently and both gazed up at the full moon as its light fell upon them. Thomas took off his coat, and as he put it around her, Rachel smiled at him and thought about how nice he was.

Thomas noticed a sprinkling of very faint freckles on her nose. "I like your freckles."

Rachel covered her nose with her hand. "Oh no, not enough make up."

"What do you mean?"

"I don't like them," she declared. "When I was younger, they were more prominent, so I was teased a lot at school. Over time, they've faded, but I guess I'm still a little self-conscious about them."

"Well, I like them," reassured Thomas gently moving her hand away from her face.

"Okay," she said liking the feel of his touch.

Thomas let go of her hand and pointed to the big dipper, and as Rachel looked on with him, she went back and forth about the best way to ask him and decided on a lead in question first.

"Do you have any plans next Saturday night?" she asked hesitantly.

"No, I don't think so."

"I'm having a party. Would you like to come?"

"Can I say no?" teased Thomas.

"Nooo," said Rachel with a grin.

"Then I guess it's a yes," replied Thomas.

Rachel stood excitedly and beckoned Thomas to join her. "Come on, I have an invitation inside, and I'll get it for you," she said grabbing his hand and leading him down the path. When they got back to the patio, she returned his coat, thanked him, and said she would meet him back at the table. As she crossed the dance floor, she could still smell his Trussardi cologne on her, and thought about how wonderful he was.

When Thomas returned to his seat, there was a scotch and cigar waiting for him. Mr. Collins, who was talking to Jessica, broke off their conversation when he noticed him. "Glenfiddich and a cigar," he said turning in his seat and wearing a grin. "Compliments of me," he continued as he stood.

"Thank you," acknowledged Thomas smiling back.

"The drink's for now, cigar is for later, when we're outside" he said, then touched his glass with Thomas's, and patted him on the back. "I know some people would say that after a meal, a Napoleon brandy would be more suited with a cigar," queried Jack glancing at Thomas for a response.

"Perhaps, Mr. Collins, that would be the right thing to do, etiquette and all," replied Thomas carefully. "But you look like a man who likes to do whatever he wants, so you will drink your Glenfiddich, and not worry too much about what others think," said Thomas, pausing for effect, "especially when you're paying for it."

Mr. Collins laughed. "You have a good eye for people. You should be a salesman," he said leaning forward. "Forget these fancy, pretty, decorated meals. There's a place I know that serves steak the size of your fist, has fifteen different types of scotch, serves every brand of beer, and twenty televisions, all with sports," he whispered. "One day I'll take you there because I know you'll appreciate it."

"Okay, Mr. Collins," replied Thomas glancing up at him as he sipped his scotch, not sure if he was being serious or not.

"Jack, call me Jack," he clarified, "we'll talk later."

As Thomas watched him walk around the table, it was only then that he suddenly realized the size of the man. He was at least six feet four, two hundred and sixty pounds, but solid, and his fist hid the glass he was holding.

"I'm back," said Rachel sitting next to him, picking up her champagne, and taking a sip as the DJ played Kool & The Gang's 'Celebration.'

"Do you want to dance?" asked Thomas.

"I'd love too," she replied.

Thomas followed her to the floor and watched her body move to the rhythm; it was mesmerizing. After the fourth song, they went back to the table and joined her mom who was sitting alone. Thomas asked them what they wanted to drink and left. On the way back, he met Jack standing and talking with Jessica close to the dance floor.

"Hi, Jack, I know you'd appreciate another Glenfiddich," he said handing him the glass.

"Don't forget we still have to smoke those cigars," he said gesturing to his pocket.

"Let me know when you're ready," he replied then turned to Jessica, "A rum and coke for you."

"Thank you," she said pleasantly. "We'll be back at the table in a minute."

Thomas left them, put a Heineken and glass in front of Rachel's empty seat, before sitting, drinking a mouthful of scotch, and watching the people dancing.

"She's gone to powder her nose," answered Jessica sitting. "Why don't you go smoke that cigar with Jack, he said he would be out in a minute, and I'll wait here for Rachel and let her now."

"Thanks, I think I will," said Thomas standing and picking up his scotch.

"And in return, I'll take a couple of dances when you get back," she teased.

"It would be my pleasure," replied Thomas then excused himself.

Jessica watched Thomas leave, she liked him, he reminded her of someone she once knew a long time ago. She quickly looked around for Rachel and wanted her to hurry back before he returned.

Chapter 5

Thomas was glad to get outside again and feel the breeze on his face, looking around he realized he was alone, and quickly glanced inside for Jack, who was nowhere in sight. He noticed someone was about to talk on the microphone, and from what he could make out it, a fundraising activity was about to take place. He finished his drink, placed it on the patio table, and decided to take a stroll to the bench and sit for a minute or two. As he got closer, he spotted a solitary figure sitting on the bench, and it sounded like she was crying. Thomas turned to leave.

"Don't go," asked the voice softly.

"Is everything okay?"

"I'll be fine in a minute," she replied drying her eyes with a tissue. "Please come over and sit next to me."

"All right," he said joining her. "My name's Thomas."

She looked at him. Her eyes were blue like the Caribbean Sea, her light brown hair was shoulder length, and parted to one side with a fringe draped over her cheek. As she moved it away from her face, the moonlight captured her flawless skin and perfect features; she was beautiful.

"Hi, Thomas," she said managing a smile. "My name's Olivia."

He looked at her inquisitively. "Have we met before?"

"Yes," she said surprised he remembered. "It was several months ago."

"Okay, don't tell me," he said wondering where.

"Need help?" she teased.

Thomas nodded slowly.

"The month was May."

Thomas thought aloud. "Where was I in May?"

She gave him that look of 'need another clue.'

"All right, I'll take another one."

"Twenty-third," she offered.

"Keep them coming," replied Thomas motioning with his hand.

"Saturday night about eight p.m…intermission…"

Thomas gestured again with his hand for more hints.

Olivia was about to give him another when she quickly realized something. "Hold on a second, you know," she said tapping his arm playfully, "you're just messing with me!"

Thomas chuckled. "Giselle, intermission, you were with Mrs. Peterson. Honestly, it just came to me."

"Yeah, sure," she replied laughing with him.

"I was with my grandmother in the Patrons Lounge, and I was coming back with some drinks, and my grandmother turned around and introduced me to Mrs. Peterson and then you, Olivia Taylor. As I recall, you stayed for a few minutes and had to leave." As he was telling her this, he thought back and remembered Olivia catching him staring at her or at least he thought she had. But tonight, there was something about her that was slightly different, but he couldn't quite put his finger on it.

"You do remember," she said delightedly.

"I do, but there was something different about you then?"

"You mean my jeans, sweat top, and no make-up," she said horrified he had remembered that part. "Please let me explain, I had danced in the matinee that day, and had planned on enough time to go home and change, but I was delayed leaving and never made it home. I knew that was the reason why you were staring at me, I felt so embarrassed that I had to leave and go back to my seat. I really wanted to explain it to you then but decided on a hasty retreat instead, and I promised myself that when I saw you again, I would put you straight. You must have thought—"

"It was your hair, you had it up in a ponytail, that's what's different."

She gave him a blank look. 'Really, my hair! That's it. But weren't you staring at me, at my clothes?"

Thomas didn't want to tell her that he was staring at her because he thought she was the most beautiful woman he had ever seen. "No, I was staring at you because I thought you looked cute, natural."

"Cute, naturally," she repeated unsure. "Really?"

"Really," he confirmed. "But I've seen you since then."

"Yes, you have, at your grandmother's funeral," confessed Olivia sadly staring into the darkness. "Your grandmother was a very special lady, she taught me from the time I was five to fifteen, and I owe her a great deal," she revealed glancing over at him. "She used to talk about you all the time and even brought in pictures of you." Olivia stopped and fondly thought about those days with a smile.

"You spoke well of her tonight."

"Thank you," he replied and remembered something she had told him. "At Giselle, when you were walking away, my grandmother said to me that you would be a principal dancer this year. Are you the new principal dancer I've been hearing about this evening?"

"I am," she replied humbly. "Penny, who has been instructing me for the last ten years, is over the moon." Olivia looked down and suddenly wanted to cry but contained herself. "Actually, the only other time I've seen her as happy was tonight," she said glancing at Thomas. "That was something quite special you did for her."

"Thank you," he replied.

Olivia didn't know how to ask and decided just to blurt it. "Would you like to come to my opening night?"

"Well, I—"

"I'll buy the ticket."

"I'd—"

"There's a reception afterwards, please, say yes."

Thomas went silent, rubbed his thumb and index finger on his chin, and pretended to be thinking really hard. "Hm, I think I have plans that night."

"You don't even know the date," responded Olivia realizing he was being playful again and pushed his hand from under his chin.

"I wouldn't miss it for the world, and I'm honored that you asked me, but on one condition, I'll buy my ticket."

"No, please, let me buy it, I'd like to," she pleaded. "Please, let me."

"All right."

"Yay!" she said cheerfully.

Someone had opened the patio doors to let the night air in and the faint sound of someone singing badly inside could be heard.

"What's that?" asked Thomas.

"It's one of our fundraising events. The First National Ballet dancers are approached by guests, and for a hundred dollars, you can request the dancer to perform a talent that they think they have, such as sing, juggle, and so on, or you can just opt for a dance with them. Some talents are good; some not so good. Right now, someone has paid to hear Francis Gray sing, or should I say, try to sing!" she said chuckling as they listened.

"Is he singing a George Michael song? It sounds like he's singing 'Faith.'"

"Yes, he is, and he thinks he looks like him."

"Does he?"

"I guess so, but you'll have to judge for yourself."

"Do you have a secret talent?"

"Well, I usually just accept a dance," she said, and couldn't believe what she was about to say, "or I can sing?"

"I'd like to hear you sing," replied Thomas.

"What song?"

"I'd like you to choose."

"Okay, I'll choose one especially for you," she said then studied him momentarily. "Can I ask you something?"

"Anything."

"Do you believe in fate?"

"No."

"That was quick. Why not?"

"I like to believe our life is in our own hands and we are in control of it."

"So, we are responsible for our lives, no one else?"

"Yes, I believe so," he reconfirmed and wondered why she had asked.

Olivia sat back, gazed up at the stars, and thought. He didn't know about tonight, the award, and why she had been crying. About Francis, about her mother, her father, and how complicated her life was. She wanted to tell him everything, and she knew she may never have this chance again, but would he understand? How could she expect him to? He hardly knew her. She wanted to confide in him, tell him everything, but she couldn't bring herself to do it because she was scared. Besides, being scared and crying about it seemed so much easier, although much more painful.

"It's a beautiful night," said Thomas interrupting her train of thought.

"It is."

"Just think how long it has taken the universe to give us this moment, right now."

"I never thought about it that way," she said contemplating it. "The moon, the stars, the trees, the garden, and us, on this bench, right now. It's really quite amazing when you think about it that way."

"And if you hadn't asked me to join you, we would have missed it."

"We would have," she acknowledged happily.

"I'm glad you're smiling."

"You're to blame" she said light-heartedly and was about to kiss him on the cheek.

"Olivia, is that you back there?"

"Yes, Penny," she replied. "I can call her Penny now, rather than Ms. Daily, she insists I do," she whispered as she stood and searched through her handbag. "Thomas, you have to put the donation in this envelope, but let me write your name, my name, and the song on it, first," she said jotting it down. "Here you go." She stopped and held onto it momentarily. "Promise me you won't read it. I want it to be a surprise."

"I won't. I promise."

"Okay," she said. "You need to give this to the DJ, he'll call me up, and then I'll put the envelope in the basket."

"Olivia!" called out Penny.

"I'll be there in a minute," replied Olivia, "she needs my help, I'll see you inside." She started to leave, stopped, and turned around. Her knee-length black evening gown showed off her ample breasts, slim hips, and lovely long legs. She hesitated, then convinced herself to walk back to him, lean over, and kiss him on the cheek. "Thank you, for everything," she whispered and quickly left.

Thomas stared at the ground and wondered why Olivia had been crying, he didn't like seeing anyone upset, especially her. He slowly got up, and as he strolled back to the patio, thought about her kiss.

Chapter 6

"Thomas where have you been, I've been looking for you everywhere?" asked Jack. "Come with me to the bar and let me buy you a drink."

"Okay, but I've just got to go talk to the DJ first," he replied. "I'll meet you there."

"It's all right, I'll come with you, the DJ is on the way," said Jack walking with him.

When they arrived at the platform, Jack stopped to talk to a couple while Thomas waited on the steps for the DJ to notice him. He casually glanced around the ballroom and could see Rachel, she had her back to him, and was talking and laughing with someone. The DJ eventually saw Thomas and waved him up, he handed him the envelope, then met Jack and walked over to the bar.

"Scotch, Thomas?"

"Thanks, Jack."

"Two Glenfiddich's," said Jack to the bartender.

After he dropped them off and they moved off to the side.

"Do you play golf?" asked Jack.

"I do," replied Thomas taking a sip of his drink.

"Any good?"

"I'm okay," replied Thomas. He was a fine golfer but knew enough not to give a fellow golfer the upper hand, especially when he knew what the next question was going to be.

"What's your handicap?"

"I didn't have one this summer," said Thomas. "I didn't get too many chances to play under the circumstances."

"Oh yeah, of course, sorry," replied Jack remembering the funeral.

It was another deception; Thomas had played more this summer than any other. Playing golf had actually helped him take his mind off his grandmother's passing and her funeral. In fact, he had played twice last week. "What's yours?"

"You know, I haven't been out enough this summer to rank myself," said Jack. "I've been busy, too."

Thomas laughed and Jack joined in.

"I'll give you a call and we'll play one day. The loser can pay for lunch."

Thomas couldn't resist. "I like my steak medium rare and my beer cold, Jack."

"You're a cocky S.O.B!" stated Jack grinning. "And I like that!"

"I knew you would."

Jack looked over at the crowded dance floor then back at Thomas. "What do you think? Fifty bucks a dance."

"You're not my type, Jack."

Jack chuckled. "It's a fundraiser event, to dance with one of them or get them to sing, recite Shakespeare, whatever, it costs a fifty."

"I thought it was a hundred?"

"No, fifty, which means for the next two hours it's going to cost you a fifty every time you want to dance with Rachel, and that's per song."

"But Rachel isn't a ballet dancer?" queried Thomas.

"First, it's the dancers, then throughout the evening they add people to the list that are well-known in the community, celebrities, television personalities, musicians, models, and such. It adds variety, plus it helps with the fundraising. They just announced it a few minutes ago."

Thomas realized he had been outside and was about to ask Jack about Rachel.

"Here you are, I was wondering where you had gotten to," said Rachel approaching him.

Jack jumped in. "I've just been telling him about the fifty dollars a dance, he was out of the room when they announced it, drink Rachel?"

"Heineken please, Jack," she replied as she watched him walk over to the bar.

"So, you're well-known in the community?" asked Thomas. "You must do a lot of volunteer work?"

"Yes, I do," she said with a smile, convinced he had no idea.

Jack returned holding a tray of beers and whiskeys. "Let's head back to the table and get this party started." As they followed Jack, Rachel put her arm through Thomas's, then sat close to him.

For the next hour, Thomas danced with Rachel and her mother, listened to two ballerinas sing, and drank and swapped golfing, fishing, and eating stories with Jack. Occasionally, he looked around to see if he could spot Olivia, but she was nowhere to be seen.

Rachel excused herself, and Thomas watched her leave before turning to talk to Jack, she returned several minutes later.

"Thomas," she said getting his attention, "I would like you to meet my closest and dearest friend, Olivia Taylor."

"Hi, Thomas," said Olivia.

"Olivia, nice to see you again," he said standing, leaning over, and kissing her cheek. He was right, her skin was soft.

"You two know each other?" asked a surprised Rachel.

"Prior to tonight, the last time we met was at the ballet last season, Thomas used to take his grandmother," said Olivia smiling. "Did you know she taught me for ten years?"

"No, I didn't," replied Rachel.

"I'm what you might call, a friend of the family," she said glancing over at him.

"Really?" said Rachel wondering why she had never mentioned this before.

The music lowered and the DJ spoke softly. "Olivia Taylor to the DJ, Olivia, to the DJ."

"Please, excuse me."

"Of course," replied Thomas.

"Make sure you come back and sit with us, we have so much to talk about," said Rachel squeezing her hand.

"Don't worry, I'll be back right after I sing."

"Sing! You're singing?" asked a shocked Rachel.

"I am," confirmed Olivia gracefully strolling away.

Both Rachel and Jessica glanced at one another dumbfounded.

Thomas wasn't sure what was going on. "Is she that bad?"

Jessica moved over and sat next to him. "I'm not one for gossip, but since this happened many years ago and everyone else here knows, I don't see any harm in me telling you the abbreviated version," she said candidly. "When she was younger, Olivia and her father were very close, and he used to take her to her ballet classes and was the one who enrolled her in the First National Ballet School. Now during this time, her father was a famous opera singer, and still is, but back when they were together, he used to sing duets with her, and she became an exceptional singer. Here's the sad part…Olivia's father started to have an affair with one of the opera co-stars, and was eventually caught by her mother, who in turn, threw him out. He tried for custody of Olivia but lost. Olivia, devastated by what her father did, didn't want anything to do with him, so heartbroken, he moved to New York City. Shortly after, when Olivia was eighteen, her mother remarried, and Olivia moved out. Her mother bought her a place and gave her money every month, then moved to San Francisco, and we've never seen her since. I think the humiliation of what had happened, and everyone knowing, was too much for her. Her father was, or I should say is, a really nice man and I liked him a lot, actually we all did, and I still find it difficult to believe he did what he did."

"Why?"

"Because he loved Olivia so much, she was his life, and you could never imagine him hurting her like that. He just didn't look like the type, then again, what does the type look like," she said with a heavy sigh. "Unfortunately, after her father left, Olivia never sang again, well, at least never publicly."

What have I done? thought Thomas. Wait a second, I didn't suggest she sing, she offered, something wasn't right.

The music went off and the murmur of the crowd took over. "Ladies and gentlemen, to sing for us now, Ms. Olivia Taylor." There was an unusual silence as people surveyed the podium to confirm that the DJ must be mistaken, as he offered Olivia the microphone, they realized he wasn't.

"This song is for someone very special," she said before handing it back to him.

Olivia sang 'Think of Me' from the Phantom of the Opera. It was beautiful, effortless, and flawless, and Thomas felt goose bumps on his arms, and a wonderful anxiety in his chest.

When she finished, people clapped loudly, and several shouted 'Brava!' while others called for an encore. Olivia graciously curtsied, thanked them, and walked off the podium.

It took her fifteen minutes to make it through the crowd, and when she arrived, she had Penelope on her arm. As Rachel and Jessica took turns complimenting her, Penelope moved close to Thomas and whispered in his ear. "You must've been sent from Heaven, an angel perhaps, only you could have made her sing again."

Thomas had a blank look on his face. "Well, I really didn't do anything, we were just outside and…" he said glancing up and realizing she wasn't even there. Penelope had moved toward Olivia and was saying something in her ear. Thomas picked up his drink, took a long sip, and when he turned around Olivia was standing in front of him.

"Thank you," he said standing and giving her hug. "You know you should sing more often, that was beautiful."

"For you, Thomas, anytime," she said affectionately then gently caressed his arm. "When I get back, I'll pay off that dance-debt I owe you, my choice of song though."

"You don't owe me a—"

"You paid a hundred. That guaranteed you your song, and me, at least one dance," she said revealing a sly smile. "Please excuse me, and I will be back shortly for that dance." She left and headed for the foyer.

"I've never heard her sing before," admitted Rachel joining Thomas. "I was told she was really good but that was an understatement."

"It truly was," agreed Thomas.

"Would you like to dance?" she asked as a slow song came on.

"I would love to," he replied.

They moved onto the dance floor. Thomas put one hand around her waist and held her hand with the other. She moved close to him, and he could smell the sweetness of her perfume, and feel her firm breasts rub up against his chest. She rested her head on his shoulder. Tonight, all she wanted was to be a regular girl enjoying a night out, and not Rachel Carter, and Thomas was giving her that opportunity. She knew if she didn't tell him, he would find out sooner rather than later, and she would, but not tonight, she was having too much fun, perhaps tomorrow. Her mother and Jack had promised not to say anything to him, but everyone else knew, and hopefully none of them would say something and spoil their evening.

Olivia walked across the foyer and into the restroom. She made sure all the stalls were empty before locking herself in the last one, leaning against the wall, and quietly crying.

Chapter 7

It was getting late, and people were starting to leave. Rachel and Jessica had their coats in their arms and were making their rounds of goodbyes when Olivia rejoined them. Thomas glanced over at her and there was a distant look in her eyes.

"Olivia, would you like a drink of something?" asked Jack.

"Can I have one of those beers?"

Jack looked down at the ones he'd been stacking on the table all night. "Of course," he said pouring one into a glass and passing it to her.

Olivia took a long drink. "Do you know how long it's been since I've had a beer?" she asked staring at the glass.

"About two seconds?" kidded Thomas.

She tried to keep a serious face but burst into laughter, Jack and Thomas followed suit.

"I can't even remember the last time I laughed," she said glancing at them both before taking another swig. She leaned toward Thomas and whispered to him, "but that's all going to change."

Thomas was about to ask her what was going to change.

"It's time for us to go."

"Let me help you with your coat," he offered, standing, and assisting Jessica then Rachel.

"Thomas, can we drop you anywhere?" asked Jessica.

"I drove down and I'm staying here tonight," he confirmed. "I have some things I want to do in town tomorrow, but thanks for the offer."

"Do you have a room?" inquired Jessica.

"Not yet, but I asked one of the hotel staff after dinner and he confirmed they have rooms available," reassured Thomas. "I was planning on getting here a little earlier and reserving one, well, you all know how that worked out."

Jack, using his best English accent, retold the story of Alfie trying to get Thomas's attention which made them all laugh.

"Here you go, room 1710," said Jessica handing Thomas two room keys. "One is for the door, and the other is for the elevator. Bill was supposed to be back from Atlanta earlier this evening, and he was going to shower and change in the room, but he was delayed and won't be coming in till tomorrow, so the room is yours."

"I appreciate that," said Thomas, "but you'll have to let me pay for it."

"Nonsense," said Jessica disapprovingly, "breakfast is included, and there's a free bar, so order what you want and just video check out before you leave. Plus, Thomas, I feel much better knowing someone is going to use it rather than having it going to waste."

"Thank you very much," he replied sincerely.

"Time for me to leave, too," said Jack pulling his coat check ticket out of his inner suit pocket along with two cigars. He put one back and gave the other to Thomas. "For tonight."

Thomas said he would walk with them up to the lobby and pulled Olivia out of her seat to join him. As they went up the escalator and across the lobby to the exit, they talked about the night. Once there, a black stretch limousine pulled up, and Thomas followed Rachel and Jessica outside and opened the door for them. They each gave him a hug and a kiss before jumping in, and after he closed it, he watched it drive away. Suddenly it stopped, and the door opened.

"Thomas," shouted Rachel waving him over.

"Is everything okay?" he asked.

"I forgot to give you this, I've had it with me all night," she said handing him the invitation. "Don't forget it's this Saturday, and bring a change of clothes, casual stuff, you know, jeans."

"I will," he said with a smile. "I'm looking forward to it."

Rachel was beaming as he closed the door.

"Rachel, you should have told him," said Jessica pulling her close. "You don't want him to find out on his own or from someone else."

"I know, I know, but it was so nice just being regular-girl Rachel. It's not every day I meet someone who likes me just for me" she said in her defense. "We spent so much time talking about my daycare and kid's camp ideas, it was amazing, and he actually listened to me and was supportive."

"I understand," replied Jessica sympathetically, "but he needs to hear it from you first. Promise me you'll tell him before the party."

"I promise, Mom," she said putting her head on her shoulder. "He's so charming, thoughtful, caring, and sexy."

"He is," replied Jessica.

A taxi pulled up, Jack jumped in, rolled down the window, and stuck out his head. "Have a good night, Thomas. I'll give you a call and arrange a day for us to play that round of golf. What's your handicap again?"

"Nice try, Jack," replied Thomas with a chuckle and a wave as it drove away. I guess Taxi Jack can't afford a limousine, thought Thomas, putting the invitation in his suit pocket. He went inside and strolled over to Olivia. "Can I have the honor of escorting you back?"

"Yes, young sir, you can," she said happily putting her arm through his.

The music was still playing, and there were quite a few people dancing, when they sat down at their empty table.

"Are you doing anything tomorrow?" asked Thomas.

"No, not really," she replied sipping her beer.

"Would you like to walk around town with me?"

"What time?" she asked interestedly.

"Well, let me see, I'm going to have breakfast in the hotel at about ten, go to Mass at the cathedral at twelve, then walk around town from about one, onwards. So, we could meet me at one?" he suggested and waited. "Or later, I don't want to pressure you."

"No, you're not. I want to meet you. It's just that I haven't been to Mass for a long time, and would like to go, but feel a little…awkward."

"Then meet me after?"

"But I would like to go," she said apprehensively.

"Okay, then come with me." He could sense by her silence that she was anxious and unsure. "Olivia, trust me, I'll be with you, and you will be okay."

She smiled to herself at the thought of how nice it would be to go with him. "Okay, I'll meet you outside the cathedral at eleven forty-five."

"Great," replied Thomas.

"Ladies and gentlemen, these are the last three songs of the evening, and we will be slowing it down. Thank you for a great night and have a safe drive home."

"I'll take that dance now, Thomas," said Olivia.

They walked onto the dance floor, and he placed his hand around her waist, and with his other hand, held hers. She let go and put both her arms around his waist, Thomas responded by placing his arms around her and pulling her close. She slowly put her head on his shoulder, and he could feel her warm breath on his neck. She closed her eyes, swayed to the music, and wanted him to hold her forever.

Before the end of the third song, Thomas pulled away slightly, and Olivia lifted her head. He gazed deeply into her eyes; she was so beautiful. She looked at him, at his lips, and wanted him to kiss her. Thomas thought about it.

"Goodnight, ladies and gentlemen, and thank you," said the DJ breaking their trance.

They slowly let go of one another and strolled off the dance floor. "How are you getting home," asked Thomas.

"Taxi, I only live five minutes away."

They left the ballroom, picked up their coats, and Thomas helped Olivia put on hers then put his over his arm. They went to the lobby and waited for a cab, and one came almost immediately. They went outside, Thomas opened the door, and she quickly kissed him on the cheek before jumping in. "I'll see you tomorrow."

"Eleven forty-five," he confirmed cheerfully, then closed the door, and looked on as the cab drove away.

Inside, Olivia smiled happily and thought about seeing him tomorrow.

Thomas went to his car and grabbed his overnight bag. The room was on the top floor, and was in fact a suite, and had two bedrooms with en suites, a sitting area with a fireplace, a wet bar, and an entertainment system. He took a quick shower, put on a hotel bathrobe, then poured himself a drink and sat in front of the fireplace. He took a long sip, thought about the night, and was worried he had entered into a world that he didn't belong in. Maybe I should have never opened the door to the ballroom, he thought, but if he hadn't, he would have never met her. Who was he kidding, he was an unpublished writer working in a distribution center, what would she see in him? And what could he have, that she could possibly want? He had nothing to offer her, and she had everything she needed.

Chapter 8

Thomas arrived at the cathedral at eleven thirty. He walked across the street to a small park, sat on the wooden bench, and waited. The sun was full in the sky and the leaves in the park were green and motionless. He watched the people walking back and forth and noticed Olivia standing across the street, called her name, and waved. She waved back and strolled towards him. She was wearing light blue jeans, a navy blouse, and her hair was pulled back off her face with a hair clip. And as she got closer, Thomas noticed how her deep blue eyes shimmered in the sunlight.

"Good morning," she said sitting next to him and putting her jacket on her lap. "Have you been here long?"

"No, I just got here a few minutes ago."

"It's a beautiful day," she said looking around. "Look at all this color."

"I know, I was just admiring it, I think this is the best seat in the house," he said glancing at her. "You look great."

"Thank you," she replied blushing.

"Are you ready to go inside?"

Olivia quickly grabbed his arm. "Thomas, I haven't been to Mass for a long time and I'm a little nervous."

Thomas gently placed his hand on hers. "You'll be fine, come on." They both stood up and Thomas held her hand as they crossed the street.

With his help, they followed the missal throughout the service, then he found the songs in the hymnbook and listened as she sang. During Holy Communion, she refused to take it until she went to confession, so she looked on as Thomas went up. On the way out, they shook hands with the priest, who wished them a wonderful day.

"Thomas, will you come with me again next week?" she asked eagerly.

"I would like that," he said looking at her. "I used to bring my grandmother here every Sunday."

"I used to come with my father, and we used to sing the hymns together," she said sadly, but smiled as she thought of those fond memories.

"Well, unfortunately, I'm tone deaf," he said and chuckled.

"You are pretty awful," she replied and playfully poked him in the side.

"Does your father live around here?" he asked, not wanting her to wonder why he never asked about her family.

"No, he lives in New York City, and I haven't talked to him in a very long time," she said quietly. "We don't get along."

"What about your mother?"

"She remarried and moved to San Francisco. I see her once in a while, either she comes to visit or I go out there," she explained glancing at him. "I heard you parents passed away."

"Yeah, they were on a plane in Europe, it had engine problems, and it crashed," revealed Thomas.

"I'm sorry."

"That's okay, it was a long time ago, and I was only eighteen," he said slowing down. "My grandmother took it the hardest, and never really recovered from it, that was the year she stopped teaching."

Olivia remembered that because it was the same year Penny took over her classes, but said nothing, instead, they walked in silence for a while.

"Can I ask you a personal question?" asked Olivia putting her arm through his

"Of course."

"What was is it like for you? You know, not having your parents?"

"I miss them; I miss them a lot, and there's not a day that goes by when I don't think of them or miss them," he confessed. "I would have loved to have gone fishing with my dad, played golf with him, watched sports on TV, or just been able to talk to him life. Or talked with my mother as she cooked dinner, watched one of her favorite musicals with her, or have her meet some of my girlfriends and show embarrassing photos of me. All those simple things that we take for granted." He suddenly stopped and thought for a minute. "Do you know what I miss most of all?"

Olivia shook her head.

"Sunday dinners, no matter how busy we were, we always ate Sunday dinners together. We used to talk and laugh; it was a lot of fun."

"That sounds wonderful."

"It was," he said and started to walk. "How long has it been since you talked to your father?"

"Nine years."

"That's a long time."

"I know, but he really hurt me."

Thomas put his arm around her and gave her a comforting squeeze as they approached a young man playing a sax in the parkette entrance.

"Hey, young lovers how about I play you a love song?" asked the saxophonist.

"We're just friends," replied Thomas removing his arm.

"How about a couple's song then?"

Thomas placed five dollars into the hat on the ground.

"Okay, lovely lady, what will it be?"

"Do you know 'Unforgettable' by Nat King Cole?" asked Olivia.

The saxophonist smiled and started playing.

Thomas whispered in her ear. "Do you know the words?"

She nodded.

"Will you sing for me?"

She looked at him. "What? Here?"

"Please, for me."

Olivia sang, and halfway through, the saxophonist stopped and sang with her. His deep rich voice complimented Olivia's, and a small crowd started to gather and clapped when they finished.

"Thank you," said Olivia to the saxophonist.

"Anytime, pretty lady," he said, then turned to the people putting money into his hat. "Thank you, thank you."

"That was one of my father's favorite songs," said Olivia as they walked onto Second Street and headed south towards the harbor front.

"It's so beautiful down here, especially at Christmas time with the colorful lights, the snow falling, and the outdoor ice rink playing festive music," said Thomas.

"I know, it's so magical" she replied.

"We used to come down here and ice skate, and afterwards, just north of here, about fifteen minutes that way," he said pointing. "There's an English pub called The Duke, and we used to go there for dinner. I'll take there one night, you'd enjoy it."

"I'd like that," she said enthusiastically.

"Do you golf?"

"I've played a couple of time but I'm not very good, I'm more of a putt-putt golfer," she acknowledged, and hoped she hadn't put him off taking her, and giggled at her unintentional pun.

"What's so funny?"

"Oh nothing, just thinking about me golfing" she said. "Maybe I just needed the right instructor. Would you take me and teach me?"

"First lesson is free!" he joked.

"Deal!" she said, happy with the way their conversation was going.

"Did you know Jack wants me to play him?"

"I'd heard," she replied. "Apparently he's really good, and he's always telling Penny about his handicap, I think that's what he called it, last week it was fourteen."

"Fourteen, really!" replied Thomas. "I asked him last night what it was, he said he didn't have one, and that he hadn't played in a while. I knew he did."

"Oops! Sorry Jack."

"Don't worry, it will be our secret," promised Thomas. "What do you like to do?"

"I like to swim, there's an indoor pool where I live, so I swim quite a lot. I also like to ski, skate, do aerobic classes, and I read quite a bit. I also like watching old movies, actually no, I love watching old movies."

"What kind?"

"Romance, musicals, westerns, mysteries, you name it."

"Me too."

They walked and talked for an hour about their favorite movies and ended up at the theater where Olivia performed.

"What does it feel like dancing on stage?" asked Thomas.

She contemplated for a minute. "It feels like I'm dancing in Heaven."

"Do you ever get nervous performing in front of all those people?"

"I'm always nervous, but not a worried type of nervous, it's a different kind. More of an excitement nervousness, like butterflies, does that make sense?"

"Definitely."

"Come on, I'll take you on a personal backstage tour," she said taking him by the hand. She said hello to the security guard at the entrance then showed him around the building ending the tour on the stage.

"Wow!" exclaimed Thomas as he looked out at all the empty seats. "I can't even begin to imagine what it would be like if this was full of people."

"Five thousand plus," confirmed Olivia.

"That's incredible," said Thomas shaking his head, then stopped and gave her a curious look.

"What?" she asked moving close to him.

"Will you dance for me?"

"Now?" she asked.

"You know what, you don't have to, I'm being too pushy."

"Nonsense, I would like to."

"Will you get in trouble?"

She smiled. "No, well, maybe," she said mischievously, and quickly took off her jacket and handed it to him. "Hold this, I'll be back in a minute."

Thomas watched her leave. She looked good in jeans.

Minutes later, she came back wearing ballet slippers tied over her jeans, and her hair in a ponytail. "I always keep a pair here," she admitted. "What ballet?"

Thomas was amazed at her sudden confidence. "What about Romeo and Juliet?"

"One of my favorites," she replied.

"Should I go sit down there?" he said pointing to the seats.

"No," she said motioning off to the side, "there's a chair over there, put it on the stage right about here, front and center stage."

He placed the chair down and sat as she left the stage.

Her head poked around the curtain. "Are you ready?"

"Ready."

She danced for thirty minutes, and for her finale, she stopped in front of him and did fifteen pirouettes then stood back and curtsied.

Thomas put her coat on the floor, clapped his hands, and yelled, "Brava! Brava!" He then walked over to her and kissed her hand. "You dance like an angel in Heaven."

"Thank you," she replied and curtsied once more. "I'll be back in a minute."

Thomas picked up her jacket, put the chair back, and met Olivia in the middle of the stage. She was smiling to herself.

"Can I be let in on your secret?" he asked.

"One day, perhaps."

They left, walked down around the harbor, and talked about sports, television shows, and music. An hour later they were back at the theater.

"I promised Kate I would be home for dinner."

"What's she like?

"You'd like her, she's a lot of fun, and far less serious than I am."

"Oh, knowing that, then I'm sure I will," said Olivia teasingly. She liked the fact that he mentioned that his sister would like her, but what about her brother? she thought. "I really enjoyed today."

"So did I," replied Thomas.

"Would you like to come over for dinner on Friday? We could go for a swim, listen to some music, and watch some old movies."

"Yeah, I'd like that. Is there something I can bring?"

"You can bring the movies."

"That's it?'

"That's it!"

"Where do you live?" he asked.

Olivia pointed to a block of condominiums across the street. "Count twelve floors up, and look over to the far-left corner, that's mine."

"What's your number?"

"1211. The door man will call up, then let you in."

"Actually, I meant your phone number, although I would need your condo number too," he said a little embarrassed.

She smiled and produced her cell phone. "Give me yours and I'll send you a text with mine."

Thomas told her.

"Okay, I've sent it," she confirmed.

"So, what time Friday?"

"Around six."

"All right, I'll see you then," replied Thomas.

"I had a really nice day."

"Me too."

There was an uncertain silence.

"Well, I should get going," he said leaning over and politely kissing her on the cheek. "I'll see you Friday."

"Friday," she said with a smile, then turned, and sauntered away.

Thomas thought about her as he walked back to the hotel, and Olivia was beaming when she entered her condo and closed the door behind her.

Chapter 9

"Hi, Kate, sorry I'm late."

"It's okay, I'm a little behind."

"How's the studying?"

"Exhausting," she replied rolling her eyes.

"You should have waited and let me cook," suggested Thomas.

"No, it gives my mind a rest, besides, I like cooking for you," she said looking over at him.

"I'm just going to take these upstairs," said Thomas holding up his overnight bag and suit. "I'll just be a minute."

"A girl called for you," teased Kate.

Thomas stopped and walked back to her. "Who?"

"She said her name was Rachel and didn't give me her last name. I did talk to her for a few minutes, and she sounds very nice, and seems very interesting. You'll have to tell me about your escapades last night," she said with an air of inquisition.

"You lawyers, I'm pleading the Fifth Amendment!" replied Thomas leaving.

Ten minutes later he joined Kate at the kitchen table, and over Sunday dinner, told her about the last twenty-four hours.

"I wish I would have been there. I would have loved to have seen you scampering to the back of the hall," she said laughing at the thought.

"Very funny, I knew you would get a kick out of that," said Thomas standing.

"Are you interested in either of them?" asked Kate as she watched Thomas clear the table.

"Both of them are interesting," he replied.

"You know what I mean!" exclaimed Kate.

"Rachel is breathtaking, and she could be a world-famous model, but looks aside, I really enjoyed talking with her. She wants to open a daycare or kid's camp, which is great. Olivia, on the other hand, is beautiful and graceful, and a professional ballerina. She's also sensitive, fun, and compassionate. They're both very rich and…" Thomas hesitated.

"What? What were you going to say?"

Thomas lowered his voice. "Who am I kidding? Let's review my eye-catching profile: I work in a warehouse, I'm an unpublished writer, and I have twelve hundred dollars in my bank account, no, actually seven, I spent five last night." He put down the dishes and looked at Kate. "What do I have to offer either of them? Nothing."

Kate smiled at him, grabbed his hand, and pulled him to sit down. "Thomas," she said softly. "If these girls are only worried about your dollar value, then you are right, you don't add up to much, but if you want to talk about what's in here," she said pointing to his heart. "Your kind, loving, sensitive, caring, thoughtful, compassionate, and if you want to consider about all these eye-catching qualities, then you are the richest man I know." She moved her finger to his head. "And in here, is one bright writer, the novel you've written already proves that: it's terrific. You really need to take it to a publisher," said Kate pausing and backtracking. "We both know that you worked hard to take care of Grandma and me, and you are still working hard to take care of me. You pay my tuition, the bills, and this house. You gave up university so that I could go. Thomas, you've sacrificed so much I—"

"Kate, everything I've done, and everything I do, I'm doing for you because I want to, and I wouldn't have it any other way."

"I know," she said squeezing his hand. "Thomas, talk to me."

He let out a big sigh. "Last night, when I walked into that ballroom, I felt like one of them. What it was like to be rich, famous, and worry free. In that room, for that brief moment in time, I felt like I was an equal. But today, they're still there in that room, and I'm not, I'm outside behind a locked door looking through the keyhole. Do you know what I mean? I just don't know what I'm doing or where I'm going anymore but I'm scared it's nowhere," he explained, then paused momentarily. "Kate, I met Olivia earlier on today, and she lives in a condominium in the city and is a professional ballerina. Rachel invited me to a party on Saturday with all her friends and she probably lives in a mansion. Look at me. I'm going to be out of place and out of my league! It's not like these are our next-door neighbors."

"Thomas, why don't you treat them as if they were your next-door neighbors. Why do you have to put them up on such a pedestal? Has either of them asked you to? They both know what you do! Who you are! And yet, they're still calling you or asking you over for dinner. Why? It seems as if they're accepting you more than you are them!" declared Kate who realized she had raised her voice. She made eye contact with him and whispered, "Thomas, this doesn't sound like you. Is there any harm in being friends with these girls? If you don't give them a chance, you will never know the truth, only speculation." Kate studied him. "Tommy, this isn't like you. What are you really afraid of?"

Thomas nervously looked at Kate. "I don't want to disappoint them and get hurt in the process."

Kate put her arm around him. "Tommy, if you want, you can lock yourself in this house and never see either of these girls again, but trust me, I will never let that happen," she said caressing his hair. "I want you to enjoy yourself and make some new friends. It's time you did more, socially. I'm old enough to look after myself, well, not financially," she said trying to make him laugh but was unsuccessful. "You know what I mean. Tommy, you have so much to offer, so much love inside of you, and you need to share that with someone special," said Kate stopping and thinking for a moment. "I wish Mom and Dad were here, they'd be much better at this than me."

"Kate, if Mom and Dad were here, I would still want to talk to you about this," reassured Thomas taking her hand and kissing it. "I'll keep an open mind, take one day at a time, and see what happens, okay?"

"Fair enough," she said then suddenly remembered something. "Oh, I meant to tell you before dinner, but you started talking about your night. Rachel said she was out, and since she was passing our house on the way home, would drop in."

"What time?"

"Around seven-thirty."

Thomas looked at the clock on the wall, it was seven twenty-five. "I'm going upstairs to get a quick shower, if she arrives before I'm ready, can you keep her company until I come down? Unless you have studying?" he asked.

"No more studying today, go take your shower," said Kate. "Besides, I want to meet, or should I say cross-examine, this breathtaking beauty," teased Kate.

"Lawyers," said Thomas shaking his head. He kissed Kate on top of her head, went upstairs, and heard the doorbell ring as he closed the bathroom door. Fifteen minutes later, Thomas descended the stairs and walked into the living room.

"Nice, Cannes, and St. Tropez, that must have been exciting, I've never been to either. You know, I always wanted to go to the French Riviera, and see the beaches, and sunbathe on…" Kate stopped when she noticed Thomas.

"Hi, Thomas," said Rachel merrily. "Your sister's great, and we've been having a most informative chat."

"I've promised her inside information anytime she wants," added Kate playfully as she stood.

"And I plan on taking you up on that!" confirmed Rachel standing too.

Kate walked to the closet and picked out her coat. "I need to walk to the store to get some diet coke. I'll be back in half an hour or so," she said and left.

Thomas turned to Rachel. She was wearing tight-fitting gray track pants and a zippered sweatshirt, and her blonde hair was loosely curled and hung down past her shoulders, she had no makeup on, and looked amazing.

"Casual day," she confessed noticing his eyes.

"Well, you look great, even casual," he said as they sat down.

"Thomas, I came over here because I wanted to show you something, and talk to you about it, or maybe I should tell you first, then show you," she said nervously picking up a big brown envelope from the table. "I don't know how or where to begin. I really didn't think I would be this anxious."

"Rachel," he said reaching for her hand, "why don't you tell me, and then show me."

"Just promise me you will always look at me as Rachel Carter the girl from the fundraiser," she pleaded. "Promise me?"

Thomas wasn't sure where she was going with this. "Okay, I promise."

"I am well-known in the community, and I do a lot of volunteer work, but I'm not a model waiting for her big break."

"You're not a model?"

"I am, but I am a very well-known model, and I've appeared in local, national, and international magazines, and on billboards. I usually model swimsuits and lingerie, and occasionally make-up and dresses," she said opening the envelope and pulling out four magazines. Two of them were swimsuits, one was lingerie, and the other was a woman's magazine. "I wanted you to see my pictures," she said opening up one of the swimsuit issues and placing it on the coffee table.

Thomas looked at it, and there she was in two full-size poses wearing bikinis. As she flipped through it, she stopped at three half-page photographs of her wearing one pieces. All five were taken on a beach. The lingerie magazine was quickly placed on top. There was a picture of her in a red teddy, a second of her wearing a white bra and panties with a garter, and the third was her in a short black satin night robe that was open and revealed her black bra and panties. The woman's magazine was placed on top, and she flipped through to a close up of her face, she was smiling and wearing makeup. Thomas looked up at her a little unsure.

Rachel wanted to calmly tell him her issues, but instead, she just blurted it all out. "Do you know what it's like having boys teasing you about your pictures or saying rude comments about them? Or just wanting to go out with you because of who you are or what they think you are? Or have nice boys not ask you out because they feel inferior? Or have jealous girlfriends threaten you because their boyfriends look over at me? Well, I do," she said taking a deep breath. "Last night, after I met you, I was so happy that someone was talking to me, Rachel Carter, the unknown. All night you wanted to be with the unknown, talk to the unknown, be friends with the unknown, and I was so happy," she said with a smile. "I really wanted to tell you last night, but for my own selfish reasons, I decided not to." She paused briefly. "When I found out you had a sister, I knew I had to as soon as possible because I couldn't take the chance that your sister hadn't heard of me. Which is why I never told her my last name on the phone, I wanted to be the one who told you, and explain why," said Rachel. "These pictures are what I do, not who I am." She glanced at Thomas and quickly looked away when he made eye contact.

"Rachel, did you expect me to react differently towards you when I found out who you were?" he asked, brushing her hair away from her eyes. "I'm not like that."

"What do you mean?" asked Rachel.

"Do you think that I would speak to one person any different than another because of who they were or weren't? Jack? Your mother? Ms. Daily? The bartender? The DJ? The coat check girl? I see the person for who they are; not what they are," stated Thomas.

"I should have just told you last night," said Rachel shaking her head and disappointed with herself.

"Maybe, especially when you had me believe that you were well-known in the community for your volunteer work," joked Thomas.

They both laughed.

"Thomas, last night I had my reasons, right or wrong, for not telling you. I don't want you to think I lied to you intentionally. I'm sorry," she said starting to get upset.

"Rachel," he whispered.

She continued to stare at the table as a tear rolled down her cheek.

Thomas gently wiped it away. "Rachel, I'm glad you told me, and there's no need to apologize for last night, I understand why you did it," he said lifting up her chin and looking into her eyes. "I can't ignore the fact of who you are, but I promise you, I will always treat you as Rachel Carter, the unknown girl from the fundraiser, and nothing else."

Her face broke into a smile.

"Friends?" asked Thomas.

"Friends," she replied, "and we'll become best of friends, and no more secrets, I promise." She put her arms around him, gave him a squeeze, then let go.

Thomas sorted through the magazines, found the swimsuit issues, and opened the page to her pictures. "Where were these taken?"

"These two in Nice," she said flipping through excitedly, "this one in Cannes, and these two in St. Tropez."

"Tell me about them, I never been," said Thomas interestedly as he closed the magazine and sat back.

Rachel started talking about the French Riviera and her pictures. Kate returned, brought them each a glass of diet coke, and sat with them. An hour later, Thomas walked Rachel out to her convertible Mustang.

"I'll see you Saturday," said Rachel getting into her car. She couldn't stop smiling.

Thomas waved goodbye as she drove away then went back into the house where Kate was waiting for him in the foyer.

"Breathtaking, Thomas? She's absolutely gorgeous!" stated Kate looking at her brother in dismay. "You didn't know who she was?"

"Did you recognize her?"

"As soon as I opened the door."

"If I would have said her full name, would you have recognized it?"

"Thomas, if you said you met a model named Rachel Carter, I would have known for sure."

Thomas was silent.

Kate waited.

Thomas knew what she was waiting for. "Relax, Kate, we're just friends."

She looked on unconvinced. "You said she's breathtaking, and Olivia was beautiful, I can't wait to see Olivia," said Kate heading for the stairs. "I'm off to bed, I'll see you in the morning, goodnight."

Goodnight," replied Thomas going into the living room, flipping through the magazines, and looking at Rachel's pictures. She was stunning.

Chapter 10

"Hi, Thomas, come on in. I'm sorry, I'm running a little late," said Olivia apologetically and leading him into the living room. "Have a seat, and I'll take your bag and coat and put them in the guest room" She took them off him and walked towards the CD player. Do you like Christina Aguilera?"

"Yeah, I do."

"Good," she said pressing play and making sure the song 'Ain't No Other Man' came on. "I love her voice."

"It's fantastic." agreed Thomas.

Oliva turned up the volume. "I'll be back in a few minutes."

Thomas watched her as she headed down the hallway and casually looked around the room. Several minutes later, she returned wearing light pink lipstick, and had changed into a white T-shirt and black yoga pants. She looked great.

"Would you like a drink?"

"Sure."

"Beer or wine?"

"Beer, please."

Olivia came back from the kitchen with two bottles of Budweiser, poured each into a glass, then placed them on the coasters on the coffee table. She sat next to Thomas, lifted the glasses, and passed one to him. "Cheers."

"Cheers" replied Thomas touching his glass with hers. He sipped his beer and glanced down at the table. "I like your coasters," he said picking one up. "Renoir's *Bal du moulin de la Galette.*"

"I bought them at a store in a small village out in the country. There are eight in the set and each of them has a different Renoir painting," she explained moving close to him. "Do you like Impressionist artists?"

"I do; bur Renoir is my favorite."

"What do you like about them?"

"I like their technique of using light, similar colors, and shapes to capture people and objects," he said showing her the one he was holding as she leaned closer to him. "Do you see the green leaves, yellow hats, blonde hair, black suits, and the ground and faces with yellowish-pink spots, and the sunlight through the leaves."

"What else?" she asked looking at him as he studied the coaster.

"See the pyramid shape formed when you connect the three figures, thee vertical lines are the people dancing, standing, the trees, and the standard gas lamps, and the horizontal lines are the figures in the background, the round lanterns, and the white wooden buildings," he explained then glanced up at her.

"What does the painting mean?" she asked.

"Many things," replied Thomas. "At face value, it's a typical Sunday afternoon gathering at the Moulin de la Galette in the district of Montmartre in Paris in the 19th century, where people would dress up, dance, drink, and eat galettes. But if you look closer, to me, it's the joys of being young and in love, enjoying a social get-together with friends, flirtation, voices, sunshine, color, music, dancing, and drinking." Thomas passed it to her. "What do you see?

"I see love, happiness, a celebration," replied Olivia. "Actually, it reminds me of the fundraiser, except we had moonlight and stars, not sunshine.

"A modern version?"

"Yeah, a modern version."

"I like that."

"I do too," she said cheerfully then looked at him inquisitively. "You seem to know a lot about art; did you study it?"

"No, I've read some books on it, been to the art gallery a few times, that's about it. What about you?"

"I've been to the art gallery and read the pamphlets they give you," she confessed. "I only bought these coasters because I liked the pictures."

"Well, you have good taste," he said and sipped his beer. "I like your condominium."

"Thanks," she said putting the coaster down. "Would you like a quick tour?"

"I would," he said enthusiastically.

Olivia stood up and Thomas followed her. "At the end of the hallway is the master bedroom, with an en suite, a walk-in closet, and a view of the harbor," she said going in and opening the blinds.

"That's spectacular," said Thomas gazing out the window.

"Come on," she said pulling him by the hand. "In here, is the second bedroom or guest room with a big closet. Next to which is the den, which as you can see, is currently being used as a storage area for unopened boxes of memorabilia. My plan is to eventually unpack them, hang them up, and set up a desk with a computer over there." She took him to the next room and opened the door. "Here is the main bathroom," she said closing it and holding Thomas's hand as they entered the living room. "You're already familiar with this room, but in through here is the solarium, and the kitchen."

"This place is amazing. I love the views."

"Thank you," she replied checking the oven.

"What smells good," queried Thomas.

"Hope you like lasagna?"

"It's my favorite dish," confessed Thomas.

She secretly knew that and smiled to herself. "If we go through here, we're in the dining room."

Thomas noticed the table was attractively set for two.

"I've saved the best for last," she said letting go of his hand and opened the blinds.

"Wow!" said Thomas. "This is magnificent!"

Olivia stood behind him, placed her left hand on his shoulder, and with her right pointed out the landmarks. "There's city hall, Second Street, downtown, the spire of the cathedral, and down there is the theater."

He could feel her breasts rubbing against his back, the smell of her floral perfume, and her warm breath which tickled his neck.

"We're still going to the cathedral on Sunday?" she whispered in his ear.

"Yes," he said turning around, "but it will have to be at nine, and I have to leave right after, if that's okay?"

"That's fine," she replied. "I have some errands to run on Sunday and that will give me more than enough time to complete them."

"Pick you up at eight thirty?"

"Eight thirty it is," she confirmed, then realized her hand was still resting on his shoulder, removed it quickly, and closed the blinds. "If we go through here, we're back into the living room," she said flicking on a switch to put the fireplace on. "You can see it from the living room and dining room," she noted before switching it off. "I'll put it back on later."

"This is a beautiful place, Olivia!" said Thomas sitting down with her and reaching for his beer.

"I love it!" she said taking a sip of her drink. "I thought we could finish these, go for a swim, and have dinner afterwards. Maybe listen to some music, and later on watch some movies. Or are you hungry now?"

"No, it sounds good."

"Let me go and turn off the stove," she said getting up and leaving.

"Are there change rooms?" asked Thomas.

"Yes, and lockers with keys, it's on the eighteenth floor," echoed her voice from the kitchen. "There shouldn't be many people at this time of night," she said her voice getting clearer as she came back into the room and sat down.

They finished their drinks the had another.

Thomas changed and waded into the empty pool.

A door opened and out strolled Olivia wearing a navy-blue Body Glove bikini. Her nipples were hard, her stomach flat, and her legs were long and lovely. Thomas couldn't help his stare.

Olivia's question broke her spell. "How's the water?"

"Wonderful!" replied Thomas as he swam to the deep end and turned to get a look at her from the back. "Flawless," he whispered.

Olivia stepped into the shallow end, dunked her head, and swam towards him. "You're right, it is, but I'm surprised it's empty, there are usually a couple of people here."

"Does this place have a fitness room?" asked Thomas.

"It's on the ground floor," she replied. "They use one of the rooms for aerobic classes, and I usually go Tuesday and Thursday nights. Do you work out?" She could tell he did.

"I run almost every morning, along with sit-ups and push-ups, and I have a bench at home, so I do weights once in a while. But if I had this, I'd be swimming every night," he admitted admiring it. "Do you work out here too?"

"Here, and my dance classes," she replied. "Come on, let's go to the shallow end so we can sit on the steps and talk some more."

They swam over and sat on the second, and as the water lapped over their stomachs, Thomas noticed how Olivia's bikini complemented her blue eyes.

"So, you're a writer?"

Thomas smiled. "I write."

"What have you written?"

"I'll be finishing my second novel in a month or so."

"When did you finish your first?"

"About five months ago?"

"Did you send it to a publisher?"

"No," he said shaking his head.

"Why not?"

"I guess I write for myself, you know as a hobby, and never really thought about sending it out."

"Can I read it?"

The question took him by surprise. "Do you want to?"

"I would love to!"

"I don't know," said Thomas hesitantly. "Kate's the only person who has read it."

"What did she think?"

"She really liked it and told me I should send it to someone."

"Well, I understand if you don't want me to read it, I know it's personal, but if you change your mind let me know."

"I will," he said turning towards her. "Do you have any hobbies?"

She laughed. "I love reading, seriously, remember last week you asked me what I liked to do."

"I remember," he replied.

An older couple had entered the pool area and were placing their towels on one of the tables.

"Do you want to go in the hot tub for a few minutes?" asked Olivia.

"All right."

Olivia quickly got out before him, strolled over, and sat in the hot water. She wanted to look at him as he walked towards her. "Thomas, before you get in, can you press the red button on the wall to start it?"

Thomas looked at where she was pointing and pushed it.

He's perfect, she thought.

"Do you cook often?" asked Thomas opening the wine.

"Most of the time, I rarely order in, and if I dine out it's usually on the weekends, but that's not too often either," answered Olivia from the kitchen then joined him and placed the lasagna and bread on the table. "I hope you're hungry?" she asked then grabbed the remote for the CD player and put on the Debussy's 'Claire de Lune.' Back at the table she served the lasagna as Thomas poured the wine then lit the candles and turned off the lights.

"It looks delicious," he said Thomas raising his glass and clinking hers. "To the chef!"

"Thank you, and enjoy."

They sipped their wine and ate.

"So, what have you been doing since last time we met?" asked Olivia.

"Well, I worked all week, wrote most nights, and went grocery shopping with Kate last night."

"Do you like where you work?"

"Hm, it's a means to an end."

"What would you like to do?"

"If I had a choice?"

She nodded her head and drank her wine.

"I guess write, and get paid to do it," he replied. "I think getting paid for something you truly love to do would be unbelievable."

"So, you want to be a published writer," stated Olivia.

"In the perfect world."

"And in the not so perfect world?

"Do what I'm doing now."

"You make it sound like you don't have a choice."

"To be honest with you I don't."

"Why don't you?"

Thomas was getting uncomfortable. "It's a long story."

Olivia realized she was pushing him and changed the topic. "Tell me about your sister."

"Kate's studying to be a lawyer, and she's in her last year, and I'm very proud of her. She's kind, considerate, and would do anything for anyone," said Thomas glancing at her. "You'll have to let me return the favor and come for dinner so you can meet her."

"I would like that," said Olivia cheerfully.

"I meant to tell you earlier, Rachel dropped by last Sunday evening for a couple of hours."

"Really, what for?" asked Olivia trying not to look concerned.

"Apparently she lives a half hour north of me and dropped in on her way home."

"That was thoughtful of her."

"It was," said Thomas wondering how often they hung out. "Are you two good friends?"

"We see each other at social functions, like the fundraiser, and with us being so close in age we usually sit together, talk, and dance. We also have the same interests and tastes, so we get along really well," she explained. "Day to day we don't see much of each other, and she travels a lot because of her job. Although she did ask me to go to France in the summer, but I didn't go."

"Why not?"

"I would have liked to have but I had some personal reasons."

"Oh, I see," replied Thomas wondering what they were. "Are you going tomorrow night?"

"To Rachel's birthday party?"

Thomas nodded as he took a mouthful of food.

"Unfortunately, I have a dinner party that I need to attend. Are you going?"

"I am." He didn't know it was her birthday; he should have read the invitation. Luckily, he still had tomorrow to buy her something.

After dessert, Olivia put on the fireplace, and they moved into the living room and sat in front of its warm glow.

"Thanks for dinner it was great."

"I'm glad you enjoyed it," said Olivia before taking her last sip of wine and placing the empty glass on the table. She stood up and changed the CD to The Style Council and put on 'You're the Best Thing' then turned to Thomas. "Would you like to dance?" she asked with an outstretched hand.

Thomas stood, grabbed it, and followed her around the coffee table. She put her arms around his shoulders, and he put his on her waist. As they danced, she sang softly in his ear. Thomas asked her to play the song again, and once more, and each time she sang. They continued dancing to the next three songs, after which she stopped, gazed into his hazel eyes, thanked him, then kissed him on the cheek before letting go. "I'll get us a couple beers," she said leaving, returning with two, and pouring them. "Do you want to watch a movie?"

"They're in my bag; I'll go get them."

"It's next to the closet door in the guest room."

As Thomas headed for the room, she followed him, and stood in the doorway. "I was hoping you might stay the night. You can sleep in here."

"Sure, if you don't mind?"

"No, I would like you to," she said watching him unzip his bag. "Would you mind if I put on my pajamas?"

"No, go ahead," he said continuing his search. He found them and went into the living room.

Olivia returned wearing oversized fleece pajamas, a washed face, and her hair in a ponytail. Thomas thought she looked sexy.

"I like your pjs."

"They're actually a men's small but they're big and comfortable," she said showing them off before sitting down. "Okay, what movies do you have?" she asked excitedly.

"Well, I have *The Quiet Man*, *To Catch a Thief*, *Roman Holiday*, *Casablanca*, and *An Affair to Remember*," he replied holding them up. "Which one?"

"Oh, I love them all, it's so difficult…*An Affair to Remember*."

Olivia cried at the end, at the start of *Casablanca* she rested her head on Thomas's chest, and during *The Quiet Man* she placed a pillow on his lap, laid her head upon it, and slowly fell asleep. He waited for it to finish before carefully getting up, carrying her to the bedroom, and covering her with the duvet. Then he gently removed the elastic from her hair, placed it on the end table, kissed her on the forehead, and said sweet dreams. He returned to the living room and put away the empty beer bottles, placed the dirty glasses and dessert dishes into the dishwasher, and turned off the lights and fireplace before going into the guest room.

Thomas woke up at eight, got washed and dressed, then went to the kitchen and made a pot of coffee. He opened the blinds in the solarium, sipped his coffee, and noticed there wasn't a cloud in the sky. He moved closer to the window and looked down at the world below.

Forty minutes later, Olivia sauntered up behind him. "Sorry I fell asleep; you must think I'm awful?" Her hair was wild.

Thomas smiled at it. "I guess my company is like a sleeping pill," he joked.

"Please don't say that you're making me feel bad."

"I'm teasing you, it was late, and I was asleep fifteen minutes later."

"Thanks for tidying up," she said sitting down. "Did you take the elastic out of my hair?"

"I did."

"How did you know to do that?" she asked.

"I've taken many a woman to bed," replied Thomas.

She looked at him unsure.

He laughed. "When my sister was younger, she always had them in her hair, and when she fell asleep in front of the television, I used to take them out of her hair."

"My father did the same for me," she said and thought for a moment. "It's funny how I just remembered that, here, come with me." She led him to the master bedroom, opened the drawer, and showed him a framed picture of her with her father. "This is the last picture I have of us. It was taken down at the harbor many summers ago."

Thomas looked at the picture. Olivia must have been sixteen or seventeen, and her father was a good-sized man, and looked familiar to him. "Why do you keep it in the drawer?"

"Bad memories I guess."

"Was that day one of those bad memories?"

"No, actually, that was one of my fondest."

"Maybe you should only keep the bad memory ones in the drawer," suggested Thomas.

"You're probably right," she said placing it on the end table and closing the drawer. She turned to Thomas and caught her image in the mirror. "Ahh! Why didn't you say anything about my hair? You're so mean letting me walk around like this."

"I think it looks sexy!"

"Sexy!" she exclaimed slapping his arm. "I definitely need to fix this. Do you mind if I get a bath?"

"You get a bath. I'll make you breakfast."

"But you're my guest."

"I won't take no for an answer," replied Thomas walking her to the en suite.

"Okay, what do I have in?" she asked still half asleep. "Bacon, eggs, bagels, Rice Krispies, fruit, cream cheese."

"What would you like?"

"Rice Krispies and a toasted bagel with pineapple cream cheese."

"And to drink?"

"Orange juice and a tea with milk."

"Enjoy your bath," said Thomas starting to leave then turning around. "Do you mind if I put music on?"

"Of course not, there's a television on the kitchen counter that has a radio and a CD player."

On the way out he could hear her singing 'Ain't No Other Man' as she ran the bath water.

Olivia came into the solarium wearing a white terry robe, her hair was wet, and slicked back. She looked at the food set out on the table then stood for a moment and watched Thomas who was looking out the window at the park below. "Looks great," said Olivia.

"Thanks," he said. "Feeling better?"

She nodded and smiled.

"Have a seat," he said pulling out her chair.

"You're so organized."

"Years of practice, I guess," he said as he sat. "This room is so bright, and has such a great view of the landscape, it's ideal for eating breakfast."

"You know, I never use this room, I usually eat in the living room or in my bedroom," said Olivia, and suddenly realized Handel's 'Water Music' was softly playing in the background. "You're right though, it is ideal." As she ate her cereal, she glanced up at him. "What are you doing today?"

"Well, I need to go shopping."

"I do too! We can go together," she said animatedly. "If that's okay?"

"I was actually going to ask you if you wanted to go," admitted Thomas. "You see I never read Rachel's invitation, and I didn't know it was her birthday, so I need to get her a gift. Maybe you could help me pick something out?"

"Okay, as long as you help me pick out an outfit for tonight?"

"Deal," said Thomas.

"Let's eat up and get going," said Olivia elatedly.

Chapter 11

"I'm glad we decided to walk, it's so nice out," she said putting her arm through his. "Do you know what you want to buy Rachel?"

"No, do you have any suggestions?" asked Thomas, who had this fear that Rachel would be opening these really expensive gifts in front of everyone and then his not-so-expensive one.

"Not really, she pretty well has everything," she replied. "I bought her a Versace sweater if that helps."

Oh great, thought Thomas.

"Knowing Rachel, she's probably not expecting you to buy her anything, with it being last minute and all," suggested Olivia.

"I'd feel awkward going empty handed."

"Well, if you feel obliged, I would suggest something not too expensive, but thoughtful."

Thomas glanced up to the sky, thank you, then turned to Olivia. "Such as?"

"Perfume."

"Do you know what kind she likes?"

"I do, and the best part is, she'll know you would've had to have asked someone to find out what her favorite was, which means you were being very thoughtful." Olivia couldn't believe she had just said that, but this wasn't about Rachel was it, this was about Thomas. "You can buy it at the store that I am going to."

Thomas paid for the perfume, followed Olivia up the escalator to the top floor, and walked to the far-right corner.

"Hello, Ms. Taylor, nice to see you again. What are we looking for this morning?" said an attractive lady in her early thirties.

"Hello, Janet, I need an outfit for a dinner party that I'm going to tonight."

"You're in luck, we had some new designs arrive this week. What color were you interested in?"

"What do think Thomas?" asked Olivia.

They both turned and looked at him. "With it being so close to fall, I would suggest an autumn color, something like beige or light brown," he suggested.

"And style?" asked Jane.

"Because Olivia has shapely legs, I would suggest a dress above the knee, in the event that it's more formal, a pantsuit."

"Excellent!" said Janet impressed. "You have a keen fashion sense, Mr.?"

"Carlyle."

"Mr. Carlyle," said Janet and turned to Olivia. "I have several items you can try on. I'll be back in a minute."

"Come here often, Ms. Taylor?" asked Thomas.

"Once or twice," she quipped. "She usually calls me Liv when I come alone, I guess with you being with me she has to be formal."

"Has to be?"

"Policy, until you let her know she can call you Thomas, it will be Mr."

Janet returned holding several items. "I'll put these in change room number one. Will you need my help getting in and out of the garments?"

"No, thank you."

"Please, follow me," she asked politely and led them into a large room. At one end, there was a sofa and coffee table, at the other, a semi-circled wall with full-length angled mirrors, and in the middle, the changing room door. Janet opened it and hung the outfits inside.

"Can I get either of you a drink, tea, coffee, juice or sparkling water?"

"I'll have water," replied Olivia.

"Same, please," added Thomas.

"I'll be back in a minute Ms. Taylor and Mr. Carlyle," she said and left.

Olivia noticed Thomas looking around. "This room is usually reserved for small groups," clarified Olivia. "The other change areas aren't as large as this, then again, I'm usually on my own."

Janet returned with two bottles of water and glasses of ice. "Here you go Mr. Carlyle."

"Please, call me Thomas."

"Thank you, Thomas. Liv, would you like yours on the table also?"

"That would be fine."

Janet opened the bottles and poured the water. If you need me, there's a button over there by the changing room door that will buzz me outside. Otherwise, I'll drop by in fifteen minutes or so just to see how you're doing. I'll knock once, and when I leave, I'll lock the door behind me, so you won't be disturbed," she explained and departed.

"Wow! She's never done this before; she probably thinks you're a fashion designer!" joked Olivia.

They both laughed.

"Although I must admit, you do know the current fashions, and you're going have to tell me later how you know so much," she said dropping her coat on the sofa. "Let me go and try these on."

Olivia came out in a fitted beige dress that was cut above the knee, had a V-neck, and long sleeves. It emphasized her face, neckline, chest, waist, and when she turned around, her bottom.

"You look stunning!"

"Thank you," she said looking in the mirror. "I love it!"

She changed into the next dress, which was light brown, cut below the knee, had a boat neckline, and was short-sleeved.

"Wow, that looks good too!"

She stared at herself in the mirror. "I quite like this one," she said before strolling to the table and having a drink of water. "I'll try on the pantsuits next."

The beige pants were well-fitted and straight down, and the jacket was light and single breasted. She took off the jacket to reveal a cream silk blouse that you could just see her bra through.

"Classy."

She moved around the mirrors and smiled.

The next pantsuit was light brown with a double-breasted jacket and a black blouse.

"I like this too, but I think this is more of businesswoman's outfit," said Olivia unsure as she moved around the mirrors.

"Maybe," replied Thomas, "but it looks really good on you, and you would definitely stand out at the dinner party."

Olivia slowly nodded her head in agreement. "Well, that's all four," she confirmed heading towards him. "I'm having such a great time and you're probably ready to go."

"Are you kidding?" said Thomas getting up and meeting her. "Not at all, I've never done anything like this before, and I'm really enjoying myself."

"Really?"

"Cross my heart."

"All right," she said convinced he was. "You said you would help me pick an outfit, so, which one?"

"Well, I really like all four, and you could easily wear any one of them and be a hit,' he said thinking. "But since you only need one, I'll narrow it down to two. The first dress and pantsuit you tried on."

"I liked both of those too, but which one?"

"Why don't you try them on again so we can have a good long look at each of them before you make up your mind?

"Are you sure?" she asked happily.

"Definitely, go on," he said playfully pushing her away before sitting back down on the sofa.

There was a knock at the door, then a click. "How's she doing, Thomas?" asked Janet sticking her head in.

"Fine, she's down to two and going to try them on again."

"Okay, I'll come back in a half hour or so. Do you need any more water?"

"No, we're fine thanks."

"I'll be back shortly," she said pleasantly and left.

Olivia came out in the dress. Thomas stood up and slowly walked around her. "It's stunning…elegant…graceful…and you look beautiful!"

She looked in the mirror and moved in a circle so she could see all the angles. Thomas moved out of her way, went to the table, and picked up his water. Olivia joined him and had a sip of hers. "Do you mind if I take a few minutes and cool off?"

"Take all the time you need."

They sat in silence for a minute or two as she drank some more water.

"You will have to let me buy you lunch?"

"Honestly, you don't have to do that."

Olivia stood up, dramatically sauntered to the changing room door, opened it then glanced over her shoulder with an insubordinate look. "I want to, and I'm not taking no for an answer, so there," she said in a spoilt voice, then childishly stuck out her tongue before closing the door behind her.

Thomas chuckled at her entertaining antics.

When she came out in her pantsuit, Thomas slowly circled her again. "Classy…sophisticated…delicate…and, beautiful!"

Olivia admired herself in the mirrors while Thomas went back and sat down. Satisfied, she left, and came out holding the two outfits.

"Well, Thomas, decision time?"

"As a friend, I would have to say either one, they're both gorgeous and look fantastic on you."

"Thomas!" she pleaded then thought. "Okay, if you were my date?"

"The dress."

"The dress?"

"Definitely!"

"Can you hold these while I put on my coat?"

Thomas held the outfits while she put on her coat, then took them off him, and pressed the button.

The door unlocked and opened. "Have you decided?" asked Janet.

"Yes, I have."

"Is there anything else you will need Liv?" she asked as they walked to the sales counter.

"I wanted to look at some underwear?"

"If you've decided on one of the dresses may I suggest a thong, we have some new ones in, and they are silk, comfortable, and very discreet. I wear them all the time."

"They sound nice."

Thomas was a little uncomfortable. "Listen, I'm going to wait for you outside. Why don't you meet me by the front entrance?"

"Okay," she replied and felt bad for embarrassing him.

"Bye, Janet."

"Bye, Thomas," she replied. "Will I be seeing you at the Winter Collection show at the Convention Center?"

"Yes, yes you will," he said coming back. "You know, I thought it was you, why didn't you say something earlier?"

"I wasn't sure at first either."

"Do you still have the same seat?" asked Thomas.

"I do," replied Janet.

"I'll make sure to say hello and try not to fall onto your lap again. Which, by the way, was my sister's fault, she tripped me on purpose."

"That was your sister?" asked Janet. "She's very pretty."

"I'll make sure to pass your compliment on," he said slowly walking backwards, "bye for now, and take your time Olivia." Thomas turned around, he wasn't too sure of the way out, so just went straight.

"You have a charming boyfriend, Liv, and handsome," complimented Janet. "You make a great couple.

"He isn't my boyfriend, we're only friends," said Olivia glancing back at Thomas asking someone for directions.

Twenty minutes later, Olivia met Thomas outside, and they walked three blocks south to a small, cozy pub. Olivia was radiant.

"Two for lunch?" asked the hostess.

"Yes, please," replied Thomas.

A waiter arrived and sat them down at a table with a view of the street, took their drink order, and promptly returned with a pint of Smithwick's for Thomas and a diet coke for Olivia.

Thomas looked at the menu then over at Olivia whose menu was unopened. "You're not eating?"

"I already know what I want, fish and chips, they serve the best here."

Thomas closed the menu and gave her a doubtful look. "I've already had the best fish and chips in the city, and they weren't from here."

"Judging by your dubious face, your demeanor, and tone, I believe that sounds like a challenge, not only to my culinary palette, but the Hidden Cove pub?"

"That it is," he replied. "Remember last week when I told you about my favorite pub, The Duke, they have the best in the city."

"Ah yes, The Duke, maybe one day I will actually see this piece of Heaven," she said humorously. "They probably serve the best imported draught beer, too."

"Oh, so you have heard of it," responded Thomas grinning and drinking his beer.

"What am I going to do with you?" she asked smiling back and shaking her head. "Did you know Janet was interested in you?"

"Did she say so?"

"No, but I could tell?"

"How?"

"The way she spoke, her body language, and the way she looked at you. Plus, the fact that she gave us that room! At first, I thought she was trying to impress you because she thought you were a fashion designer, but looking back, it was because she liked you."

"Liked me?"

"Yes."

"Do you think I should pursue it?"

The question caught Olivia off guard, "Well, I'm not sure? It's your decision."

"My decision?"

"Yes."

"Well, let's see…she's attractive, has a nice figure, and is very friendly. Wouldn't you agree?"

"I would."

"And you would be comfortable with me dating her, your fashion consultant?"

"Of course," she lied.

Thomas sat back in his chair to give her the impression that he was considering it.

Olivia sipped her drink and tried her best to look uninterested.

Thomas broke into a loud laughter.

"What's so funny?" asked Olivia, who wasn't in good humor.

"I think you may be jealous?"

"I am not," she insisted, but she was.

"In any case, Olivia, I'm not interested."

"Not interested? Why not?"

"Janet has a girlfriend," revealed Thomas, "she's a lesbian."

Olivia looked at him in disbelief then suddenly realized he had been leading her on all along. "All this time you knew this, and yet, you led me to believe…" she said and was searching for the right word, "otherwise! Why? You! You…conniver!

"Conniver?" asked Thomas.

"Yes, conniver, manipulator, schemer, deceiver!" she said trying not to laugh.

"Any more or is that it?"

"No, I think I've made my point," she said giggling.

"Next time, Olivia, why don't you tell me how you really feel," joked Thomas.

"Enough," she said laughing with him.

"The reason I didn't want to tell you was to see how you would react," explained Thomas, "you know, jealous and all."

"I was not!" she said hitting his arm.

"Okay, I'm teasing, you weren't," said Thomas holding up his arms and surrendering.

"Put your arms down, you goof," she said taking a sip of coke and loving their banter. "How did you know Janet's a lesbian?"

"Kate and I went to the Fall Fashion Show, and as we were going to our seats, Kate was messing around and tripped me up, causing me to fall onto Janet's lap. Our seats ended up being next to hers, so we struck up a conversation, during which she introduced us to her girlfriend. I guess Janet just assumed Kate was my date, and that's why she was surprised to hear this morning that she was my sister."

"Oh, I see," said Olivia putting all the pieces together, "and that's how you know so much about fall fashion."

"Actually, Kate's the fashion guru, and she loves those shows. So, I go with her, and afterwards she talks nonstop about the latest styles, trends, and colors."

"Sounds like you're a good listener."

"What?"

"It sounds like you're…Oh, stop it you!" said Olivia realizing he was pretending not to hear her.

The waiter brought their lunch, and as they ate, they talked about the pub's decor and ambiance.

Olivia waited till the waiter took their empty plates away before asking him. "So, what did you think?"

"Not bad, but—"

"Not as good as The Duke?" finished Olivia.

"One Friday night, I'll take you to The Duke, and then we can have a vote on which is better, okay?"

"All right," agreed Olivia liking the fact that they had all these dates, well activities, planned.

Back at the condominium, Olivia took her shopping bags to her bedroom, while Thomas collected his from the guest room and waited for her by the front door.

"So, tomorrow?" she asked walking towards him.

"I'll be here at eight thirty," he reconfirmed. "By the way, I left you the DVDs in case you wanted to watch one of them."

"Thanks," said Olivia smiling but knowing she wouldn't watch them without him. "Enjoy the party, and make sure you say Happy Birthday to Rachel for me."

"I will and have fun at your dinner party."

"It won't be as exciting as Rachel's bash, but I'm sure it will be nice," she confessed, wishing she could bail out of it.

"I had a fantastic time last night, and today, thanks again," he said wondering if he should kiss her goodbye.

"Me too, we'll have to do it again soon."

"I'd like that," he said hesitating. "Well, I should go, I'll see you tomorrow morning."

"I'm looking forward to it," she said opening the door and watching him go down the hallway to the elevator. She wished he had kissed her goodbye, but on the bright side she was seeing him tomorrow, why rush it.

Chapter 12

Thomas pulled onto Carter Lane, drove for fifteen minutes then slowed down and stopped when he reached two large wrought iron gates. They were attached on either side to twenty-foot brick walls that ran the length of the property. On the left wall was a gold-plated plaque that read, 'The Carter Estate' and on the other, '#1 Carter Lane.' He continued through the gates on a paved road that separated sixty-foot oak trees that ran parallel with him as he drove.

Ten minutes later, he veered off to the right and realized he was in a roundabout. In its middle, was a beautiful water fountain that had statues of dolphins and fish squirting water out of their mouths. To his left, and off in the distance he could see the mansion and followed the road to the front driveway. He cautiously pulled up, showed the vested attendant his invitation then gave him his name. The man perused the guest list and checked off his name and then instructed Thomas to drive his car to the valets located in front of the garages. He proceeded in that direction, turned off his car and handed over his keys, then took the slip and watched as they drove it onto a field that was doubling as a parking lot.

Thomas strolled towards a table where he was told by the hostess to continue past the front of the mansion and follow the posted signs on the path. He reached the pathway, which was lined with eight feet hedges, and followed the arrows to the back of the house before walking down numerous steps onto a lawn that led him to the grounds.

Thomas stood in awe. In front of him were three enormous canopy tents, and in the distance, tall maple trees that encircled an exceptionally large pond. He continued on, and was met by a young, vested lady who notified him that Tent A was the bar, Tent B was serving food, and Tent C was where the music and dancing would take place.

Thomas sauntered over and went inside Tent A. To the left, were long rows of tables, behind which, were fifteen bartenders serving drinks. In the middle, were groups of people sitting around a multitude of picnic tables. And to the right, were high tables that guests were sitting and standing around. Thomas walked over to the bar and asked a pretty young girl with red hair for a Heineken. She came back with his beer and offered

Thomas a glass, which he politely refused. He turned away from her and glanced at his watch; it was six thirty. What to do now? he thought.

"There's a gift table in Tent C," said the redhaired girl motioning to his wrapped gift and card.

"Thanks," replied Thomas facing her.

"There's also a live band playing there later tonight, and a DJ," she revealed. "The band is excellent."

"You've heard them play before?" asked Thomas interestedly.

"Many times, my husband's the lead singer," she said proudly, "and I'm not saying they're good because of that."

"I believe you," said Thomas wondering why she was in this tent. "So why aren't you working in that tent?"

"There's no bar service," she said wiping the table as she spoke "I was lucky to get this job." She glanced around, leaned forward, and whispered, "I don't work for this catering company, Robby, that's my husband, he spoke to the manager and got me on the staff for tonight. I would watch him in a heartbeat, but we could use the extra money," she said unconsciously touching her stomach.

Thomas noticed. "What's the band called?" he asked taking a sip of his beer.

"AtlasX!" she said excitedly.

"AtlasX?"

"They wanted a universal sounding name with an edge."

"I like it," said Thomas.

"So do I," she said with a cute smile.

"My name's Thomas."

"Hi, Thomas, I'm Tracy."

"So, Tracy, what type of songs does AtlasX play?"

"Well, tonight they'll be playing those songs that you typically here at weddings and parties, you know, the type of songs that everyone knows and caters to all age groups."

Thomas nodded his head. "Yeah, I know."

"But when they play the clubs, they play their own songs, and they're brilliant," she said earnestly. "He's a huge Bon Jovi, actually, we both are, and that's one of the groups he gets his inspiration from, and he loves singing their songs."

"Do they take requests?"

"Definitely, if you ask him for a song, he'll play it!"

"Okay, I will. What song should I ask for?"

"Always," said Tracy without hesitation, "that's our song. He sang it to me on our first date, on the night we got engaged, and it was our wedding song." She leaned over again. "Can I let you in on a little secret?"

"Sure," replied Thomas leaning in.

"It's our first wedding anniversary tonight," she said excitedly. "If you ask him to sing it, he will, and I'll hear him from here, or I may even leave for a few minutes and sneak a peek."

"It's a shame you have to work tonight," said Thomas feeling sorry for her.

"It's okay, I'll see him during his breaks, and after we finish. As long as we're together, that's all that matters," she said happily. "And he's promised me the world when he gets his record deal, and I know he'll give it to me."

Thomas realized how in love she was. "Let me see what I can do for you," he said and suddenly sensed someone standing behind him waiting to be served. "I'll let you get back to work, nice meeting you, Tracy."

"You too, Thomas, see you later," she replied then turned her attention to the man waiting in line.

Thomas strolled into Tent C, which was much larger than the previous one, noticed the gift table, and placed his down on it. He wandered around and spotted the band at the far end of the tent setting up on the stage. He guessed Robby to be the one with the black, shoulder length hair, in black leather pants, testing the microphone. Off to their right, the DJ was setting up, and in the middle of the tent, was a spacious, raised wooden dance floor which was surrounded by tables and chairs. With the exception of the band, the DJ, Thomas, and a group of five older couples in their sixties, the tent was quite empty, and he decided to go for a walk.

Thomas strolled down to the pond, which was more like a small lake, and onto the dock. He looked at the speedboat, then out onto the pond, and could see a medium-sized, man-made wooden raft which he assumed was there for people swim out to and sunbathe on. He left the dock and sat under a large maple tree, as he sipped his beer, he wondered if Rachel still swam in the pond and sunbathed on the raft. Then he thought about Olivia in her sexy bikini and how beautiful she looked in her dress. He pondered where she was tonight and if she had a date, but concluded she would have said something. He wondered if there was a reason why she hadn't said anything more about her dinner party; maybe there was nothing to tell. Wherever she was, he hoped she was having fun. He took another sip of his beer and listened to the murmur of the crowd growing louder and wondered where Rachel was. "She's probably finishing getting ready," he said to himself. He really liked her and couldn't wait to see her again.

Thomas decided to go back and socialize with some of her guests, so he finished his beer, got up, and headed for the bar tent.

"Thomas," he heard as he walked in, and looked around. "Thomas over here!" said Jack waving him over.

"Hi, Jack," said Thomas. He was glad to see him.

Jack stood, put his arm around him, and gave him a squeeze. "I've been looking for you. Did you just get here?"

"About twenty minutes ago, I had a walk around."

"Here's your Heineken, Thomas," said Tracy. "I'll take that empty back."

"Thanks, Tracy."

Jack looked at Tracy sauntering away then at Thomas.

"A friend," he said reading Jack's mind.

"Nice friend to have," replied Jack. "Come, sit down, and meet some of my new friends."

He sat next to Jack and looked across the table.

"Thomas, this is Tiffany, Elle, and Leanne," said Jack. "Girls, this is Thomas."

"Hello," said Thomas.

"Hello," replied the three exceptionally pretty girls.

"From what I understand, these are three of Rachel's model friends," whispered Jack. "Have you had a really good look around?"

Thomas followed Jack's eyes and picked up on what he was saying, with the exception of the older married guests, a high percentage of the girls were young and extremely attractive. "Are these all models?" asked Thomas.

Jack laughed, then whispered, "they're either models or rich kids who can afford to look good."

When Taxi Jack made comments like that, Thomas wondered who he really was, not that it actually mattered, because Thomas really liked Jack. Yet, there was something about him he couldn't quite put his finger on.

"So, we still on for Friday morning?" he asked. "I know it was short notice calling you yesterday."

"Yeah, I got the day off, but maybe we should make it a week Friday so I can give you a chance to improve your fourteen handicap!" suggested Thomas cheekily.

Jack was caught off guard and choked on his whiskey, making Thomas laugh out loud.

"How did you find out?" he asked wanting to know.

"I have friends," bragged Thomas.

"In low places," stated Jack.

"In the right places," corrected Thomas.

The three girls, who had been talking amongst themselves, stood up in their micro dresses and excused themselves. Jack and Thomas watched them strut away.

Jack turned to Thomas. "I heard you stopped by and saw Barry Levinson late Wednesday afternoon."

"Yes, I did, he called me and asked me to pick up a laptop for him. So, I dropped one off," he said glancing at Jack. "How did you know?"

"I ran into him late Thursday," he replied. "He said the technician had come by and set it up for him."

"Yeah, the warranty he has includes the setup as well as the technician explaining all the bells and whistles."

"Barry says he really likes it and that you got him a thirty per cent discount."

"I did," replied Thomas.

"He wanted to talk to one of the sales reps at QTech about getting a hundred more for his employees, and to ask you if you knew someone he could contact."

"Sure, a good friend of mine is a sales rep, I'll give him a call on Monday."

"I'll be seeing Barry tomorrow and I'll let him know," said Jack. "Did you know he's a corporate lawyer?"

"I did."

"That he's the owns that firm?" continued Jack.

"I had an idea," replied Thomas.

"Well, he's getting the laptops for all the lawyers and paralegals."

An attendant interrupted their conversation. "Please, ladies and gentlemen, I ask that everyone make their way into Tent C."

Thomas and Jack sauntered into Tent C and stood in the back.

"Familiar territory for you, eh, Thomas," said Jack amusing himself by recalling the fundraiser.

"Ha, ha," replied Thomas unamused and making Jack laugh louder.

"Ladies and Gentlemen, if we could have your attention, please," said a man in his fifties wearing a custom-made blue suit. His hair was short, gray, and parted to the side.

"That's Rachel's old man, Bill," whispered Jack.

"Thank you. As you know today is our daughter's twenty-seventh birthday, and I'm so glad that you are all here to help us celebrate this special day with her. As parents, Jessica and I couldn't be any prouder. So please, raise your glasses to our beautiful daughter, Rachel." With her mother on her arm, Rachel walked out from the crowd towards her dad; she looked incredible.

Everyone sang a chorus of happy birthday, as the four-layer cake decorated with white and pink flowers and twenty-seven lit candles, was carried out and placed in front of her. Rachel closed her eyes, made a wish, and blew them out as the crowd cheered. She waited for them to stop before speaking. "I would like to thank you all for being here tonight. It is so wonderful to look around the room and see so many of my dear friends and family. Again, thank you for coming, and for all your wonderful presents." She stopped and turned to her parents. "Thanks, Mom and Dad, for throwing me this beautiful party, and for making this day so special." Rachel then looked at the crowd. "Now it is time for everyone to eat, drink, dance, and have fun."

"Let's party!" yelled a voice in the crowd making everyone laugh.

Thomas could see her smiling face through the crowd then watched it disappear as everyone surrounded her. The lights lowered, the DJ said his congratulations, and started the music. The tent was now full of young people on the dance floor and older ones sitting around watching them. Jack left to go speak to an acquaintance and Thomas approached a heavyset girl named Veronica, who was sitting alone, and asked her to dance. He danced a couple of songs with her, thanked her, then noticed Jessica and asked her for a dance. After which, Jessica introduced him to Bill, who said they would get together later and have a talk, then excused himself. Thomas left Jessica with her friends and went outside for some fresh air.

"Thomas there you are!" said Rachel. "Have you met my friends Tiffany and Leanne?"

"Yeah, I met them earlier on, hello again."

"Hello, Thomas," they replied.

Rachel took his arm, told her friends she would see them later, and strolled with him down to the water's edge where she stopped and looked at him. "Thomas, I'm so glad you're here!"

"I wouldn't have missed it for the world, Happy Birthday," he said hugging her and giving her a kiss. He held her hands, stood back, and admired her. She was wearing an above the knee, tight-fitting brown dress that showed off her curves, and her blonde hair was curly and fell past her shoulders. She looked like a super model. "You look great, and I like your dress, only you could get away with a dress like that."

"Thank you," replied Rachel blushing. "You look very handsome. I'm going to have to keep an eye on my friends tonight," she said grabbing his arm again and starting back. "Are you enjoying yourself so far?"

"I am, this is great."

"Is there anything I can get you? Or anything you need?" she asked.

"No, what more could I ask for, besides, it's your birthday I should be taking care of you. Is there anything you need?"

"No, I have everything I need," she said squeezing his arm.

Thomas remembered something, stopped, and glanced over at her. "Actually, there is something you can do for me," he said and told her.

They went to the bar, got a drink then went to Tent C, and danced to the DJ's music. Some of Rachel's friends joined in and they all danced together. After the DJ finished his set, there was a short intermission while the band did some last-minute preparations. Rachel excused herself from the group, and when she reappeared, the dance floor was empty, and she walked across it with Tracy to the front of the stage. Rachel asked Tracy to wait, while she went onto the stage and talked to Robby, then walked off and stood next to her.

"Ready boys?" asked Robby to the band.

"Ready, Robby," they replied.

Robby looked excitedly at the crowd. "At the request of our birthday girl, Rachel, and to get this party started, we will be rocking with a set of three Bon Jovi song…One, two, three."

The music started and Rachel danced with Tracy, then pulled Veronica up, then Thomas. In no time the dance floor was packed as Robby did Jon Bon Jovi justice. On the third song, Rachel pulled up a seat next to the steps leading up to the stage for Tracy to sit on. Robby walked down them, sat, and stared at Tracy, then started to sing 'Always.' Tracy started to cry.

Rachel walked up to Thomas, looked deeply into his eyes, and asked him to dance with her, which he accepted.

At one o'clock, the party came to an end. Veronica had met a guy from her university days and was sitting at a corner table talking with him. He reminded Thomas of Buddy Holly. Jack had gone up to the mansion with Bill and Jessica, AtlasX and the DJ were taking down their equipment and loading it into their cube vans, and the caterers were starting to clean up.

"Do you want to go for a walk?" asked Rachel.

"I'd like that," replied Thomas.

"Around the pond?"

"Around the pond it is," he confirmed.

"First, let me tell Veronica," she said and came back shortly with a bottle of champagne and two glasses. "Let's go."

"Rachel, Thomas," said a voice from behind, they both turned, it was Tracy calling them and she was with Robby.

"I wanted to thank you Rachel for letting me spend the evening with Robby and still getting paid, that was so nice of you," she said giving her a hug. She then hugged Thomas and whispered in his ear, "I know you were behind all this, thank you." She kissed him softly on the cheek.

"Thank you, Rachel, and congratulations," said Robby, then thanked Thomas and shook his hand.

"You guys were great tonight," said Thomas.

"Thanks," he replied. "It makes a big difference having that someone special in the crowd," he said putting his arm around Tracy.

Tracy put her head on his shoulder. "You two make a good couple," said Tracy to Rachel.

Thomas and Rachel quickly glanced at one another.

"We're going back to our place to spend some time alone and enjoy our anniversary," said Tracy.

"Yeah, it's time to get out of these pants," added Robby.

Everyone laughed.

"I didn't mean it that way."

"They know honey," said Tracy, "besides, that's my job."

They laughed again.

"Robby, not to sound odd, but those leather pants look great. Who made them?" asked Thomas.

"You're looking right at her!"

"Tracy, you made these?" asked Rachel.

"And the vest!" added Robby.

"Yeah, I'm studying to be a designer, part-time."

Thomas glanced over at Rachel. "I always wanted to wear leather pants but never had the nerve to get a pair."

"You would look great in them," replied Rachel with a seductive wink.

"Thanks again," said Tracy realizing it was time for them to go.

"Here," said Rachel handing Tracy the champagne and glasses, "you two have a romantic evening."

"We can't accept this," said Tracy.

"Once Rachel's made up her mind, there's no changing it," confirmed Thomas.

Tracy hugged her, then they said goodbye, and Rachel and Thomas watched the happy couple leave.

"To the bar," said Rachel.

Tent A was empty, but the beer and champagne were still in the ice filled containers. Rachel picked out a bottle of champagne and two glasses out of a crate. They went outside and walked on the grass around the left side of the pond till they came to a paved trail that Rachel said circled the pond.

"Are you cold?" asked Thomas.

"No, I'm fine," she replied. "I'm still warm from dancing."

"Are you and Veronica close friends?"

"We used to be closer, but I haven't seen her for a while. That's why I asked her to stay over tonight and go riding with me tomorrow." She glanced at Thomas "She thinks you're great."

They walked quietly for a few minutes.

"What about Olivia? Are you and her close?"

"Not really, at social events we are, but not everyday life," she answered, then thought for a moment. "I asked her to go to France with me in the summer, she wasn't dancing and had no summer plans, but she said she couldn't. Something to do with a personal matter. I thought we could have been closer, you know with neither of us having sisters and always being at the same social functions, but she always keeps her distance. It's like there's something else, I'm not sure what and I can't explain it, but something. I asked her to come tonight, but she couldn't make it because of a dinner party, I was kind of hoping she would." Rachel stopped. "Well, here's the guesthouse."

"This is a guesthouse?" asked Thomas. "It looks like a Cape Cod beach house."

"Actually, it's a replica of the one my grandmother owns in Cape Cod," revealed Rachel. "I love this place, it's peaceful and quiet, and I sometimes come here when I want to be alone."

"I can see why you would."

They walked up to the front door; she bent down and reached for the key under a garden gnome and opened it. They went inside and Rachel turned on the light. It was a beautiful, open-concept design.

"There's a living room area with an entertainment center and gas fireplace, a dining room, a desk and chair with a computer and phone, and a kitchen," said Rachel as Thomas followed her into it and watched her put down the bottle and glasses on the island before following her through the patio doors onto a large deck.

"What a magnificent view of the pond and trees," said Thomas strolling to the end and leaning on the railing then noticing steps to his far right.

"Those take you to the lower-level deck," said Rachel joining him.

"You can't see the main house from here," noticed Thomas.

"We had it built here for privacy," she smiled. "Come on I'll show you the lower level."

He went inside and followed her downstairs. There was a full bar, billiard table, poker table, and dartboard. It had a rich red carpet and oak paneling, and the sofa, love seats, and armchairs, faced a large brick fireplace. They walked over to the patio doors and went outside. This deck was longer and wider than the one above and Thomas noticed the steps from the deck above came onto this one.

"Look at this Thomas," said Rachel partially lifting the cover up. "It's a ten-person hot tub. We have this on all year." She replaced the cover and grabbed Thomas's hand. "Let me show you upstairs." They went inside and climbed the stairs to the top floor. There were two bedrooms and a bathroom at the back of the house, and a master bedroom with an en suite at the front. She led him into the master. "There's a double bed with a thick down filled duvet and several large pillows, and," said Rachel opening two French doors, "a large balcony that has two Adirondack chairs." They walked onto it, and she stood close to him. "What do you think?"

"This is inspirational!" declared Thomas.

"Wait till you see the loft," she said closing the doors behind them, walking out to the hallway, and ascending a smaller set of stairs.

The loft was a small room that had a desk, chair, and three bookcases filled with encyclopedias. There were two reclining chairs facing a large round window that offered a view of the pond. The floor was hardwood, but under the recliners was a large Persian rug, and in the corner was a small electrical heater.

"Now, this is inspirational!" exclaimed Thomas.

"I know you're a writer. So, I thought you might want to come by here on weekends or weeknights and use it. It's peaceful, quiet, and inspirational! We never use this house, and most of our guests stay in the mansion, but we do have maids come in and clean it twice a week," she said looking at him. "You could come and go as you please, all you would have to do is let the butler know when you would be here, and he'd make a notation on his board to make sure there was food and clean sheets." She stopped and smiled. "I thought this would help you with your writing and give you some personal space."

"Are your parents okay with this?"

"I haven't asked them, but I'm sure they wouldn't have a problem with it, like I said, it never gets used, and most of our guests stay in the

East Wing, that's where Veronica, Jack, and a couple of other guests are staying tonight," she explained.

"And me," added Thomas.

"I thought you might prefer to stay here tonight, a kind of trial run," she suggested. "I had the maids clean it up for you, make up the master bedroom, and there's food and beer in the kitchen."

"Did you fix this loft up for me?"

"Maybe," she said with a crafty grin.

Thomas looked around; he loved it. "And you, where are you sleeping?"

"I was going to stay here, in one of the two bedrooms," she replied. "Unless that makes you uncomfortable?"

"No, not at all, but I have to leave early in the morning to go to church, but I'll be back for lunch."

"That's okay, I thought you may have needed a lie in, so I promised Veronica I would go riding with her tomorrow morning. She'll be taking off after lunch, which means we can spend the afternoon together," she explained. "Now, what about other nights?"

"I'd love to come here, this loft is perfect, and the view is incredible," he said looking out of the window then remembering something and turning to her. "But you need to clear it with your parents first."

"I will, I promise," she said happily. "Now, let's go drink that champagne and celebrate in the hot tub!" He followed her into the master bedroom where she opened a chest of drawers, pulled out a pair of swimming shorts, and handed them to him. "Thomas, all you need to do is pull the cover right off, and the button to turn it on is on the outside wall under the deck stairs. And while you're doing that, I'll grab the towels, champagne, and glasses," she said heading for the door. "I'll be down shortly."

Thomas sat in the hot tub, and something caught his eye, it was Rachel's silhouette opening the patio doors. She turned on two small floodlights, closed them, and strolled over to Thomas. Her curly blonde hair was tied back in a ponytail, and she was wearing a yellow high cut Nike bikini which fit her perfectly in all the right places. As she leaned down to place the champagne bottle and glasses next to Thomas, he noticed her round breasts had a light sprinkling of freckles on them. She quietly slipped in beside him as he opened the champagne, filled the two glasses, and handed her one.

"What a beautiful night," he said glancing up at the star-filled sky.

"Gorgeous," she said gazing at him, "and what a dreamy way to end a perfect evening."

Chapter 13

"Good morning, Robert," said Thomas to the doorman after reading his nametag.

"Good morning, sir. Can I help you?"

"Can you call Ms. Taylor and let her know Thomas is here."

"Certainly," he said picking the phone, dialing the number, and waiting. "There' no answer. Is she expecting you?"

"Yes, at eight thirty."

Robert looked at his watch. "It's eight thirty-five, let me try one more time," he said dialing again. "Sorry, sir, there's still no answer."

Thomas stood wondering what to do. He placed a brown envelope on the counter and decided to wait a few more minutes. Suddenly he heard laughter coming from outside and recognized the voice, it was Olivia's, he then heard a male voice, and they were heading towards the entrance door. Olivia hadn't noticed him.

"Robert, here she comes, she's with another man," said Thomas frantically looking around for a place to hide.

"Behind the wall," said Robert, pointing over Thomas's shoulder.

Thomas hid.

"Good morning, Rob," said Olivia.

"Good morning, Olivia, Frank," replied Robert.

"Haven't seen you at The Stallion recently?" he asked.

"One of the doormen and his wife just had a baby, so I've been pulling night shifts and double shifts," he explained. "Hopefully I'll be back there in a couple of weeks."

"I'll let the others know," said Frank, as he and Olivia moved away from the desk towards the elevator.

Thomas shifted further back so he wouldn't be seen.

"I had such a good time last night," she said smiling.

"It was a lot of fun," replied Frank. "You know I love you."

"I love you, too," replied Olivia.

Thomas peeked around the wall to see her kiss him on the lips.

"Are you sure you're okay with this?" she asked.

"I'm sure," he replied.

The elevator doors opened, and Olivia and Frank sauntered in. Thomas walked out into the lobby and noticed she wasn't even wearing the dress he had chosen but the pantsuit. Olivia turned around, and just before the doors closed, caught a glimpse of Thomas.

He turned and headed for the front door.

"Your envelope?" said Robert picking it off the counter.

"Throw it away," he replied scurrying out.

Thomas walked around for twenty minutes, before returning to the park outside of Olivia's building and sitting on a bench shaded by a tree and away from the noise of the street. Overhead, a light breeze rustled the leaves in a melancholy harmony that echoed his own sadness. A laughing couple pushing a stroller walked past and out of sight. Typically, he would have been happy for them, but not today. He peered through the leaves and could see Olivia's condominium, and wondered what they were doing up there. He hung his head and put his hands over his face, he didn't want to think about it anymore, it was too painful.

Chapter 14

"Here is your tea, sir," said the butler startling Thomas, and placing the tray on the table closest to where he was standing.

"Thank you," he replied managing a smile.

"Would you like me to pour, sir?"

"No, I can take care of that."

"Mr. Carter will be with you shortly, is there is anything else I can get for you?"

"No, that's fine, thank you."

"Enjoy, sir," he said and departed.

Thomas poured his tea, stared out the window at the gardens, and thought about Olivia's deception. "You hadn't seen that one coming," he said to his reflection.

"Sorry to keep you waiting," said Bill Carter closing the doors behind him, walking over to Thomas, and shaking his hand. "Quite a view," he said as they looked out.

"I was just admiring your gardens," admitted Thomas.

"Our gardener is from England, and he's magnificent, you should see what he does to this place in the spring," said Bill moving away from the window and motioning to an armchair. "Please have a seat." Bill waited till Thomas sat, then occupied the chair opposite him.

"Did you enjoy yourself last night?" asked Bill.

"I did, thank you," he replied. "It was a wonderful party."

"It's been quite some time since I've seen Rachel have so much fun," stated Bill getting to the point. "I don't know if you are aware of this, but at one time Rachel and Veronica were the best of friends, in fact, quite inseparable. But unfortunately, Rachel has started spending less time with Veronica, and more time with her model friends," he said crossing his legs. "I don't know if you met these 'so-called friends,' if you haven't, take it from me, they're very one dimensional and dull-witted. Unlike Veronica, who is down-to-earth, well-balanced, intelligent, and far much better suited for Rachel," explained Bill pausing before revealing his own selfish motives. "With her father and uncle being business partners of mine, having Rachel and Veronica, shall I say close, benefits us all. If you know what I mean?"

Thomas smiled, he knew exactly what he meant, and when to listen.

Bill continued. "The reason I have a golf game with her father and two of his business associates this afternoon is because he saw his daughter and Rachel dancing the night away, having fun, and becoming friends again. And with them going horseback riding this morning, I can go to the clubhouse and tell them they are getting along famously and have never been closer," he revealed, then collected his thoughts. "Thomas, who do you think I have to thank for this? My daughter? That it was her initiative that made this happen?"

Thomas nodded.

"No," said Bill theatrically clasping his hands, then motioning them toward Thomas and grinning. "Actually, you."

"Me?" asked Thomas surprised.

"Rachel sees you dancing and talking with Veronica, the next minute, she is. Then they socialize all night, and before you know it, they're making plans to go riding. Let's face it Thomas, Rachel likes you, Veronica likes, my wife likes you, even Veronica's father likes you," he said standing and walking around to emphasize the next point he was about to make. "You see Thomas, to Veronica's father and his associates, family is very important, and just as important, is how their family members interact with other family members. So, it's imperative to Veronica's father, that his family and my family get along, especially Veronica and Rachel, and when they do, it makes conducting business that much easier."

And you, what do you want? thought Thomas.

"As far as I'm concerned," continued Bill as if reading Thomas's mind, "I also like the way things are working out, and I would like them to continue that way. Do you know what I mean?"

Thomas didn't. "I'm not sure," he replied honestly.

"Over the last week, my wife has seen a positive change in Rachel, and I noticed it myself for the first-time last night," confessed Bill. "Jessica and Veronica's father believe you're the reason behind this transformation, and they also say it's because of your friendship with her," said Bill quickly glancing at Thomas. "You two are only friends?"

"Yes, Mr. Carter," answered Thomas.

"As I said earlier, I truly believe Rachel removing herself from these modeling playmates and having more practical friends is a good thing. I know Veronica is one such friend, and I believe Thomas, you are another. Would you agree?"

Thomas nodded in agreement, and without him saying it, realized what Bill wanted was for Rachel and Veronica to continue to be friends, and keeping Thomas in the picture would benefit his cause. It had nothing to do with disliking Rachel's model friends.

"Well, thanks for taking the time to speak with me," said Bill ironically and respecting his silence. "Rachel and Veronica will be back from their ride at twelve-thirty, and Rachel said that they would have lunch with you in the guesthouse." He picked up the phone and asked the butler to come in, then turned to Thomas, it was time to ensure he played his part. "Rachel has asked if you can use the guesthouse, Jessica and I have agreed that you can, and it's for your use for whatever period of time you need and for often as you like."

"Yes, Mr. Carter?" asked the butler.

"Please make sure Mr. Carlyle has a key to the guesthouse, and there is a golf cart available for him when he's here, and that all the necessary cleaning and stocking is done as required."

"Yes, sir, is there anything else?" asked the butler.

"Not at this time," replied Bill and waited for him to leave before looking at Thomas.

"Thank you, Mr. Carter, for your hospitality and generosity," he said graciously.

"It's my pleasure, and please, call me Bill," he said slowly walking toward Thomas. "I have to be honest with you, I am somewhat uncomfortable with this arrangement, but I trust you will not compromise our generosity or my daughter in any way?" asked Bill, who didn't want Rachel and Thomas becoming romantically involved, and if he had it his way would have refused him access to the guesthouse, but he needed Thomas around to play his part and keep everyone happy.

"No, sir," replied Thomas.

"Good," said Bill quickly changing the topic. "So, you're a writer?"

"Yes."

"What do you like to write?"

"Fiction."

"I love to read, although my preference is mystery," he professed. "There are over two thousand books in here: fiction, nonfiction, mystery, romance, reference, and several first additions. Anytime you want to borrow one, help yourself," he offered then pointed. "There is a computer over there just next to the staircase. You can use it to look up a title, its location, and to sign it out. I'm a stickler for details."

"Thank you," said Thomas appreciatively. He strolled over and glanced up at the fifteen feet of bookshelves and the accompanying sliding ladders that ran along its horseshoe design. There were more books on the second floor, which could be reached by a black, wrought iron circular staircase off to the left.

"This is where I come for my piece of mind," stated Bill studying Thomas. "If you ever want your writing critiqued or considered for publication, let me know, I have some friends in the business."

"Thanks for the offer," he said joining him.

Bill glanced at his watch. "Eleven forty-five, I have to get going, I have a one o'clock tee off. If you like, you can stay here and have a look around or head to the guesthouse?"

"I think I'll make my way to the guesthouse," replied Thomas.

"Fine, I'll walk you to the back door."

Thomas followed Bill, then strolled out onto the brick patio, and took the path to the guesthouse. As he walked, he reflected on Bill using Rachel's friendship with Veronica for his own personal gain, and it didn't sit well with him, overall, he found Bill unsettling. He decided not to read too much into it, and just be thankful for the offer of the guesthouse. He was looking forward to seeing Rachel, but when he arrived the house was empty, so he went upstairs and lay on the bed and within minutes he was asleep.

"Good afternoon, sleepy head," whispered Rachel sitting on the edge of the bed in track pants and a sweater.

"What time is it?" asked Thomas.

"Two thirty, you've been asleep for at least two hours."

"Two hours. Why didn't you wake me?"

"Well, two reasons, first, you were sound asleep and looked so peaceful, and second, it gave me and Veronica time to make lunch and talk some more," she explained. "We've saved some for you. Why don't you take a shower while I go warm it up for you and I'll meet you downstairs?"

Fifteen minutes later, Thomas ambled into the kitchen.

"Why don't you go sit outside and I'll be out in a minute."

Thomas sat at the patio table, the sun was warm, but a cool breeze blew occasionally across the deck.

"Here you go, it's homemade chicken noodle soup with a ham and cheese sandwich. We made the soup from scratch," said Rachel pleased with herself and taking as sip of her diet Pepsi.

Thomas tried the soup. "Wow, this is delicious!"

"I'm glad you like it," said Rachel happily.

"Where's your partner in crime?"

"She left after lunch, and asked me to say goodbye, she really likes you."

"I like her, too, she's a nice girl," confirmed Thomas.

Rachel silently watched him eat, after he finished, she picked up his dishes and asked him if he wanted a drink with dessert. She returned with a cup of coffee and chocolate chip cookies.

"From scratch?" he queried.

She nodded and smiled. "Do you like them?"

He hesitated, then made a face. "Not bad."

She gave his bicep a playful squeeze. "Not bad, they're the best in the country."

"Okay, okay, they're the best."

She patiently stared at him.

Thomas had a feeling there was something on her mind. "You know Rachel, I think we should just sit here a while, enjoy the silence, and this lovely day," he teased. "What do you think?"

"Well, okay," she replied sadly and stared out at the pond.

"Unless there's something you wanted to talk about?"

"No, nothing in particular," said Rachel realizing he knew there was and that he was tormenting her.

"Are you sure?"

"Positive," she replied, finishing her drink.

"Well, I guess I won't tell you something I found out this morning."

"There's nothing that you could have heard from the time you left me this morning, till now, that would mildly interest me or that I don't already know about."

"Okay, I guess a conversation with your dad in his study would be uninteresting, or perhaps you already know what we talked about," said Thomas indifferently as he gazed at the pond. "What a magnificent day."

"You spoke to my dad in his study? He never lets strangers in there. What did he say?" asked Rachel excitedly.

"Oh, I'm a stranger now!"

"You know what I mean! What did he say?"

"I'm sure nothing that would interest you," he replied.

"Thomas," she said pulling at his arm, but he was too strong, so she stood up and went behind him. "Thomas, if you don't tell me," she whispered sensually into his ear, "then I will have to do something that won't be nice, in fact, it will be very, very naughty." She lightly blew in his ear then gently nibbled his earlobe.

"What's that?" asked Thomas aroused.

"This!" she said pulling on his sweater, pouring the glass of ice down his back, and swiftly running inside. Thomas quickly jumped up, opened up the bottom of his sweater to let the ice cubes fall out, then chased after her. He listened to her footsteps above, climbed the stairs, and went into the master bedroom. Thomas looked under the bed, in the closet and out on the balcony, before going inside and into the en suite. He could hear her breathing in the shower stall and slowly tiptoed over, quietly put his hand around the curtain, and turned on the cold water.

"Ahh!" Rachel yelled as she turned it off and opened the curtain. "Someday when you're not expecting it, I'll get you for this!" she warned as her long hair hung over her face, and her sweater clung to her breasts, revealing her hard nipples.

Thomas pulled her wet hair aside exposing her sparkling green eyes. "I'll get you a towel," he said turning to go.

"Since I'm already wet, I might as well get a hot shower. If I throw my clothes over, will you hang them over the chair?"

"All right," said Thomas returning with a towel. Her clothes were on the floor, and the shower was running. He picked up her track pants and sweater and hung them over the chair, then her white bra and silk panties. "I've left the towel on the sink," he said glancing at the curtain and catching her silhouette. Her hands were over her head washing her hair, her back was arched, and her full breasts were accentuated. He could even see the outline of her small waist and curvy legs.

Rachel stuck her head around the curtain. "Thanks, I'll only be a minute."

"Okay, I'll wait for you in the bedroom," said Thomas promptly glancing away unsure if she had caught him or not. He left the bathroom, and decided to go onto the balcony, and gazed at the pond.

"What are you thinking about?" she asked standing next to him.

"Just how peaceful it is here," he said turning to her. She was in a bathrobe and had her wet hair brushed back. "We should go inside before you catch a cold. Are you going to dry your hair?"

"I should but I'm too tired," she replied.

"Come over here and sit down at the makeup table," he said leading her by the hand, then left and came back with the hair dyer, plugged it in, and started to dry her hair.

"You're very gentle," she whispered. "I have a feeling you've done this before."

"Many times," he replied.

"Who was the lucky girl?" she teased.

"My sister, Kate."

"She's lucky to have a brother like you, I wish I had one."

"She's more than a sister, we're best of friends," acknowledged Thomas, then finished drying her hair. "All done."

"That was so wonderful," she said yawning. "Now I'm sleepy!"

"Why don't you lie down on the bed and have a nap?"

"Lay with me just till I fall asleep?" she asked pulling him onto the bed.

"Okay," he replied laying down next to her.

She moved closer, put her head on his chest, and fell asleep soon after. Thomas looked at the ceiling, thought about the hot tub last night, and what they talked about. He gently placed a pillow under her head and left the room.

Rachel woke up and went downstairs. "There you are," she said entering the room still in her robe. "What time is it?"

"Four," answered Thomas hitting the que ball. "Do you feel better?"

"I do, thanks for lying with me," she said strolling over to him. "Are you staying for dinner?"

"I can't, I promised Kate I'd be home for six," said Thomas. "Which means I'll have to leave in an hour."

"We never did go horseback riding. Maybe next time?" she asked.

"Next time," he confirmed, "and after we've both had a good night's sleep."

"I enjoyed last night, especially the hot tub, that was a lot of fun," she said smiling.

"It was," agreed Thomas.

"I'm glad you enjoyed it, next time you come, we'll go swimming," stated Rachel.

"Swimming?" questioned Thomas. "In the pond?"

Oliva laughed. "No, silly, we have an indoor swimming pool connected to the house," she said grabbing his arm. "Why don't I take you for a walk and I'll show you around the estate?"

"I'd like that."

"Okay, let me get dressed," she said strolling away, "besides, it will give us a chance to talk."

They walked out the front door and continued around the other side of the pond back to the estate. Rachel was wearing a white sweater, black leggings and Nike running shoes. Her blonde hair was loose and blowing in the breeze. Thomas wondered if she ever looked bad in anything she wore.

"Are you interested in what your father and I talked about?"

"Not really."

"No," said Thomas surprised.

Rachel grinned and glanced at Thomas. "I saw my dad before he left to go to his golf game, and he told me what you two talked about."

"So, you already knew?"

"Yes, I did, he wanted to meet you and…" She stopped.

"And?" asked Thomas.

"And nothing, said Rachel looking straight ahead.

"Rachel!" exclaimed Thomas. "Tell me."

"Okay, he thinks you would be a good friend for me to have but he's somewhat wary about us, you know the way fathers are." She caught herself. "Oh, I'm sorry about the father thing."

"That's okay, don't worry about it, I know what you meant. I act the same way with Kate," he admitted. "I got the feeling he was a little uncomfortable about it."

"Well, he told me he liked you; my mother doesn't have a bad word to say about you, and Jack acts as if you and him are best friends. Then there's Veronica, who thinks I should lock you in the guesthouse and never let you go. Oh, that reminds me, Veronica has a date with the guy from last night, the one with the black rimmed glasses, looks like Buddy Holly."

"Buddy Holly!" exclaimed Thomas chuckling. "I'd forgotten all about him."

"Actually, his name is Johnny, but everyone calls him Buddy. Anyway, she really likes him, and she's seeing him again on Friday."

"Good for her," said Thomas.

Rachel hesitated "She was hoping we would meet up with them."

"Friday night?" asked Thomas.

"Yes, Friday night."

"I can't, I'm playing golf with Jack, and after I'm going to his place for dinner."

"Oh, too bad," said Rachel sadly. "She'll be disappointed, too."

"Any other day would be fine?" suggested Thomas. "How about Saturday?"

"Let me find out," said Rachel. "Do you know when you're coming over again?"

"I'll have to talk to Kate tonight and work out a schedule," explained Thomas. "Once I've done that, I'll give you a call and check it out with you, I want to make sure you're going to be here."

Rachel smiled. "You should bring Kate with you one day."

"Thanks, I'll mention it to her, although I fear she will exhaust you with her questions on modeling."

"I love modeling, and especially talking about it, so I look forward to it," she said putting her arm through his. "You know I talked with Veronica this morning and we're going to look into running a children's daycare together. We'll have to find out how to set one up, the legal implications, staffing, location, and so on. So, we're going to set up meetings over the next couple of weeks and get more details, and, we're going to do it on our own."

"That's terrific," he said enthusiastically. "What about modeling?"

"I'll continue with the it for now, and if later on a decision needs to be made, I'll worry about it then. Besides, it could take six, twelve, maybe eighteen months to set up a daycare. In the meantime, I'll just have to balance the two."

"You seem excited," said Thomas, then suddenly realized this is what had been on her mind and had been waiting to tell him.

"I am," she replied, stopping, and facing Thomas. "I do have one concern."

"What's that?"

"My parents."

"You haven't told them?"

"You're the first. I'm telling them tonight and I'm a little bit worried about their reaction, I was hoping you might be able to help me out on how I should approach them," she said anxiously.

"I would just tell them the same way you told me, and I think you'll find them very supportive," said Thomas confidently.

"You think so?"

"I'm sure of it!" he said reassuringly.

"But I want to do it on my own, and that may cause some problems, because I know they'll want to help and get involved. Especially my father," she said as they started to walk. "I don't want to hurt their feelings, but I really want to do this on my own. What do you think I should do?"

"I think you should be direct with them and tell them what you want to do, how you are going to do it, and how you feel about it. I'm sure they'll respect that."

She looked unsure.

"Explain to your parents what you and Veronica are planning to do, stipulate that you want to do it on your own, and if down the road you need their help you will ask," said Thomas thinking momentarily. "Then tell them you will set a couple of hours aside, you know, biweekly or monthly, and sit down with them and give them an update. Your dad is a businessman, he'll appreciate that, and so will Veronica's father. You can let them know your progress, identify any roadblocks, and ask them for some suggestions. They'll have some good ideas, but ultimately, you and Veronica decide if and how you want to use that information and proceed," he explained. "Just consider your father and Veronica's father business advisors, which they will love, and your mother more of a personal advisor, meaning she's the one you talk to about setting up the physical business, she'll love that. That way everyone will feel a part of it, but you and Veronica will be the ones in charge and in control." Thomas stopped and waited. "It's only a suggestion; there are probably better ones out there."

"No, I really yours a lot," she said placing her arm through his. "Where did you come up with that?"

Thomas laughed. "Kate and I have dinner every Sunday, and it gives us time to talk about different things while we eat. We discuss anything and everything, and basically give each other suggestions as to what we should or shouldn't do. I guess it's our version of a family meeting. Most of the time we just listen to each other," he said stopping momentarily. "It's nice to have someone to talk to but it's great to have someone to listen to you."

"I know, it does," said Rachel glad she had him.

They walked in silence for several minutes until they came to a clearing and could see the lights inside the mansion.

Rachel slowed down and pointed. "Can you see the left of the house and the windows of the study?"

"Yes," confirmed Thomas.

"Follow those windows to your left. Can you see the corner of the house?"

"Yes."

"If you look closely, you can see a wall jotting out just past the corner, and a slight sloped roof from the second story of the house."

"I see it."

"That's the roof, and the pool's in there, and there's an outdoor deck on the other side."

"It looks big," suggested Thomas. "Is it?"

"It's a fair size," she replied. "It has a slide, diving board, and there's also a whirlpool and sauna." She pointed off to the left to a rooftop between several trees. "That's the servant quarters, only the butler and his wife live there, the maids, gardeners, and stable hands live off the property. To the extremely far left, is the stables." They started to walk again. "You will see them better as we get a little closer."

As he listened to her, Thomas noticed there wasn't a tone of snobbery in her voice.

"I hope I'm not sounding like I'm bragging."

"Not at all, actually, I was just thinking about how you don't sound like that at all."

"I just want you to be familiar with the surroundings, especially since you'll be spending time here," she said seeking reassurance.

"I know and I appreciate everything you're doing," he said putting his arm around her. "I'm really looking forward to coming here."

She looked at him delightedly.

"You're still a nobody to me," he joked.

Rachel giggled. "I pretty sure the word you were looking for was unknown."

She showed him around the estate for half an hour, and on the way to Thomas's car, pointed out the place where she fell off a horse when she was eleven, and a trail that took you to a beautiful picnic spot that overlooked the valley.

"I'll give you a call after I've talked to Kate," he said opening the door, "either tonight or tomorrow."

"Okay," she said then remembered something. "I almost forgot to tell you, I received a call from Tracy earlier, she said her, and Robby enjoyed the champagne and had a lovely romantic night and wanted to thank us. She said she would call and let us know when Robby was playing at a local club and would reserve a table for us all."

"Really!"

"I told her that would be great and to call me when she found out," said Rachel. "I thought that was nice of her."

"That was," replied Thomas hesitating. "Well, I should get going." He leaned over and kissed her on the cheek.

She pulled him close and gave him a long hug. "I had a great time."

"So did I," he said getting into his car. "Call me anytime."

"Thanks, I will," she replied standing back.

As he drove away, he looked at her in his rear-view mirror.

Rachel watched the car till it was out of sight then turned around and had the happiest of smiles on her face.

Chapter 15

During dinner, Thomas talked about the last two days omitting Friday night at Olivia's and Sunday morning. While Kate spoke about her studying, then how she needed to get into a law firm part-time to gain some experience, and how it would help her before and after the bar exam. She also revealed she had submitted resumes and still had a few more to drop off but hadn't had any replies to date. Thomas told her to be patient and that she would hear back soon. Then they talked about Thomas spending time at the Carter's, and Kate coming with him one afternoon. She said she was looking forward to horseback riding, but more importantly, talking about modeling with Rachel.

After dinner, Thomas placed the plates in the dishwasher and walked into the living room with two cups of tea.

Kate waited till he sat down. "Thomas, what happened with Olivia?"

Happened? What did she know? he thought. "What do you mean?"

"Olivia's been calling all day, and she sounds really upset, and I noticed during dinner, you deliberately left out Friday night. Did something happen? Did you have a disagreement? I don't want to pressure you into telling me, and I understand if you don't want to talk about it."

Thomas had tried to forget what had happened but was having a tough time doing so. He needed someone to talk to, and Kate was that someone. So, he told her about dinner at Olivia's, shopping, and what he witnessed on Sunday morning, the only thing he left out, was his name.

"Hold on," said Kate, "I'm confused. Do you want to be more than friends?"

"What do you mean?" asked Thomas.

"Are you in love with her?"

"In love with her?" questioned Thomas. "No. Why would you think that?"

"It's just the way you speak of her, it's very passionate," said Kate, "and you seem to really like her."

"I'm just confused," said Thomas putting his hands on his head.

"She sounded really upset on the phone. Maybe you need to talk to her about it?" suggested Kate.

Thomas looked at Kate. "We're supposed to be friends, you know, honesty and trust, she's probably calling to apologize for not telling me."

Kate put her arm around him. "Thomas, if that's the case, then at least you will know the truth, but until you hear what she has to say, you're just jumping to conclusions. You really need to give her a chance to explain…I know that you are upset, and maybe you have every reason to be, but you said it yourself, you're friends."

"I don't want to talk about it anymore," he said standing and starting for the stairs, "I need to lay down, I'm tired."

"She is calling back at eight. You should talk to her."

He climbed the stairs to his bedroom and closed the door.

At eight o'clock Thomas picked up the ringing phone. "Hello."

"Hello, Thomas, its Olivia, don't hang up."

Silence.

"Thomas, you don't understand what's going on. Please, give me a chance to explain. Please."

"Is your explanation going to answer the questions I have about your trust, honesty, and our friendship?"

"I don't know, Thomas," she replied uneasily. "I was wrong, and I should have told you, but I need to explain some things to you first so you can fully understand—"

"I've been open and honest with you all along, and you've had ample opportunity to talk to me about this."

"Please, just give me a chance now! This isn't easy for me. I wanted to tell you, in fact, I was going to explain it all to you this morning."

"Well, you don't have to now, because I've figured it all out on my own."

"Thomas, I need to see you, talk to you, and explain. Please, give me that."

"I'm sorry Olivia, I can't see you right now."

She started to cry. "Thomas, you say you are my friend, why are you treating me this way?"

"Well, I guess I can't be trusted either, goodbye, Olivia." As he hung up the phone, he glanced over at Kate standing in the doorway.

"Thomas, you didn't even give her a chance?"

He was silent.

"Why not?" she asked waiting.

He remained silent.

"Thomas, this isn't you," said Kate. "You always like to give people the benefit of the doubt. Why are you acting this way towards her? I really think you need to listen to what she has to say and try to understand where she is coming from. Friends are friends, through rights and wrongs, good times and bad times."

"Kate, maybe I don't want to know the whole story. You know, how they met, how she's in love, how he's such a nice guy, and how I would like him once I got to know him, and how we could all be good friends and hang out together."

"Who's he?"

"George Michael," replied Thomas chuckling a little. "Francis Gray."

"I see," said Kate studying him. "Thomas, do you love her?" she asked, then suddenly realized something. "Or are you acting this way because you are in love with Rachel?"

Chapter 16

"Thomas," called Rachel coming from the direction of her house.

"Rachel, how are you?" he asked putting his arm around her as they strolled the path to the guesthouse.

"Good, I just had to go the kitchen and get a French loaf," she explained showing him. "I was hoping I would meet you on my way back."

"I couldn't ask for a more beautiful escort?"

"Escort?" she asked giggling at his choice of words. "You make me sound like a call girl."

"Well, I did call you to say I was coming," he jested.

"Yes, you did, and here I am," she said playing along. "How much?"

"One million dollars for the night?"

"Sounds like a bargain."

Thomas stopped. "You're right, I'll take nothing less than two million."

"Wait, what? You want me to pay you!" she asked chuckling.

"In cash!" he clarified.

"You should consider yourself extremely honored to serve this vestal temple," she said standing back in tight jeans and sweater, posing, and then turning around to show off her cute behind before facing him.

As he went around the back of Rachel, he slowly examined her, then stopped, put his arms around her waist, and whispered in her ear. "Any man would consider himself very fortunate to have you in his arms."

Rachel was blushing and realized she was nervous. She wanted to turn around and kiss him wholeheartedly but remembered what she had talked to him about in the hot tub after her party. She was confused and wondered if he was just teasing her.

Thomas pulled away. "Now, get you behind up to that shack and cook me some vittles, woman!" he joked slapping it.

It took Rachel by surprise and turned her on a little. She playfully rubbed her bum and started to walk away then glanced over her shoulder. "Are you coming?" she asked mischievously.

Thomas caught up to her.

"How was your day?"

Thomas told her about it and asked how hers was as they entered the guesthouse.

"Well, I did some running around this morning, then spent the afternoon cooking, as you so eloquently put it, your vittles," she said with a chuckle and leading him to the stove. "Homemade pasta sauce, and in the fridge Caesar salad, plus a fresh French loaf from the bakery," she said putting it on the counter. "I'll put the noodles on, which gives you fifteen minutes to shower and change."

"Really?" he asked sniffing himself.

"Really!" she kidded covering her nose and pushing him in the direction of the stairs.

"Wow, this looks great," said Thomas admiring the food on the table.

"I'll just be a minute," she said opening a bottle of wine then joining him and pouring it. "Help yourself."

Thomas filled his bowl and waited till she had done the same. "To the chef!" he said listing his glass.

"Thank you," she replied clinking his glass, taking a sip, then starting to eat. "I was happy to receive your call last night, and that you're going to be here every Tuesday and Thursday."

"Yeah, I'll head here straight after work."

"And Kate's okay with it?"

"She's busy studying, and to be honest with you, I think she's glad to get me out of her hair."

"Well, her loss is my gain," said Rachel with a smile.

"Out of the frying pan," teased Thomas before taking a mouthful of food and not making eye contact.

"Oh, and into the fire!" she finished acting unimpressed. "No dessert for you, mister."

"I'm just having fun with you," he said sincerely. "I appreciate everything you've done, and I was looking forward to coming here."

"Me too," she said cheerfully. "You don't mind if I hang around with you upstairs while you write, do you? Otherwise, I can stay down here."

"Of course not, I would like the company."

"Good, because I bought some magazines to read."

After dinner, Thomas went up to the loft to set it up. He placed the desk diagonally with the window so he could see the trees and pond outside as well as inside the room, then opened the window.

Rachel joined him moments later, sat on the recliner, relaxed back, and put her feet on the footrest. "Yes?" she asked noticing him staring then sipping her wine.

"Are you okay with the window being open?"

"I actually like it; you can hear the outdoors."

"All right," said Thomas turning to his laptop and typing. When he eventually stopped, he didn't realize two hours had passed. He glanced over at Rachel who was still reading and playing with her hair.

She felt his stare and looked over at him. "Can I help you?"

"Do you know, when a girl twirls her hair around her finger, it means she is sexually frustrated?"

"Oh, really?" she asked, and with both hands messed up her hair, then peeked at him through the strands in front of her face. "That's because, Thomas, being so close to you, all I can think about is your hands roaming freely all over my naked body." She sexily blew her hair away from her inviting eyes. "Take me, Thomas, I'm yours."

"Sure, Ms. Vestal Temple!" he replied so matter-of-fact that she burst out laughing.

"That was my best attempt at seducing you," she said throwing a cushion at him.

He picked it up and sat in the recliner next to her.

"How did you make out?"

"Almost ten pages."

"Ten, that's it?"

"Ten's not bad, sometimes it can be a paragraph, other times twenty pages. It all depends on where you are in the story."

She knew better than to ask him what it was about. "Actually, now that I think about it, I had no predetermined number in my head, so I'm not sure why I was surprised when you said ten. I guess a lot of people think you just sit down, and the words just fill up the pages."

"Yeah, it's a slower process than most people realize," he admitted, "but I love it." He glanced at her empty glass. "I guess you could use a wine?"

"You're finished for the evening?" she asked excitedly.

"I am," he confirmed going to the desk, putting his stuff, and closing the window.

Rachel grabbed his hand, led him downstairs, and poured two glasses of wine. "Now, first off, I did not make the dessert, but I picked one that I believe you will love," she clarified. "It's a cheesecake. So, tell me, what type is your favorite? No, wait a second, close your eyes." She waited till he did, took the cake out of the fridge, and returned. "Okay, tell me?"

"Chocolate!"

"Open your eyes," she said merrily. "It's my favorite, too."

She cut them a slice each, then took him out onto the deck and turned on the gas fire pit, before sitting next to him on the sofa.

"This is delicious."

"It's so good," said Rachel finishing hers, then taking Thomas's empty plate, placing them on the end table, and picking up her wine.

"You have a gas fire pit outside?"

"Uh-huh."

"A wood fireplace on the lower level?"

"Yep."

"A gas fireplace on the main level?

"We do."

"And central gas heating throughout the guesthouse?"

"This is true," she answered unsure why he was asking all these questions and took a drink of her wine.

"What's with the small electrical heater in the corner of the loft?"

Rachel was so caught off guard by his question that she did a spit take all over her shirt. "Oh, thanks very much," she said chuckling and standing, "now I'm covered in wine."

Thomas stood and tried, unsuccessfully, not to laugh.

"I'm so glad I'm here for your amusement," she said gently pushing him. "Come on, I need to change."

Rachel turned off the fire pit and Thomas grabbed the dishes and put them in the dishwasher while she refilled their glasses. He then followed her upstairs into the master bedroom, Rachel went into the en suite, and Thomas continued on through the two French doors onto the large balcony and sat on the Adirondack chair sipping his wine.

"That's better," she said coming out in flannel pajamas and taking a seat. "It's such a lovely night. Look at all those stars."

Thomas agreed with a nod then turned to her. "You bought that heater for me, didn't you?'

"I did," she confessed. "I just imagined you typing at the desk with the window open, the late autumn leaves falling, and you with your little heater next to you keeping you warm. I know, I'm silly."

"Not at all, I think it's cute, and very considerate," he said in her defense and tenderly squeezing her thigh. "I like who you are, so don't change, ever."

"Thank you," she said shyly and thought for a moment. "You know, I always wanted a brother or sister, or both, when I was younger. I used to ask my mom if I could have one, she would put me off and say maybe one day, but one day never came and I eventually stopped asking."

"You have me now," said Thomas reaching for her hand.

Olivia held it tightly then put her head on his shoulder. "Forever?"

"Forever, and ever."

"Promise."

"I promise."

Chapter 17

"Nice car, Jack," said Thomas as they headed north in his convertible Cadillac.

"Thanks," he replied. "It's quite a drive. Have you ever been behind the wheel of a Cadillac before?"

"Never," said Thomas.

Jack pulled over. "Here you take over."

Thomas changed seats, put the car in drive, and accelerated. "Wow! What a drive!"

"If you're ever looking around for one, let me know, I can get you a great deal," said Jack candidly.

"Thanks for the thought, Jack, but I don't think I'll be taking you up on that offer anytime soon," replied Thomas.

"Thomas, if you think small, you'll always be small," preached Jack then turned towards him. "If you had a choice of any car and price wasn't an issue, what would it be?"

Thomas thought for a while. "A metallic blue convertible Aston Martin, fully loaded with blue leather interior, six speakers and a CD player," said Thomas looking around, "and maybe one of these in silver, with black leather, and fully loaded. And for when I go skiing, a red Dodge Durango, with cloth interior, again, fully loaded." He glanced over at Jack. "I believe that would do it."

"That's more like it. Always dream big, and always think big. It's all about confidence and believing in yourself," he said patting Thomas on the shoulder. "I must admit, you look good behind that wheel."

"I feel good, Jack," replied Thomas with a grin. "So, where are we going?"

"The Devil's Valley," replied Jack. "Have you ever played there before?"

"No, but I've heard of it. Isn't it an exclusive private club?"

"That it is."

"I heard it has a fifty-thousand-dollar membership?"

"Try seventy-five," corrected Jack.

"How long have you been a member?"

"Five years," he replied. "Since you knew my handicap, I figured I needed an advantage."

"Jack, I hate to embarrass a man on his home turf," said Thomas confidently.

"You're a cocky little bastard. I can't wait to beat your ass," he stated with a chuckle. "Here, let me put on some tunes."

With the top down and the sun shining, Thomas and Jack drove to The Devil's Valley.

They refused caddies and drove the cart to the first tee. Jack turned to Thomas. "Lunch."

"Lunch?" he asked.

"Loser buys lunch at the clubhouse," confirmed Jack. "Unfortunately, we won't have time for the Steak House today."

"Deal," said Thomas shaking his hand.

Jack flipped a coin, and Thomas won the toss and elected to shoot second. He never shot second again.

Thomas glanced over the menu and the prices. "Glad you're paying Jack."

"You play a hell of a game. Where did you learn to play like that?"

"After work and on weekends, I caddied for a few seasons at The Eagle and became friends with the old guy that owned the place and used to help him out. You know, some painting here and there and cleaning the golf carts, and in return, he let me play for free. So, I played when I could, and watched when I wasn't," he replied. "The old guy, his name was Marvin, passed away and his wife ended up selling the place. It was never the same after that, so I started playing the public courses."

The waiter came by for their order.

"Thomas, do you mind if I order for the both of us?"

"No, go ahead," he replied closing his menu.

"The filet mignon is excellent, and the baked potatoes are the size of my fist," he said clenching his hand to the size of a melon. "Two filets medium rare and double top shelves, Bob."

"I'll be back with your drinks in a minute Mr. Collins and Mr.?"

"Carlyle, please, call me Thomas."

"Thank you, I'll be back in a minute."

Bob returned with two double whiskeys. "Here you go Jack, Thomas, enjoy. Lunch will be about fifteen minutes."

They ate lunch and moved into the lounge that overlooked the eighteenth hole and ordered two more drinks.

"Look, it's Barry Levinson, he's about to chip onto the green," said Jack. "I'll bet you one he takes three strokes to sink the ball."

"I'll take that bet, and I'll say two or less, and let's make it a five," said Thomas with a grin.

"Easy money," he replied.

Barry's chip almost went in, and his second shot was just a formality. Jack glanced over at Thomas. "Nice call."

"Jack, I'll let you in on a little secret," he said leaning toward him. "When I dropped off his laptop, he talked about his golf game, and how many times on the eighteenth he's been this close to chipping the ball in for an eagle."

"He told me his score last week and it was horrendous."

"Come on, Jack, you can't win on short game alone," said Thomas cheekily. "He also told me his long game is his weakness."

Jack took out his wallet and gave Thomas five one-hundred-dollar bills and then from the inside of his jacket gave him an envelope.

"What's this Jack?" asked Thomas looking at the bills.

"You won," said Jack with a puzzled look. "I always pay my debts."

"Jack, do you have a five-dollar bill in your wallet?" asked Thomas.

Jack opened up his wallet. "Here you go."

Thomas took the five and gave him the five hundred back. "Sorry Jack, I meant five dollars."

Jack put the money back in his wallet. "You're lucky you won kid, or I would have been looking for the five hundred," said Jack with a stern face that quickly broke into a smile. "Always make sure you clarify your bet first."

"You too," replied Thomas.

They both laughed.

"What's this?" asked Thomas pointing to the envelope with his name on it.

"It's for you," said Jack. "Commission."

"Commission, for what?" he asked.

"The hundred laptops Barry bought. He got a great discount and a first-rate service contract, and it only ended up costing him two hundred and fifty thousand and he had budgeted for three, which means you saved him fifty. This is your two per cent finder's fee on the three," explained Jack.

Thomas opened the envelope, inside was a check for six thousand dollars and a note from Barry thanking him. "I can't take this. I did it as a favor and wasn't expecting anything in return," he said putting the note in his pocket and the check back into the envelope and passing I to Jack. "I'll keep the note, and you can give this back to Barry."

"Thomas, this is business, and in my business, we pay people finder's fees. If we don't, we get a reputation, a bad reputation," clarified Jack. "You have no choice but to accept it."

Thomas looked a little unsure. "I wouldn't tell anyone."

Jack knew that. "What you did for Barry was the favor, but what you did for his firm, is business. And what you do with the money is up to you, with one exception, you can't give it back," stated Jack firmly. "Don't take this the wrong way, Thomas, we still appreciate what you did for us, and you taking this money doesn't take away from that." He slid the envelope back to Thomas. "This business transaction is concluded, and we thank you."

Thomas looked at him oddly. "Jack, what's all this 'we' and 'in my business.' How do you fit in?"

"I'm the silent partner of Levinson and Associates, so you saved me money, too," replied Jack. "At dinner tonight, me and you, we'll have a talk, for now, let's enjoy our drinks."

Again, Thomas wondered who Taxi Jack really was. "Okay," he replied and took the envelope.

They talked for half an hour about golf, cars, and casinos, and Jack was talking about Las Vegas, when they were interrupted.

"Hello, Jack, Thomas," said Barry. "How did you play today?"

"Not bad," replied Jack not giving anything away. "Thomas has a sweet swing and played a good round."

"Nice chip onto the eighteenth," complimented Thomas.

"It was but my long game is still suffering, though, I keep slicing to the left. Luckily, the eighteenth's a dog leg," he said with a chuckle. "Did you get my envelope?"

"Yes, I did," replied Thomas. "Thank you."

"I was scheduled to be in court, but last night they opted for an out of court settlement, and it freed me up today. If I would have known, I would have given it to you myself," he explained. "Anyway, I wanted to come by and say thank you," he said reaching out his hand and shaking Thomas's, "and also give you this." He handed Thomas a brown envelope.

Thomas took it and read the name, "Kate Carlyle."

"Kate is your sister?" asked Barry.

"Yes, she is."

"There is a paralegal position opening up in our firm," he said sitting down. "It's a lower-level entry position, mostly filing, documentation, some time in court, and attending meetings. It's part-time, basically whatever time she has available during the days, nights, and weekends. We'll give her time off to study for the bar exam and after she passes, we offer them a full-time position." Barry hesitated then continued, "I'm not going to beat around the bush, I oversee all applications and three met our requirements, Kate was the best candidate of the three. She had the best grade point average and everyone we talked to spoke exceptionally well of her. A select group of lawyers, myself included, made the final decision, and considered her to be the best candidate. She secured the position on her own merits and should be very proud. The fact that I know you and that she is your sister never factored into our decision-making process. In that envelope is an offer, if she accepts, she will have to come in for a set of interviews, which are formalities." Barry stood up. "I was going to call her on Monday but I when I found out I might bump into you here today I thought you might like to pass on the good news. It will also give her time to look over the offer this weekend and get back to me with a decision on Monday."

"I'll forward it on and let her know to call you," said Thomas stunned.

"Thanks," said Barry. "If you will please excuse me, I have to meet an associate in the dining room. Thanks again, Thomas, and see you tomorrow, Jack." He shook their hands then left.

Thomas looked curiously at Jack, "Did you know about this?

"I had nothing to do with it, and this is the first I've heard of it," replied Jack genuinely. "I know nothing about running a law firm, that's Barry's job, I'm just a partner who cares about the bottom line. But I will tell you this, Barry doesn't do favors for anyone when it comes to hiring, there's too much at risk. So, believe him when he says they screened all the applicants, and trust me, they left no stones unturned," said Jack. "Business is business." He then motioned Thomas to lean over and whispered, "in this room sit some of the richest men in the city, in fact the country, and if they're here on a weekday, it's all business. If it's after four on a Friday or a weekend, then it's mostly social. Remember, Thomas, money never sleeps."

Thomas glanced around the room. All the men were in deep discussions, some were going through documents, others had their briefcases open on the table. There were only a couple of women.

"Why are there so few women?" asked Thomas.

"Powerful women do business differently than men. They like to dress up, go for lunches, dinners, and shows. It wouldn't be good business for a woman to beat a man at golf or as you put it, on his home turf. Men have egos and women don't, this gives them a distinct advantage. But don't be fooled, women are just as shrewd as men when it comes to business, if not, shrewder," explained Jack "One more drink, then we'll head back to my place."

"Where do you live Jack?" asked Thomas.

"At the J.C. Condominium Tower, downtown. I'm leaving my car here overnight in the garage and I'll pick it up tomorrow after I've beaten Barry. We'll get chauffeured home from here, and I'll arrange to have your clubs dropped off at your house."

The name of the condominium tower sounded familiar to Thomas; he must have passed it before.

As they were leaving the bar, Thomas noticed many of the members made a point of going out of their way to say goodbye to Jack. Outside, a stretch Rolls Royce pulled up to the front doors and Jack and Thomas jumped in. It had a bar, television, CD and DVD player, and a phone.

"This yours, Jack?" asked Thomas.

"One of them," he replied. "Same chauffeur though, here, let me get you a beer." He grabbed two and passed on to Thomas then put on Ray Price's, 'For the Good Times.'

Thomas listened as Jack sang along. When it ended Thomas commented. "That's a sad song, powerful, but sad."

"Sure is," replied Jack. "It was one of my mother's favorites. She used to sing it all the time. I guess she was sad, but I like to think about her, and that song reminds me of her, that's why I play it a lot." He looked out the window and thought about her then turned to Thomas and changed the subject. "Now me, I like Dean Martin." He put on one of his CDs. "Now, just sit back, enjoy your beer, the ride, the music, and me," said Jack as he sang along with Dean.

Chapter 18

An hour later, they passed the theater and pulled into the parking garage of the J.C. Condominium Tower. Thomas now remembered where he had seen that name before, it was engraved on the front of Rob the doorman's desk. They walked onto the elevator; Jack inserted a card and pressed the nineteenth floor. On the way up, the elevator stopped on the twelfth floor, Thomas's heart was in his mouth. He hadn't spoken to Olivia since the phone call last Sunday and here he was in her building. A young man walked on and pressed sixteen. The elevator door closed and opened on the sixteenth to let him off, then again on the nineteenth. Thomas and Jack walked off, and ten feet in front of them, was a set of heavy wooden doors. Jack opened one with a key and walked in as Thomas followed behind.

"Welcome to my home in the city, Thomas," said Jack.

"Is this floor all yours?" asked Thomas.

"Well, all floors are mine, but I just live on the nineteenth," replied Jack. "J.C., Jack Collins"

Thomas never put the two together. He quickly thought back to the fundraiser, watching Jack get into the taxi, and calling him Taxi Jack.

"Let me quickly show you around," offered Jack leading the way. "To the left we have two bedrooms, each are a decent size and have their own en suite. You can leave your bag in this one, it has the best view. Back here I have a recreation room with a pool table, dartboard, and wet bar." Jack went behind the bar, opened the refrigerator, grabbed two beers, and gave him one. "Down here is the laundry room, and if we walk this way, we're back at the front door. Let me show you the rest. Here is the dining room, through here is the kitchen, the living room, and the master bedroom. The master bedroom is the same size as the two other rooms put together, and the en suite in here has a big oval tub and separate shower. This door here, leads into my office."

"Jack this place is incredible," said Thomas in awe.

"I'm glad you like it," he replied as they walked into the living room. "Dinner isn't for another couple of hours, and I need to take a shower, put on some fresh clothes, and make some calls. If you like, you can watch the big screen TV, have a lie down, or get a shower. I'm going to be in my office for a while, so you have the place to yourself. There's a bar here in the living room, and you know about the one in the recreation room, so help yourself to a drink. And in case you want to go for a walk, here are the keys, and the elevator card. The doorman knows you're my guest so you can get back in without disturbing me." Jack glanced at his watch. "It's just a few minutes passed five, and I'll be finished by six thirty."

"Thanks, Jack, there's more than enough here to keep me busy," replied Thomas.

Jack left and Thomas walked to his room. It felt weird being seven stories above Olivia's condo. He missed her and thought about going down to talk to her but decided against it. Instead, he lay down and fell asleep.

"Thomas," said Jack knocking on the door. "Thomas," he said slowly opening it."

"Hi, Jack," acknowledged Thomas stretching.

"It's six forty, I thought you might have fell asleep. Get a shower, get dressed, and come join me."

Thomas strolled into the living room at seven. "Jack," he called out.

"In here," he answered from the kitchen. "I'm just putting the racks of lamb into the oven. You do like lamb?"

"I love it," replied Thomas joining him, "preferably not glazed."

"A man after my own heart," commented Jack. "Baked and topped with mint sauce."

Thomas smiled at his passion. "You like cooking?"

"I rarely get the chance to these days, but when I do, I do," said Jack, happily. "Tonight, we're having lamb, mashed potatoes, and carrots."

"Hope you're better at cooking than you are playing golf," teased Thomas.

"Ha, ha," replied Jack sarcastically. "In case you're wondering why I'm putting three in, Penelope Daily is coming for dinner, is that okay?"

"Of course."

"Here open the wine and pour a couple of glasses," he said handing him the corkscrew, "and not those sample sizes, fill them up."

Thomas pulled out the cork, poured, and handed Jack a glass. "Cheers."

"Cheers," replied Thomas.

"Jack, Jack," called a voice from the hallway.

"Penny, I'm in the kitchen with Thomas," he shouted back.

"There you are. Hello, Thomas," said Penelope kissing him on the cheek.

"Hello, Penelope," replied Thomas.

"Please, call me Penny," she requested and moved close to Jack. "Hi, Jack, how are you doing?" she asked kissing him on the lips.

"I just put the lamb in the oven, I'm slow-roasting them so they should be ready in about forty-five minutes. Did you bring dessert?"

"Yes, it's on the hallway table, I'll go and get them." She returned moments later with a baker's box. "I'll put them in the refrigerator," she said looking at Thomas. "He loves his chocolate éclairs."

Thomas smiled awkwardly he didn't know they were a couple.

"Let's go in the living room," suggested Jack, "I'll put some background music on, and we can have a talk."

"Thomas, how was your round of golf today?" asked Penny.

"I enjoyed it immensely," replied Thomas, "and it's a beautiful course."

"What he is actually saying, is that he immensely enjoyed beating me on it," interjected Jack. "He'll have to give me a rematch so I can remove that victorious smile off his face," he stated, sitting down next to Penny on the sofa, and opposite Thomas. Jack quickly glanced over at Penny then back at Thomas and suddenly became very serious. "Listen Thomas, there's something I, actually Penny, needs to talk to you about. I don't like getting involved in these sorts of situations, neither does Penny, but when it effects people that you love and care about, and their life and careers, sometimes you have no choice but to." Jack continued but in a more light-hearted tone. "Before I let Penny talk, there are some things I would like to share with you first, so if you could keep this confidential, I would appreciate it."

"Definitely, Jack," confirmed Thomas.

Jack leaned forward and spoke. "When I was ten my father left, and it wasn't till years later that I found out he took off with another woman, and needless to say, I never seen him since. Leaving my mother to take care of me and my brother. To make end meet, she worked a full-time job during the week and a part-time one on the weekend. We were poor, but we were happy, because we had each other. We lived just down the road from here," he said pointing. "When I was sixteen, my brother was struck by a drunk driver and killed, and when I was eighteen, my mother died of cancer. Here I am, eighteen, with no family and no money. I couldn't afford to rent the place we lived in, and I had little education, so I took a job driving a taxi, I soon realized that I was working hard to make someone else rich, and set my sights on me being the one getting rich. I eventually bought my own taxi, then another, and another, till I owned my own taxi company. I ran that for a few years, before buying another company and then another. I quickly realized that running one company was the same as another, and today, I own many companies. I got out of the day-to-day operations, and I hire people to do that for me now. As you know, I'm also a silent partner in several big firms, and like I said, I don't get involved in their day-to-day business, all I'm interested in is the bottom line, the profit. Today, I'm semi-retired from the acquisitions of businesses, and have a company that does that for me now," explained Jack. "Thomas, when I was eighteen, I had a hundred dollars to my name. Do you know what I'm worth today?" he asked.

Thomas didn't answer. When he waved goodbye to him in the taxi leaving the fundraiser, he would have guessed Taxi Jack wasn't worth much, with what he knew now, he guessed forty million, and that was a high estimate.

"Four hundred and fifty million," stated Jack.

Four hundred and fifty, thought Thomas.

"And why was I so successful? Because at eighteen, I turned my fear, anger, loneliness, and poverty into drive and determination. The world owed me, and they were going to pay. It had nothing to do with power, fame, and fortune. In fact, I'm a very low-key individual and private about my businesses, my partnerships, and my personal life," he stopped momentarily and took a sip of his drink. "Seven years ago, I realized I had achieved all that I had wanted to. So, I withdrew my active participation in my businesses and all the day-to-day decision-making and passed them on to a very loyal and longtime employee of mine named Ernie Harris, and semi-retired. A year later, I looked around and realized I had nothing in my life, no wife or girlfriend, no children, and the only friends I had were business associates, I was depressed for a year." He glanced over at Penny and held her hand. "I've known Penny for a long time, almost twelve years now, and she was always there for me. and helped me get through that tough period in my life. She gave me purpose and meaning to my life, and was compassionate and loving, and I owe her more than words can say." He kissed her hand and looked at Thomas. "For the last six years, Penny and I have been companions."

"And lovers," added Penny.

"And lovers," repeated Jack. "Nobody knows about us, not family or close friends, except Olivia, and now you. When we first got together, we decided to keep it private and that hasn't been easy," said Jack glancing at Penny who smiled and shook her head. "Thomas, you haven't been around enough to notice, but we never show up together, sit together, or leave together." Jack filled their wine glasses. "Penny has her own place on the sixteenth floor where she lives but she spends most of her time up here with me. We cook and eat dinners together, go out for meals, and on vacations. When people we know bump into us, they just look at us as a couple of old friends having a drink or a bite to eat. At the fundraiser, we danced a few songs and spent some time together, but nothing that can be categorized as a romance." Jack stopped, took a drink of his wine, and stared at Penny. "The only regret I have is that we didn't find each other sooner, especially since we both talked about how we would have liked to have children." He held her hand again and tears were forming in his eyes.

Penny placed her free one on his cheek, wiped a tear away, smiled, and faced Thomas. "I had liked Jack since the first day I met him," she admitted. "You must understand, he was a different man then, a little difficult, a little rough around the edges but he had a kind look in his eyes, similar to yours Thomas. We were both so busy in our own little worlds that we never took the time to share it with anyone else," she said glancing over at Jack. "I'll never forget the first time we went out; he was like a big high school football player out on his first date, shy and nervous, but always the gentlemen." She gently played with is hair. "He has missed out on so many of the good thing's life has to offer, as have I, but in the last six years we've made up for it." She turned her attention to Thomas. "Jack has a great deal of admiration and respect for you, in fact, he hasn't stopped talking about you since the fundraiser. What comes so natural to you, is sometimes, so difficult for Jack." She leaned toward Thomas. "Do you remember when you let me present your grandmother's award?"

Thomas nodded.

"It was an exceedingly kind and unselfish act, and you were a gentleman in the truest sense of the word. You had made me so incredibly happy, and when I was presenting, I looked over at Jack and I could see how happy he was for me. Your simple gesture made it possible for me, for us, to both feel that way. After the fundraiser, we were both sitting right here having a drink, and Jack talked about how open and honest you were, that you were never judgmental or condescending, but respectful, and treated everyone equally. Thomas, for you to fully comprehend why Jack was so impressed by this, you first need to understand that Jack came from a vastly different world than you or me. He had to deal with two-faced people, liars, cheats, thieves, backstabbers, and believed in an eye for an eye retribution, not literally thankfully. And because of this, he ended up with major trust issues. But over these last several years, he's changed and become a lot more acceptable of people and trustworthy." Penny paused and looked at Jack. "We've recently realized that we have both done something wrong and would like to change it and make it right."

Jack took over. "Thomas, when I look back at me and you at eighteen, we were both in the same situation: no parents and little money. Yet, you turned out completely different than me. Why do you think that is?"

Thomas thought momentarily. "Because I had a sister that I was responsible for and my grandmother," replied Thomas. "I had family, and they needed me."

"I believe that, too," agreed Jack. "When I look at you, I see someone who has both feet on the ground, and there is no doubt in my mind, that thirty years down the road you won't turn around, like I did, and look back and have regrets. Do you know why?"

Thomas shook his head slowly.

"Because when your sister starts working full time, I'll bet you she'll give you the opportunity at the life she had, university, and such. Everything you gave to her; she'll give right back to you without hesitation. Am I right?" questioned Jack.

"She's already said so."

"Well, let me tell you a story about Henry and his daughter," he said quickly taking a drink. "Henry was a very loving father, and his daughter meant the world to him, and he would do anything for her. He had a soaring career and was well-off. Unfortunately, his career meant that he was away for extended periods of time, and his wife, whether it was because of loneliness, lack of attention, perhaps both, started to have an affair. To cut a long story short, Henry caught her and asked that she leave him and his daughter alone and offered her a great sum of money to do so, but she refused. Their marriage was over, but she was clever woman, and several months later she had a private investigator take compromising pictures of Henry with his new girlfriend. After which, she took him to court seeking a divorce and full custody of their daughter. She won, and Henry's name was smeared over the papers. A year or so later, he moved away to protect his daughter from any further embarrassment." Jack looked at his empty glass, fetched another bottle of wine and filled everyone's, then sat down and had a sip. "That was over nine years ago, and only Penny and I know the truth, and now you."

"And your grandmother," added Penny.

"My apologies, and your grandmother, God rest her soul.

"Sadly, everyone else believed the story in the papers to be true," stated Penny. "We keep in touch with Henry to let him know how his daughter is keeping and see him from time to time."

"What about his daughter?" asked Thomas.

"She still doesn't know the truth, and Henry had asked us to promise him that we would not tell her or anyone, especially her. Of course, she knows we still keep in contact with him because he is still our dear friend," explained Penny.

"But you're telling me?" questioned Thomas.

"In retrospect, it was a promise we should never have agreed to, and we were wrong. Worst of all, so was Henry," acknowledged Penny. "At the time, his daughter didn't want anything to do with him, and he felt responsible for the mess he had made of their lives. So, he thought, we thought, we were doing the right thing," said Penny looking over at Jack. "We want to correct this wrong and give her a chance at a relationship with her father."

"So why not just tell her?" asked Thomas.

"We want to, but we want to keep Henry's promise. He's a very good friend of ours and we value his friendship, and he trusted us not to say anything to her," replied Penny.

"So why tell me?" asked Thomas.

"We want you to help us," she replied.

"How can I help you?" queried Thomas confused.

Penny reached over and held his hand. "Henry's daughter is Olivia."

Thomas felt his heart pounding and thought, of course, Olivia, why hadn't he realized it sooner? He looked at them. "I really don't think I can help you."

"Thomas, I know something has happened between the two of you, and I didn't need Olivia to tell me, her body language speaks volumes. But neither Jack nor I are here to discuss your personal life, that's between you and her, but your relationship aside, I'm concerned about Olivia, and extremely worried about her well-being," said Penny with a troubled look. "I know, she is not your concern, so if you prefer me to stop, I will, and trust me, there will be no bad feelings between us," stated Penny.

Thomas gazed down at his wine glass, thinking, and recalled what Kate had said to him last Sunday. 'Friends are friends through rights and wrongs; good times and bad times.' He glanced up at Penny. "I would like to listen to what you have to say."

Penny let a relieved sigh followed by a smile. "Thomas, we understand that we may be asking a great deal of you, and maybe more so, if we knew the situation between the two of," she said taking a sip of her wine and continuing where Jack left off. "After Henry left, Olivia threw herself into her dancing, and she was one of the finest pupils the school has ever had. She had drive, determination, but also fear, loneliness and anger, and it flowed through her veins and into her dancing. Her technique was exceptional, and she has won too many awards to count. At the age of twenty-two, Olivia became a second soloist; at twenty-four, a first soloist;

and this year, she will become a principal dancer at the company. She will have reached the greatest goal a ballerina can achieve." Penny paused and softly asked. "At the fundraiser, when I said only you could have made her sing again, was I right, were you the friend she sang for?"

"She said I could pay for a dance or hear her sing; I asked her to sing," explained Thomas, then smiled as he remembered how she had charged him a hundred dollars so that she could get a dance as well.

"I am going to tell you something about that night that no one, not even Jack knows, in fact, not even her. After she sang, she left the room and went to the restroom. I followed her in moments later and heard her sobbing in the last stall. I waited outside the door and told people a staff employee was mopping up the wet floor, and to use the other one. When I heard her walking inside, I went in, and acted as if I knew nothing. Casually, I asked her if she was okay, she replied everything was fine, although she did miss her father. Just like that, out of the blue. That was something I never thought I would ever hear her say. Thomas, you need to understand that Jack and I were never even allowed to mention her father in front of her." Penny drank a mouthful of wine. "No doubt you have heard that since her father left, she has never sung in public?"

"I have said," said Thomas nodding his head.

"The following Monday, Olivia, tells me how she went to the cathedral with you, sang hymns, and how she sang with a street musician in the park," said Penny looking for confirmation.

"Yes, she did, she sang, 'Unforgettable' and said it was one of her father's favorite songs," replied Thomas.

"For the last nine years, this girl has not wanted to know her father, hear her father's name, or sing. Not only is she singing now, but singing her father's favorite song in the street," said Penny in amazement. "I walked into her condominium this week and I see she has a picture of them on her end table."

"I'm a little confused. Why does that worry you?" asked Thomas.

Jack spoke. "When she dances in three weeks, she will have reached the goal that every ballerina dreams of and aspires to, but when she looks down at the audience and around at her colleagues, she will suddenly realize that she will have no family or close friends to share in her joy. Like me, the next day Olivia may wake up and wonder what she has done with her life, and like myself, fall into a deep depression, or perhaps worse," answered Jack.

"It could ruin her career and more importantly, her life," added Penny.

"Thomas, I have Penny, and you have Kate. Right now, she's all alone, and has no one. She's very fragile and vulnerable."

"What about her mother?" asked Thomas.

"Her mother isn't coming," answered Penny with a laugh. "She's quite out of the picture."

"Olivia thinks her mother bought her place and helps with her expenses," said Jack. "Her father, as a favor, asked me to get her the condominium so she could be in the city and close to work, and paid for it. He also has his money come through one of my law firms to make it look as if it's coming from her mother," revealed Jack.

Thomas looked at them, then down at his glass and drank his wine. "This is incredible," he said shaking his head slowly. He understood their concern for Olivia, and this was about Olivia, not him. Friends in good times and bad times, he thought, and glanced up. "How can I help?"

Penny jumped from her seat and kissed Thomas several times on the cheek. "I prayed you would!"

"So, what do I need to do?"

"Let's have some dinner first and talk about it after we have full stomachs," suggested Penny smiling happily and dancing into the kitchen.

"That lamb was delicious Jack," complimented Thomas sitting on the sofa in the living room.

"I'm definitely a meat and potatoes kind of guy and I especially enjoy my lamb," replied Jack joining him.

Penny stuck her head out of the kitchen. "That's all the cutlery and plates in the dishwasher. Some coffee?"

"All the champagne's gone," commented Jack tipping the Bollinger upside down. What do you want, Thomas?

"Can I have a brandy?"

"Chivas Regal and a cigar," stated Jack.

"If you're smoking cigars go out on the balcony," insisted Penny from the kitchen.

"Follow me, Thomas. Penny, are you coming?"

"Just let me make a coffee and get my cardigan, and I'll be out in a minute."

Jack poured the drinks at the bar and picked out two cigars from the box, then opened the sliding doors and switched on the balcony light, before walking out onto the large balcony.

"It's quite a view from up here."

"It sure is," replied Jack following his gaze. "Come over here and have a seat," he suggested placing the drinks down on the table, giving Thomas a cigar, and a box of matches.

They smoked and drank in silence for several minutes.

"Jack, I have to be honest with you, when I saw you a couple of weeks ago and you left in a taxi, I thought you were on the lower end of the millionaire's club. And it wasn't the taxi alone that brought me to that conclusion, I think talking with you that night contributed to most of it, and you leaving in the taxi just confirmed it."

"What do you think now that you know I'm a multi-millionaire?" asked Jack.

"That you didn't spend enough money on golf lessons," said Thomas cheekily.

Jack laughed.

"I actually gave you a nickname."

"Really! What?"

"Taxi Jack!" replied Thomas chuckling.

"Taxi Jack, I like it, you were closer than you thought," commented Jack and wondering. "Why are you telling me?"

"I don't know. I guess to show that I also make mistakes in judging characters," replied Thomas.

"You judged me all right that night. You knew I was a whiskey drinking, meat and potatoes, king of guy," stated Jack sucking on his cigar. "Let me ask you a question. What do you think of Bill Carter?"

"I only met him the one time, besides he's your friend," replied Thomas feeling uncomfortable.

"He's a business associate and not a friend," confirmed Jack. "Never mix the two up."

"I really don't have to worry about mixing those up," joked Thomas.

"Consider yourself lucky, then," he said. "So, tell me, what you think of him?"

"Well, there's something about him that I just can't put my finger on. It's difficult to describe," he replied. "He has that look in his eyes."

"Always remember that when you're around him," said Jack, "and always be on your guard."

"What are you talking about?" asked Penny joining them.

"Bill Carter," answered Jack.

She ignored the topic. "Rachel's very attractive," she said sitting. "You know I think she's becoming more her old self, for a while there she was becoming a little stuck up," commented Penny. "I know her mother was worried."

"I think she likes old Thomas here," teased Jack. "He wasn't too far out of her eyesight at the party."

Thomas blushed. "We're just friends," he confirmed, then looked at them both. "Can I ask you two a question?"

"Of course, dear," said Penny.

"How come you want to keep your relationship quiet?"

"When we first got together, Jack was in the news quite a bit because he was a well-known businessman, and anything he did or said ended up in the papers. If the media found out he was in a relationship, it would have been in all the papers, and I would have been hounded day and night by the press. I didn't want any part of that and knew I wouldn't have been able to handle it, so I asked Jack to keep it private. He promised me he would, and he has."

"Thomas, I was used to publicity, and I know what reporters can be like. At the time, I believe we made the right decision, but since I've been semi-retired and Ernie took over, people aren't as interested in me anymore. We've been talking recently about making it public, but it's really up to Penny," said Jack grabbing her hand.

"Maybe one day," suggested Penny uneasily.

Thomas decided to change the subject. "Okay, what do you want me to do?"

Jack leaned over and answered. "Tomorrow, we need you to go to Manhattan, talk to Henry, and convince him he needs to come here and tell Olivia the truth."

"That seems easy enough," said Thomas. "I'll go, tell him what you told me, and say if he doesn't tell her, you will."

"Unfortunately, Thomas, it won't be that simple," said Penny. "As I mentioned earlier, we made a promise to Henry, which means when you talk to him, you will have to act as if we never had this conversation and don't know the details of what happened."

"Which means, you will need to figure out a way to get him here, get the two of them talking, and hope that he tells her himself," conveyed Jack.

Thomas was taken aback. "How am I going to do that?"

"You have until tomorrow night to think of something," replied Jack, "and Thomas, trust me, you will. Just keep in mind what's important: getting him here with her."

Thomas stood up, stared out at the city lights, and wondered how in the hell he was going to do what they asked. He ran his fingers through his hair, thought about the task at hand and Olivia, then suddenly turned around. "I'll get him up here Sunday," he said confidently.

"Next Sunday?" asked Penny. "How will you do that?"

"How indeed?" asked Jack intrigued.

"Not next Sunday, this Sunday, and I don't know how, yet," clarified Thomas. "Jack, you mentioned Manhattan?"

"I did," said Jack captivated. "Tomorrow morning my private jet will fly you to La Guardia where a limousine will be waiting to take you to your hotel in Manhattan and be available for your entire stay. Henry is performing in Otello at the Opera House tomorrow night, and you have a box reserved. The rest is up to you."

"You have all this arranged?" asked Thomas curiously.

"We were counting on you," replied Penny.

"And if I need to get Henry on a plane on Sunday?" he asked.

"Call me Saturday night, and I'll have the tickets waiting for him at the airport, and one of my limousines will pick him up when he arrives. Now, you will need to tell him it's one of yours, and I'll make sure the chauffeur asks about you," specified Jack.

"All right," said Thomas. "Can my sister come with me?"

"Of course, I'll arrange for her to be dropped off at the airport tomorrow morning."

"Thanks, Jack."

"Thomas," he said sternly, "I'll be paying for all expenses, no exceptions."

"Okay," he said, then thought about something he had said to Olivia about friendship and honesty. "If there comes a time when I need to tell Olivia about this, I have your permission to tell her everything?"

Penny stood up and walked over to Thomas. "If that time comes, and I hope it does, you have our permission."

"Thank you."

"I need to make some phone calls," said Jack getting up. "What time did you want to leave in the morning?"

Thomas told him and Jack went inside.

"Thomas," said Penny moving closer to him. "The week after the fundraiser, Olivia danced like I've never seen her dance before, so full of positive energy, love, and compassion. The rest of the group stood back in awe and watched. I thought I had seen Olivia dance her best until that week." She held his hand and was about to say something else.

"Maybe you should give Kate a call first?" suggested Jack.

Chapter 19

"My private cell number is stored under Taxi Jack, call me when you have some news," he said handing Thomas a cell phone and an envelope.

"Anytime," added Penny.

"Will do," replied Thomas grinning as he thought about Jack using his nickname. Thomas boarded the private jet, turned, and waved goodbye, then sat down next to Kate.

"Thomas, what's going on?" she asked.

"Once we've taken off, I'll explain everything."

The plane taxied, took off, and when they reached cruising altitude, the flight attendant offered them coffee which they accepted. Thomas turned to Kate and explained what was going on.

"…and as for you Kate, you're just along for the ride and to take some time away from your studying, do some shopping, and relax."

"Thomas, are you okay with this?"

"Don't worry, I'm fine."

After the flight attendant brought their coffees, Thomas opened the envelope, and took out a sheet. As he read over the information, he summarized out loud: "Two rooms, two nights…The tickets for Otello would be waiting for us at the box office and we should get there an hour prior to the start of the show…Jack has suggested several restaurants to dine at with instructions and how to get preferential seating and service…He's also listed two men's clothing stores and five women's, each with a person's name next to them." Thomas glanced over at Kate. "I think Jack has traveled to New York City before."

Kate nodded.

Thomas looked inside the envelope and took out the platinum credit card and cash, then read the written notation out loud: "Thomas please use the credit card and cash for any expenses occurred. Make sure you and Kate make time to go shopping and buy some nice clothes, especially for this evening. I have noted the stores to visit, and they will take care of you. When ordering at the restaurants, make sure it's the best on the menu. Enjoy, and thank you, Jack and Penny."

"How much money is there?" asked Kate.

Thomas counted it. "Five thousand dollars."

"How expensive is New York City?"

"I don't know," replied Thomas putting the card and cash in his wallet.

Kate smiled. "I'm looking forward to it, especially Fifth Avenue."

They landed an hour and a half later, picked up their bags, and were walking towards the exit when Kate noticed a man in a black suit holding up a sign 'Mr. Carlyle.' They approached him and forty-five minutes later arrived at the hotel, and within minutes were following the bellboy to their tower suites. The bellboy dropped Kate off first, then Thomas, who thanked him and gave him a twenty. He decided to go see how Kate was settling in.

Kate grabbed his hand and took off with him around the suite. "It has a living area with a sofa, chair, big screen television, a stocked wet bar, and a fireplace," she said turning it on and off. "In here, is the bedroom with a king size bed, a flat screen TV, and walk-in closet. Through here is the bathroom, it has an oval Jacuzzi tub for two, which I'm definitely going to use, a shower stall, and look, bathrobes." She took him back to the bedroom. "Thomas, this is gorgeous," she said flopping on her bed and looking up at him. "So, what are we going to do?"

Thomas glanced at his watch. "It's seven thirty. Why don't we have some breakfast, go shopping on Fifth Avenue, and have some lunch?"

"Can I order breakfast to my room?" asked Kate jumping off the bed. "I want to have it over here on the table by the window."

"Sure, call me in an hour," said Thomas, "I'm going to have a nap first."

"How can you sleep!" exclaimed Kate. "I'm going to have breakfast, take a walk around the hotel, find out the best places to shop, then come back here and have a nice hot bath and then…"

They walked across the Grand Lobby, out the front doors, and onto the street.

"Okay, it's ten thirty," said Thomas. "Let's do some shopping." And started walking. "You have to be back at the hotel for three because—"

"Thomas you're going the wrong way!" said Kate heading in the opposite direction and laughing at him as she waited for him to catch up. "Why do I have to be back by three?"

"I booked you an appointment at The Spa. Facial, manicure, pedicure, hair, and makeup."

"The Spa!" cooed Kate.

"They also suggested if you take down your outfit for this evening, they will help you get dressed."

"Really?" asked Kate surprised.

"Today, I think we should just concentrate on buying clothes for tonight and take tomorrow and Monday to shop for ourselves. Is that okay?"

"Of course, it's okay," replied Kate happily. "Let's go!" She put her arm around Thomas and picked up the pace.

They walked along Fifth Avenue, visited the stores that Jack had put on his list, and asked for the people whose names he had provided; they were treated like royalty. In between, they stopped forty-five minutes for lunch. Back at the hotel, Thomas walked with Kate to The Spa then went to his room.

He hung up his black Hugo Boss suit and shirt then placed his brogues underneath them, then sat down on the bed thinking of a way to get Henry to meet with Olivia. He wasn't any further along when he met Kate in the lobby at five thirty. "I must say you look absolutely breathtaking."

Kate twirled for him in her Marchesa gown. "Why thank you Thomas," she replied elatedly.

"Did you enjoy dinner?"

"It was delicious, and the restaurant was first class."

"It was," agreed Thomas.

"I was speaking to a lady in the restroom, and she said that there was a three-month waiting list. I couldn't resist, and told her we just showed up, and got a table within minutes," said Kate giggling. "You should have seen her face. Then she turns to me and asks me straight up who I was to be getting that kind of treatment."

"What did you say?"

"I told her that it was none of her concern and to mind her own business," replied Kate.

"Did you?" asked Thomas looking a little surprised.

"I was going to," said Kate. "Instead, I told her…" She stopped.

Thomas glanced over at her and could tell by the tone of her voice that she had said something at his expense. "Okay, Kate, let me have it, what did you say?"

"I told her that the man sitting with me at my table was one of the most influential men in New York City, and that if she didn't know who you were, then she obviously socializing with the wrong circle of friends."

"You didn't"

"I did"

"And?" asked Thomas.

"That you are the richest man in the country."

"And?"

"Next please," said the box office attendant.

"Saved by the attendant," said Kate smiling at Thomas. "I was only having a little fun; besides, she was a snob."

The lady handed them the tickets, and told them they had an eight-seated box to themselves and access to the members' lounge. They thanked her and moved off to the side.

"Kate, I don't know if I feel comfortable with you being a lying lawyer?" asked Thomas dryly.

Kate made an unamused face. "Very funny."

"I still don't know how I'm going to meet Henry," said Thomas. "Any crooked suggestions magistrate?"

"This is going to be an ongoing joke all night, isn't it?"

"You know it!" replied Thomas with a grin. "Let's go to the stage door and see if I can talk to the doorman, maybe he can pass a note on."

The stage door was packed with fans waiting to catch a glimpse of the stars. They managed to move up to the door and get the attention of the doorman who told them he wasn't their mail service and were moved to one side by a muscular security guard who was throwing out five teenagers.

"If I catch you trying to sneak in here again, I'll call the police," said the guard in a deep voice. "Now go home."

"We just wanted to see the show," answered back one of the girls.

Thomas watched their sad faces walking away.

"Poor things," said Kate.

"We have extra seats," said Thomas.

Kate gave him a smile. "Go on!"

"Hey, kids," he shouted. The teenagers turned around as Thomas and Kate approached them. "How would you like to see the show?"

"Really mister?" asked the same outspoken girl.

Fifteen minutes later, Thomas and Kate strolled into the Opera House with the children, who were speechless as they walked into the main foyer. Thomas went to the bar and ordered two glasses of champagne and five cokes.

"So, what are your names?" asked Kate.

The girl spoke. "My name is Katrina, this is my brother Ethan, this is my best friend Shawna, and this is my friend Bobby, and my brother's friend Michigan."

"How old are you?"

"We're all eighteen, except Ethan and Michigan, they're seventeen."

"Do you like opera?" asked Kate.

"Yes, we sing in the New Baptist Church of Harlem Choir."

"Choir?" asked Thomas.

"Yes, sir, and we've never seen an opera before," explained Katrina. "But tonight, is a very special night!"

"Why's that?" asked Kate.

"There is a Black man named Rufus Williams playing the lead, Otello, it's his debut night and he's from Harlem."

"That is special," said Kate.

"What are your names?" asked Shawna.

"My name is Kate. and this is my brother Thomas."

"Thank you for letting us sit with you," said Michigan.

"You're welcome," replied Kate.

"Shall we go see what our seats are like?" asked Thomas.

"Yes, sir," they replied.

On the way to their box seats, he picked up seven opera glasses and programs. The five teenagers sat down and leafed through them then tried out their glasses.

Kate smiled and squeezed his arm. "You're a kind person, Thomas."

"Thank you, but unfortunately, I'm quickly realizing my kindness in not going to get me any closer to meeting Henry," he whispered. "Any suggestions?"

"I've been thinking about that, and I believe crooked people would say you're doing it the hard way," suggested Kate.

"What do you mean?" he asked.

"Why wait outside by the stage door with the common folk? Use your influence," suggested Kate "Sometimes a little grease goes a long way."

They watched the opera and were mesmerized, and Rufus and Henry were unbelievable.

During the intermission, they went and bought some drinks and a snack for the kids, then Thomas excused himself and spoke to the usher.

"How did it go?" asked Kate.

"He's going to get the note to Henry," replied Thomas.

"How will you know if he got it or not?"

"In the note, I asked Henry to give me a sign," said Thomas slyly. "You'll have to wait and see."

As the curtain fell, the kids stood up and applauded as loud as they could and joined in the calls of 'Bravo!' After the third curtain call Rufus came from behind the curtain and spoke to the audience.

"I would like to thank you all for coming to my debut tonight," he said looking down at the front row. "My dear mother and brother, thank you for being part of this special night with me." He then looked up. "And to you, the audience, thank you," he said bowing. "As many of you know, I was born and raised not far from here in Harlem, and tonight, I am very honored to have five special guests here from the New Baptist Church of Harlem Choir. They are Katrina, Shawna, Ethan, Bobby, and Michigan. Can you shine the light up there?" said Rufus pointing to their box.

The teenagers were in shock.

"Stand up and wave," encouraged Thomas.

They stood and waved, and the two girls blew Rufus a kiss.

The light returned to Rufus. "Thank you." he said blowing one back before bowing. He looked at the crowd, thanked them once more, bowed, and went behind the curtain. The crowd applauded till the house lights came on.

Kate turned to Thomas. "Subtle sign."

"I thought you would appreciate it," acknowledged Thomas, and on the way out, gave the usher the other half of the five hundred.

"Are you going to be okay getting home?" asked Kate.

"We'll be okay," said Katrina. "Do you live in New York, Kate?"

"No, why?"

"Never mind," said Katrina.

"She was hoping you would take us again," said Shawna.

"You know what Katrina, why don't you give Kate your address and phone number and we'll see what we can do," suggested Thomas.

"Okay," she replied. "Can we have yours so we can send you a thank you note?"

They swapped information then said goodbye.

"Where to now?" asked Kate.

"The hotel lobby bar," said Thomas.

"Do you have a plan?"

"No, and I only have an hour to come up with one."

They strolled into the hotel, went up to the front desk, and Thomas asked if he had any messages.

The receptionist noticed the program in Kate's hand. "Did you enjoy the opera?" he asked.

"Immensely," she replied.

"Our manager is the biggest opera fan," he revealed.

"Really, is he here?" asked Thomas.

"Yes, he is."

"May I speak to him?"

Thomas spoke to the manager in private. When they returned, he walked them to the lounge and sat them at a partially secluded table. He left, spoke with the waitress, and returned shortly after. "I will make sure your guest is brought over to your table upon his arrival. When you leave for your room, the waitress will inform me, and the food and drink you have ordered will be delivered to your room soon after. Is there anything else I can do for you Mr. Carlyle?" asked the manager.

"No, thank you, you have been most helpful," replied Thomas.

The manager left and the waitress brought a bottle of Dom Pérignon placed it in a bucket of ice and left three glasses on the table.

"What did you say to him?" asked Kate.

"I promised him that Henry Taylor would sing here tonight and that he would get his picture taken with him."

"How on earth are you going to pull that off?" asked Kate chuckling.

"I'm not sure," said Thomas laughing nervously with her.

"But why get the manager involved?" asked Kate.

"He's the senior manager, and I may need a favor from him or one of the junior managers while we're here," said Thomas.

"If you pull this one off, I'll—"

"You'll what?"

"I'll sing after he does," said Kate confidently.

"You're on! But you sing to him, and right after he does?"

"Agreed!" said Kate shaking his hand. "I've finally got you Thomas, and when you lose, we shop all Sunday and Monday in women stores only! And you call me Ms. Carlyle and carry my bags!"

"Okay, but you have to sing one of your favorite singer's songs. A Carrie Underwood one!"

"Thomas, you can even pick the song! That's how confident I am," stated Kate.

"Agreed," said Thomas letting go.

The waitress appeared and asked if they would like the champagne opened and poured. As they drank, Kate grinned behind her glass at Thomas.

"Enjoy it now while you can, sister," he said, "because I will be later."

"I wanted you to know what an honor it is to have you here tonight, Mr. Taylor," said the manager. "If there is anything you need, please don't hesitate to ask for me."

"Thank you," replied Henry watching him leave then turning to the table. "Thomas Carlyle?"

"Yes, and this is my sister Kate, please have a seat," he said, and was now convinced he had met Henry before. "Would you like some champagne?"

"Please," said Henry.

Thomas poured a glass and filled theirs up.

"You sang beautifully tonight," complimented Kate.

"Thank you," he replied nervously then looked at Thomas. "You're a friend of Olivia's?"

"Yes, I am."

"Is she okay?" inquired Henry. "Your note asking me to meet you tonight makes me believe she isn't."

"Yes and no," replied Thomas.

"Pardon me for my directness but please tell me," begged Henry.

Thomas told Henry about his cheating wife on him, the divorce, and him taking care of Olivia financially.

"How could Penny and Jack do this to me?" asked Henry upset. "They shouldn't have told you, they gave me their word, and I trusted them.

"They didn't tell me," said Thomas reassuringly.

"If not them, then who?" asked Henry confused. "They are the only ones that know."

"Unfortunately, they are not the only ones," replied Thomas. "Henry, I met you nine years ago. Do you remember me?

He looked at Thomas carefully. "No."

"I didn't remember you either until I saw the picture of you and Olivia taken in the summer at the harbor front, you had a beard."

"And?" asked Henry.

"Do you remember Margret Carlyle? She danced at the First National Ballet?" asked Thomas.

"Of course, she was a good friend of mine," he replied. "I heard she had passed away in the summer."

"Yes, she did," said Thomas. "We are her grandchildren."

"Oh, I'm so sorry, I didn't know. Please forgive me, and my deepest sympathies," said Henry. "She was a fine lady."

"Thank you," said Thomas, hesitating momentarily. "One night, you came to my grandmother's house with Penny, you spoke to them, and told them what I have just revealed to you. I was in the house that day. Do you recall my grandmother introducing me when you walked in? I was doing my homework in the kitchen," said Thomas trying to refresh his memory.

"Vaguely."

"You tried to talk low, but I overheard you, and it was only by chance that I saw the photograph of you and Olivia, that I made the connection.

Jack and Penny, they only confirmed my suspicions after I had approached them."

Henry thought for a while. "You're right, I do remember that night and meeting you, and having a conversation with Margaret and Penny," he said contemplating. "But how did you know about my financial arrangement with Jack?"

Thomas sipped his champagne and thought, good question. He put his drink down slowly to give himself more time to think. "When I confronted Jack and Penny with what I knew, they just filled in the blanks," he replied. "It's important that you realize that I knew most of it anyway, Jack and Penny had no option but to tell me everything. If they didn't, I told them I would tell Olivia. So, they agreed."

"So why are you telling me this?" asked Henry.

Thomas repeated what Jack and Penny had told him about Olivia.

"I understand what you are saying, and you are right to be concerned. Many people throw their heart and soul into their work, so much so that work is their life; and life is their work. There needs to be a healthy balance between work and your life, but when there is no balance at all, you can quickly fall apart," whispered Henry who stopped and looked at Thomas. "What should I do?"

"Can I suggest we finish these drinks then go to my room where we can speak privately?" asked Thomas glancing around. "I believe your celebrity status is drawing attention."

"Yes, I believe you are right," said Henry quickly surveying the bar. "Hopefully they haven't taken our serious conversation in the wrong way."

"I've been watching the clienteles, and most of them are just excited because they recognize who you are, I wouldn't be too concerned," said Kate reassuringly. "But I agree with Thomas, we should go to the room."

"Henry, I have a suggestion that may put their minds at ease," said Thomas. "I'm sure my sister and the people here would be honored to hear you sing, and I believe if you do so, you would remove any doubts they may have."

"That is an excellent idea," replied Henry.

"Let me check with the manager and confirm that it's okay," said Thomas leaving and returning minutes later. "He said it would be a privilege to hear you sing, and asked if he could possibly have his picture taken with you first, and be permitted to take several while you perform?"

"Of course," replied Henry.

Thomas motioned the manager over.

"This is quite an honor Mr. Taylor," said the manager standing next to him while the waitress took their picture. "Thank you," he said shaking his hand, then turned to the people in the lounge. "Attention, attention, ladies, and gentlemen. As many of you have already noticed, we are graced tonight with one of the greatest opera baritones of our time, Mr. Henry Taylor, and he has graciously accepted my offer to sing one song for us tonight."

Henry stood as the onlookers clapped. "This song is dedicated to this beautiful and delicate angel sitting next to me, Kate," he said motioning to her, then sang Rossini's 'Largo al Factotum.' As the waitress took pictures the manager cried, and after Henry finished, everyone clapped and shouted 'Bravo!' to which he graciously bowed and said, "thank you."

Thomas waited for the clapping to subside before getting up. "Ladies and gentlemen if you could please give me several more minutes of your time. It is a long-standing tradition in our family that when a man sings to a lady, she in return must sing to him. So, without further ado, please let me introduce my sister, Kate Carlyle, who will be singing Carrie Underwood's, 'Last Name.'

Kate was in shock. She didn't think he would follow through with it, and not only that, she had expected him to a least pick one of her love songs, not the one about a girl getting drunk in Vegas and getting married to a man she'd just met. As Thomas helped her up, Kate gave him a horrified look, then turned around. Everyone was staring at her, waiting, there was no way out. She glanced across the table. "For Henry," she said, then sang as the waitress took pictures. When she finished, everyone clapped loudly, and Kate curtsied. Henry stood, and gave her a kiss on the hand, and joined in the clapping. Thomas contained his laughter as he stood and shouted, "Brava!"

They finished their drinks and went to Thomas's suite, and the food arrived shortly afterwards. "Compliments of the manager," said the waitress, who set up the food and drinks on the table, then took the tip from Thomas on the way out.

"Is it possible for you to leave tomorrow, meet Olivia, and tell her everything that has happened?" asked Thomas.

"I can, and I will, but why must I tell her?" questioned Henry.

"I believe if you go and start to build a relationship with her, and she finds out all this information later on, you will lose her again, but this time for ever," said Thomas. "She would feel like you had..."

"Deceived her," added Kate helping him out.

"I see what you mean" said Henry thinking. "What happens if I tell her, and she sends me away?"

"Well, you won't be any better off than you are today in regard to your relationship with her, with one exception, the burden you have been carrying around all these years will be lifted."

"You're right, in my heart I know you're right, but in my mind I'm worried," he said anxiously. "Can I ask you a question?"

"Yes."

"What happens if I don't tell her?"

"When I arrive back Monday night, I will," said Thomas bluntly. "I can't keep this secret from a dear friend of mine and still call myself her friend. I have no promise to keep with you, Jack, or Penny, but I do with Olivia. You may not like the position I am putting you in, but honestly, I don't care."

Henry studied him. "Thomas, you are a decent man for giving me this opportunity, you could have easily skipped coming to see me, and told her. Instead, you came here first and faced me man to man, and I truly appreciate your candidness," he said sincerely then slowly leaned back in his chair and rubbed his chin. "Tell me, are you in love with my daughter?"

Kate quickly glanced at Thomas.

"She is in love with another."

"That was not my question."

"No, I am just her friend."

Henry stared at Thomas for a while. "Then you are a good friend, and she is lucky to have you, and with all my heart, I thank you."

"Henry, you must make me one promise?"

"Anything," he replied sitting forward.

"You must never let her know that I was here, or that Jack and Penny know of this."

"Okay," he replied. "I believe that is for the best and it is a promise I shall keep."

"Thank you," he said relieved. "Now, let's eat and plan tomorrow."

They talked for another forty-five minutes, and at one thirty, Thomas walked Henry down to the lobby and outside to his limousine. Henry shook Thomas's hand and thanked him again. After Thomas watched him leave, he went back to his suite, and sat next to Kate.

"Thomas, why are you doing this?" asked Kate.

"What do you mean?"

"You know what I mean," said Kate softly.

"Olivia has a chance of being with her father and having a relationship with him."

"Is that the only reason?"

"It is," he replied.

Kate decided to change the subject. "You would make a good lawyer, too."

"What do you mean?"

"I don't believe that you overheard Henry's conversation."

"I refuse to answer that statement on the grounds I may incriminate myself," he replied. "Besides he wants to tell her."

"How do you know that?"

"No one was putting a gun to his head. He could have told me to go ahead and tell her, and left, but he didn't."

"I hope everything works out for them."

"Either way, it can't be any worse than it is today."

"I guess not," agreed Kate.

"By the way, nice singing," he said chuckling.

"I'll get you back for that," she cautioned.

"You haven't yet, and you never will," he said then put his arm around her. "If it's any consolation, you sang it great, and I would never have embarrassed you like that if I didn't think you could carry a note. And I must admit, I loved your choice of songs," teased Thomas breaking into a laughter. "Not only did you have to sing after him, but to him, and about getting drunk and married in Vegas," he said making himself laugh louder.

"Go ahead and laugh it up. I'm going to pay you back one day," she promised with a determined look.

"Oh, I'm shaking!" replied Thomas laughing even louder.

Kate laughed with him. "Okay, okay. So, what are our plans for tomorrow?"

"There's a church around the corner, let's go to Mass at nine, then come back here and have breakfast in the room that way I can give you your surprise before we go shopping."

"Surprise! What surprise?" asked Kate.

"Come on, Kate," he said standing and ignoring her. "I'll walk you to your suite."

She opened her door, went inside, and turned to him. "Any hints?"

"Goodnight, Kate," he replied closing her door behind him and leaving.

When Thomas got back to his room, he called Jack and told him what had happened then hung up the phone and got ready for bed. He wasn't happy about lying to Henry or threatening him with telling Olivia, but he believed it was for the best. He thought about Olivia and wondered what she was doing at this very moment, and decided she was probably sleeping peacefully in bed and smiled but it disappeared when he realized Frank was probably lying next to her. It quickly returned when he thought about

Rachel and being with her at the guesthouse and how much fun they had, then he recalled what she had said in the hot tub and wondered if she meant it, it didn't seem like it. Thomas stopped thinking, closed his eyes, and eventually fell asleep.

Chapter 20

The next morning Thomas ate breakfast in Kate's room. She had opened the curtains and doors, and a gentle breeze blew in.

"There's a balcony through there," said Kate pointing towards them.

Thomas looked through the sheers and could see the silhouette of the railings.

"Thomas, I can't keep my eyes off it, what is it?" she asked gazing at the envelope.

"Come and sit with me on the sofa?"

She followed him and sat down.

"On Friday, after I had played golf with Jack, Barry Levinson dropped by our table," said Thomas.

"The man who you got the laptop for?" asked Kate.

"The same, and he gave me this envelope," continued Thomas. "He said he was going to courier it to you on Monday but knew he was going to see me and asked if I would hand it to you."

"What is it?" asked Kate.

"Do you remember what law firm he works for?" queried Thomas.

"Levinson and Associates," answered Kate.

"Are they well-known?"

"Thomas, they are one of the best law firms in the country, and one of the most respected, and they have some of the biggest accounts in the city," she replied. "I was going to drop off my resume there this week."

Thomas handed her the envelope and watched her open it. "Thomas it's a job offer for a paralegal," said Kate excitedly. She reviewed the document and read out loud the key points: "It's a part-time position, whatever hours I have available during the week and weekends, with a minimal of fifteen hours. Oh my God, look what their paying me hourly," she said showing him. "Once I pass the bar exam, they will hire me on as a lawyer, salary to be discussed, but no less than one hundred and twenty-five thousand. There will also be a signing bonus of twenty thousand dollars." She glanced up. "Thomas, am I dreaming?"

Thomas pinched her arm.

"Ouch. Why you? That's two I owe you," she said then stared at him curiously. "You had something to do with this?"

"I would like to say I did, but I didn't," he admitted. "I went to drop off his laptop, and thought while I was there, I would drop off your resume at Human Resources. I ended up giving it to Barry's administrative assistant and she said she would pass it on for me."

"Really?"

"That's all," he declared. "Apparently, a group of lawyers, including Barry, reviewed three potential candidates. They were very thorough on their research, and even spoke with your professors, and thought you were the best and chose you. Barry was extremely specific on why they chose you and said it was all in there," said Thomas pointing.

Kate flipped through the paperwork. "There's a letter here explaining why they chose me and basically says what you just said," confirmed Kate. She put her hand on her head and broke down crying then leaned over and placed her head on Thomas's shoulder as he put his arm around her. "This is one of the happiest days of my life."

"I think it's only going to get better," suggested Thomas.

Kate wiped her eyes and looked at him. "What do you mean?"

"Remember when I gave Jack the contact's name and number for Barry?" asked Thomas.

Kate nodded.

"Barry ended up buying a hundred units and gave me a two percent finder's fee. At first, I said I wouldn't accept," he explained.

"Thomas those companies have reputations."

"That's what Jack said. So, they gave me six thousand dollars, of which I am keeping one thousand aside, but the other five is for you to buy clothes for your new job," he said giving her the money.

"Really!" said Kate excitedly.

"Really."

"But Thomas, you shouldn't spend all this money on me there must be things you would like to buy."

"Kate, the money is yours, and I want my sister looking her best. Please take it?" he said squeezing her hand. "Besides, nothing would make me any happier than seeing the smile on your face as you're going from store to store trying on clothes and buying them."

"Thank you, Thomas," she said hugging him.

"Oh, before I forget, Barry asked that you call him by tomorrow to let him know your decision. If you accept, he will arrange the interviews, and they're just a formality."

The cell phone rang, and Thomas picked it up. "Hello," he said and waited for a reply. "Hi, Jack." Thomas listened for five minutes. "So he arrived, was dropped off at the cathedral, and met her." Thomas listened.

"Thanks, Jack, let me know when you hear anything else. Oh, by the way, is there any way Kate can get in touch with Barry today?" he asked. "He is, okay, I'll put her on." Thomas covered the mouthpiece as he passed the phone to her. "Barry is with Jack."

Kate gained her composure. "Good morning, Mr. Levinson," she said and listened. "Yes, I did, and it's a very generous offer," she replied and listened. "I accept," answered Kate. Kate listened and reconfirmed, "Tuesday at four, that's fine." She listened again. "Oh, okay, thank you. I'll put Thomas back on," she said passing him the phone.

"Barry," said Thomas. "Jack, it's you." Thomas listened then said, "Goodbye."

"Ahh! Barry gave me five thousand dollars to spend on clothes for accepting their offer," said Kate animatedly.

"Jack said to put it on his card and Barry will reimburse him," confirmed Thomas. "Looks like you have ten thousand dollars to spend on clothes," said Thomas grinning.

Kate stopped and grabbed his hand. "Thomas, I owe all this to you."

"I didn't get you the job, you did."

"Not the job, the opportunity," clarified Kate.

"You deserve it Kate, you've worked hard for it."

"I'm the luckiest sister ever! Promise me you will never leave me alone in this world?" she asked.

"Never," he replied then held her for a few moments before pulling away and looking into her eyes. "Do you ever feel guilty?"

Kate hesitated. "A little," she whispered. "You've sacrificed so much for me, and I know you wanted to go to university, and that you don't like your job. I just feel that you've missed out on so many things for me."

"Kate, the reason I asked is because I never want you to feel guilty, ever," he explained. "I haven't missed out on anything, we've only postponed them, right?"

"Thomas, you would give me the chance to take care of you and pay for you to go to university?"

"If your offer still stands?"

"Always," replied Kate sincerely.

"And if down the road I decide on another path, and refuse your offer, you will be comfortable knowing that you gave me the opportunity?" he asked.

"Definitely!" confirmed Kate. "All I want is what's best for you, and for you to have no regrets."

"No more guilt then?"

"None," replied Kate.

Thomas yawned playfully. "Well, I think I'll have a lie down."

"Nice try, Fifth Avenue awaits!" exclaimed Kate.

Thomas laughed. "Look out Fifth, here comes Kate."

"Very funny," she replied Kate heading for the door. "No, seriously, let's go."

On the way out, Thomas stopped to talk with the manager, and six hours later they returned to Kate's suite which had bags and boxes everywhere.

"And I still have three thousand left to spend tomorrow," she said ecstatically.

"I'm sure you won't have a problem," replied Thomas.

"You will have to thank Jack for giving us the names of the people in the stores, they were definitely an asset," said Kate. "What time do we have to leave tomorrow?"

"Whenever you want, the jet is on standby, all I have to do is give them a call."

"Can we leave tomorrow night so we can see the lights of New York City?"

"That's a great idea. In fact, the later we leave tomorrow the better, we can miss the rush hour traffic."

"What are we doing tonight?"

"I thought we could go out and get something to eat," he replied. "One of the restaurants on Jack's list is supposed to be fantastic."

"I'll leave it in your capable hands," she said heading towards her bags.

"All right, and when we come back you can give me a fashion show," suggested Thomas. "How does that sound?"

"Like you have a long night ahead of you," replied Kate.

Chapter 21

The cell phone ring woke Thomas up. "Hello," he said. "Hi, Jack," he replied. Thomas listened and suddenly sat up in bed. "Thanks, Jack, I'll talk to you when I get back." He glanced at the clock, it was eight, and had been sound asleep for ten hours. "I must have been tired," he said then called in sick to work before walking over to the sofa. Still half asleep, he put on some music, and sat down. Suddenly, there was a knock at the door. "Who is it?"

"Henry."

"Good morning," he said opening it.

"Did I wake you?" he asked apologetically.

"No, I was already up."

"I brought coffees and muffins. Is your sister here?" asked Henry surveying the suite.

"Kate's next door," replied Thomas, "and won't be awake for another hour. She's resting up for her second day of shopping."

"I wanted to come by and thank you from the bottom of my heart, I am reunited with my daughter, and it's all thanks to you," he said kissing Thomas on both cheeks. "A debt, I am afraid, which has no adequate payment."

"Would you like to tell me what happened?" asked Thomas.

"That's another reason why I'm here," confirmed Henry. "Your limousine picked me up, by the way your driver asked how you were enjoying New York City, then he drove me to the cathedral. I went in and spotted Olivia close to the back. So, I sat behind her and waited till they asked you to shake hands as an offering of peace. She turned, and when she realized who it was, she gave me the biggest smile and hug. I moved around and sat next to her. After church, we walked to her place, and we talked along the way. I told her about Manhattan, and she talked about her ballet. When we arrived, she made us something to eat, and we talked some more. Shortly afterwards, I told her everything, and she got upset and ran to her room crying. I thought that was it. I followed her and asked if she wanted me to go. She said no, so I closed her door and waited in the living room. Olivia came out of her room and ran to me crying, she said, 'Daddy, I've missed you, don't go." Then held me for what seemed like hours. We talked about it some more, and agreed that the past was the past, then she asked that we start off slow to which I agreed. After dinner, she drove me to the airport, and before I left, told me she was coming to New York City this Friday for a week."

"I'm so glad it all worked out," said Thomas.

"I'm so happy!" Henry cried. "I have my little Liv back."

Thomas put his arm around Henry and comforted him.

"No more tears, there have been too many tears," he said wiping them away then glancing at Thomas. "I owe you my life, and I ask myself, what can I give a man who has everything?"

"Honestly, Henry, you owe me nothing," replied Thomas. "I'm delighted for you both."

"You are humble as well," stated Henry. "I hope Olivia realizes what a good friend she has in you, which reminds me, she asked why I decided to come and see her, now, after all these years. I told her it was time she knew the truth, that I couldn't carry this burden and guilt around anymore, and that I missed her and wanted to be a part of her life."

"Thank you," said Thomas sincerely.

"Is there anything I can do for you that can match the magnitude of your kindness and thoughtfulness?" asked Henry. "Anything?"

"Actually," said Thomas thinking, "there are a couple of things. Let me get dressed and I can explain to you on the way down to the lobby."

They got off the elevator and sauntered over to the front desk. Thomas picked up three envelopes then sat down with Henry on a sofa in the lobby. "If you are uncomfortable with any of this, please let me know?"

"I will," replied Henry.

"I would like you to call Ms. Brown at the number on this envelope, she runs the New Baptist Church of Harlem Choir, and arrange to meet with her and the five children listed next Sunday, and give them this," he said handing Henry the envelope. "If you could spend an hour of your time with them, I would be very grateful."

"I would be honored. Can I ask what's inside?"

"Under Ms. Brown's name, I have reserved eight sets of tickets, one set per matinee, per month. They're all paid for; all she has to do is go to the box office and show them her identification. I've also listed the operas and the dates on the sheet," explained Thomas. "If you could let them know that this is from your company and not me, again, I would be very grateful."

"Okay," said Henry studying him. "You are a kind and a curious person Thomas."

He smiled and gave the second envelope to Henry. "This contains a picture of you with the manager, and ones of you singing. The manager has put some notes on each of them and asked if you would write the notation on the identified picture and sign them."

Henry wrote and signed the pictures then put them back inside the envelope.

"That's it," said Thomas. "Consider us even."

"For the time being," stated Henry.

"It was very nice meeting you and hopefully I will see you soon," said Thomas.

"You can count on it," said Henry pleasantly, "I plan on visiting Olivia regularly."

They both stood and shook his hand. Then Henry gave Thomas a hug and whispered, "thank you again, from the bottom of my heart."

Thomas watched him leave then went upstairs and called Jack's cell, spoke with Penny, and told her the good news. He then had breakfast with Kate, took her shopping, and had dinner with her at the hotel. At nine, they flew over New York City, and gazed down at the lights.

Kate turned to Thomas. "This is the best weekend I've ever had, and I won't forget this, ever," she said joyfully. "Me, Olivia, Henry, the teenagers, you're something special, I don't know how do it?"

"It's only time and money," replied Thomas.

"Money you no longer have," pointed out Kate.

"Sis, I wasn't expecting it in the first place," acknowledged Thomas.

Kate glanced out the window. "I thought it was funny seeing the hotel manager meticulously instructing the bell boy on how to put up the signed picture of him and Henry," she said laughing.

"You want to hear something funnier?" asked Thomas.

"Sure," she said facing him.

"I signed the picture of you singing with your name, and when I gave him the envelope, I told him you were a famous actress and that you were playing on Broadway next month in a new production."

"You're not serious?"

"The manager said he was sorry he didn't get his picture taken with you as well but did mention that he's hanging it right next to Henry's."

"Thomas!" shouted Kate punching him in the arm. "You're a rotten scoundrel!"

Thomas chuckled loudly.

"That's three I owe you!" quantified Kate.

Jack's limousine picked them up and dropped them off at home. Thomas realized he would be going to work tomorrow and unloading skids of computers. Privately, he despised his job, but this was the first time he was actually regretting going in, and wished he could quit. He knew he needed to make some changes in his own life; the sooner the better.

Chapter 22

"Hello, Francis."

"Thomas?"

"Yes, it is."

"After I buzz you in, walk up the three flights of stairs, there's only one door at the end, that's mine."

The buzzer sounded, Thomas opened the door, and started climbing the steps. He had received a call from Francis on Thursday asking, actually pleading, to meet him for a drink, dinner, and a talk. Thomas didn't really want to, but when Frank asked what he had done, Thomas realized nothing and agreed to come to his place on Saturday afternoon.

"Thomas, how are you?" asked Francis shaking his hand.

"Good Francis. How are you?"

"Please, call me Frank, only my mother calls me Francis," he replied. "I'm doing fine, and I'm so glad you decided to come. Please, come in. Here let me take your coat."

Frank hung up his jacket in the hallway then led him into the living room. "I'm making a Martini would you like one?"

"All right," he replied nodding his head.

"Make yourself comfortable while I'll get the drinks," he said leaving the room.

Thomas sat down and surveyed the room. It was exceptionally clean and attractively decorated.

Frank returned and noticed Thomas looking around. "It's not much They call it a one-bedroom bachelor apartment. There's this room, the kitchen, a den, a bedroom, and a bathroom."

"I like it, it's cozy."

"Well, it's perfect for me and I love the location. Why don't we go outside onto the balcony, and I'll show you what I mean?"

Thomas followed him.

Frank put their drinks on the table and leaned on the railings. "I love this time of the day, when the sun is shining, and people are walking back and forth."

Thomas stood next to him and followed his gaze down to the street and the people.

Frank pointed to his left. "If you look down there, you can just see a row of small stores. There's a grocery store, pharmacy, butcher shop, florist, and video rental store. A little further past, in the park, they have an outdoor farmers market every Saturday that sells fresh vegetables. In the opposite direction," he said pointing to his right, "there are bars, pubs, and a couple of dance clubs. If you like, I can take you for a walk before dinner?"

"I would like that," said Thomas enthusiastically.

"In the meantime, let's sit down, have a drink, and enjoy the sun," he said motioning to a patio chair then sat after Thomas did. "Do you like retro music? You know, from the eighties?"

"Yeah, I do."

"Do you mind if I put some on?"

"No, please do."

"This is a mixed CD, it has Erasure, Frankie Goes to Hollywood, Depeche Mode, The Cult," he said turning on the portable CD player. "One of the clubs down the road has, 'Saturday Retro Nights,' and they play all this type of music. They even ask people to come on the stage and lip sync and mimic famous singers and give a prize to the best. They're not professionals, just people in the club, but if you look too good you get booed off the stage for being a poser. If you're interested, you should stick around, it's a lot of fun," he said observing Thomas as he took a sip of his drink. "How's the Martini?"

"Excellent."

"I worked part-time in a very trendy cocktail bar, it even had a lounge singer, you know one of those guys that plays the piano and croons Frank Sinatra and Dean Martin songs as well as Top 40 hits. It attracted the after-work crowd, and because of the atmosphere, customers ordered lots of Martini's. I had a great time working there," confessed Frank thinking back. "Everyone thought I looked like George Michael; they even called me GM. Oh! Did you hear me singing at the fundraiser?"

"I did," recalled Thomas, it was while he was sitting outside with Olivia, which now seemed like a lifetime ago.

"Unfortunately, it's not one of those occasions where people remember you because you sound good."

Thomas smiled. "You're like me, tone deaf."

"You weren't supposed to agree with me," said Frank chuckling.

Frank talked about his parents, who lived east of the city, and how his father owned three garages and his mother, who had retired this year, had worked in an office. He explained how he fell in love with dancing while on a school trip to see the Nutcracker when he was seven, and shortly after, started taking dance lessons. "My parents, mostly my mother, supported me. She took me to my lessons, while my father wasn't as involved. He had played sports when he was younger, and had aspirations of me following in his footsteps, and envisioned himself going out to my games, cheering me on, and bragging to his friends over a couple of beers. Instead, he sits in a theater with a buttoned-up shirt and listens to people yelling 'Bravo!' and throwing roses on the stage. He never talks to anyone about me. Luckily, I have a younger brother who took a great interest in sports, football actually, so it helped me out." Frank thought for a moment then continued. "When my father talks about my brother, Ted, and his athleticism, there is so much pride in his voice, and you can see it on his face, with me, it's the opposite. He also has this fear that I'll walk in one day with a boyfriend and announce that I'm gay," said Frank laughing and sipping his drink. "My mother on the other hand, loves watching me, and she's never missed me dance yet. When she comes to my rehearsals with Olivia, she brings us, and all the other dancers a packed lunch. At first, I was horrified, but everyone thought it was great, and I realized that she just wanted to be a part of my life. And, in her defense, she does make the best lunches," admitted Frank nervously taking another sip. "I have a sister who's the middle child, let me see Ted's almost eighteen, so Stephanie is twenty-three, and she's studying to be a veterinarian. She's a truly kind, gentle person who loves people and animals, and will make an excellent vet. Ted, on the other hand, is going to get an athletic scholarship to whatever college he decides to go to and has promised my dad he would get his degree and take over the family business. Something else my father wanted me to do." Frank took a big gulp of his drink. "Thomas, I love dancing, and I don't know what I would have done if I had had two left feet," he said smiling.

Thomas felt bad for him. "Sometimes you just have to give people time, and they'll come around eventually," he suggested referring to his father.

"I know, and I wait patiently," acknowledged Frank studying him. "Olivia was right."

"About what?"

"She said I would like you."

Thomas came here with a preconceived notion of disliking Frank Gray and was hell-bent on making sure he continued to do so after he left, he no longer did. He lifted up his glass to Frank. "Friends."

"Friends," replied Frank letting out a sigh of relief. "I'm so glad, I was so nervous, and I had this image of me opening the door and you punching me on the nose," he admitted holding his right hand on his chest as he spoke. "Okay! Enough! Let me bring out the pitcher of Martini's."

As they drank, Thomas talked about his parents, about Kate, his work, and his writing. After they emptied the pitcher, they left the apartment, and went for a walk.

"What do you call this area?" asked Thomas.

"The Village," replied Frank. "They wanted to recreate a community-type atmosphere with houses, duplexes, triplexes, stores, markets, and pubs. I think they did an excellent job."

"I like it, and it does have a great ambiance," said Thomas taking it all in.

As they walked, he noticed Frank knew everyone, and that the stores they entered were small and the owners were the ones who served the customers. When they picked up the bacon, Thomas was introduced to Gary the butcher; when grabbing eggs and bread at the grocery store, he met Steve; and at Thom & Gerry's Florists, he met Thom and Gerry. They strolled around the market for a while, bought some fruit, then walked back to Frank's.

"Let me drop this stuff off, fill out the card for Mrs. Waters, and we'll head out for a drink and dinner," said Frank.

Upstairs, Thomas listened to Frank put away the items then watched him fill out the card and put it with the flowers. On the way down, they stopped at the first-floor apartment door and dropped them off. "Mr. Waters' wife broke her hip, and he takes a nap in the afternoon before heading back to the hospital to see her. They're a sweet couple and great landlords," explained Frank as they walked outside. "We'll go to The Stallion, it's a ten-minute walk," he said glancing over at him. "Do you like pub food?"

"I do," he replied.

"And English beer?" asked Frank. "They pour a good pint of Tenants."

"It's sounding better by the minute," replied Thomas with a grin.

"They also have the best fish and chips in the city," stated Frank waiting for his reaction.

"The best fish and chips in the city!" repeated Thomas laughing.

"Olivia told me to say that," said Frank laughing with him. "Actually, this place has the best roast beef, mashed potatoes, and Yorkshire pudding in the city, and their sticky toffee pudding is to die for."

Along the way a couple approached them holding hands. As they got closer, they recognized Frank. "Frank, how are you? Long time no see.

Give me a hug," said a man with long brown hair, embracing him and kissing him on the cheek. "You remember Blair?"

"Of course, nice to see you again," said Frank giving him a hug and kiss on the cheek.

Frank turned to Thomas, "Greg, Blair, this is a friend of Olivia's and mine, Thomas."

"Hi, Greg, Blair," he said unsure what to do, so he decided to wait and see.

"Hello, Thomas," said Greg shaking his hand.

"Hi, Thomas," said Blair doing the same.

"Where are you off to?"

"The Stallion for dinner," replied Frank. "What about you guys?"

"We're going to the Eros Bistro," replied Greg.

"Fancy place, what's the special occasion?" asked Frank.

"Third year anniversary," they replied in unison and squeezed each other's hand.

"We're all meeting at The Bear tonight for drinks, and everyone is going to be there, you should try and make it," suggested Greg.

"I'll try," replied Frank.

"We'll be there about nine, and we're going to The Saddle afterwards for their 'Retro Night,' so come over and help us celebrate."

"Sounds like fun, I'll try."

"Thomas, you're more than welcome too," added Blair.

"Thanks," said Thomas.

They said goodbye, continued down the street, and a few minutes later strolled into The Stallion. They sat in an isolated corner booth where they ordered Tenants and roast beef dinners. During dinner, Frank talked about Greg and Blair, and how they were in the Jets gang in the stage production of *West Side Story*, and that they sang and danced wonderfully. Frank explained how he had known Greg since he moved to The Village five years ago and was one of the first people he met. After they ate dessert and drank their coffee, Frank leaned back and stared at Thomas.

"If it's okay with you, I would like to talk to you about Olivia and me?"

"All right," replied Thomas, unsure as to whether or not he wanted to hear what he had to say.

"I originally thought about telling you as soon as you walked into my place but decided it would be better if we got to know each other first, and I'm glad I waited," declared Frank.

"Me too," he replied.

"Thomas, I'm not too sure what you know?" queried Frank waiting for his response.

"What I know is what I heard and saw in the foyer. Which was Olivia saying she loved you, you saying you loved her, and you two kissing. I also noticed Olivia was still in her clothes from the evening before, and then heard her telling you she had a great night, While I was standing there looking like Humphrey Bogart as he read the note from Ilsa at the train station in *Casablanca*," replied Thomas realizing he was sounding a bit melodramatic and chuckled.

Frank joined him.

"I'm glad we're enjoying my misery," joked Thomas.

"Thomas, why are you miserable?" asked Frank.

"She betrayed our friendship."

"Anything else?"

"I guess I was hoping she would have been more open and honest with me."

Frank leaned forward. "The conversation we are going to have, is probably not going to answer those questions, and I believe you will need to speak with her about those concerns, but I will try to clear up the circumstances around the events that you witnessed and hopefully shed some new light on them."

"Okay," replied Thomas.

"Before I start, please remember that Olivia wanted to tell you this herself."

"I understand," confirmed Thomas.

"You are right, I do love Olivia and she loves me, and we've known each other for an exceptionally long time, and this season we'll be dancing together. We have a great friendship, and she has helped me through tough times, as I have helped her. Not only with the day-to-day challenges of life but inside the world of ballet, I'm referring to the training, the steps, and the pressure, and we have the highest respect for one another. I compare our love to the love one has for a sister or a brother or a dance partner, and the kiss was one of friendship," Frank said and stopped when he noticed Thomas's face. "You don't look convinced," he said thinking. "Okay, let's go back to what you had seen. I've explained why we love each other, and that the kiss between us was one of friendship. Oh, the clothes, okay. The dinner party was at Penelope Daily's, she lives in the same condominium tower on the sixteenth floor, and we both stayed over. You've been to Olivia's place, well Penny's is the same accept she has three bedrooms, which means Olivia and I slept in separate rooms."

"Why didn't she just go home?" asked Thomas.

"Penny and I were up talking about a problem I'm having with one of my routines, it didn't involve Olivia and it was late, so Penny told her to go lie down and she fell asleep. Penny and I talked into the early hours, and she invited me to stay. That morning, we left Penny asleep, went for a walk, and got a cup of coffee."

"Why were you both going upstairs?" probed Thomas.

"We were going back to Olivia's apartment."

Thomas grinned and thought, at last.

"Thomas, you're still not getting it," said Frank. "All night long, all Olivia talked about was you. How you went swimming, ate dinner, had a romantic dance, watched old movies, and went shopping in the afternoon. She was on cloud nine, and I hadn't seen her this happy in an awfully long time, in fact, since I've known her. That night she asked if we could break off our 'so called' relationship, and I agreed. Looking back, we should never have done what we did in the first place, it was all a charade, but she was trying to help me out. The reason she was so happy that Sunday morning was because she was going to tell you, and I was going to help her explain. That's the reason she said she loved me and kissed me." Frank paused, noticed Thomas was still confused, and continued to clarify. "I see Olivia as a beautiful person, an incredibly good friend, and I love her because of who she is, but when I look at her, all I see is a female, a dance partner. I am not, nor ever will be, physically attracted to her," he said staring into Thomas's eyes. "Thomas, I'm gay."

Thomas felt like he had been hit with a baseball bat.

"Rumors had started to fly in the media about me being gay. My father called me up and asked me, and I quote, 'If I was a fairy?' I told him no and made up a lie saying I was dating Olivia. I spoke to Olivia and told her what I had said, she suggested that we keep the role-playing going until I was comfortable confronting my parents and the media. After which, we could break up and I would 'come out of the closet' as the term goes." Frank got the attention of the waiter. "Crown Royal and seven," he said and glanced over. "Thomas?"

"Same," replied Thomas, "but make them doubles."

Frank waited for the waiter to drop them off, took a sip, and continued. "For the last six months we've been acting out this make-believe relationship. She even goes with me to my parents' place, and we talk as if we're dating. In public, we're together quite a bit anyway, so it was easy enough to pull off."

"But I never read anything in the papers about you two being a couple, then again, I'm not one for reading the society pages," confirmed Thomas.

"No, you're right, people aren't as interested in two local celebrities dating, but if one's gay pretending to be straight then gets caught with another man, that's news."

"But today being gay is more accepted than it's ever been?" he asked.

"Honestly, Thomas, I'm not worried about the media or the public, it's my family, actually my father, and hearing him say, 'I told you he would end up becoming a great, big puff,' good old dad," said Frank glancing nervously at Thomas before taking a big gulp. "I've been celibate for quite some time because I'm very choosy about the man I want to be with, and I guess it all comes down to the fact that I want to be in love. Most of my life, I've had a tough time looking at myself in the mirror, and being Catholic makes me feel hypocritical. So, I have my father, falling in love with a man, my lifestyle, and my faith all pulling me in different directions," revealed Frank. "What Olivia and I were doing was postponing the inevitable," he said with a distant look. "Anyway, enough about me, this is about Olivia. Do you see now how wrong you were about her? She wanted to tell you everything herself and I really think you need to meet with her and talk about all this."

"Does Olivia know we were going to be discussing this?" asked Thomas.

"I told her I would try talk to you, and she'll probably call me after she gets back from New York City on Thursday to find out what happened," replied Frank.

Thomas took a long drink and contemplated. "Do you mind if I talk to her first?"

"No, not at all, I think that would be best," said Frank reassuringly.

"Are you going to be all right?" he asked.

"Thomas, my faith is my faith, and my lifestyle is my lifestyle, and no one can ever take them away from me. I also know the media will find out eventually, but I'm not concerned about them," he said leaning forward. "But in saying that, I also know I have to tell my family before it goes public, and I am worried about their reaction, mostly my dad's. In fact, I'm terrified. I'm a realist, and know I have to face them sooner than later, the only issues are when, where, and how," he said taking a long drink, managing a smile, then excusing himself to go the restroom.

While he was gone, an image came to Thomas of Frank in the last stall sobbing, and he felt sorry for him. He decided to talk to him tomorrow about his apprehensions and would just hang out with him tonight as a friend.

When Frank returned, they quietly sipped their drinks.

"What time do we have to meet your friends at The Bear?" asked Thomas.

Frank grinned; he was glad he was staying. "They said around nine, we could head over there now and save some seats, it's just across the road."

"Where's the club?" asked Thomas.

"Down the road," he replied.

"Do you mind if I crash for the night?"

"The sofa is a pullout bed and it's yours," said Frank happily. "I was hoping you would stick around."

They finished their drinks, paid their bill, and went to The Bear.

On the way Frank asked, "When are you going to call Olivia?"

"Thursday," replied Thomas.

Frank put his arm around him as they crossed the street. "Good."

They sauntered into The Bear, Thomas sat down, and Frank stood over him. "What should we have to drink?"

"Something that describes our newfound friendship," he suggested.

"I know the perfect one," said Frank going behind the bar and mixing their drinks. He came back minutes later holding a pitcher, two cocktail glasses, and filled them. "This is my own creation, it's smooth and strong, I call it a Careless Whisper. Appropriate don't you think?"

"Very!" said Thomas taking a sip. "Mm, it's delicious."

"I'm glad you like it," he said putting the pitcher down and sitting next to him in the booth.

"Do they always let you go behind the bar?" queried Thomas.

"They should, I'm the silent partner, but don't mention that to any of my friends tonight they don't know. I just make sure when they run a tab that twenty-five percent is taken off the total. The other owner, Stuart, he's the one behind the bar, he runs the place and tells them that the discount is because they're regulars here. I find it works out better this way," explained Frank. "I only go behind the bar to make drinks for my special guests, and because I make the best."

"You certainly do," replied Thomas taking a drink and looking around. "Why are these places all named after animals?"

Frank laughed. "The Bear is not referring to the animal, it refers to a particular type of gay man: big sized, with belly's, hairy chests and backs, beards, and mustaches. Look at Stuart, he's a bear."

Thomas glanced over. "I see what you mean." He didn't need to ask what The Stallion referred to.

"Does me being homosexual bother you?" asked Frank.

"No. Does me being heterosexual bother you?" joked Thomas.

They both chuckled.

As the place started to fill, Thom and Gerry joined them, they were a couple, Greg and Blair, then Gary, Steve, Phil the lawyer and his friend, Josh, Miguel the designer, Pat the engineer, and Lawrence the teacher. Thomas drank and listened as the friends caught up, then joined in once the conversations turned conventional.

"Miguel, I like your biker's jacket," he said admiring it.

"Thanks, I design and make them, this one is Frank's," he replied showing it off. "What I do is wear them for a few days to soften them up and give them that lived in look, there's nothing worse than a wrinkle free biker's jacket. I wore this tonight so Frank can take it home with him." He then leaned over and whispered, "it's good marketing too."

Thomas nodded approvingly. "What happens if the size is too small for you?" he wondered.

"I'd just get one of the girls to wear it," replied Miguel.

"If I were to give you a size, could you make me one for a friend?"

"Sure!"

"How long would it take?"

"For a friend of Frank's, Friday, with a good discount," he answered. "What size?"

"A woman's small," said Frank interrupting. "Right?"

"Right," confirmed Thomas.

"Excellent! The women's design is similar to the men's but a little less brass, softer leather, and classier," explained Miguel, "and they look absolutely marvelous."

"Do you want me to pay you now or give you a deposit?"

"Like I said, you're a friend of Frank's, you can pay on delivery," said Miguel.

"Did you know that Miguel and several of the others are in the Village Choir?" whispered Frank.

"What's that?" he asked.

"Just tell him you'll order the jacket on one condition, they sing."

Thomas turned to him. "Miguel, I've been speaking to my legal advisor here, and he suggests that before I place that order the Village Choir should sing a song, you know, to seal the deal."

"Your legal advisor will do anything to hear us sing and I mean anything," replied Miguel winking at Frank. "Deal!" He glanced down the table. "Okay, it's that time."

Miguel, Thom, Gerry, Lawrence, Blair, and Greg stood up and arranged themselves off to one side.

"Any particular request?" asked Greg looking at Thomas.

"What do you know?" he asked.

"Shout them out, and we'll tell you if we know it or not."

"As Time Goes By."

Once they started harmonizing, the bar music and televisions were turned off, and everyone went quiet. They were amazing, and everyone clapped loudly when they finished.

"How Deep is Your Love," requested Frank leaning toward Thomas. "They sing this and 'Yesterday' beautifully."

When the song ended, the choir took requests from around the bar, and pitchers of beer started arriving at the table from thankful patrons. Thirty minutes later they stopped singing and started drinking.

"Frank, they're really good," said Thomas.

"They sing at the hospital, usually the cancer and children's wards, and at nursing homes. Last year Miguel lost his nephew to leukemia, and while his nephew was in hospital, Miguel and the group used to go in and cheer him up by singing his favorite songs, and that's how it started. His nephew was a great kid, and he loved to sing, and after he passed away, they decided to keep on singing in his memory," he explained. "They go almost every Sunday afternoon, and during the Christmas holidays, in fact, tomorrow they're going in to see Mrs. Waters."

"That's really nice," said Thomas impressed.

Twenty minutes later the choir stood up again and the place went quiet. Greg spoke. "For our encore, we are going to sing four more songs, and we'll take two requests from this table, Frank and Thomas, and two from the bar." Customers quickly put up their hands. "The young lady in the black dress and the man with the black hair leaning on the bar. Ladies first, what will it be?"

They sang, 'Can't Hurry Love' for the lady, and 'Green, Green, Grass of Home' for the man, and 'Yesterday' for Frank.

"Okay, Thomas, what's it going to be?" asked Greg.

"You're the Best Thing," replied Thomas, and as they sang, he thought about Olivia.

They arrived at the nightclub at ten thirty, walked past the lineup, and straight in. Greg had reserved a table close to the dance floor but far enough so people could talk, and there were bottles of champagne chilling in buckets. They all sat down, except Greg, who remained standing and started to open a bottle, and as he did, he spoke. "I would like to thank you all for being here and helping Blair and I celebrate our three-year anniversary. From this point on, the remainder of the night is on us, so after the champagne is gone, feel free to order what you like from the bar, we're covering the tab. Again, thank you and enjoy." He popped open the champagne, cheered, and filled the glasses.

Lawrence stood and spoke for several minutes describing how Greg and Blair met, and how they made such a wonderful couple. He finished his speech by asking everyone to lift up their glasses and join him in a toast. "To Greg and Blair, and their happiness, and their love."

Everyone repeated, "to Greg and Blair," then drank.

Thomas glanced over at Frank and caught something in his eyes. Was it sadness or perhaps loneliness? Or was he thinking about his family and how different their reaction would be to this kind of celebration? Frank caught Thomas's stare, quickly smiled, and stood up. After he got everyone's attention, he talked about Greg and Blair and congratulated them on their union, commitment, and happiness.

One by one they all got up, gave a speech, and offered their congratulations and best wishes.

Miguel leaned over the table. "If anyone asks for these two empty chairs, don't let them have them, I have two friends arriving shortly." He then whispered, "you'll be expected to stand up and speak."

Thomas had no idea what to say and decided to keep it simple and wish them all the best and sit down. But as he rose, he recalled a poem by John Donne's called 'The Good Morrow' and recited it perfectly for them. They all clapped and cheered as he sat.

"Thomas, that was beautiful and quite appropriate," said Blair acknowledging him before facing the group. "I would like to thank you all for sharing this special time with me and the man I love," he said pulling Greg up and kissing him full on the mouth.

The table, with the exception of Thomas, cheered Blair on, and was feeling a little uncomfortable. Was it because he had been caught off guard by this unexpected action? Surely, he wasn't expecting any couple to turn around to him and give him a heads-up that they were about to kiss so that he could prepare himself accordingly. No, that wasn't it. Was it because they were kissing? He thought for a while. It wasn't that. He was a firm believer that individuals should show affection openly for the ones they love. Was it because it was two men, and he was heterosexual? Was that it? What about his religious beliefs, they must definitely play a role? He wasn't too sure about his reasons why, but one thing was for certain, they were in love, they were happy, and that was all that mattered. The chanting stopped when the kiss did, and the conversation around the table resumed. As Thomas sipped his champagne, Blair, Greg, Thom, and Gerry went onto the dance floor, and as he watched them moving, laughing, and having fun, he suddenly realized that the worst feeling a human being could have, was to be on a planet with over six billion others, and yet feel so alone. He glanced over at Frank, and his heart went out to him; he had only just understood what he must be going through.

"This is one of my all-time favorite songs," said Frank.

"Want to dance?" asked Thomas.

"Are you okay with that?" he asked.

"I've danced with friends before at a club, I don't see any difference."

"I'll make sure no one tries to cut in on me," joked Frank.

They danced to Talk Talk's 'It's My Life' and halfway through the song Thomas spoke. "Isn't it ironic that you like this song?"

"That's the reason I like it so much," commented Frank.

They danced to two more songs, sat down, and neither of them noticed Miguel's friends had arrived.

"Hi, Thomas."

"Janet, how are you?"

"I'm doing well. I wouldn't expect to find you here," she said brushing her cheek with his.

"I'm a friend of Franks," he replied.

"Do you remember my girlfriend from the show, Betty?"

"I do, but I didn't remember her name, hello, Betty."

"Hello, Thomas," she said shaking his hand.

"Is Olivia here?" asked Janet.

"No, she's in New York City."

"Oh, that's right, she was in the store a few days ago buying an outfit for her trip. I was surprised not to see you with her?"

Thomas was silent.

Janet continued. "Last time, when you were waiting outside, she told me how much fun it was having you around and how she was going to beg you to come with her again."

"I've just been really busy," said Thomas.

"Well, she only tried two outfits on and ended up asking me to pick one. She looked so miserable, so I asked her how she was, and she said she was fine. Then she told me she was seeing her father this week, and hadn't seen him for some time, and I replied you should be happy then. She forced a smile, but she wasn't herself. I don't think she was there more than twenty minutes," revealed Janet surprised. "When I saw her walking away and compared it to the last time she was with you, I knew there was something upsetting her. Is she okay?"

"I don't know, I haven't seen her for a while, you would have to ask Frank," suggested Thomas.

"You haven't seen her for a while," repeated Janet. "Maybe that's it?"

Thomas quickly changed the subject. "When I went with her, she thought you were trying to pick me up."

Janet laughed. "I was only being playful, I thought she knew."

"She didn't."

"Really!"

"I had some fun with her for a while, before I eventually told her."

"Did you like her in the dress?" asked Janet.

"I thought she looked beautiful."

"I think you two make a good couple."

"We're just friends," confirmed Thomas.

Greg and Blair were getting up again to dance and pulled Thomas up with them, Janet, Betty, and Miguel followed.

Throughout the night, they had individuals go on the stage to lip-synch and take off various artists. Frank did George Michael, and Thom and Gerry did Erasure. Thomas was dancing with Frank and Miguel when Billy Idol's "Rebel Yell' came on. Thomas unbuttoned his shirt, started pumping his arm, and singing with a sneer like Billy Idol. Miguel whispered to Frank, who headed toward the disc jockey while Miguel took Thomas back to the table. "It's time," he said.

"Time for what?" asked Thomas.

"Billy Idol to hit the stage," said Miguel taking off Thomas's shirt and putting on Frank's biker's jacket then glancing over at Janet. "We need to do something with the hair."

Janet took out her brush, gel, and styled Thomas's dirty blond hair.

The music died and a voice came over the speakers, it was Frank's. "Ladies and gentlemen, tonight, flown in from merry England via New York, for a special one night only guest appearance, the one, the only, Billy Idol."

"That's you," said Miguel.

"Here," said Janet giving him a shot of tequila.

He downed it and headed for the stage. 'Rebel Yell' started again, and Thomas imitated Billy Idol to almost perfection. After he'd finished, he jumped off the stage, and could hear the group's chanting of 'Billy, Billy,' getting louder as walked towards them, and from that point on, he would always be affectionately known to them as Billy. And they chanted once more, when he went onto the stage for his runner-up prize of a bottle of wine, which he gave to Blair and Greg, the three phone numbers he gave to Frank.

When the night ended, they all gave Thomas a hug goodbye and told him they would see him soon.

Janet pulled him to one side and whispered, "I hope you work it out with Olivia, you two look good together."

"I hope so, too," replied Thomas giving her a kiss on the cheek.

As Frank and Thomas staggered away the group chanted, "Billy, Billy, Billy!"

Thomas turned around, sneered, and gave them one more Billy Idol pump, which was met with loud cheers. Out on the street, they meandered back to Frank's place. Once there, he pulled out the sofa bed and gave Thomas some blankets.

"I usually sleep in on Sundays, make some breakfast, and go to church at noon over at St. Theresa's, you're welcome to join me?"

"Thanks, I will, but I have to leave after church," said Thomas taking off the leather jacket and passing it to Frank. "I'll need to borrow a shirt, mine never made it back to me."

Frank chuckled. "I'll give you one in the morning."

"By the way, your friends are great."

"They like you, too," replied Frank. "Have a good sleep."

"Goodnight."

"Night."

Thomas woke before Frank and made himself a coffee, then put on his pants and sat outside on the balcony. He thought about Olivia in New York City and was happy it was working out with her and her father. Then he thought about the way he had treated her and what she must think of him.

Half an hour later Frank walked onto the balcony and passed him a shirt. He quickly looked down at the street before turning to Thomas. "Come inside, and I'll make some breakfast."

Thomas followed him into the kitchen, sat down, and listened to him talk about dance as he cooked. After they ate their bacon and eggs, then went to Mass, and on the way back, Frank confided in Thomas. "I need to talk to my parents."

He nodded and listened.

"Sooner than later," he said half-smiling. "That'll be fun."

Thomas noticed the worried look in his eyes.

"Last night, you were right, it is my life," stated Frank as they walked past his apartment and stopped at Thomas's car. "It's time I started living it."

"Frank, if you like, I can go with you to your parents," he offered. "I don't want to interfere in any way, but if you need me, I'll be there."

"You would?"

"Yeah, definitely, if you want me to."

"Thanks, I was fearing going alone," he said relieved. "I'll give you a call, okay?

"That's fine."

"Do you think Olivia would come as well?"

"I think you already know the answer to that," said Thomas.

"Yeah, I do."

Frank gave Thomas a long hug and was so glad he met him. "You're going to talk to Olivia?"

"Thursday," he reconfirmed.

"Good, make sure you do, because you two have a lot to talk about, and thanks, again," he said sincerely.

"Call me when you have a day and time," said Thomas getting into his car and lowering the window. "Thanks for last night, I had a great time, and we'll do it again soon."

"You can count on it," said Frank pumping his arm back and forth and chanting, "Billy, Billy, Billy!"

Chapter 23

Thomas parked his car, and as he strolled along the path to the guesthouse, a young man in a two-piece blue suit slowed down as he approached and stopped him. "Thomas?" he asked.

"Yes," he replied a little confused.

"I'm Mathew Walker, the lawyer that's helping Rachel and Veronica with the daycare."

"I know the name, Rachel's mentioned you," confirmed Thomas. "How's everything going?"

"Slow," he replied. "I came by to give them information on the municipal and federal by-laws."

"Red tape," suggested Thomas.

Mathew nodded his head. "Yeah."

"Well, I'm sure once they get passed the bureaucracy it will speed up," assured Thomas.

"Definitely," agreed Mathew. "Are you here to do some writing?"

"Yeah. Is Rachel in the guesthouse?"

"She is."

"I'll see you again," said Thomas shaking his hand.

"Good luck," said Mathew unsure as to what else to say to someone who writes.

"Thanks."

Thomas walked to the guesthouse and was ascending the stairs when he met Rachel coming down dressed in jeans and a tank top.

"Thomas!" she screamed and gave him a big hug, "I've missed you. How are you? You look tired?"

"I am, it's been busy at work," he explained noticing her hair and touching it. "Wet."

"I just got out of the shower."

"You always look so fresh and smell so good," he commented sniffing in. "I passed Mathew, he stopped and said hello."

"He's a nice guy," she said grabbing Thomas's hand. "Come downstairs to the kitchen and I'll make you my famous ham and cheese sandwich."

"That would be great," he said following her.

"Do you remember when I asked you if you could come out with me, Veronica, and Buddy, and you were busy," she said grabbing the items from the fridge. "Well, they couldn't change the date, and Veronica asked Mathew to come, and he said yes, and we had so much fun together. I went out with him again last weekend," she said waiting for his reaction.

"Did you have good time?"

"Yes, he took me for dinner, and we went for a drink afterwards."

"You like him then?"

"He seems really nice."

"Seems?"

"Thomas, I've only been on one date," she said placing the sandwich in front of him.

"You look happy," suggested Thomas.

"I am, but that's because you're here."

"How is he with you being a super model?" teased Thomas.

"He's great, and very understanding," acknowledged Rachel, "like you." She stared at him anxiously.

Thomas noticed it. "What's the problem?"

"I want you to meet him, you know socially, and let me know what you think of him. It's important to me that you like him because your friendship is more important to me."

"Why don't you arrange something this Saturday," he suggested.

"Tracy called me yesterday and said AtlasX was playing in a club in the city, I'm sure she said it was this Saturday," said Rachel excitedly.

"Saturday it is," said Thomas.

"Yay!" she shrieked and kissed him on the cheek. "I'll call Mathew, Veronica, and Buddy, and you can ask Kate. I'll let you know the details tomorrow," she said walking away.

"Where are you going?"

She put her thumb to her ear and pinky to her mouth. "To call people, make plans," replied Rachel. "Nothing like the present."

Thomas grinned and shook his head. "I'm going up to your house to return a book I borrowed from your father's study," he said getting up.

"I'll meet you up there in fifteen minutes," said Rachel disappearing up the upstairs.

Thomas strolled to the mansion, entered through the back door, and entered the study. He signed the book back in on the computer, walked over to the shelf, and returned it to its original place.

"You have a nerve!"

Thomas turned and looked at Bill Carter; he was furious. "You said I could borrow your books," he replied confused.

"Not the books, you idiot! I'm talking about you fucking my daughter in my guesthouse!" said Bill storming towards him and stopping inches from his face.

Thomas could smell booze. "What are you talking about?"

"I was suspicious of you when I first met you. No money, working in a two-bit warehouse, and I thought to myself, this guy is on the game. So, I humored my wife and Jack, and said I'd agree to what Rachel wanted but made a point of keeping a close eye on you. Then I hear from the servants that you've been fucking my daughter in my guesthouse. Everyone said you would be a good friend for my daughter, but I was right all along, you were only interested in poking my daughter's rich pussy in hopes of getting a windfall. I knew you were too good to be true, you fucking bastard!" screamed Bill.

"Honestly, I don't know what you're talking about."

"Thirty minutes ago, a staff member came by and told me he could hear you and that slut fucking in the hot tub!" yelled Bill as he tapped his forehead on Thomas's nose.

"Bill, what's going on? Who are you calling a slut? And why do you have members of our staff spying on our guests?" asked Jessica standing in the doorway.

"Jessica, I have no idea what he's talking about," pleaded Thomas to her.

"You don't speak to my wife with that filthy mouth!" barked Bill head-butting Thomas above the right eye; a half inch slit opened, and the blood poured.

Thomas wasn't expecting it and his knees weakened, and with his arms, he desperately leveraged himself against the bookshelf. Jessica shouted at Bill to stop then ran to get help.

"Time to taste some rich man's fists," said Bill punching Thomas to the ground. "Get up! Get up!"

Jessica quickly returned to witness Bill punching and kicking Thomas. "Bill, stop!" she screamed running over to him, he turned, and pushed her hard to the ground.

Bill put his attention back on Thomas, stood over him, and kicked him repeatedly. Bill suddenly felt a strong hand on his right shoulder turning him around, a fist the size of a melon swiped across Bill's face and the distinctive cracking of his nose filled the air. Bill, knocked out, fell with a thud to the ground. Jack went to Thomas and helped him up.

"Is he okay?" asked Jessica.

"I have to get him to a hospital, he'll need to be looked at, and stitched up. I'll take him in my car," said Jack leveraging a disoriented Thomas on his shoulder. "Call the hospital and let them know I'm coming," instructed Jack, "and get rid of that piece of shit you call your husband."

"What's happening?" asked Rachel coming up behind her mother. When Jessica turned toward her, she noticed Thomas's face covered in blood, and leaning on Jack. "Thomas!" she cried. "What happened?"

"Quick, get a towel from the powder room," said Jessica leading her in that direction.

Rachel grabbed a towel and met them in the hallway. Jessica took it from her and put it over Thomas's eye.

Outside, Jack walked Thomas to his car and carefully placed him on the passenger side, then looked over at them. "Rachel, call his sister and tell her the hospital, Jessica, I'll call you later on your cell phone," said Jack wiping his forehead. "You two leave immediately and stay somewhere safer tonight."

Jack dragged Thomas through the emergency entrance and were seen to straight away. While Thomas was getting examined, Jack went into the hallway and called Jessica to find out what had happened. After getting the details, he walked back and waited outside the room.

"Are you a family member?" asked the doctor.

"No, a close friend of the family," replied Jack.

"I'm his sister," said Kate joining them. "How is he?"

"He's stable. He has five stitches above his right eyebrow, some bruised ribs, bruising on his face, hands, arms and legs, and a mild concussion. I've given him a mild sedative for the pain and will be keeping him in for a couple nights as a precaution," he replied. "I believe this man was beaten. Would you like me to call the police?"

Kate looked at Jack. "What happened?"

"Doctor, can we have a minute?" he asked.

"Take several, I'll be around."

Jack walked Kate to the waiting room, explained to her what had just happened, told her about Jessica and Bill, then asked her for a favor. Kate listened, agreed, and they went back to speak to the doctor.

"Thomas had tripped and fallen down several steps. Jack found him unconscious on the ground and brought him here," said Kate convincingly.

The doctor looked at her hesitantly, then glanced at Jack. "Is this what happened?"

"As God is my witness," lied Jack.

"Okay, I'll make a note of that in his file," he said, "you may want to get those steps looked at."

"Will do," replied Jack.

"Can we see him now?" asked Kate.

"You can, we've moved him upstairs to room 312."

They walked into the semi-private room and over to its only occupant. Kate looked at him and wept. Jack, after seeing his swollen right eye, the stitches, and bruises, wished he had punched Bill a few more times. He picked up a chair and moved it next to the bed for Kate, she sat and picked up Thomas's bruised hand and kissed it.

"Can I get you a cup of coffee?" asked Jack.

"Please, Jack," she said wiping her eyes. "Do you think they'll let me sleep in that bed tonight?"

"Sure, they will," said Jack. "I'll take care of it."

Jack called Jessica, told her about Thomas's condition and hung up, then called Penny. Afterwards, he spoke to the nurse then picked up two cups of coffee.

"Thomas has the room to himself, and you have the use of the bed for as long as he's here," confirmed Jack.

"Thanks," she replied and started to cry. "He could have killed him."

"I know," he said gently putting his hand on her shoulder and thinking Bill's finished. He sat with Kate until ten, got up, kissed her on the head, and said he and Penny would be back early tomorrow morning. At midnight, Kate lay on her bed looking over at Thomas; he hadn't moved all night and his breathing was so light. She eventually dozed off.

"Kate, Kate, is that you?" asked Thomas.

She woke up and was disorientated for a minute then remembered where she was and turned to see him awake. She swiftly jumped out of bed and went to his side. "How are you?"

"Thirsty."

"Let me call the nurse," she said pressing the button.

"Where am I?"

"In hospital," she answered.

The nurse came in. "How are you doing, Thomas?"

"Thirsty."

"Good, I'll get you some water."

"My head and body aches, too," added Thomas.

"I'll get you a mild sedative it will take the pain away and will help you sleep," she replied and left.

Thomas closed his eyes and opened them when she returned. "Take these two pills and drink some water, slowly," she warned.

Thomas did, then closed his eyes.

The nurse glanced at Kate. "You should let him sleep. I'll leave the water in case he wants more, make sure he drinks it slowly," she said and departed. It was 3 a.m. when Kate went back onto the bed, and slowly fell asleep.

Thomas was sleeping when Rachel came into the room.

"What do you think you're doing? Get out? Haven't you done enough?" said Kate in a stern voice trying to hold back the tears.

"I'm so sorry Kate, I didn't mean for any of this to happen, I feel so bad, please, don't send me away," she begged.

"Get out? Get out or so help me I'll throw you out!" said Kate confronting her.

"Kate," whispered Thomas.

"Thomas," said Kate running to his side. "How are you?"

"Kate, come closer," he said softly. "I know your upset, but she is my friend, and had nothing to do with this, don't blame her."

Kate cried and spoke in between sobs, "I know…I'm just frightened."

"Rachel's your friend too," said Thomas trying to smile. "Ouch!" He waited a moment then spoke again. "I love you, and I'll always be here for you, I'm not going anywhere."

Thomas slowly closed his eyes. Kate turned to Rachel who was bawling, walked over, and put her arms around her.

Ten minutes later, Jessica came in and stood over him teary eyed. "It's all my fault."

"It's not," replied Kate.

"Kate," she whispered, "many times I've looked in the mirror and seen my face like Thomas's, and I never did a thing to stop it from happening again. If I would have, maybe this would never have happened," she explained crying and walking away.

Kate followed and held her. "It's not your fault," she said reassuringly. "Come and be with Thomas, he likes it when you hold his hand." She sat Jessica down in her chair then left to get them coffees.

Jessica held it and looked at the bruises. She knew her marriage to Bill was over. She glanced at Rachel who was sitting at the end of the bed. "Did you know?"

"About Dad?" Rachel asked. "About the abuse?"

"Yes," replied Jessica.

"When I heard the yelling, it reminded me of bad dreams that I used to have when I was younger, and I remember you were never around for days after those dreams. I wanted to tell you about them, so you could make them go away, instead, I went to Dad, and he told me they were just bad dreams. Looking at Thomas, I understand why you weren't around, and that they weren't bad dreams at all."

"I didn't want you to be a part of it, and I was scared that if you knew, he might hurt you, too. I should have made him leave a long time ago, and this time I will, I promise."

Rachel stood behind her mother, leaned over, and placed her arms around her, then rested her chin on her shoulder. Jessica lifted her free hand and tenderly caressed her daughter's face.

"Maybe we can spend some time together, like we used to?" suggested Rachel. "We could go horseback riding?"

"Can I go as well?" asked Thomas.

They both looked at him.

"How long have you been awake?" asked Jessica.

"Long enough," he replied.

"How are you feeling?" asked Rachel.

"Thirsty," said Thomas.

Rachel held the straw to his mouth, and he drank a little.

"Can one of you get the nurse?" he asked.

"I'll go," said Jessica leaving.

"I don't think I can make it Saturday," said Thomas trying to grin.

"It's okay, I got the wrong date, it's a week Saturday that AtlasX are playing. So, you're not getting out of it that easy, mister."

"Then I'll be there," said Thomas winking with his good eye.

Rachel couldn't hold back the tears and cried over his chest. "It's my fault! I should have never left you alone in the house."

"Rachel," whispered Thomas, "it's not your fault, never blame yourself." He couldn't lift his hand to comfort her. "Rachel, look at me, look at me." He waited till she did. "I need you, remember were friends, like brother and sister."

She smiled at him recalling that.

"Come closer, closer."

She leaned over and close to his mouth.

"I can see right down your top," he said.

She put her hand over her shirt and playfully hit his arm. "Some brother!" she exclaimed.

"Ouch!" said Thomas.

"Sorry," she said kissing it better.

"How are you doing?" asked the nurse.

"My eyesight is fine," said Thomas glancing over at Rachel.

Rachel shook her head and rolled her eyes.

"Actually, I wondered if I could have some more of those pills?" asked Thomas.

"The doctor will be here in about ten minutes, he's making his rounds, can you wait till then?"

"That'll mean I'll have to listen to this blonde bore me with talk about her super-sex life," said Thomas.

"Thomas!" said Rachel embarrassed.

"You should be so lucky to have such a beautiful woman at your bedside," said the nurse in Rachel's defense.

"He calls that a sense of humor," said Rachel. "That's it, I'm taking my flowers and fruit basket back."

The nurse was still shaking her head on the way out.

"Thomas, I'll get you for that," said Rachel sternly.

"Kate's first in line with three," replied Thomas, "you're next."

When the doctor walked in, Rachel and Jessica left. "Good morning, Thomas, I'm Doctor Reed, I treated you last night and I'm here to have a look at you." He pulled the curtains around the bed and examined Thomas. "You're doing fine, the swelling will go down over the next day or two, and the bruising will take a little longer. After you leave, make an appointment to see your family doctor in a week to ten days so he can examine your stitches. Later this morning, you should get out of bed, go to the bathroom, go for a walk," he said making notes on his chart. "I'll be back tomorrow, same time, and I'll probably release you then. You should take a couple of weeks off, and if you need a note for work, I'll give you one tomorrow."

"Can I have some pills for the pain?" asked Thomas as the doctor pulled back the curtain.

"I'll have the nurse bring you some and let her know that anytime you need them you can have them. I'll also give you a prescription tomorrow," he said thinking, then quietly spoke. "Thomas, your sister claimed that you fell down some steps, and Jack confirmed that he found you at the bottom unconscious and brought you here. Is that true?"

Thomas glanced at Rachel and Jessica outside. "Yes, I was distracted, mistimed the step, and fell forward. The next thing I remember is waking up here."

"Mistimed the step?" repeated the doctor.

"Yes," confirmed Thomas, knowing Jessica and Rachel would be safe and Bill was fucked.

"All right, I'll see you same time tomorrow."

"Thank you, Dr. Reed."

The doctor opened the door and said to the people outside, "he's all yours."

Kate came in alone and closed the door, "What did he say?"

"That I need to get out of bed and go for a walk, take the pills whenever I need them, that I should be released tomorrow, and to take a couple of weeks off work and relax," summarized Thomas.

"That's positive news," said Kate.

The nurse came in with the pills and some cold water.

Kate went outside and gave them the update.

After the nurse left, Penny and Jack came in.

"Oh, poor Thomas," said Penny placing some flowers and chocolates on the side table. "Are you feeling better?"

"A little," he replied then looked at Jack. "Thanks, I owe you one."

"Forget it, we'll talk about it later, you just get well," he said with a nod. "I'm going to go outside to give you two sometime alone. Oh, by the way, Thomas, if you want you can use my rustic cabin up north for the weekend, week, whatever, and you can have it all to yourself or invite your sister up or a friend."

"Thanks, Jack, I just might take you up on that offer," said Thomas as he watched him leave and close the door before turning to Penny.

"Thomas, I know I thanked you last week over the phone for what you did for Olivia, but I wanted to thank you again in person. And once you're better, you should come by for dinner one weekend, and we can talk about it some more."

"I look forward to it," replied Thomas. "I was going to call Olivia this Thursday and see if she wanted to get together and talk." He paused momentarily. "Did you know about Frank and what they were doing?"

"Yes, I thought it best that one of them told you," confirmed Penny. The last thing you needed was another person getting involved, and since you didn't want to give Olivia the chance to explain, she asked Frank to. Besides, who would you have rather heard it from, me or one of them me?" She touched his face gently. "You should call her."

"I will, although I was hoping to look a little better when I saw her," he confessed. "I don't want her to see me like this."

"In you, Olivia sees what's in here," she said pointing to his heart, and then his temple, "and what's in here."

"Thanks, Penny," said Thomas feeling a little better.

Penny kissed him on the cheek and left. Outside, she could see her crying in Jack's arms.

Thomas closed his eyes for a moment and fell asleep.

He woke a few hours later and noticed Jessica sitting forward in her seat softly crying. He lifted his hand and played with her hair. She looked at him and he gently brushed his fingers over her cheek. "An attractive woman like you deserves to be caressed," whispered Thomas.

Jessica smiled. "Rachel and Kate have just gone down for some lunch."

"Good. That means you can help me out of my bed, and we can go for a walk around the ward; I'll be the envy of all the patients," said Thomas gradually moving his legs over to the side of the bed then taking Jessica's arm as she helped him stand. She then picked up a robe from the end of the bed and put it on him. "Let me go to the bathroom first," he said carefully ambling in its direction and closing the door behind him. He had forgotten he hadn't seen himself in the mirror and was shocked by his reflection. He quickly composed himself, used the bathroom, then came out and put his arm through Jessica's. They went out of the room, down the hall, and stopped at the refrigerator to get a juice and continued. Thomas noticed the television room was empty and decided to stop there for a rest. Jessica helped him then sat beside him.

"Is it okay if I talk to you candidly about me, Bill, and Rachel?" asked Jessica realizing now was as good a time as any.

"Of course," said Thomas.

Jessica took a deep breath and began. "Thomas, when I first met you at the fundraiser, you reminded me so much of Bill when he was younger - charming, charismatic, independent, proud, confident – but also very caring and sensitive. The difference between you and Bill today, is that you see all the good in people, while Bill is the opposite, and is very judgmental and quickly jumps to conclusions; usually the wrong ones." She glanced at the finger that once occupied her wedding ring. "I first met Bill when I was twenty and he was twenty-five, and I fell in love with him the first time we met. He didn't have much money at that time, but he was smart, ambitious, and worked extremely hard. We got married, and I had Rachel when I was twenty-five, and everything was great," she said managing a smile before turning serious. "Bill hit me for the first time when Rachel was around five, you know, Thomas, I can't even remember why he did, but I guess no reason could justify what he did. For the next few years, he continued to hit me once in a while, you know, a slap or two here and there. Afterwards, he was always sorry, and would buy me flowers, perfume, jewelry." She looked at Thomas. "One thing many people don't know about him, is that he is extremely jealous and possessive, and used to get so angry if a man talked to me or even casually gazed in my direction. And I could tell just by that look in his eyes, that I was going to get it when I got home, especially when he'd been drinking. You slut, smack! Whore, smack!" Jessica nervously played with her hands. "He beat me up when Rachel was eleven; his slaps had now been replaced with clenched fists. The next day, when he was sober, he would apologize, take me away to our cottage and cater to my every need. I thought maybe it was the pressure of the job, but I soon realized it wasn't that all and that he had a serious problem, and when he started drinking, he had two." Thomas reached over and took her hand; she clasped her other around his and held it tightly. "I wanted to have more children, and give Rachel brothers and sisters, but for obvious reasons I didn't. She always asked for one, and when I didn't give her a satisfactory reason, she thought I was being selfish, and I honestly believe she despised me for it. You see, Thomas, I came from a family of three sisters and two brothers and would have loved her to have siblings growing up like I did. But she didn't know about the beatings, nobody did, and I wasn't about to tell her that was my reason why I couldn't give her one." Jessica loosened her grip and gently caressed his hand. "As Rachel grew into her late teens, they weren't as often, and when they did happen, I'd learned how to protect myself, mostly my face. But one day Jack surprised me at home and saw my face healing from a beating I'd taken a few days earlier. He went straight to Bill and threatened to kill him if he touched me again. Jack came back, told me to call the police, and throw him out but I didn't listen. After Jack left, Bill hit me again. After that, I moved out of our room, and Bill started to travel more often. I know he has a girlfriend, but I didn't mind, it's kept his attention and fists off me for the last few years." She let out a heavy sigh. "When we were out in public, I used to put on a performance with Bill, especially around Rachel, but over the last couple of years I dropped it. Rachel suddenly noticed I had stopped loving her father and started to take his side. She was even spending more time with him. Rachel never knew what was going on between Bill and me, and it really affected her indirectly, and over this past year, she distanced herself further from the both of us. She also changed, and became a spoilt, confused girl, and I was worried about her welfare, and I honestly thought she was going to move out and leave me alone with that monster."

"Why didn't you just tell her?"

"Don't get me wrong, she always loved me, and we had a relationship, but I thought if I told her she would think I was lying to get back at Bill and trying to pull her onto my side. And I didn't want to drag her in the middle of our problems and into harm's way," she replied. "Bill didn't even notice the change in her personality, and that she was becoming someone else, but I did, and every day that went by she became more distant and more confused. I became extremely worried for her well-being, and decided after the fundraiser, I was going to tell her the truth about Bill and me in hopes of getting my Rachel back. Then she met you, and just like that, she became the old Rachel again." Jessica removed her hand, reached for her juice, and took a sip, then continued. "Over the last few weeks, I've noticed Rachel's transformation back to her old self, and we've started to become close again, what I didn't realize was how much this was infuriating Bill. He started drinking more, and I could see that look in his eyes and the tone in his voice when he spoke to Rachel, and I never wanted her to fall victim to his rage like I had. So, the morning after the party, I decided it was time I spoke with Jack and told him everything. He threatened Bill, and said if he came near me again, he would not only beat him senseless, but do something far more severe; Jack and his associates would withdraw all their money from everything they were partners in with Bill and tell investors to keep away from him. It would cripple Bill financially. Later on that morning, when Bill spoke to you and said you could use the guesthouse, it was because Jack and I had told him earlier that he had to. Bill didn't want you anywhere near Rachel or our house, he saw you as a threat, and our ally. But Jack and I knew that you being around Rachel would help her get back to her old self and keep her safe. In hindsight, I should have told Rachel a long time ago and had Jack throw Bill's ass out onto the sidewalk."

"Why didn't you leave him? Was it the money?" asked Thomas.

Jessica had a surprised look on her face then laughed. "All that money is mine. The estates, the house, the cottage, they're all mine. My net worth is over a hundred million and Bill can't touch it. My father never liked Bill and would only let me marry him if he signed a prenuptial contract. He also wanted the six children to run his business after he died, no spouses, so he made us all equal partners and applied the condition that it was only transferable to our direct offspring. Which means when I die, Rachel gets everything I own. Today, my two brothers and sister run the business; I'm not interested. Anyway, Bill signed the prenuptial without hesitation because he knew he could use my influence and contacts to succeed in his own ambitions, which he did. Plus, he knew I had liquid assets and would be receiving profits from the family business. So, with the help of my connections, Bill has done well for himself. In fact, Bill would have to give me my share of his twenty-five million." Jessica paused momentarily. "Funny, when I think back, if it were up to me, I would have married Bill without my father's prenuptial stipulation," she admitted glancing at her vacant finger again. "To answer your question, why I didn't leave him? I was in love with him, but not anymore," she said finishing her juice then looking over at Thomas. "Which brings me to yesterday. I didn't know this at the time, but Bill was having the guesthouse spied on by the servants who were there to clean it and stock the cupboards. You know, observe the goings on, stains on the sheets, that sort of stuff, and report back to him. Yesterday afternoon, one of the groundskeepers was cleaning the guesthouse garden and said he saw Rachel talking to someone in the kitchen. Several minutes later, the same man went to ask if he could have a drink of water, only to see the kitchen was empty, so he went back to work down by the side of the house. Ten minutes later, he hears the sliding door open and Rachel and a male entering the hot tub and having sex. What had actually happened was that Rachel had been talking to Mathew, Veronica, and Buddy in the kitchen. Mathew and Rachel went outside on the porch to say goodbye, while Veronica and Buddy headed downstairs to the lower level and start to get hot and heavy. Rachel comes in and goes upstairs to take a shower, she is notorious for taking long ones, and she told me later she wanted to look nice for you. Anyway, Veronica hears the shower go on, knows Rachel will be in there for a while, and with the noise of the shower, knows Rachel wouldn't hear them. Veronica and Buddy get naked, get into the hot tub, and have sex. They hear the shower go off and go back inside. Half an hour later, the groundskeeper is telling Bill in the study what he heard. As Bill is listening, he's staring out the window and sees you coming from the direction of the guesthouse with a book in your hand. He thinks it was you and Rachel in the hot tub, well, you know the rest." She stopped and was about to cry but gained her composure. "Not to take anything away from what he did to you, but I believe if he had seen Rachel approaching and confronted her in the study, he would have beaten her, and she's so fragile she may never have…" Jessica put her head down and cried.

Thomas placed his arms around her and waited till she finished. "But it's over with now, she's fine, I'm fine," he said reassuring her. "So, what's next?"

Jessica wiped her eyes. "Jack, Penny, Kate, and now you, know everything, and let me tell you it's not easy for me, I'm a very private woman."

"I understand," said Thomas comforting her.

"I'm going to take Rachel away, and tell her everything, she only knows bits and pieces. Tomorrow, Jack, his associates, and their lawyers are going over to see Bill to end their business relationship with him. Me, I just want to get rid of him, so I'm going to give him some breaks. I'll let him keep his twenty-five million, a million in cash, his car, and personal items. All he has to do is sign an agreement that says he will move out of the city, leave me and Rachel alone, and can't try to get any more money from me before, during, or after our divorce. He will also have to admit to the beatings. In regard to Rachel, she will have to decide if she wants to visit him or not, I wouldn't stop her, but she would need a chaperone," said Jessica. "I've given Bill until noon on Wednesday to be out of the house."

"Will he sign?" asked Thomas.

"If he doesn't, he would be a fool. He's not expecting what I'm offering him, and he'll know he will be getting much more than he deserves." replied Jessica. "Trust me, this will suit him just fine, our marriage will be over, and he can go live with his girlfriend, Suzy." She thought for a minute and realized she had to say something. "Thomas, he could have seriously injured you, even killed you, you are still within your rights to press charges and sue him?"

"No."

"No?" questioned Jessica. "You could make a small fortune fast."

"I'm not interested."

"Why not?"

"Correct me if I'm wrong, if I press charges, your life and Rachel's would be splattered all over the newspapers and the media would hound you day and night throughout the trial? Isn't that why you just want to get rid of him, give him some breaks, and have him sign an agreement?"

"Yes," confirmed Jessica.

"Well, I wouldn't want you two to have to go through all that, no amount of money is worth it. Rachel's my friend, and Jessica, so are you."

"Thanks, Thomas," she said resting her head on his shoulder and sitting in silence momentarily before changing the subject. "Rachel told me that your eyesight was okay," she said chuckling.

Their laughing subsided and the mentioning of Rachel's name reminded Thomas of something. "Jessica, I thought the groundskeeper would have confused Rachel and Mathew having sex because he was leaving when I was arriving."

"No, not Rachel," said Jessica lifting her head and looking at him, "she's very particular about certain things, especially sex. So, I knew it wasn't her, besides, she loves you and wants to—"

"Here you two are!" said Kate with Rachel coming in behind her. "We've been looking for you everywhere."

"Thomas, they dropped off your lunch in the room, and mother, I brought you a sandwich and tea," revealed Rachel standing next to her.

"Well, let's have lunch," he said to Jessica as he stood up awkwardly, and with her help, walked back to his room.

Kate and Thomas told them about New York City. In fact, they spoke about it so much, they talked Jessica into taking Rachel there next week for a long weekend.

"Make sure you stay in the same hotel as we did, and you will see the famous face of one Kate Carlyle gracing its walls and make a point of asking Richard the manager if this Broadway star stayed there," said Thomas chuckling.

"I'll make sure we do," replied Rachel looking forward to it.

"I still owe you for that," said Kate, "and one day I will get you back, you'll see."

"Kate, your idle threats are more painful to hear than my body," he jested.

"Ha, ha!" replied Kate unamused.

Thomas was released Tuesday morning, and Kate drove him home.

"I'm glad you're okay," she said glancing at him." You look so much better than you did last yesterday."

"I feel better," he said staring out the window. "You must be behind in school?"

"Don't worry, I'll catch up," she promised.

"How was your first day of work?"

"Well, it was a Saturday, so quiet, but it gave the skeleton staff a chance to show me around and meet some of the lawyers I'll be working with. I'm back again tonight, Thursday, and Saturday, and I'm looking forward to it," said Kate excitedly.

"I'm glad," said Thomas grinning at her enthusiasm. "Jack offered me his cabin."

"You should go; you have two weeks off."

"I was thinking about staying home for a few days till I get back on my feet then heading up there Thursday."

"That's a good plan," she admitted, "I can help you out while you're here."

"Did you want to come up Saturday after work?"

"Thanks for the offer but I will get more done studying at home."

"That's okay, I thought you wouldn't, I just wanted to ask and make sure," he said thinking. "I'll probably stay there for a week, put my feet up, and relax in Jack's rustic cabin."

"Rustic cabin!" repeated Kate giggling. "Good luck!"

Chapter 24

Thomas watched Jack's chauffeur drive away as he picked up his bag. He could have driven but Jack insisted he take it easy in the back seat of his Bentley. He turned around and scanned the so-called rustic cabin, what he beheld, was a spectacular log chalet which he guessed to be over three thousand square feet.

He climbed the wooden steps onto the large porch and looked over at the several chairs, tables, and two-seated chair swing before lifting up the doormat and picking up the key. He opened the front door and went into the main room. It had a magnificent brick fireplace, above which was a shield and two crossed swords, two large sofas, a tree-trunk coffee table with a glass top, a couple of armchairs and end tables, and a rifle lamp, which Thomas thought must have been a gift. The floor was hardwood and was partially covered by a wilderness rug that resided in front of the sofas and under the coffee table. Over to the far-left, was a long wooden bar and stools, and to the right, was a dining table and chairs, behind which, was a spacious kitchen with an island, breakfast bar, and a rectangular table with six. To the right of that, was a sunroom with a view of the pool.

Thomas strolled past the bar and into a large recreation room that had sofas and recliners facing large windows offering a stunning view of the lake, boathouse, and dock. There was a pool table at the back of the room, and to his left was an entertainment system with a flat screen television. Thomas noticed two doors leading out to a deck, opened one, and peeked out. There was a barbecue, patio table and chairs, and a hot tub, as well as six steps the length of the deck that invited you down to a manicured garden and a path that led you to the lake.

He closed the door and went past the pool table into the hallway. The door on the left was a bathroom and on the right was the laundry room. He continued and opened the door on the left and went into a sizeable bedroom. It had two big bay windows with a double bed against the wall, an end table with a phone on it, a chest of drawers with a mirror, and a large television. He opened a door on the left and glanced around the full-sized bathroom, then the next one, which revealed a walk-in closet. Thomas strolled to the windows and gazed out at the lake before leaving and heading down the hallway. The next three rooms were similar in size and set up as the first one, and before checking out the last, one ascended the stairs to the loft.

When he reached the top, he looked over the railing at the main room and front entrance. When he turned around, he noticed there were only two doors on the floor, he went through them and stared in awe at an incredible master bedroom. It took up the whole upstairs area, had a four-poster king size bed, two end tables, a tallboy, and chest of drawers, entertainment center with a flat screen television, and gas fireplace. He walked over and opened two French doors that revealed a long and wide walk-in closet. He then strolled over to another set, and went into a stunning ceramic tiled en suite, that had a two-man oval tub, shower stall, large mirror, and two sinks. He glanced out the windows that encircled the tub, at the trees and lake. Thomas went back into the bedroom and sauntered over to two glass doors that led him out onto a balcony that wrapped around the cabin, and had a spectacular panoramic view of the pool, deck, garden, dock, and lake. He closed the doors behind, exited the bedroom, and descended the stairs.

Thomas walked into the last bedroom. It was the same room as the others except it had a large desk and leather chair. He put his bags on the bed, took out his laptop and placed it on the desk, then unpacked before laying down on the bed. He glanced at the clock, 10 a.m., he picked up the phone and called Olivia, it rang unanswered. He tried again thirty minutes later, and still no answer, and decided to try later on. Thomas took two pills, closed his eyes, and fell asleep.

He got up and spent the afternoon sitting on the deck, gazing out at the lake, and wondering if Olivia was intentionally ignoring his calls. The sun was starting to set, and he decided to barbecue something while there was still daylight. He went into the kitchen and read a note that Jack's retired next-door neighbor Jim Jones had left. It informed him that he had filled the refrigerator, freezer, cupboards, and the bar, and that the fireplace was ready, all he had to do was open the flue and light the newspapers. He had also signed his name, left his phone number, and said to call him if he needed anything else. "P.S, I've left two T-bone steaks defrosting in the refrigerator, the barbecue is gas, and just needs to be turned on and lit. Two?" pondered Thomas, maybe he's stopping by for dinner. He went onto the deck and lit the barbecue, then back inside into the main room, before going behind the bar and grabbing a Heineken from the refrigerator. He placed it on the bar, and was so busy looking for an opener, he hadn't noticed the solitary figure standing in the doorway. He eventually found one, opened the bottle, and took a swig.

"I knocked, you must have been outside, so, I came in."

"Olivia," he said softly.

She stood there still with her small suitcase in her hand wanting to run to him. "I hope you don't mind me intruding…I called your house and spoke to Kate…then I called Jack…I had to see you…and now, I'm here," she explained nervously.

"I called you; you weren't answering."

"I was on my way here," she replied. "Why were you calling me?"

He walked from behind the bar and toward her. "I needed to talk to you."

"Over the phone?" she asked cautiously.

He stopped in front of her. "I was going to ask you if you wanted to join me here."

There was an uncomfortable silence.

"I've missed you," said Thomas.

Olivia fought back the tears. "I've missed you!"

"I'm so sorry. Can you ever forgive me?"

"Thomas, I'm the one who should be asking you for forgiveness, I wasn't honest and up front with you, and I shouldn't have let you find out the way you did."

Thomas stared at her beautiful face. "I should have given you a chance to explain, and I didn't, I'm sorry."

"I'm sorry, too," she replied, "and I'm making you a promise right now, that by the end of the night you will know everything about me, and you always will, there will be no more secrets."

"All right," replied Thomas with a smile. "I've been doing a lot of thinking, and I really need to talk to you, too.

"Okay," she said feeling happier.

"I've really missed you."

"I've missed you," she confessed and couldn't hold back the tears anymore.

Thomas held her in his arms. He loved the way she felt, the smell of her hair, and her soft skin on his cheek. When he felt her tears, he pulled away and tenderly lifted her chin up, then looked her in the eyes. "No more tears," he said gently wiping them away.

"Thomas, they're not tears of sadness," she said giving him a radiant smile.

"Good," he said caressing her face.

"Let me put my suitcase and coat in the bedroom and change into something more comfortable."

"I'll wait for you on the deck."

"I'll just be a minute," she replied then studied his stitches, "I heard what happened." She reached up and kissed them tenderly "Kissing them better," she explained then turned and left.

Olivia came onto the deck wearing jeans, a thick beige sweater, and her hair in a ponytail, she walked to the first step and asked him to join her before sitting. Thomas grabbed the beers, gave her one, then sat down on the fourth step and looked up at her. The sun was setting on her face, and a delicate breeze blew a few strands of her hair around; she looked gorgeous.

"What are you thinking about?"

"How beautiful you look?"

She blushed and glanced down at the garden. "Do you want to go for a walk?"

"Sure."

"What about the barbecue?"

"I'll turn it off," he said standing and going to the barbeques, when he returned, he followed her down the steps onto the garden path.

"As you know I haven't been completely honest with, and unfortunately, there is more. In a good way," she quickly clarified with a cheery tone in her voice. "You don't know this, but your grandmother used to talk to our ballet class about you all the time, it was Thomas did this, and Thomas did that. She even showed us photographs of you and your sister. And when she instructed me alone, I would always ask after you. She would talk about you, and even bring in her photo albums, and show me all the pictures. I even remember you coming in and picking her up. I guess I was young and had a crush on you," she admitted pausing and collecting her thoughts. "After your grandmother left and Penny took over, she told me about your parents' death, you becoming the man of the house, and taking care of your grandmother and your sister. I know that your parents had no life insurance, hadn't left you much money, and how you had to work to pay the bills. I also know how that because you had to work you couldn't attend university but are paying for your sister to go, and so on." She stopped and looked at him. "I never got to see any more pictures of you, but throughout these last ten years, I've heard everything about you through Penny. Last year, by chance, I had heard that your grandmother was going to the ballet on Saturday evenings and that you were taking her. So, last May was no accident," she confessed as they continued down the steps to the beach area. "I wanted to see you and meet you. Well, you already know this part of the story, I was so late, and never had time to change and ended up wearing jeans and a ponytail, then caught you staring at me. Thomas, I wanted to look so nice for you and here I was looking awful. I was horrified! I wanted to crawl under something and hide, instead, I exited stage left," she said laughing with him at her choice of words. Olivia then went quiet momentarily and thought as they strolled along the beach and onto the dock "After I saw you at your grandmother's funeral, on the way home I concocted a plan, and spoke with Penny about it. I asked her who was giving your grandmother's award, and she said she was going to ask you and Kate to present it together. I thought if you were bestowing something on behalf of your grandmother you would certainly come, but it almost backfired when Kate agreed and said she was coming alone. Then for whatever reason, Kate called Penny and told her she couldn't make it, and that you would be presenting. I was so happy. I made sure you were at our table and sitting next to me. I had some anxious moments when you showed up late, and even stood up to wave you over to your seat, but Alfie called you to the podium. Then after he left the stage, you were standing there alone, and I wanted to come up and bring you back to our table, but I was nervous and scared. As it turns out, stunning Rachel walks up with her perfect body wearing a tight fitted sexy dress, and she's all smiles as she escorts you back to her table and sits you in her absent father's seat. That night, I'm outside, and start thinking about everything that's happened. You've done the most wonderful thing for Penny letting her present the award, so she's happy; I'm role-playing being Frank's girlfriend, so he's happy; and you're laughing and dancing with Rachel, so she's incredibly happy, and I'm totally miserable. Everything went wrong, nothing had gone to plan, so I started to cry. Then you appeared and made me smile. Do you remember what you said?"

"Something along the lines of just think how long it has taken the universe to give us this moment, right now."

"Yes, and I believe it's the most romantic thing anyone has ever said to me," she admitted shyly.

They reached the end of the dock and watched the setting sun's rays dance across the water and make it glisten.

Olivia moved close to Thomas. "I've never sung for anyone since my father left, never. Many people have asked me to, including Penny, but the pain was too deep. I sang for you because you asked me to, and because I wanted to, that's the reason I picked that song, I wanted you to think of me. Afterwards, I made a decision, I was going to take control of my life and be responsible for my own actions. What was it you said to me? 'You believe our life is in our own hands and we are in control of it.' Do you remember?"

"I do."

"Well, I thought there was no time like the present. So, I told Frank that the dinner party was the last time we would be role-playing as a couple, and we would talk about it then. Then, I came back and sat alongside Rachel because I wanted to be with you. Later, after we danced, and you agreed to meet me the following day, I was so happy, and I wanted to tell you about Frank then but realized it was too soon. I know, I've had many opportunities since, but I had convinced myself to wait till after the dinner party. That night, rather than us just ending it and you not knowing about it, I decided I needed to tell you everything, so I spoke to Frank, and he agreed to accompany me when I did. On Sunday morning, my plan was I would talk to you and tell you everything, and once I did, you would understand, and we would move on. Unfortunately, it was too late."

"Olivia I—"

She put her finger on his lips. "Please, let me finish, you need to hear this."

"Okay."

"At the fundraiser, after I sang, I went into the last stall in the restroom and cried. I met Penny and I told her how I missed my father," she said then looked deeply into Thomas's eyes and softly brushed her fingers over his cheek, "and that I loved you." She smiled at Thomas. "I love you, and I've loved you for a very long time, in fact, I fell in love with you the first time I saw you."

"Olivia, I love the way you wear your hair, your blue eyes, your soft skin, your radiant smile, your beautiful body, and long legs. I love your sincerity and your sensitivity. I love the way you make me feel. I love the way you sing, the way you dance, the way you dress. I love shopping with you. I love the way you like old movies. I love the way we talk, laugh, and dance. I love you," whispered Thomas. "I love you, completely."

"Oh Thomas, I love you so much!"

They held each other tightly, then looked into each other's eyes, and when their lips came together in a soft, gentle kiss, their love was unified. They separated momentarily, and as the sun set behind them, they came together in a long, passionate kiss.

They held hands and walked back to the cabin.

"I have a secret, also."

"You do?" asked Olivia. "What is it?"

"You know when Penny visited my grandmother, she always spoke of you, so I know quite a bit about you, too. She used to bring pictures of you to show my grandmother and talk about how much you had grown. That time we met in May, I was staring at you—"

"Oh, don't remind me," she said chuckling.

"Not at what you were wearing," he clarified. "I was staring at you because I thought you were the most beautiful person I had ever seen, and I was hoping you were going to be at the fundraiser."

"Do you think your grandmother and Penny set this in motion and we just picked it up and ran with it?" suggested Olivia.

"I wouldn't put it past them."

They walked quietly in the garden for a few minutes. Thomas stopped, and faced Olivia, the light from the cabin was enough to make her eyes sparkle. He held both her hands. "I'm not too sure how to say this any other way so I'll just ask," he said hesitantly.

"Go on, ask," she said encouragingly.

"What happens when we're together in public?" queried Thomas. "You being who you are and me being who I am?"

She moved close to him. "Thomas, I knew what you did before we ever met. If you stay in the same job till the day you die, I will always be proud of you, and love you. You are the love of my life and have qualities that no man will ever match, and my love for you is stronger than anyone's words." She kissed him softly on the cheek and noticed something in his eyes. "Thomas, is there something else?"

"This afternoon I was on the deck, looking out at the lake, and I asked myself what I was doing here? And I realized this is crazy."

"What is?"

"Olivia, I'm socializing with people who have millions of dollars. They lend me their guesthouse, I eat their food, and spend their money. Take this weekend for example, I got a ride up here in a Bentley, have this chalet, and there's bottles of Bollinger in the refrigerator. I drive to work in a beat-up second-hand car and work in a warehouse, come home to a sixteen hundred square foot house, and work out my pennies."

"And?" asked Olivia.

"I'm in over my head," said Thomas. "What happens when people move on?"

"What do you mean?"

"I'm always going to be me."

"Which is why I love you," said Olivia.

Thomas grinned. "I like hearing that."

"Thomas, if Jack, Jessica or Rachel gave you a million dollars would you take it?"

"No."

"If they said, here, take this million we want you to be comfortable around us and be one of us. Would you take it?"

"No."

"If you had an opportunity of making money from one of them, would you?"

"No," replied Thomas.

"Why not?" Olivia asked.

"Because I consider them my friends," replied Thomas.

"So, you think they are using you, and they're not your friends?"

"No, I don't know, I'm confused. I know they like me because of who I am, but who I am doesn't make me money."

"No, Thomas, it doesn't make you money, it makes you friends, and it makes you who you are," said Olivia. "I know Jack has told you his life story. Do you ever wonder why he did that? Did you know that Jessica's father sent her to public school and brought her up learning to respect people and value money? He had her working on the ground floor making minimal wage, and Jessica did the same with Rachel! Here's something else, Jack said that Jessica's father was one of the most respected businessmen he even knew. He ate lunch with his employees, played golf with them, and he even had picnics on his estate for them and their families. Jessica's father and Jack are new money. Do you know what that means Thomas? They weren't born into it; they made it on their own. If you think they are not your friends then you are blind."

"I know they are."

"Then what is it?" asked Olivia. "What's really eating at you?

"I hate my job," he blurted out.

"That's it, this all comes down to that," said Olivia giggling.

"Oh, you think that's funny," he said nodding his head.

"I do," she said and laughed some more.

"Why's that?"

"Thomas, you really are confused! If you don't like something and it makes you unhappy then quit!" stated Olivia simplistically. "And do something that will make you happy."

"Olivia, I have a few hundred dollars in my account, I have Kate, her education, the bills."

"Why don't we go back to the house, get another couple of beers, put on the steaks, and you can tell me what you've been up to then I'll tell you what I've been doing. And once we're all caught up, let's talk about how we can help you out, okay?"

"All right," he replied. "It feels good to have someone to confide in," he acknowledged kissing her.

"That's another reason why I love you because you tell me the way you feel," she said pulling him down onto the lawn and kissing him fervently.

They eventually made it to the deck and made dinner. During the meal, Thomas talked about Rachel's birthday party, the Sunday afternoon at Rachel's guesthouse, playing golf with Jack and having dinner at his place. Kate's job, going out with Frank and his friends, the fight and Jessica being abused. He intentionally missed out New York City and the topics leading up to it because of the promise he made to Penny and Jack. Even though they had agreed to let him tell Olivia when warranted, and that time was now, he wanted to hear from her first on how it went.

"So, Billy Idol's been busy?" asked Olivia.

"Don't you start with that!" said Thomas.

"I wish I had seen you."

"I wish so, too. Maybe I'll give you a private performance."

"Promise?"

"Promise," replied Thomas. "So, what have you been doing?"

"Well, I cried a lot, rehearsed a lot, and exercised more than I should have. I did some reading and read one piece in particular that was very exceptional. Oh, and my father came from out of the blue and visited me. He spent the day and night with me before flying back to New York City. We talked, we cried a lot, and we came to terms with everything that had happened. We're taking it slow but I'm glad we're working it out because I missed him. Actually, I went to New York City last week and he's going to come back up in a few weeks." She caressed his face. "If I would have known what had happened to you, I would have flown back sooner."

"I know you would've," said Thomas.

"Thank you."

"For what?"

"You know what," she replied.

Thomas decided to quickly change the subject. "What did you do in New York City?"

"Well, I'm glad you brought that up!" she said cheerfully. "While I was there, my father had invited the members of the New Baptist Church of Harlem Choir for a tour of the Opera House and held a class on the stage for them with Rufus Williams. At the end of the class, Rufus asked the kids how they liked the opera last Saturday night and the teenagers talked about how much they enjoyed it. Then one of the girls stands up and tells this amazing story of how they tried to sneak in, got caught and thrown out, and how a brother and sister named Thomas and Kate let them sit with them in their private box. And how she had wished they were going to be here because she had a letter she wanted to give to them. My father said he would make sure that they got it and took it from her, then gave them tickets compliments of the Opera House. This same girl puts up her hand,

I think her name was Katrina, and she said, 'You mean compliments of Thomas and Kate, don't you?' My father looked over at me and I gave him an interested look. So, he came clean and told them how Thomas had asked him to present the tickets and set up this class for them. I thought to myself, Thomas in New York City and meeting my father, that's a coincidence, or was it?"

"I took Kate there as a surprise, and told her about her job offer, then took her shopping, and to the Opera," said Thomas casually. "The teenagers were so upset, so we invited them with us."

"And you met my father how?" she asked.

"Good question," he replied thinking quickly. "It was actually by coincidence, we bumped into each other at the hotel, and I found out he was your father. One thing led to another, and he agreed to give them the tickets, as a favor, nice man. Another beer?"

"No, thanks," she replied.

"I need one," he said hastily getting up, taking off inside to the bar, and opening a beer.

Olivia leisurely followed him in. "You met him on what day and gave him the tickets when and where?" she queried.

"I think Monday. Yes, Monday."

"And it was just a coincidence that he flew out on the Sunday to see me and bumped into you when retuned on the Monday?"

"Yes, it was, he actually said that he'd just got back from seeing you."

"Thomas, tell me the whole story," she said moving slowly towards him and backing him up against the wall. "I love you," she said kissing him. "Now, tell me!"

"Okay, okay, no more torture," he joked.

"Oh torture, is it?" she said kissing him again, again, and again.

"I give in, I surrender, I'll tell you."

She led him outside, they sat on the steps, and he told her everything.

"Did you really see my father at your grandmother's?" she asked.

"Yes, I recognized him from the picture of you and him."

"Did you hear him talking to them that night?"

"He told Penny and my grandmother that night at my house."

"Then you heard him?" she asked.

"After your father left, I went into the living room, and heard my grandmother say to Penny that your father was in a bad situation. From what Penny and my grandmother had talked about, and the few words I had overheard in between that night, I made an assumption, and told him that I had overheard him that night. So, to answer your question, not exactly, I had headphones on and was listening to music most of the night.

But when I got back from New York City, I spoke to Penny on the phone about that night and what I had told your father, and she that my assumption was correct because that's what they were talking about."

"I see," she said.

"Olivia, Penny did tell me that you said you missed your father, but she conveniently missed out the part about how you were in love with me; it must have slipped her mind."

"Must have," she said nonchalantly.

"Olivia, the only reason I did what I did, was for you."

"I know, and you've made me so very happy."

"We'll have to tell Penny and Jack that you know," said Thomas.

"We will. I'm your date for dinner, am I not?" asked Olivia.

"Dinner?" asked Thomas confused.

"Dinner at Penny's next Friday?"

"I asked someone else already and they said yes," he said in a serious voice.

"You have," said Olivia sadly.

Thomas laughed.

"Why you?" she said standing in front of him, pushing him on the deck, and lying on top of him. As they kissed, she realized she had the man she loved, and her father, back in her life, and she couldn't be any happier.

"Thomas," she whispered. "Tell me, what do you want to do?"

"If I had a choice?" he asked.

"If you had a choice and no financial worries."

"I would be a writer, I love writing," he replied. "You know the enjoyment, freedom, and excitement you feel when you dance, that's how I feel when I write."

She rolled off him, and with one hand holding up her head she gently caressed his chest with the other and spoke quietly. "When your sister is working full time, can't you leave your job and write? I'm sure she would want to do that for you?"

"She's already offered," said Thomas, "but she won't be full time for at least another eight months," he replied, "and I don't know if I can last that long."

"I have almost eighty thousand dollars in a savings account you can have that," said Olivia. "In fact, I want you to have it."

"No, I couldn't take your money."

"Why not?" she asked.

"It's your money, and Kate wouldn't be comfortable with the idea either."

"Then ask Jack for an interest free loan?"

"It's called a handout!" said Thomas.

She corrected him. "It's called a hand up."

"I couldn't face looking at Jack knowing I owed him money; besides, I would rather borrow from you."

"But you wouldn't have to, and if it were up to me, you could have the money."

"I know," he replied.

"Thomas, let me help you, I really want to," she pleaded. "I just want you, us, to be happy."

"I know you do, and I appreciate your offer, but I don't feel comfortable accepting it."

"What about this?" asked Olivia sitting up excitedly. "I'll be your silent business partner, and I'll invest eighty thousand dollars in you, you write, and I'll send your manuscripts off to publishers," she said proud of herself.

Thomas thought. "Can we put something in writing, like a business contract that indicated it was your money, and that any money we made went to paying off the loan and anything over would be split equally."

She looked at Thomas. "If you want."

"Maybe we can register it as a company and write something up legally."

"Thomas, whatever you want, we'll look into it next week," she said waiting for another condition, but none came. "So, is it a, yes?"

"It's a yes, business partner," he said pulling her over. "Thank you."

She kissed him avidly. "So, what are you going to do Monday?"

"Quit!" he confirmed. "And you should come to the house and meet Kate," said Thomas suddenly realizing something. "Kate, I'll have to tell her, and she will have to be okay with all of this."

"You should, and the sooner the better," replied Olivia.

"No, we should," confirmed Thomas.

"Okay, we should," she said correcting herself. "I'm so happy for you!" She placed her head on his chest, and he put his arm around her.

"I'm happy, too," he said gently squeezing her. "Don't you want to read my novel first before you commit?"

"I already have!" she exclaimed.

"What? How?"

"That exceptional piece of work I was talking about was yours. You left it with the doorman and told him to throw it out, but he's a friend of mine so he kept it and gave it to me."

"What did you think?"

"I read it three times and cried every time, I loved it!" replied Olivia "We should send it off to a publisher this week."

"All right."

"Maybe Kate can help us put together a business contract," she suggested. "We could put together a rough outline and show it to her."

"That's a great idea, I love you."

"I know," she said giggling. "Tomorrow night, why don't we celebrate, I'll cook."

"That sounds wonderful," said Thomas.

They kissed then went inside.

Olivia quickly ran into the bedroom and came back holding DVDs. "Tonight, is musical night, first, *Gigi*, then *Seven Brides for Seven Brothers*, *West Side Story*, and *Singin' in the Rain*. But before you press play let me go put my pajamas on," she said cheerfully dancing out of the room.

They laid together on the sofa and watched the first two movies. Olivia fell asleep at the beginning of the third, and Thomas carried her to bed, then went to his room and slept soundly for the first time in what seemed like a lifetime.

Chapter 25

"Can I come in?" asked Olivia tapping on the door.

"Yeah," replied Thomas stretching.

She walked in with a breakfast tray and placed it on the end table. "Good morning," she said with a kiss and sitting on the bed. "I fell asleep on you again."

"I don't mind, I was tired, too," he said surveying the tray of food. "What do we have here?"

"We have Kellogg's Corn Flakes, a bagel and cream cheese, orange juice, and tea. If you sit up, I'll put the tray on your lap, then lie next to you," she instructed.

Thomas helped her with the tray and waited till she was next to him before handing her a bowl of cereal.

"What should we do today?" she asked eating.

"I don't know," he replied unsure. "What time do you want to have dinner?"

"Around Seven"

"And time to prepare?"

"Start at five thirty," she said thinking. "Do you want to go for a ride and have a picnic?"

"That's a great idea," he said enthusiastically.

They finished breakfast, got ready, and met in the kitchen. Then picked out cheese, cold cuts, fruit, yogurt, cookies, and bread, and placed them on the counter. "What are we going to put this in?" pondered Olivia.

"I know," said Thomas heading down the hallway and coming back with a wicker picnic basket. "I spotted it yesterday in the laundry room."

"It doesn't look like it's even been used," commented Olivia opening it. "It has plates, cutlery, cups, and napkins.

They filled it and Thomas was about to close it.

"Wait! I know what's missing," said Olivia walking over to the bar and returning with a bottle of red wine. She placed it in the designated spot and closed the basket. "All done."

They went outside, jumped into her BMW, and started to drive. Along the way, they stopped off at small towns and strolled around the antique shops, bookstores, and markets, before continuing to their final destination. Olivia pulled into the entrance to the state park and drove to a secluded spot. She spread out a blanket under a large tree, sat down, took off her shoes, and placed them next to her handbag, then watched as Thomas carried the picnic basket and portable CD player over; she liked the way he looked in his jeans. Thomas put the items down, sat next to her, and gazed at her brown hair blowing in the breeze and the sun lighting up her face; she looked like an angel. Olivia turned towards him and kissed him for a lengthy period of time before pulling away.

"Will you dance for me again," he whispered.

"Okay," she replied softly, and placed a CD in the player, "let me get set first, then put on the music." She scanned the grass to make sure it was clear of obstacles, then took off her socks and sweater and threw them to Thomas, before getting into position. "Okay, play the music."

In her jeans and T-shirt, she danced gracefully to Tchaikovsky's 'Swan Lake.' Thomas was hypnotized. After she finished, she curtsied while Thomas clapped loudly and offered her a dandelion, which she graciously accepted with a polite bow of the head.

"I love watching you dance."

Olivia smiled and grabbed his hand. "Why don't you come around me, here," she said positioning him behind her. "We are going to perform a partnered pirouette, which means as I turn my body clockwise you help me by rotating my waist, and when I say now, you stop me by holding my waist. The trick is that I need to be facing the audience, who are, Mr. Blanket, Mrs. Picnic Basket, and their daughter, Ms. CD Player."

Thomas tried and finally got it right on the fifth time. On the sixth, he purposely stopped her early so that she was facing him then kissed her. As Olivia wrapped her legs around him, he carried her to the blanket, lay down on top of her and kissed her ardently. His hand slowly went up and down her body, and she responded by caressing his back then grabbing his bum and pulling it towards her. Olivia could feel his hardness and rubbed her pelvis up against it as he pressed against her. She wanted to make love to him more than anything in the world, and knew waiting would be difficult, but worth it. She slowly stopped, and breathing heavily, she looked deeply into his eyes and gently played with his hair.

"I have something for you," she said leaning over and turning off the music, then reaching over for her handbag and pulling out a paperback.

Thomas rolled onto his back and looked at the paperback. "*100 Best-Loved Poems* edited by Philip Smith," he read then gave her a gentle kiss. "Thank you."

"I picked it up at the last bookstore we were in," she revealed, "and I wrote an inscription inside."

Thomas turned to the front page and read:

> *Thomas,*
> *With all my love,*
> *Olivia.*

"Read something for me?" she asked.

"Okay," he replied sitting up.

Thomas reviewed the table of contents as Olivia put on her sweater and socks then snuggled into him.

He picked Lord Byron's, 'She Walks in Beauty,' and as he recited it, gazed down at her. "That's you," he said after he finished.

Olivia was beaming. "Please, read another."

Thomas read several.

She pulled him on top of her and kissed him. "Thomas, will you read some of your novel to me one day?"

"If you would like me to?"

"I would."

"Then I will."

Oliva held him tightly. "I love you, Thomas, I love you with all my heart and soul," she whispered.

"Thomas, put on some music, the CDs are next to the stereo, and open a bottle of champagne," shouted Olivia from her bedroom.

He put in a CD, poured two glasses, and placed them on the tree-trunk coffee table, then lit the fireplace, before sitting on the sofa and watching the glowing flames.

Olivia sauntered into the room wearing her hair in a French braid and the dress that Thomas had picked out. "Do you still like it?" she asked twirling.

"You look absolutely stunning!" exclaimed Thomas admiring, her "Dance with me?" he asked pressing play.

'You're the Best Thing,' said Olivia holding him closely. "I love this song."

"Me too," he replied.

"I think this is our song," they said at the same time making them laugh.

"Did you go back and get this dress for me?"

"Go back?" asked Olivia confused.

"When I saw you that Sunday morning, you were wearing the pantsuit."

"Did you think I only bought the pantsuit?" she asked and realized by the look on his face that he did. "Thomas, I bought the pantsuit for the dinner party and this dress for you, this is the first chance I've had to wear it."

"That's why Janet asked me if I liked the dress," recalled Thomas.

"Yes, and I bought the underwear she suggested, too," she revealed with a mischievous smile. "They're pure white, and I'm wearing them as I speak, along with the matching bra."

An image of Olivia in her white thong and bra ran through Thomas's mind as she put her head on his shoulder and softly sang the words. When the song finished, she kissed his cheek, and led him to the sofa.

"Do you want to eat in front of the fire," he asked.

"Yes, that would be so romantic," she said excitedly. "Let me move the cutlery and napkins over here."

"No, he said grasping her hand, you sit and have some champagne, I'll grab them."

She sat, picked up the glass of champagne, and watched him walk there and back.

Thomas put the items on the coffee table and noticed her stare. "What are you thinking about?" he asked, joining her.

"Nothing, I was just watching you," she replied.

"A toast," said Thomas, "to the most beautiful girl in the world."

"And to the handsomest man."

They touched glasses and took a sip.

"Dinner is warming in the oven, so we can have it whenever we are ready."

"Let's wait a while," suggested Thomas. "I'm enjoying this."

"Me too," she agreed sipping her champagne and thinking back to the picnic. "Thomas, I've never been in a serious relationship before. I mean I've had boyfriends, but I've never been in love. I love you; I know it, I feel it in my heart and in my soul, and I want to give you all of me. And today at the park, I wanted to make love to you so badly it hurt," she confessed then paused briefly. "In this day and age what I am about to say is going to sound so old fashioned, that I'm hesitant to even say it, but you need to know."

"It's okay, tell me," he said reassuringly.

She glanced at him nervously. "A long time ago, I made a vow that I would wait until my wedding night to give myself to the man I was going to spend the rest of my life with. I'll admit it, being around you isn't making it easy for me to keep that promise, and I feel that one day I may break it. But whatever happens, I don't want you to think I don't love you wholeheartedly, because I do."

"Olivia, I will never think that I love you, and I want you to keep that promise, and if the time comes for us to break it, then look out, because it'll be amazing."

Her face lit up. "Oh Thomas!" she cried and hugged him.

They ate dinner in front of the crackling fire, drank champagne, slow danced, and talked all night. When the flames had turned to ash, they slowly stood, and walked down the hallway to Olivia's bedroom. When they arrived, she turned and kissed him. "I'll see you in the morning, goodnight."

"Goodnight," replied Thomas going to his room, and into the bathroom. He inspected his stitches and noticed the swelling had gone down, but there was still a light shade of yellow around his eye. His hands and body still had vague signs of bruising, but the stiffness was completely gone. As he took his shirt off, he thought about Olivia undressing, and wondered what she looked like in her underwear and in the nude. He desperately wanted to make love to her, too, but she was well worth the wait.

Chapter 26

The next morning Thomas woke up, got dressed, went into the kitchen, and cleaned up. As he was making coffee, he heard Olivia's bath running, and went to her door. "Can I bring you something?"

"No, I'll be out in fifteen minutes."

As he walked away, he could hear her singing 'You're the Best Thing' and smiled. He poured a cup of coffee, went out onto the deck, and leaned on the railing. Olivia would be leaving tomorrow morning, and he would be alone, and he wondered when he got back how often she would want to see him.

"Good morning," she said kissing him.

"Morning, did you sleep well?"

"Somewhat restless," she replied. "I tossed and turned all night."

"Same here."

"You were so deep in thought when I came out. What were you thinking about?"

"You, us."

"Really. Good or bad?"

"Neither, I was just thinking about you leaving tomorrow," said Thomas staring out at the lake. It was a cool day, and the sky was cloudy.

"Are you worried about what happens next?" she asked cuddling into him.

"I'm not worried, just a little unsure," he said pulling her close to him.

"I'm the same," she confessed glancing up.

"I need to tell Kate what's going on, and I would like us both to be there."

"We should," she agreed.

"It's important to me that you two get to know one another."

"Thomas, I want to spend time with her, get to know her, and us to become good friends," she said eagerly. "So, what should we do?"

"Well, we need to tell her how about us, me quitting my job, about setting up the company, and what our plans are."

"What are our plans?" she asked.

"I don't know," he replied as they looked out at the horizon. "I'm not sure what's next."

"Thomas, I have to leave tomorrow, and I know I love you and you love me, and that I'll be seeing you on Friday night," she said turning to him. "I know I will be dancing on air next week, but when I come home at night, you won't be there and I'll be alone, and I'll miss you. Thomas, I don't want to crowd you or be selfish but…"

"But what?"

Olivia smiled. "I want you to come home with me tomorrow and stay at my place for the week. You could write during the day when I'm out. We could have dinner together. Maybe you could meet me for lunch sometimes. And when you need to work at night, tell me, and I will leave you alone. Maybe you could schedule to write when I'm at my evening workout classes. Free nights, we could watch television or go to a movie or for a swim."

"That sounds wonderful," said Thomas. "What about the following week?"

"I don't know. Can we take it for a week at a time? All I want to do is be with you, and if I had it my way, I would have you there forever."

"I want to be with you, too," he said drowning in her deep blue eyes.

"Then just leave with me tomorrow."

Thomas thought momentarily. "Okay, I will."

"Yay!" she said clapping her hands.

"How about this?" he asked "Why don't we leave here early tomorrow morning, go to my house, and have dinner, compliments of Kate's cooking. Then we can talk to her and bring her up to speed on everything that has happened and ask her about the business contract and get some advice. If you want, you can stay the night, that way you get to spend some time with Kate and see where I live and where I write. Then Monday morning, we'll go to your place where I will stay for the rest of the week," he summarized.

"Now, that's a plan!" she said excitedly.

"When do you want to tell Penny and Jack about us?"

"Penny knows I'm up here this weekend, and when she sees how happy I am on Monday, she'll have an idea what went on and will probably tell Jack. We'll just confirm it with them Friday at dinner," said Olivia. "What about Rachel?"

"This weekend she was going to find out about her father, and I was going to give her a call in the middle of the week to see how they were doing. And next Saturday, I promised to go out with her to a bar to see a group playing."

"On a date?" asked Olivia.

"That came out wrong. Rachel and Mathew, Veronica and Buddy are going. Rachel asked Kate and me to go, and I was going to ask Frank as well. I wasn't sure about us," he said looking at her. "Would you like to go with me on Saturday and make me the happiest and most envied man in the world?"

"I would love to," she said putting her arms around him and kissing him.

"Can you ask Frank on Monday?"

"Of course."

"I need to talk to Rachel about us, and I would like you to be there."

"I will," she replied. "She's another person I need to talk to. She tried her best to be my friend, and I've been avoiding her like the plague, especially these last few weeks. I guess I was jealous of her spending so much time with you at her guesthouse. I thought you might have liked her."

"Olivia, Rachel and I have talked, and we're just friends. She wants to be your friend, too, that's why she asked you to go to France with her."

"I know, but I couldn't," replied Olivia staring at him uneasily. "Thomas, where have you always wanted to visit?"

"Cannes, France."

"Your grandmother and Penny used to tell me how you always wanted to go there, and how you said that one day when you had the money you would. That's where Rachel was going. I dreamt that if everything worked out between us, that one day we would go to Cannes, together. That's why I didn't want to go with Rachel, and why I couldn't tell her the real reason. I just said it was a personal matter. Is that crazy? It's crazy. I'm crazy. Oh my God! I sound like a stalker!"

"You're not a stalker," said Thomas chuckling and comforting her. "Crazy? Yes!"

"Why you?" said Olivia hitting him on the arm.

Thomas overdramatically grabbed it.

"What am I going to with you?" she asked shaking her head.

"Kiss me?" he asked, which she did.

"So, Tuesday or Wednesday we can see Rachel, Friday, Penny and Jack, and Saturday we'll all go out and see the band. How does that sound?"

"I love it, and I love you." he replied.

"I love you," she replied. "Now, while I make some brunch, you can call Jack and let him know we're leaving here tomorrow morning, then Kate, and let her know we're going there tomorrow afternoon."

After they ate, they got ready and went for a long afternoon drive in the country. They stopped at a farmer's market and bought an apple pie for dessert on Sunday. Then they pulled into a quaint restaurant and had dinner. When they got back to the cabin, Thomas started a fire, while Olivia poured two glasses of wine and met him on the sofa.

"Here you go," she said passing him one. "The fire looks amazing and it's so cozy and warm."

Thomas put his arm around her, and she said rested her head on his chest. "You'll like the band next week."

"You've heard them before?"

"Yeah, they played Rachel's party, they're called AtlasX.

"AtlasX?" asked Olivia sitting up.

"Yes."

"My friend's boyfriend plays in that band."

"Are you sure?

"Definitely! I helped them get the show."

"Really."

"Tracy used to go to ballet school with me, and we became good friends. She was a talented ballerina, and we were in the same troupe. Apparently, the band toured a lot, and she didn't get to see much of her boyfriend, she told me she wanted to spend more time with him, so she quit. He tried to convince her to keep on dancing, but she didn't listen."

"She quit, just like that," said Thomas.

"Tracy said she loved him, and he loved her, and told me her boyfriend didn't want her to give up her dream, but she said she was unhappy and had other dreams to follow."

"What did you think about that?"

"At the time I told her she was insane, and that any day he could leave her, and she would have nothing. She told me I was so wrapped up in my ballet that I couldn't possibly understand how she felt, and to talk to her about it again when I was in love." Olivia thought for a moment. "I guess she was right."

"Do you still talk to her?"

"Yeah, she calls when she's in town, but they've been on tour for a year, so I hadn't talked to her in a while. When I heard she was back, I called her and told her about the party, and that Rachel wanted to have a band. Rachel hired them, and Tracy called me hoping I would be there because she said she had some good news, I told her I had a dinner party and couldn't make it, and we would get together soon. It will be good to see her again and find out what she's been up to," said Olivia. "Was the band good?"

"They were great."

"I'm glad. I think about her often, and always hoped she was doing well, and things worked out for her."

"I'm sure they are," said Thomas and left it at that.

They talked the rest of the evening and decided to have an early night. When they stopped at Olivia's bedroom, she pulled him in, and asked if he would lie with her till she fell asleep.

When she woke up, he was gone, and she could hear him in the kitchen cooking. As she got ready, she smiled at the thought of them sleeping together, then joined. They ate breakfast, cleaned up the cabin, packed up the car, and locked it up.

Outside, Olivia kissed him. "I'm so in love with you."

He kissed her back. "I love you."

They jumped in the car and drove down the dirt road.

"How's your dancing going?" asked Thomas.

"Good. I'll be busy over the next couple of weeks," she said turning onto the main road "Did I tell you my father is coming to my opening night?"

"No, you just said he was coming to see you in a couple of weeks, that's wonderful that he'll be here for that."

"He'll be sitting next to you," she said glancing over at him. "He asked if he could, he really likes you and Kate. Oh, before I forget, remind me to give you the letters when I get to your place. They're addressed to the both of you, and I'm sure you would like to read them with Kate."

At noon, they stopped at a small turn-of-the-century church, and went to Mass. Afterwards, they had lunch in a charming country inn then took the long, scenic route back to Thomas's house. Along the way, they talked, laughed, and sang songs on the radio. It was as if they had known each other their whole lives, and in a sense, they had.

Chapter 27

They stood outside Thomas's front door; Olivia was nervous. "What happens if she doesn't like me?" she asked.

"She will, just be yourself, on second thought," joked Thomas.

"I'll get you for that." she said squeezing his hand.

They went in, Kate wasn't in the kitchen or the living room, so Thomas called her.

"I'm up here, I'll be down in a minute," she answered.

"Come on, let's have a seat in the living room," said Thomas.

Olivia followed him into the small room. "This is just as I had imagined it," she said sitting on the sofa. "I can picture your grandmother and Penny sitting here gossiping."

"And drinking tea, I'll make us some," he said going into the kitchen.

Thomas could see Olivia strolling over to the pictures on display in the wall unit. She looked at the one of Thomas and Kate, Thomas on his own, Thomas, Kate, and their grandmother, Thomas, Kate, and their parents, their grandmother and Penny, and several pictures of people whom Olivia didn't know.

"Hello, you must be Olivia?" asked Kate.

"Hello, Kate, I am, nice to meet you."

"That one of Thomas and me was taken at a fashion show he took me to," explained Kate politely.

"Is that the time he tripped onto the girl's lap?" asked Olivia.

"Yes, it was," replied Kate laughing. "How did you know?"

"He met that girl by accident in town, her name's Janet, and she works at a store I shop at, and she recognized him."

"You know what's really funny, is that I tripped him on purpose!"

"Really? On purpose?" asked Olivia.

"Of course! He's always embarrassing me in public and playing practical jokes. So, it was payback."

"I know what you mean," confirmed Olivia. "I would have liked to have seen that."

"I see you two have met," said Thomas coming in with two cups of tea.

"Yes, we've been talking about your next trip to the fashion show," replied Kate.

"I suddenly realized now would be a good time to start bribing Kate and stop her from telling you too much," said Thomas placing the two cups down. "This one is Olivia's and this yours Kate's. I'll be back in a minute."

They both sat.

"I heard you started work last weekend?"

"Yes, I went in last Saturday and met some people. Barry's great, in fact they all are. Then I was in on Tuesday and Thursday evening, and yesterday, and I'm going in tomorrow morning for a few hours," she said picking up her tea. "You're a ballet dancer?"

"Yes."

"Is it as demanding and disciplined as they say it is?" asked Kate.

"More so, but when you are enjoying what you do, it's not," said Olivia. "You going to law school, and now working part-time, that must be a challenge?"

"It will be because it will assume the remainder of my free time, but I love it, and I wouldn't give it up for the world."

Thomas joined them and sat down next to Olivia, opposite Kate.

Kate leaned over and looked at him. "Your eye looks better. When do you need to see the doctor?"

"Next week, I need to make an appointment," he replied. "How long will dinner be?"

She glanced at her watch. "The roast beef won't be ready for another hour, and I still need to make the mashed potatoes," she replied. "Is that okay? You're here earlier than I thought," she confessed.

"That's fine. I, we, need to talk to you. That's why we're early."

Kate sipped on her tea and listened for thirty minutes as Thomas and Olivia explained both sides of their stories and told her they were in love. When they finished, Kate looked back and forth at them, her eyes stopping on Thomas. "Have you felt this way all this time?"

"Yes."

"I thought so! I'm so happy for you both," she said leaning over and giving Thomas a kiss on the cheek, then Olivia.

"Kate there is something else you need to know," said Thomas.

"You sound serious Thomas?" she asked.

"I don't mean to be, I'm just anxious," he confirmed. "I'm quitting my job tomorrow."

"What!" exclaimed Kate.

"Let me explain," he said calming her down. "Over the last few months, I've started to dislike my job, and I've been waking up and going into work unhappy. You're almost finished school, and you have a job lined up, and I know you said you would help me out once you started working full time, but I can't wait any longer," explained Thomas. "I want to write full time."

"How will we? I?" mumbled Kate trying not to cry.

"Kate, Olivia and I are going to start a company. Olivia is going into a partnership with me, and she's going to invest eighty thousand dollars, which will pay for all our ongoing expenses. We still need to work out the details, but we thought we could do that tonight. The money you make from work is all yours and if you run short, we will help you out," emphasized Thomas, seeing Kate was getting upset.

"Thomas, I wanted to help you!" stated Kate. "You said I could."

"Kate, how can you help me out today?"

Kate was getting more upset. "I can't."

"Would you rather me wait?" asked Thomas. "I will if you want me to."

"Of course not," said Kate starting to cry.

"Kate the money is a business investment. Once Thomas starts making some income, we're planning on paying it off. If you like, you can help us with that when you start working full time," suggested Olivia.

"I need to put on the potatoes," said Kate scurrying out the room into the kitchen. They could hear her sobbing.

"I should go talk to her," said Thomas starting to get up.

Olivia held him down. "Let me go," she whispered and headed into the kitchen.

Thomas could hear them.

"Kate, I don't want you to be upset. I want us to be friends and get along. I offered the money to Thomas, no loan, no contract, and he said no. He wouldn't take it unless we started a business together. You know him better than I do, and how proud he is, and he's been so worried about how you would react. He cares about you a great deal. In retrospect, maybe we should have all talked about it together and come to a decision, rather than us telling you what we had decided, I guess we got carried away. All I want is for Thomas to be happy and I know you want that too." She waited a moment. "You've read his novel. What did you think?"

"I loved it, and I told him to send it out to publishers, but he wouldn't," replied Kate.

"Kate before he can move forward with this, he needs to have your blessing," stated Olivia.

"I want him to be happy, I really do, he's done so much for me, and I wanted to be the one to help him out," said Kate.

"Why don't we go back in the room, all talk about it, and come up with a suggestion that we all agree on?" asked Olivia.

"Okay," replied Kate.

Thomas stood and Kate walked into his arms. "I can't believe I'm acting this way. You have the opportunity to write full-time, and someone who is going to help you out financially and support you, and all I think about is myself. After all you've done for me, I should be pleased for you, and supporting you, and telling you to go for it," said Kate crying. "Thomas, I'm worried I'm losing you."

Olivia whispered to Thomas. "I'll make some more tea." She picked up the empty cups and went into the kitchen.

"Kate, I'll always be here, you will never lose me," said Thomas holding her closely.

"I'm sorry Thomas, I want you to be happy, and I'm actually surprised you lasted as long as you did in that job. You have so much more potential, you should do what you've planned, and I want you to. You are an excellent writer," said Kate pulling away from him. "She seems great."

"Olivia said we should all talk about it and come up with an arrangement that we all accept, she's right, and we should have done that at the offset," said Thomas.

She came into the room with three cups of tea, a sugar bowl, and a creamer on a tray. Thomas and Kate stared at her.

Olivia noticed them. "What's wrong?"

Thomas helped her with the tray and put it on the coffee table. "My grandmother used this set all the time, neither myself nor Kate has used it since she died."

"Oh, I'm so sorry!" exclaimed Olivia. "I'll put it back."

"Don't worry about it," said Kate smiling. "We should have never stopped using it, my grandmother would have wanted us to, it has some fond memories and I'm glad you did."

"Let me serve," offered Olivia feeling a little better. She added the milk and sugar then passed the cups one at a time. "So, what should we do?" she asked sipping on her.

"How about I write, Olivia takes care of the publishers, and Kate's our lawyer," suggested Thomas.

"Really?" asked Kate.

"We were going to ask you to set up the contract for us," declared Olivia.

"The only question is the finances?" asked Thomas.

"You've always taken care of them and it's Olivia's investment," said Kate.

"Then Olivia and I will do the finances, and around the last day of each month, we all meet and review them."

"Is that okay, Kate?" asked Olivia.

"That's fine with me."

"Kate, can you put together a contract that we can all review and sign?

"I can," replied Kate keenly.

"Olivia researches publishers that are accepting unsolicited manuscripts and sends my first novel out."

"Will do."

"And I will finish my second."

"Are there any other plans for the company?" asked Kate.

"Well, I thought we should concentrate on trying to get my work sent out and hopefully published, then finishing my second novel, and sending that out. Maybe down the road we could look at helping other local writers get published or maybe publish them ourselves; eBooks seem to be gaining in popularity. I think we have lots of options but first things first."

"How should I set up the contract?" asked Kate.

"That we three are owners of Company X. That all profits will first go to pay back the eighty thousand and anything above and beyond will be split. Fifty per cent for Olivia and twenty-five each for you and me." answered Thomas.

"Wait a minute, I'm not going for that," replied Olivia, "fifty for you and twenty-five for me and Kate."

"Twenty-five is too much for me," replied Kate.

"Okay, okay," said Thomas. "Twenty-five percent each and twenty-five percent back in the company. Agreed?"

"Agreed," they both replied.

"You'll need to name the company and register it," said Kate.

They went silent.

"Why don't we all think about names and let's say…," said Olivia glancing quickly at the time, "at ten o'clock we put forward our ideas and vote on the best one."

They all agreed.

Kate stood up. "I need to put on the vegetables."

"Can I help?" asked Olivia.

"You sit here and take it easy," replied Kate.

"I would really like to help."

"I could use a hand," smiled Kate.

They went into the kitchen and Thomas was left alone. "I guess I'll watch some television," he said turning it on. From the kitchen he could hear them talking and laughing, and he was glad they were getting along.

"That was delicious," said Thomas.

"It was," agreed Olivia. "Kate, how did you like New York City?"

She quickly glanced over at Thomas.

"It's okay, she knows," confirmed Thomas.

"I had a wonderful time, the hotel was beautiful, and the shopping was magnificent. I loved the Opera, and your father is an amazing singer."

"Did you know Kate sings quite well, too?"

"I didn't know that," replied Olivia.

"He's teasing you," clarified Kate. "Let me tell you what kind of person you're in love with," said Kate telling her every detail of the story.

Olivia laughed. "You sang 'Last Name' to my father."

Thomas joined in laughing with Olivia.

"I'm glad you two find it so funny," said Kate blushing. "So, here we are leaving, and guess whose picture they are putting up on the wall next to your father's? Mine!"

"I told the hotel manager that she was a famous singer and dancer on Broadway and secretly signed her name on the picture, so they put it on the wall next to your father's."

They all chuckled

"The letters! Let me go and get them," said Olivia going to the hallway, searching in her bag, and coming back with three. "Who wants to read them?"

"Thomas can," said Kate.

Thomas took the envelopes and opened one. It was a card and read:

Dear Thomas and Kate,

Thank you for letting us in to see Otello. We are all grateful for your kind generosity. We've put one of the programs and our tickets in our display case in the church hall where we practice so that we will always have one good copy. We leave the others out so that people can read them. We put a thank you note next to them with both your names. I have enclosed a picture so you can see what I'm talking about. I have also included a picture of the five of us. When you are back in New York City, I hope you will come visit us and see us practice. Please write and send us a picture of you and Kate. Maybe one day we can come and visit you.

Your friends,

Katrina, Shawna, Bobby, Ethan, Michigan.

They looked at the pictures.

"We'll put these in the wall unit," said Kate.

Thomas opened the next envelope.

Dear Thomas and Kate,

We have just come back from buying this card with Olivia. I knew she was going to see you shortly and we wanted to thank you both again. Henry Taylor spent the afternoon showing us around the Opera House and later on Rufus Williams joined us, and we spent an hour practicing on the stage with him and Mr. Taylor. We were all very excited and nervous. They have agreed to set up a class one Sunday a month and someone from the company will take us through a practice.

At the end of the day, Mr. Taylor gave us our surprise. We cried when we found out we had been given tickets to see an opera once a month. Mr. Taylor had tried to say it was the company, but I spoke up. We all know it was you and Kate that set up the meeting and got us the tickets. Mr. Taylor explained to us that you wanted to remain anonymous. Oops! Sorry! I asked why because you were our friend. Olivia explained the whole story. We like her a lot, too. Olivia bought a digital camera, and we took some pictures of us, and we have included them. We are in our Sunday best. We will write to you often.

Thank you,

Katrina, Shawna, Bobby, Ethan, Michigan.

They looked at the five smiling faces. The girls were wearing dresses, and the boys were in dress pants, shirts, and ties. There were also pictures of them with Rufus and Henry, with their teacher, and with Olivia. The last one was with all of them.

Thomas opened the final envelope it was a note:

Dear Thomas and Kate,

My name is Ms. Lydia Brown, and I teach the children their lessons. I wanted to send you a short note and thank you for your generosity. Unfortunately, it's so much easier for these children to get mixed up with gangs, drugs, violence, and the wrong side of the law. Your kind gesture has given them an inspiration to aspire above all that. I can see the difference in their faces, in the way they talk, and when they sing.

Myself, and the piano player Leroy 'Lenny' Johnson will be chaperoning the children to the shows. We have one ticket over so each month we will be treating the mother of one of the children to a show. I hope one day we will meet, so that I can thank you in person. You are always welcome to visit, and we look forward to meeting you. The children took a picture of me and Lenny, and I have included it.

God bless, Lydia Brown.

They looked at the picture.

"That was so thoughtful," said Thomas.

"It was," added Kate taking the pictures, card, letter, note, and envelopes. "I'll put them over here on the wall unit," she said, and after she did, went into the kitchen.

Thomas stood, put his arms around Olivia, and gave her a kiss. "What did you tell the teenagers?"

"That you thought I was in love with someone else and how much I loved you," she replied kissing him.

From the corner of his eye, Thomas saw Kate walking in and back out. He shouted after her and she came back.

"Kate, you and Olivia sit down and have a chat, I'll clean up," ordered Thomas pushing them onto the sofa. "Why don't you show her around? Olivia is sleeping in my room tonight," he said then glanced over at Olivia. "You can drop your bag in there."

Kate gave Thomas a surprised look.

"Yes, you heard me right, Kate. She's sleeping in my room tonight. Better put on some earplugs because we are going to be doing the dirty dance all night long. You know what I mean?" As Thomas said this, he thrusted his pelvis back and forward and made it into somewhat of a dance. "Do you have a problem with that?" he said emphasizing the word 'that' with a big thrust.

They both looked at each other and laughed.

"Do you really know what you are getting yourself into?" asked Kate.

"I'm starting to wonder," replied Olivia watching Thomas as he strolled away and accentuated his wiggle.

He turned his head around. "Can't help but look!"

"More in disgust," replied Kate.

"You have potatoes mashed into your jeans," added Olivia.

"Where?" asked Thomas as he stretched back to look.

They both laughed at him and walked out of the living room.

Thomas took a little longer than usual to clean the kitchen so that they could have some time to be alone and talk. The phone rang and he picked it up.

"Hello."

"Hello, Thomas."

"Rachel, it's so good to hear your voice. How are you?"

"I'm okay. How's your eye?"

"The swelling's gone down, and there's a slight bruising around the stitches, but I'm in no pain and doing fine. How was New York City?"

"We had a wonderful time. We shopped in all the stores on Fifth Avenue and bought loads of clothes, did some sightseeing, went to The Spa, I took my mother to a show, and you're right, the hotel was fantastic. We just got back a couple of hours ago. I was with my mother and Jack in the kitchen, and he's been telling us what happened with my father and our lawyers."

"How's she doing?"

"Okay," she replied. "She told me everything, and also told me that you, Kate, Jack and Penny know."

"Yes, but only because of what happened to me."

"I know."

She sounded sad. "Are you okay?"

"I'm a little confused, but I'm surviving. My dad signed the documents, packed up his stuff, and left, just like that, he didn't say goodbye or even leave a note."

"You have to give him time. He's a little confused, too. Your mother said you can see him whenever you like."

"Yes, but that will be quite some time," she said hesitating. "I need to talk to you. Are you comfortable coming up to the house?"

"Yes, of course."

"Why don't you come up on Thursday? Jack's going to be here, and he needs to talk to you, too, it has something to do with my father and his lawyer, and he wants my mother and me to listen in as well. Is that okay?"

"Of course, it is."

"I'll let Jack know before he goes."

"I need to talk to you about a few things, and I have some news."

"Really, I'm curious!" she said.

"We'll talk Thursday."

"Okay, Thursday. I'll see you then. Oh, I almost forgot, they had your picture up in the hotel as well."

"What?" screamed Thomas.

"Remember you said to look for Henry's and Kate's pictures on the wall, well we did, and found them. There was also a picture of you there. It said, 'Country's Richest Man, Thomas Carlyle.' Remember Kate said one day she would get you back."

"That Kate, I'll get her for this," said Thomas.

"My mother and I thought it was great. We went and asked for the manager so that we could tell him we knew the people on the wall. Well, it seems that the bellboy and the doorman had already recognized me and told the manager, so when he came out to speak to us, he asked if he could take a picture with me and put it up. I said yes, and it's right next to yours," said Rachel. "I took a picture of it, and I'll show you on Thursday. Oh, before I forget my mother said to say hello."

"Tell your mother I said hello, and I'll see her on Thursday."

"Will do, bye."

"Bye, Rachel."

Thomas hung up and went upstairs; they were sitting on his bed. He sat next to Kate and put his arm around her. "Are you ready to do some explaining?"

"For what?" she asked mystified.

"Picture! Wall! Hotel! New York City!"

Kate bolted for her room. Thomas chased after and Olivia followed behind. She was hiding under her blankets on her bed. Thomas slowly walked up and pulled the blankets off. Kate's hair was covering her face, and she was trying her best not to laugh.

"You think you are so funny? You think you've outsmarted me?" asked Thomas.

"What? What did she do?" asked Olivia.

"You tell her Kate. It's your moment."

Kate moved her hair from her face and looked at Olivia. "In New York City I asked the manager at the hotel to take a picture of Thomas, so he took one of him in the hotel restaurant drinking champagne. I told him he was the 'Country's Richest Man, Thomas Carlyle' and I wrote that on the picture and signed his name," explained Kate laughing out loud and putting the blanket back over her head.

Olivia laughed with her.

"Laugh it up you two, I'll be in my room sulking," said Thomas. But before he left, he turned, and looked at Kate, "I'm going to get you good for this, and you too Olivia, for laughing so hard," he said ominously.

Kate stopped and threw the blankets off her face. "No, Thomas, please, no."

He strolled out of the room and Olivia had a puzzled look.

Kate turned to her. "When he says he's going to get us good, he's going to get us good, wait and see!" she warned melodramatically.

They glanced at the door, then each other, and burst out laughing.

"I like your room," said Olivia to Thomas's back.

He turned around from his desk and motioned her over.

She closed the door and went to him. As he lifted her onto his lap, she wrapped her legs around the back of the chair. He kissed her neck, her cheek, her ear, and her lips. She pulled herself against him and he could feel her breasts on his chest. He gently picked her up, placed her on the bed, and lay on top of her. Again, he kissed her neck, her cheek, her ear, her lips. She was breathing heavily. Olivia let his hand roam freely up the side of her body and brush against her breast. She let out a soft moan. He then moved it slowly down between her thighs and gently rubbed. She moaned louder, opened her legs, and didn't want him to stop. Thomas suddenly rolled off and stood up.

"You'll be sleeping in this bed tonight," he said.

She quickly realized what he had done. "Why you, you…" She couldn't think of a word, instead, she gave him a malevolent look, and threw a pillow at him.

"Who is laughing now?" he said with an evil chuckle as he walked toward the door. "I warned you."

"That is so cruel I'll get you for that," she said hopping off the bed and chasing him down the stairs. He jumped onto the sofa, and she jumped on top of him. She pinned his arms down and sat on his lap. "If that's the kind of games you play, then beware, because now I'm a player, too," she said kissing him then laying her head on his chest. She could hear his heart beating. "I love you."

"I love you."

She lifted her head, glanced up at him, and softly asked, "Don't ever leave me?"

"I won't."

"Promise me?"

"I promise."

She kissed him on the nose, moved off of him, and sat on the floor. "So, who told you about the picture?"

"Rachel, she called before."

"How is she?"

"She's okay. A little confused. She says she wants to talk to me, and that Jack needed to talk to me about her father and wanted Rachel and her mother to be there as well."

"That's strange. Did she say why?"

"She didn't know. She said her father had signed all the paperwork, had moved out, and was upset that he didn't say goodbye or leave a note."

"I feel sorry for her. When are you going up?"

"Thursday night. I thought we would both go."

"Do you think that's a good idea?"

"You don't?"

"I would feel out of place."

"Well, I don't want you to be uncomfortable."

Kate interrupted them. "Have you thought of some names?" she asked walking into the room in a nightgown and robe. "I have some paper and pens," she said placing them down before going into the kitchen and coming back with a tray containing warm slices of apple pie and glasses of milk."

"I forgot about the pie," said Olivia.

"Grab a piece, a fork, and a milk," said Kate watching them then placing the tray on the table and taking hers.

"Mm, this is so good," said Olivia.

"Oh my God, it is," agreed Kate.

"We should have got two," said Thomas.

They threw the dirty dishes and glasses onto the tray and Kate placed it on the floor then gave them each a paper and pen. "I thought we could each write down three names and then put them all together in a list so that we have nine in total. We make three copies of the list, and we each go through the list marking the company names one to nine, one being the best. Then we combine the three lists and add them up. The two company names with the lowest points are put together and we decide the best," explained Kate. "The company's main goal is supporting Thomas's writing and helping him get published, and potentially in the future, helping local writers get published or publishing their novels and eBooks. Also, the company is going to be registered as a general partnership business, which simply means the three of us our partners, equal owners, and have an unlimited liability in the business. So, we'll probably want to keep all that in mind when we come up with names."

"Great job, Kate!" said Olivia impressed.

Thomas nodded approvingly. "Let's get started."

Kate and Olivia sat around the coffee table while Thomas remained on the sofa as they went through the elimination process.

"Okay, we have our two finalists, and we each picked these as our top two choices. First, was Carlyle Enterprises and second, 'Carlyle Publishers."

They went back and forth for a few minutes with no decision.

"Okay," said Kate. "Why don't we go around the table and say a few words about which one we like best, or if undecided, talk about both. And if we are still unsure, we will do a final vote on paper, one pick each."

Thomas and Olivia agreed.

"Thomas, you're first," instructed Kate.

"Overall, I think Carlyle Enterprises sounds very strong, modern, and leading-edge, and can encompass everything we want to do…were Carlyle Publishers makes us sound like all we are is a publishing company which is something that we may or may not do down the road…so hearing myself now, I pick Carlyle Enterprises."

"Thanks, Thomas, Olivia?"

"I agree with what Thomas said. If publishing is something that we take on later we can offer that as one of our services. So, I pick Carlyle Enterprises."

"I also agree, Carlyle Enterprises gives us the option of offering one or multiple services when we deem necessary," stated Kate happily. "Now we have a company to register."

"Let's have a celebratory drink, teas all around," said Thomas heading into the kitchen.

Olivia followed him. "Can I help?"

"You can get the milk out the refrigerator."

"Thomas, is everything okay?"

He shook his head. "Not really."

"Tell me what's wrong?"

"We said we would both go talk to Rachel."

"I thought maybe you wanted to go alone under the circumstances," she replied.

"But I want you to be there with me."

"I'll go," she said smiling.

"You will?"

"I just needed to make sure you wanted me to go, and you do, and I love you all the more for that," she kissed him and walked out the kitchen.

"What about helping me making the tea?"

She stuck her head back in. "I only wanted to know what was on your mind," she said blowing him a kiss. "I'm going to put on my pajamas I'll be down in a minute."

As they drank their tea, Kate and Olivia made plans to go shopping Wednesday night and talked about the latest fashions while Thomas listened on.

"It's getting late, and I have an early morning, please excuse me," said Kate standing. "It was wonderful meeting you, Olivia, goodnight. Goodnight, Thomas.

"Goodnight," they replied and watched her leave.

"I like your sister, she's different than you, she's nice," joked Olivia.

"Do you remember what happened on my bed?" he cautioned.

"I do," she said moving over and sitting on his lap. "I wasn't going to stop you."

"You weren't."

"No," she said gazing into her eyes and running her fingers through his thick hair then stopped and placed her head on his shoulder as he held her. "You feel so good," she whispered, "and so warm." She slowly drifted off.

Olivia woke up the next morning in Thomas's bed and lay there for a while looking at the posters of the French Riviera. She eventually got up, went downstairs, and watched Thomas sleeping peacefully on the pull-out sofa bed. She quietly got under the sheets, lay next to him, and fell asleep. When she stirred his arms were around her.

"You're nice and toasty," said Thomas.

"And you are lovely to cuddle in to," replied Olivia.

"What time do we need to leave?"

"Nine. I'll get up now and take a shower. Has Kate left?" she asked.

"Yes, you have the upstairs to yourself," he said pulling her close to him. "I'll go up when you've finished. Do you want something to eat?"

"Can we pick up a coffee and bagel on the way?"

"That's a good idea."

Olivia turned round, kissed him on the lips, and got out of bed. Thomas watched her climb the stairs; she stopped halfway up, looked back at him, and smiled then continued.

Chapter 28

She closed the condominium door behind her, and took Thomas into the guest bedroom, where he put down his bags and coat "I have a surprise for you, now close your eyes, and walk behind me. Here, hold my hand." They crossed the hallway, Olivia opened the door, and walked in with Thomas trailing. "Okay, you can open them."

Thomas looked around. The room that was once full of boxes now had a desk and chair, sofa, and posters of Nice and Cannes.

"Come and sit down," she said pulling him in. "There's a cordless phone, a modem under your desk so you can get the internet, a color printer, paper, pens, pencils, dictionary, and thesaurus," explained Olivia. "How does the chair feel?"

"Very comfortable," he replied.

"Over here I framed the front page of the novel that you gave me. I like what you wrote on it," she said, then read it out loud:

"Dear Olivia,
When I asked you for a song? You sang,
When I asked you to dance? You danced.
Thank you. Your friend always,
Thomas Carlyle."

"That's so sweet," she said with a cute smile. "And you have a good size window for light," she revealed opening the blinds.

"You did all this for me?" he asked.

"Do you like it?" she asked waiting for his approval.

"I do; I do. When did you do all this?"

"Thursday."

"Thursday?" queried Thomas.

"I arrived home just after eight in the morning, emptied all the boxes, and cleaned up the room. Then I went and did some furniture shopping, and the room was finished by three," said Olivia proudly then noticed his peculiar look. "You're wondering what I would have done if it hadn't worked out?"

Thomas nodded.

Olivia sat on the sofa. "It wasn't that big of a gamble. I already knew what you had done for my father and for me, and you did that even before knowing the truth about me and Frank. You could have tried to convince me that you did it out of friendship, but I wouldn't have believed you. Your actions speak volumes," she said leaning forward. "Thomas, I'm tired of waiting for things to happen to me. I'm tired of relying on other people's help to get me what I want. I'm tired of being in love with you and not being with you. You've helped me so much. On Thursday at the cabin, do you think if you had said that we can be friends I would have put my hands in the air and said okay. Not a chance! I had driven up there to tell you everything. I wanted you to know how I felt and that I was in love with you. You needed to know, and I wanted to tell you." She stood, walked over to him, then knelt down and whispered, "you are the only person I have ever loved, and will ever love, and I will continue to love you till the day I die. I want you to hear me say it and believe it." She paused momentarily. "Thomas, I've been alone and lonely for such a long time, but those few weeks we didn't talk, and I didn't see, were the loneliest. I was devastated, and I've never cried so much. Then you go and do something so wonderful for me and make me realize maybe all isn't lost," she said glancing up at him. "I love you and I want to be with you and grow old with you."

Thomas stared into her beautiful blue eyes, "You sing for me, you dance for me, and now you help me, support me, and do this room for me. I love you, and I love who you are." As he stood, he pulled her up, and hugged her. "I will always love you, and no other, till the day I die."

They kissed for a while then Olivia suddenly pulled away. "I have to get going or I'll be late!" she said quickly kissing him again. "Let me get my bag from my bedroom, I'll be back in a minute."

Thomas sat, twirled around in the seat, and stopped facing the desk. He noticed a framed picture lying flat and picked it up. It was a recent picture of Olivia, just her face, taken outdoors. Thomas read what was written on the picture in pen. 'Love Olivia.'

"I didn't want you to see that, I meant to take it away," said Olivia embarrassed and coming towards Thomas.

"Why? Is it for me?"

Olivia blushed. "It was for you, but I changed my mind and thought it was too forward."

"Too forward would be a picture of you naked," replied Thomas. "Can I have it?"

She giggled and nodded yes.

He opened the frame's flap and put it on the desk. "There, you will be with me always."

"It was taken by my father in Central Park, I'm glad you like it," she said smiling. "I'll be back by six. Help yourself to the kitchen." She hesitated. "Thomas, I want you to consider this place yours, too."

"I will."

"Oh, don't make dinner! I'll pick up some Chinese food on the way home."

"That sounds great."

"I'll be thinking of you," she said kissing him bye.

Thomas watched her walk out of the room and then heard the front door open, close, and lock. He looked at her picture briefly before bringing in his laptop, plugging it in, and typing. The words flowed.

There was a banging on the door. Thomas looked at his watch and realized the time. He walked out of the room and unlocked the door. Standing there was Olivia holding two bags of Chinese food and her workout bag. Thomas took the bags of food, Olivia put down her bag, and closed the door.

"With both your hands occupied I now have you just where I want you," she said putting her arms around his waist and kissing his lips.

"How was your day?"

"I was dancing on air," replied Olivia letting go, standing on her toes, lifting her arms up in the air, and tilting her head to one side and smiling. She giggled and relaxed. "How was your day?"

Thomas put the bags down. "I was tap dancing on the keyboard," he said positioned his hands above his chest in a typewriting pose, darting his fingers up and down, and tilting his head to one side and grinning at her.

"Oh, very funny!" she said chuckling.

They sat in the solarium and ate. Thomas told her that he had written all day, and figured another four to six weeks, and he would be finished. Olivia talked about her class, and how the sister of one of the dancers had fallen on the weekend and broken her leg. After they finished, they went for a long walk around the harbor and talked, then stopped in a coffee shop, ordered hot chocolates, and continued their walk.

"You should come and watch my rehearsal one day?" suggested Olivia.

"I would like that," replied Thomas.

"Thursday I'm rehearsing with Frank, come down, and we could all go for lunch."

"Okay, what time?"

"Eleven till twelve."

When they got back to the condominium, Olivia took a bath, while Thomas lay on her bed and read a magazine article on Peter Gabriel. She came out of the en suite, wearing a terry bathrobe and a towel around her head, and lay next to him.

"Is it a good article?" she asked.

"Yeah, I really like him, I have his solo albums and the ones when he was lead singer for Genesis."

"He sang with Genesis?"

"He did, from 1967 to 1975, I brought a couple of their CDs with me, *Selling England by the Pound,* and *The Lamb Lies Down on Broadway.* I listen to them when I write," explained Thomas sitting up. "A few years back there was this guy at work, we were paired together to unload the trucks, and he was always playing this music. So, I asked him one day who it was, he told me, and got me hooked on them. He was a great guy and a good friend, but he moved out west. Before he did, he bought me these CDs."

"That was nice of him."

"Yeah, it was," replied Thomas. "Do you want to hear one? It's progressive rock," he said unsure.

"I'll listen while I do my nails and get my clothes ready for tomorrow."

Thomas left and came back with the CD player and put on *Selling England by the Pound* then went to his room, got his accounting book, sat at the dining room table, and looked it over. Olivia walked in an hour later wearing a short pink nightgown and matching silk robe, and her hair was pulled back with a clip; she looked incredibly sexy.

"No pajamas?" queried Thomas.

"I don't wear them all the time, and I never get to wear these sets. Especially ones, shall we say, that hides the least," she teased as she crouched down at the coffee table and purposely let her nightgown fall to the side so Thomas could see her inner thigh. She pulled out a pad and paper from the bottom drawer and slowly stood. Thomas looked at her long, lovely legs as she strolled over to him. Olivia stood behind him, put her arms around him, and whispered in his ear. "I'm not wearing underwear either," she said licking his earlobe, then softly kissing his neck, before sitting down next to him.

"Getting me back for last night?" asked Thomas.

"This is just the beginning!" she purred and licked her lips. "Unless?"

"Unless what?" asked Thomas turned on.

"Let's talk figures."

"Figures?" questioned Thomas.

She smiled. "Let's do it!"

"Do what?"

"Let's do the finances," she said chuckling.

"Oh, okay," he said opening up his book.

"I liked the CD."

"You did."

"It was different than what I'm used to, but I liked it. Especially the one that starts off with the grand piano."

"Firth of Fifth," replied Thomas. "That's a great song."

"Is that what it's called? Can I take that CD with me tomorrow so that I can listen to it when I'm doing my stretching and warm-ups? It has so much emotion, I just love it!"

"Of course, you can," he said then looked down at his book. "Okay, let's talk finances. Not taking any other income into account, the eighty thousand will cover the monthly outgoings and expenses for almost three years. On top of that, you keep your own money, Kate keeps hers, and I have two hundred dollars salary a week."

"Thomas that's not much, you should have put more down, you must have had more money than that when you worked?" asked Olivia.

"Olivia, at first there were times I had no money for a couple of weeks, even when I did, it wasn't much. I gave most of it to Kate, she needed it more than I did. Over the years, I managed to save some here and there, and put some aside to play golf. Besides, if I need more, I'll ask you and Kate for a raise," he said lightheartedly. "Why how much do you have each week?"

Olivia was silent.

"I'm sorry I shouldn't have asked, that's your personal business, forgive me," said Thomas embarrassed and changing the subject. "I figure if Kate works at least fifteen hours she'll clear this much a week, which should be more than enough for her. She bought enough clothes in New York City to last her and the female population of Manhattan to spring. I almost forgot; I still have the seven hundred dollars in savings that I haven't included. We can use that for a celebration if things work out."

"Thomas, stop!" yelled Olivia.

He had been so busy looking down at his book and working out numbers that he hadn't realized Olivia was crying. "What's wrong?"

She got up, took off to her bedroom, and closed the door. He could hear her crying. Thomas didn't know what to do as he sauntered up to her door and knocked. "Are you okay?"

"I'll be fine in a minute," replied Olivia. "I'll see you in the morning."

"Okay, I'll give you some time alone," he said leaving confused. He picked up his book, turned off the lights, went into his room, and shut the door. He lay on the bed wondering what was wrong.

Twenty minutes later he heard footsteps passing his door, the lights in the living room went on and shone under his door. Suddenly, there was a knock.

"Come in," he said.

Olivia opened the door "Thomas, can you please come into the living room so we can talk?" she asked then walked away.

Thomas got out of bed and followed her into the living room. She was sitting at the dining room table with a folder in front of her and sat next to her.

"First," she said, "I'm sorry I told you to be quiet. Please say you'll forgive me."

"I do. It's okay," he replied.

"It's not okay, I was wrong."

"Okay, I forgive you."

She managed a smile then spoke. "You made me realize something, but first I want to explain this folder," she said opening it. "This is my finances and net worth, I want you to take it, and read through it," she said sliding it to him. "But for now, I want to give you a verbal summary." She took a deep breath and started. "This condominium is mine and it's worth five hundred and seventy-five thousand dollars. My father bought this for me, and until last week, I thought my mother was responsible. Throughout the years, my father sent me money to live on, again, I thought it was my mother. I had so much left over each month that Jack offered to have someone set up an investment portfolio for me, which he did, and I currently have over two hundred thousand dollars in investments. My BMW is paid for, and with my salary and the money that I don't invest, I easily clear easily over two thousand a week. Most of it I save, which today is the eighty thousand, and the rest, I spend. There are two reasons I am telling you this: the first is, I want you to know my financial status, and the second, I want the eighty thousand dollars to be our money or our company's money, whatever, as long as you agree you won't repay it back to me. It makes me feel like we have a prenuptial agreement for our relationship, and I don't want that. Thomas, if I had it my way you could have as much of my money as you needed. I love you and I want to help you, and I know if you were in my shoes, you would be saying the same to me. So, I want the repayment off the contract." He just stared down at the table. "Thomas, please look at me. The reason I agreed to do the finances with you and send your work to the publishers is so I could be with you, and be a part of your dream. And I want you to watch me rehearse and perform, or ask me to dance or sing, or about my day and be a part of my life and my dream," she explained holding his hand. "Am I making any sense?"

"You are," he whispered then waited a moment. "And if I say no to what you're asking?"

"I would go ahead with what we had agreed to, the only difference being you would know how I feel," replied Olivia. "Thomas, I really want it to be ours."

"Olivia, I need some time to think about all this?" he said getting up with her. "I want you to know that I love you for what you're doing, not just the money, but for being honest and talking to me. The more I'm with you, the more I love you," he declared holding and kissing her. "I'll see you in the morning," he said slowly walking away, stopping, and turning to her. "What if we were married?"

"I don't want a prenuptial relationship or marriage. Everything we have is ours, that's what I believe," stated Olivia. "And you?

Thomas nodded. "The same."

Olivia watched him leave, sat down, and wondered if she had done the right thing telling him, but she felt awkward loaning the man she loved money.

Early the next morning, Thomas came into her room, and kissed her on the cheek.

"Thomas," she said still half asleep and lifting up the blankets, "lay next to me and hold me." He slid in next to her, she rested her head on his chest, and fell back asleep. Olivia started to stir and woke Thomas up.

"Did you think about it?' she asked.

"Olivia, I love you, and I want to spend the rest of my life with you. So, everything you have, I have, we have, is ours."

"Oh, Thomas, I want to spend the rest of my life with you, too," she said pulling him close. "I love you more than anything in this world. Thank you."

Chapter 29

Olivia walked around the condo looking for Thomas and realized he was out. She went into her room, lay down, and wondered where he was. Suddenly, she heard the front door open.

"Thomas!" she called out.

"Where are you?" he asked.

"In my room," she replied.

He came in, jumped on the bed, and gave her a passionate kiss. "Take a bath and put on something sexy we have reservations for eight; I thought we would go out and celebrate," he said rolling off the bed and heading for the door. "I'm going to get a shower."

Olivia got out of the bath and stood naked in front of the mirror. She dried her hair leaving it parted to the side and loose to her shoulders, then put on a black bra and matching thong, followed by a short, black, spaghetti strapped dress that went straight up and down. She leaned over, and put on her makeup, before going into the bedroom, putting on her high heels, and picking up the matching handbag. Oliva strolled back into her en suite and sprayed herself with perfume before throwing it, and her lipstick, into her handbag. She went back into the bedroom and looked at herself one last time in the full-length mirror and was pleased with her Manhattan purchase and what she saw." I bought this outfit for such an occasion, she thought to herself, and was extremely happy with it. Olivia strolled down the hall, into the living room, and noticed Thomas wearing a black two-piece suit and tie. "You look very handsome," she said going to him.

"Wow!" responded Thomas. "You look stunning."

"Thank you."

"So where are we going?" asked Olivia.

"We are going for dinner up town at La Petite Maison."

"Very chic," she replied.

Thomas ordered champagne and made a toast. "To Olivia, who is talented, beautiful, smart, and sexy, and to our happiness, health, and love; to us."

"To us," replied Olivia who was radiant.

They got up and danced to the pianist's renditions of famous love songs, and on the way back, Thomas stopped by and made a request then joined her. As the server filled up their champagne glasses, the pianist played, 'You're the Best Thing.'"

"Did you request this?" asked Olivia.

"Yes, I did," he replied.

"Dance with me?" she asked.

"First, I need an answer from you," said Thomas standing up, then going down on one knee, and opening a small blue velvet box and staring into her eyes. "Olivia, make me the happiest man alive, and give me the pleasure of your hand in marriage?"

Olivia was taken totally by surprise, for her, everything was happening in slow motion. She looked deep into his eyes and from the bottom of her heart said, "I love you, and I will love you forever, and it will make me the happiest woman alive to be your wife. Yes, yes, yes!" Neither of them had realized that the pianist had stopped playing, the staff had stopped serving, and the patrons had stopped eating; they were all watching them and clapped when she accepted.

Thomas took the one-carat marquise diamond ring out of the box and placed it on her finger. Olivia stretched out her hand and admired it; she thought she was dreaming. She stood with Thomas, put her arms around him, and kissed him tenderly.

"For the two newly engaged couple let me start that song over," said the pianist.

While they danced, Thomas promised Olivia, he would love her for as long as he lived, and Olivia cried tears of joy. When they left the dance floor, they agreed that 'You're the Best Thing' would be their wedding song, because it was their song.

Once inside the condo, she grabbed his hand, led him into the living room, and sat down next to him. "Thomas, I still think I'm dreaming?" she said admiring her ring.

"If you are, don't wake us up.,"

Olivia pushed him back, put her leg over him, and straddled his lap. Then looked into his eyes, caressed his cheek, and kissed him gently. "Mrs. Olivia Carlyle, I like the way that sounds," she whispered. "You know people are going to ask us the date?"

"I thought you should pick it," suggested Thomas.

"One minute," she said getting off him, going into the kitchen, and returning with a wall calendar and opening it up on the coffee table. "One, three, six, or twelve months?"

"Not twelve, too long," he replied.

"Not one," replied Olivia, "too soon."

"Six isn't bad," suggested Thomas.

"But three is just right!" she said excitedly. "January!"

"January it is!" agreed Thomas.

"Now, what date?" she asked. "What's your lucky number?"

"Seventeen."

She looked at the calendar. "It falls on a Saturday," she said elatedly.

"January 16 it is!" confirmed Thomas. "Now, what kind of wedding do you want?"

"Small. Family and close friends only," she replied.

"Where?"

"If we have it here, we can have the ceremony at the cathedral and the reception at the La Petite Maison, that place is beautiful, and we could rent it for the day. Or," she said thinking, "we could get married on a Caribbean Island, like Antigua, Anguilla, St. Lucia, or Virgin Gorda, and fly guests down. What do you think?"

"They both sound great," replied Thomas.

"I guess we need to know how many guests we are inviting, then decide," she said thinking out loud. "One minute," she said grabbing a pen and paper.

They quickly put a list together.

"Approximately twenty-five, maybe thirty," estimated Olivia. "So, we can do either. You know what I just thought; we need to tell Kate and my father."

"Kate's coming here tomorrow to meet you to go shopping, we can tell her then."

"And I'll phone my father tomorrow afternoon," said Olivia. "Penny and Jack?"

"Tomorrow, tell Penny that you want her and Jack to drop by and see you for a few minutes, after you've finished shopping," suggested Thomas.

"Good idea, but that means I will have to leave my ring here tomorrow," said Olivia putting on a sad face.

"I'll keep it company," promised Thomas.

Okay," she said with an adorable smile.

"We can tell Rachel and Jessica Thursday night."

"And Frank, Thursday at lunch," added Olivia, then suddenly realized something, and sat back "What about Kate living alone out there in the house?"

"I don't know," he replied, with all the running around and getting caught up in the moment, Thomas had forgotten about Kate. "On Saturday, I told her I would never leave her alone."

"Listen, why don't we leave it for now, and talk about it with her tomorrow?" suggested Olivia.

"Yeah, that's a good idea."

"I'm so ecstatic. I love you, Thomas."

"I love you, Olivia."

Chapter 30

Kate and Thomas were in the living room when Olivia walked through the front door.

"Hello, Kate, hello, Thomas," she said joining them and giving him a kiss.

"Kate was admiring your place, so I showed her around."

"I love it, and you have such a great location," she said glancing at Thomas. "We should sell the house and buy one of these. This area would be perfect for me, the university is down the road, and I can see the law firm I work at for from the dining room window."

"They also have a pool upstairs and downstairs they run aerobic classes Tuesday and Thursday," added Olivia. "I'll show you on the way out. We should probably get going."

Kate agreed and stood up.

"Kate, one second," said Thomas whispering to Olivia who left and returned moments beaming. "There's something we need to tell you."

"Is everything okay?" she asked.

"Everything is fine," he said standing next to Olivia who lifted up her left hand up to Kate.

"We're engaged!" said Olivia animatedly.

Kate was silent, and they waited for her to absorb the words and what she was looking at. "Oh my God! Thomas, Olivia, I'm so happy for you, let me have a closer look at that," she said admiring the ring. "It's gorgeous."

"I thought you would be shocked and tell me it was too soon," stated Thomas.

"Thomas, it's a surprise but not a shock, you're both responsible, mature adults, not teenagers, and I can see how much in love you are," replied Kate. "When is the date?"

"Guess?" asked Olivia.

"Hmm, since you got engaged so quickly, I don't think you'll wait too long to get married, so I'll say in three months?"

"Yes," said Olivia.

"January?" she asked.

"January 16," answered Olivia.

Kate gave Olivia a big hug and a kiss on the cheek. "My future sister in-law," she said cheerfully, then hugged and kissed Thomas.

"Kate, I need to ask you something."

"Ask away," said Kate.

"After we're married, I will be living here," he said and felt as if his words were hanging in the air.

"I guess so," said Kate.

"I'm worried about you living at Grandmother's house alone."

"Thomas, it's our house now, let's sell it and split the money," stated Kate bluntly.

"Are you sure?" asked Thomas surprised.

"Thomas, the only reason I haven't suggested selling it before is because I thought you didn't want to."

"But I thought you didn't want to."

"If it would have been up to me, I would have sold it after she died. Without her, it's only a house," she said surveying the room. "Maybe I can rent something like this in the city, that way we can still be close, and see each other."

"That would be perfect," said Olivia.

"Well, let me look into the value of our house and see what's available in the city," said Thomas.

"I want you to know how happy I am for you both, and that you have my support, one hundred percent," said Kate reassuringly. "Now, future sister-in-law, let's go shopping."

They both kissed Thomas on the cheek and headed for the door.

"Have fun," he said closing it behind them.

"Hello, Thomas," said Jack shaking his hand, "you're looking a lot better."

"I feel better," he replied.

"Hello, Thomas," said Penny kissing him on the cheek, "you eye looks much better."

"Thanks," he said showing them into the living room. "Olivia and Kate are on their way up; they were out shopping. Can I get you a drink?"

"Black coffee, no sugar," replied Jack.

"Same," said Penny.

"I'll be back in a minute," he said leaving, putting on the kettle on, and returning moments later.

"If you're free next week, can you squeeze in another game of golf?" queried Jack.

"Any day is fine, just let me know what's good for you."

"I'll see what's available and talk to you on Friday," confirmed Jack.

"Okay," said Thomas looking at him and thinking. "Jack, are there condominiums up for sale in this building?"

"There are three. I'm selling one myself," replied Jack. "It's a one bedroom with a den on the sixteenth floor and has a magnificent view. I only had it for clients visiting from out of town, but I have no use for it anymore, so I'm putting it on the market on Monday. Why?"

"I know someone who is looking in the area and I said I would ask around," answered Thomas. "Do you mind if I ask what the asking price is?"

"Four hundred and fifty thousand."

"It's a beautiful place," added Penny, "you should have a look at it, it's barely been used."

Jack pulled out his keys, took one off, and gave it to Thomas. "Here, take a look, you can give me the key back on Friday."

"1610," said Penny.

The door opened and in strolled Olivia and Kate with handfuls of bags.

"How was it?" asked Thomas.

"We had a great time, and it was fun," said Kate from the front door.

"A lot of fun!" said Olivia.

Kate walked into the room first, Jack and Penny stood and gave her a hug, and asked her how she was doing.

"I heard you've already impressed them down at the firm," said Jack.

Kate just smiled shyly.

Olivia walked in, kissed them both, and waited for them to sit down and stood next to Thomas. "Penny, Jack, Thomas and I have some news."

Penny quickly glanced at Jack then back at Olivia.

"We're engaged and getting married January 16."

Penny jumped out of her seat and yelled, "Yes!" And ran over to Olivia and embraced her.

Jack stood and walked over to Thomas. "She's a fine lady and you're a fine man, congratulations," he said pulling Thomas toward him and giving him a hug, then went over to Olivia.

"Thomas, I've prayed for you both, and for your happiness," said Penny squeezing his hands. "Your grandmother would be so happy." She let go and sat on the sofa next to Olivia and Kate and talked with them about the wedding.

"I'll make those coffees," said Thomas.

"I'll come with you," said Jack following him. "That's great news Thomas, I know I'm not your father, but I'm as happy and proud as any father would be."

"Thanks, Jack," he replied reheating the water.

"Listen, are you going to be there tomorrow night?"

"Rachel's house?"

"Yeah."

"I am. Rachel said that you needed to talk to me," confirmed Thomas glancing at him.

"Not me, Jessica's lawyer, and you need to be there by seven."

"Her lawyer? I thought it was Bill's lawyer?"

"Tomorrow, it will be just Jessica's lawyer, Jessica, Rachel, and us, and we'll be listening to something to do with Bill. That's all I know. My lawyer is ninety-nine percent sure it has to be something to do with Bill assaulting you," said Jack.

Thomas was confused. "Jack in layman's terms."

"Jessica gave Bill such a great deal when he signed the contract that we never thought about him trying to make a settlement with you," explained Jack.

"An out of court settlement?" asked Thomas.

"More like a 'never go to court settlement,'" declared Jack.

"I won't accept it, you know that."

"Unfortunately, it doesn't always work like that."

"What do you mean?"

"What are you two plotting?" asked Olivia.

Jack and Thomas looked at one another.

"Jack was just reminding me about tomorrow night and that we have to be there at seven," answered Thomas.

"All right," said Olivia picking up two cups of coffee. "Grab the rest and come back inside."

Thomas and Jack picked up the remaining cups and followed her.

"I told Kate's to stay here tonight, it will save her driving home later on in the dark," said Olivia.

"Great," replied Thomas distracted and thinking about what Jack had just said to him.

Chapter 31

"I thought Penny ran your rehearsals?" asked Thomas walking out of the restaurant with Olivia and Frank.

"No, it's Alfie, he's the artistic director," replied Frank. "Penny helps us more one on one."

"She shares her time between the ballet school and the First National Ballet but her first responsibility is the school," added Olivia.

They crossed the street and strolled into the park, Olivia asked if they could sit on the bench for a few minutes, and sat between Thomas and Frank

"Frank, I have some wonderful news," stated Olivia.

"What?" he asked Frank.

"I thought you may have noticed at lunch," she said waving her left hand in front of his eyes.

"Olivia!" exclaimed Frank. "Thomas!"

"We got engaged Tuesday evening!" blurted out Olivia elatedly.

"That's great news. I'm so happy for you both," he said putting his arm around her and giving her a kiss. "I should have known something was up, you've had a glow about you all week. Does Penny know?" he asked then answered his own question. "Of course, she does, I saw her earlier on and she asked if I had spoken with you."

"We told Penny, Jack, and Kate yesterday, but I haven't been able to speak with my father yet. We've been missing each other's calls, so I left him a message with a time for him to call me this afternoon. I'm so excited."

"I'm so happy for the both of you," he said leaning over and shaking Thomas's hand. "You're a lucky man, she's a treasure; and Olivia, you, take care of Thomas, he's a good man."

"I will," said Olivia smiling.

"I knew you two were destined for one another," continued Frank. "So, when's the big day?"

"January 16," replied Olivia grabbing Thomas's hand.

"Not wasting any time, eh!" said Frank teasing them.

"Are you surprised?" asked Olivia.

"Surprised, a little, but I think you are doing the right thing," he replied then glanced over at Thomas. "It's your life, and life's too short."

"It is," he agreed.

They got up and started to walk back.

"I was going to ask if you two would like to come with me to my parents on Sunday afternoon for an early dinner?" asked Frank.

"Of course, what time?" asked Olivia.

"Around two o'clock."

"Why don't we pick you up and we can all go together?" suggested Thomas.

"I'd appreciate that," replied Frank hesitating then looking at Olivia. "The reason I'm going over there is to tell my family that I'm gay."

Olivia stared at Frank surprised.

"Thomas has already offered to come with me, and I wanted to warn you first, and make sure you were still okay coming with us. I don't want to put you in an uncomfortable position, so if you prefer not to come, I understand."

"Of course, I'm coming," she replied. "But why did you wait till now to tell me that you were going to say something?"

"Thomas and I had talked about it the last time we met, and I didn't want to say anything till I had a definite date, plus, you two had other things going on," he explained, then stopped, and turned to her. "Olivia, I look at you and Thomas moving ahead with your lives and making plans for your future, I'm living a lie, and I want to move ahead with my life and my future, too." Frank paused briefly, smiled, and admired them. "I want to be like you two, in love."

Olivia and Thomas knew how lucky they were to have each other but neither had realized how lonely Frank really was.

Chapter 32

Thomas unlocked the door to 1610, Olivia walked in, and he followed her into a spacious ceramic tiled foyer. She opened the two wooden doors and revealed a large closet. Then they strolled down the hallway to the first door, opened it, and looked inside at the full bathroom. They continued on, and went into a roomy den, it was furnished with an executive mahogany table, a cabinet, and chairs, and had a large window that offered a splendid view of the city They left the room, crossed the hallway, and opened the doors to the laundry room. They retraced their steps past the front door and walked into the kitchen. It was open concept and had a bleached wood table with four chairs, black appliances, a speckled gray countertop, and an island. They went through the doorway into a dining room which contained a long oak table, six chairs, a buffet, and hutch. Olivia turned on the light and a beautiful chandelier lit up the room. She turned it off, and pressed down on another switch that opened the blinds. They looked out at the city and harbor then strolled into the living room. It had a full-sized white sofa, love seat, black end tables and coffee table, and an entertainment center with a thirty-six-inch plasma television. They continued through the living room and back into the hallway. The foyer was to their left, so they went right. They opened two French doors and sauntered into the master bedroom. It had a four-poster king size bed, end tables, chest of drawers and cabinet, all in oak, a walk-in closet, and en suite with an oval tub with windows all around, and a shower stall. Thomas looked out at the harbor front and realized it was a corner suite.

"Thomas this is beautiful and would be perfect for Kate," said Olivia going into the bedroom and sitting on the bed.

"It would be," he agreed. "It's modern, has a lot of space, and a sizeable den. She would love it."

"How much is your place worth?" asked Olivia.

"Three hundred and fifty," confirmed Thomas. "After selling the house, and paying off everything we owed, including the agent, we'd be left with two fifty. Which means, if Kate bought this, the remaining two hundred we could mortgage and pay until she started working full time," he said joining her on the bed. "There may be more expenses, like furnishing the place." He quickly surveyed the bedroom. "I don't know, maybe she'd want some of this stuff, and we could buy it from Jack."

"Thomas, I'm not too sure about her taste, but this furniture is beautiful and looks brand new," stated Olivia.

"I thought the same," he said contemplating.

"What is it?"

"We would have to get close to the asking price for our house to pull this off, which means it may take a little longer to sell, but I'm sure Jack would hold it for us to we sold ours."

"Of course, he would, and he may give us a better deal," suggested Olivia.

"Probably," he replied.

"Thomas, I don't want to take advantage of them either, but they are our friends."

"I know, and I wonder sometimes if I'm too proud?" he asked.

Olivia pulled him up and put her arms around him. "No, Thomas, you're not. You value their friendship and don't want to take advantage of them, that's all," she said, then gave him a kiss and held him. "If Kate lived here, she would be close to us, to work, to university, and she would be safe, and I know you would feel better knowing that. So, just sell the house and buy this for her."

Chapter 33

Thomas and Olivia arrived at the Carter Estate ten minutes before seven and Jack came out to meet them. "They're waiting for you in the study."

They followed Jack, and Thomas immediately noticed all the bookshelves were empty and that the room had a somber atmosphere. Rachel and Jessica were sitting on a sofa and gave half smiles, and a man in a suit was behind a desk that had been set up for the occasion. They walked over and said hello to Rachel and Jessica, who didn't seem themselves, before sitting opposite them.

Jack introduced them to the suit at the desk. "This is Mrs. Carter's lawyer, Sidney Goldstein."

"Before we proceed, let me make sure everyone is present," he said glancing up as he called out their names. "Jessica, Rachel, Jack, and Thomas Carlyle." He then looked at Olivia. "Who are you?"

"She's with me," replied Thomas.

"Any objections, Jessica?" asked Sidney.

Jessica shook her head.

"Your full name, please?" asked Sidney.

"Olivia Taylor," she replied.

Sidney wrote it down. "At this time, I will ask you all to leave, except Mr. Carlyle," requested Sidney.

Everyone stood up to leave, Thomas grabbed Olivia's arm and told her to stay.

"I will have to ask the young lady to leave as well," insisted Sidney.

"I prefer she stays," said Thomas.

"It's okay, Sidney," said Jessica wanting him to get on with it.

Sidney watched them leave, stood up and went around the desk, then pulled up a chair in front of them and shook their hands. "Now Thomas, do you have any idea why we are meeting?"

"No," he replied.

"Let me start off by saying this is an informal meeting but its nature is quite serious. You are aware of the state of affairs that took place last week with Mrs. and Mr. Carter, actually between me and his lawyer?"

"We are," replied Thomas.

"Good," replied Sidney. "Then you are also aware that Mr. Carter had agreed to all the conditions and signed all the documents?"

"We are."

"Put quite simply, it was really an offer he couldn't refuse," he stated, then heisted. "We strongly believe that Mr. Carter's lawyer will be approaching you in the very near future."

"Why?" asked Thomas.

"We believe to offer you a settlement for the physical and mental damages he caused you, or to be more precise. 'a never go to court settlement.' If you were to accept his offer, he would ask you to sign papers, to which you would agree not to press charges against him, hence, not take him to court." Sidney studied Thomas briefly then came to the point. "There are two reasons for our meeting: first, I am here purely to protect the interests of Mrs. Carter, and secondly, to make sure that the meeting between you and Mr. Carter's lawyer never takes place."

"So, you're trying to beat him to the punch?" asked Thomas, and although he knew the seriousness of this meeting, couldn't help but smile at what he had said, and noticed Olivia trying her best not to giggle.

"You could say that," confirmed Sidney.

"If you are here representing Jessica, why is she outside?"

"Thomas, this is a very delicate matter, and of significant importance to Jessica and Rachel. I told them it would be in her best interests if they let me take care of, shall we say, the negotiations, and for them to keep their emotions out of it," said Sidney candidly. "That's what they pay me for."

"Business is business," stated Thomas.

"Precisely," agreed Sidney.

"All right," said Thomas a little annoyed. "Continue."

"Tonight, Mrs. Carter would like you to sign a document stating that your testimony, and any medical records from your recent injuries from Mr. Carter's violence, could be used in a court of law against him, should it be deemed necessary."

"Okay," said Thomas wondering where the document was to be signed.

"After which, a deposit of one million dollars will be put into an account of your choosing."

"What!" exclaimed Thomas. "Did you say a million dollars?"

Sidney realized they should have offered more. "Yes."

"Unbelievable," said Thomas glancing over at Olivia's stunned look. "Sidney, can we be left alone for a few minutes?"

"Of course," he said leaving with a concerned look on his face.

"Sidney, can you do me a favor?" asked Thomas.

"Yes," he said turning.

"Can you ask Jessica if she can have Rachel come in with some soft drinks?"

"Not a problem," replied Sidney closing the door behind him.

"What's going on?"

"I don't know!" she replied.

"What do you think?"

"I don't know," she said shaking her head. "A million dollars, that's a lot of money."

"A million dollars," echoed Thomas, getting up, strolling to the window, and staring out. She followed and stood behind him. "Olivia, tonight I can walk out of here a millionaire, or I can walk out of here with fifty dollars in my account."

"I thought you had seven?" she teased.

"I paid for the engagement dinner."

She laughed and Thomas joined in.

"I could walk out of here a wealthy man."

"Thomas," she whispered, "I believe you walked in here a very wealthy man, and I know you will do what's right in your heart." She kissed him on the cheek. "That's one of the reasons why I love you."

"What about Kate?" he asked. "We could buy her that condominium."

"We don't need this money to buy her the condominium," she replied then recalled something. "Do you remember when Kate wrote that line on your picture in the hotel in New York City, 'Country's Richest Man, Thomas Carlyle?'"

"I do," he said turning to her.

"It had nothing to do with money," she stated placing her index finger on his chest, "it's about who you are in here. That's the reason why she loves you and I love you, and why we both know, you will never let either of us down."

Thomas smiled at her.

The door opened and Rachel walked in with three cokes, as she placed them on the table, they went over to her. They gave her a hug then all sat down.

"How's Mathew?" asked Thomas.

"He's great. I saw him yesterday," she replied. "What have you two been up to?"

"Funny you should ask," he said.

"Why?"

"Olivia and I are engaged to be married on January 16."

"Thomas, is this another one of your jokes?" she asked.

"I know you've been waiting patiently to show her," he said turning to her.

Olivia modeled the ring.

"I love it, it's gorgeous," said Rachel embracing her. "I'm so happy for you, for the both of you, but this is so sudden."

"Rachel, I have an interesting story to tell you, and so many other things that I need to explain," confessed Olivia. "Maybe we can talk sometime?"

"After this, why don't you come up to my room and we can talk then," she said excitedly, "and you can tell me all about the wedding."

"With that being said, let's get this over with," stated Thomas standing, strolling to the doors, and opening them. "Why don't you all come in?"

Once in the study, Thomas asked them to sit down while he sat on the table. "Okay, can someone beside Sidney, no offence Sidney, please explain to me what is going on?" he asked surveying them. "Jessica?"

Jessica spoke nervously. "We believe Bill is going to offer you a lot of money if you sign a settlement with him and we wanted to talk to you first. If down the road, Bill renegades on his contract with me, your testimony could be crucial to my defense. You see I have no witnesses or medical reports. So, I needed you to sign an agreement detailing the events of his vicious attack, and to say that you would testify in court on my behalf. I need to be protected from Bill, not only now, but for the rest of my life, and you may not always be around. What if something were to happen to you, you move, or I never see you again, it's as good as you signing Bill's documents... Thomas, I'm not particularly good when it comes to these sorts of things. I just wanted to make sure you were taken care of, and I will give you anything, anything, for your signature," she said putting her hands over her eyes and crying. Rachel comforted her.

"Jack?" asked Thomas. "You're turn."

"Bill is going to offer you a lot of money, and I was just protecting Jessica's interests, and yours," he replied.

"Rachel, what did you think about all of this?"

"I told them that you would never take any money from my father or my mother, and that you would sign anything for us."

"Sidney, answer this question, if I were going to formally charge Mr. Carter, how much money could I potentially receive from an out of court settlement?"

Sidney looked at Jack, who nodded his head, then spoke. "You have a compelling case: witnesses, a medical report, and assault charges; he could have killed you. Which means he could, and probably would, receive a jail sentence. But even if he didn't, just the publicity alone would ruin him financially. So, I believe he would probably try to settle out of court for a minimal of two million."

"So, Sidney, Mr. and Mrs. Carter, in business terms, are protecting their interests?" asked Thomas.

"In a manner of speaking, yes," he replied.

Thomas studied Sidney, then looked at Jessica, then Jack, then Rachel, who smiled at him, then Olivia, who was admiring him proudly and mouthed, "I love you." Thomas slowly stood. "I need a few minutes alone?"

"We'll leave!" suggested Sidney.

"No," said Thomas, "I need some air, give me ten minutes."

Thomas went outside, sauntered over to the fountain, and thought about the situation. When he came back into the room thirty minutes later, they were all sitting very quietly, and it was as if no one had moved or spoken since he had left. Talking to Olivia later, he would find out that Jessica and Jack had agreed they had managed the situation wrongly, and that Thomas was a friend, and should have approached him as one. Sidney disagreed and told them this was the best way to handle these kinds of situations. He had been through many of these before and seen them go awry fast. The rest of the time they were silent.

As Thomas stood in front of them, he spoke. "I contemplated long and hard about what was going on here, and I took Sidney's advice, and decided to think about this rationally rather than emotionally, and have come to a decision based on that," he stated then looked at Jessica and Rachel. "I understand your situation, and what Mr. Carter is trying to do, and it must be a very difficult time for you both. Jessica, I understand your predicament and the anxiety you must be experiencing right now; it's time to get this over with so you can move on with your life." He glanced over. "Then there's Jack, I must say I'm impressed by his loyalty and friendship. He understands that Jessica has a great deal to lose, while I can do nothing, except to gain financially. So, why not help out his dear friend Jessica, and at the same time his good friend Thomas, and in the process screw Bill. Business is business," he said smiling at Jack who grinned back. "There is still the issue of my compensation, to which, I still have to make a decision on."

There was a long silence.

Sidney asked the question that everyone wanted to know the answer to. "What is your decision?"

Thomas sat back on the desk. "I'll get to that momentarily," he replied and faced Jessica. "Did I tell you that Kate and I are selling our house?"

"No, you didn't," replied Jessica confused.

"Would you know of any condominiums that are for sale in the city?" asked Thomas. "You see, I'm looking at buying one for Kate."

Jessica stared at him totally confused. "No, I don't know much about real estate in the city."

"Sidney, do you?"

"I live an hour out of town, I don't know the area," he replied.

"Jack?" he asked. "How about you?"

"Actually, there's one going up for sale on Monday, right in the city."

"The house Kate and I are selling is worth about three hundred and fifty, by the time we pay off outstanding debts, we'll have around two hundred and fifty left over. I'm going to use that two hundred and fifty as a down payment, and buy Kate a condo in the city, but I'm not too sure what the prices are in town. Jack, would you happen to know how much that condo is selling for?"

"I heard the owner is trying to get rid of it, and is very motivated, and selling below market value. In fact, I believe it's two hundred and thirty, and that includes all the furnishings and an underground parking spot. Which means the extra twenty could be used for any miscellaneous expenses or to replace any unwanted furniture."

"Jack, I would need to let Kate see the condominium, and have time to sell the house. Would there be a problem with the owner putting it on hold till Kate has had a tour of it and gives her feedback?" asked Thomas.

"Not at all, the owner is so desperate, he would even help you sell your house," confirmed Jack.

"Kate will be so happy," said Thomas smiling. "You know what, now I'm happy."

Sidney and Jessica had puzzled looks.

"Mr. Carlyle, I wonder if we could get back to the business at hand and your decision?" asked Sidney.

Jack already knew that it was over. He would explain everything to Jessica and Sidney, and have the document updated with the dollar figure removed. Everyone was going to get what he or she wanted, except Bill Carter. Jack also realized Thomas never wanted their money, after all, they were his friends. Instead, he had helped them out, and at the same time, took care of his sister. From that point on, Thomas was the son that Jack would have wanted.

"Rachel, my coke has gone warm, why don't you, me, and Olivia go into the kitchen, get some ice, and go up to your room, and we can leave your mom, Jack, and Sidney to write up the new offer, Jessica, you can bring it up to the room and I'll sign it there."

As the three stood and walked to the door, Olivia put her arm around him and whispered, "Jack's going to want to adopt you." Then affectionally nibbled on his earlobe.

"I know," he replied.

Chapter 34

Olivia and Thomas sat on the four-poster king-size bed and waited for Kate's response.

"I love it, it's perfect, and it's got breathtaking views," said Kate.

"What about the furnishings?" asked Thomas.

"Is the furniture included?"

"If you want."

"You know, I was really looking at the space and imagining it without the furniture. Can we look around once more?" she begged and took them around the condominium three more times. "Are all these countertop appliances, dishes, and pots included?" she asked opening the cupboards.

"Everything," replied Thomas.

"Kate, all the furniture and appliances are top of the line. Look at these dishes, they are Mikasa, and the ones in the dining room are Royal Doulton," pointed out Olivia.

"I don't think I would get rid of anything, and I'd bring some of Grandmother's pieces, but nothing more," she said. "Olivia, what do you think?"

"It's beautiful, it's modern, it has lots of space, and it has a den. It's perfect," answered Olivia.

"Thomas?" Kate asked.

"I agree with Olivia," he replied, "plus it's close to work, university, and us, and it's safe. You would be insane not to take it."

"Can we afford it?" she asked.

"Kate, do you want it?" asked Olivia smiling.

"I do! I do!" she said eagerly. "But I don't want to be disappointed if we can't afford it."

"Kate, come and sit around the table with us," said Thomas leading the way then opening the envelope that Jack had given him and reading through it.

"What's that?" asked Kate.

Thomas continued reviewing the documents, finished, then glanced up at her. "It's a surprise."

"Surprise?" asked Kate looking at Thomas, then Olivia.

"Last night, we went to Penny's for dinner, and Jack talked to us while she was getting ready. He told us that he was going to buy our house for her," explained Olivia.

"Why?"

"She loves it, and always has. She told Jack how she liked the location, how cozy it was, and how she would like to have a garden to grow flowers and vegetables. Apparently, she used to garden with your grandmother all the time."

"I remember she did, but I never thought anything of it," admitted Kate.

"Jack said the cottage is too far for her to travel on weekends, so he's going to buy our house for her, and surprise her tonight."

"I'm so glad," said Kate. "Especially knowing someone like Penny will be taking our house."

"So, what has he offered?" asked Olivia.

"Four hundred thousand," stated Thomas.

"I thought you said it was worth about three fifty?" asked Kate.

"I was guessing. There are several quotes in here from agents indicating what it's worth, and they range from three fifty to four; he gave us top price. On this page, it breaks down the price we've been offered, minus what we owe, minus the price for this condominium." He looked at her. "We will be left with a check for seventy thousand."

Kate quickly worked out the math. "Wait a second, we're getting this for two hundred and thirty thousand. Is there something wrong with it?"

Thomas explained what happened on Thursday night.

"One million!" she repeated.

"I didn't want to tell you over the phone and thought it would be better if I explained it to you today and surprise you with this," replied Thomas.

"I really want to live here," said Kate. "I love it!"

"Then, consider it yours."

"Welcome neighbor," said Olivia cheerfully and squeezing her hand.

Thomas sat back and stared at them. "So, what are we going to do with the seventy thousand?"

"Thomas, you keep it," said Kate immediately.

He thought momentarily. "Did you write up the contract?"

"I did, and I was going to show you after we had dinner tonight."

"Kate, if you take twenty, would that cover your expenses and bills till you start working fulltime?" he asked.

"Thomas, that's more than enough."

"Okay, you take twenty. Now that Kate is taken care of, that leaves the question of the fifty thousand," he said looking at Olivia and thinking. "How much would you say it will cost for our wedding?"

She went silent.

"What is it?" he asked.

Olivia nervously whispered. "Thomas, I wanted to ask you something when we were having dinner tonight, but I guess I'll just ask you now. Remember when I spoke to my father yesterday, and I told you how happy he was for us, and how much he liked you?"

Thomas nodded.

"He asked if he could pay for the wedding, I said I would talk with you, and let him know."

"What do you want?"

"I want him to, it would make me so happy, and him, too," she replied.

"Olivia, all I want is for our wedding to be the best day ever. So, if allowing your father to pay for it is going to add to your special day, then I say call him and say yes."

"Oh Thomas!" she cried jumping up, sitting on his knee, and kissing him.

"Maybe I should leave," joked Kate pretending to get up.

Thomas and Olivia laughed with her.

"So, I can't give away this fifty thousand," stated Thomas.

"Just, put it in your bank account," said Kate.

"No, here's what I'm going to do. I'll put the fifty thousand into the company, that's twenty-five each for Kate and me, and Olivia you put twenty-five in. That's seventy-five thousand."

"No, Thomas I—"

"Olivia!" said Thomas in a stern tone. "We will go to the bank and set up a joint account for the remaining fifty-five thousand you were going to put towards the company, all right? Besides, we'll need money for our honeymoon."

"Thomas, I like it when you get upset with me," she said getting turned on and kissing his neck and ear.

"This time I am leaving," said Kate departing.

Thomas kissed Olivia passionately for a moment then stopped. "Are you okay with that?"

"Yes, and I can't wait for our honeymoon," she replied. "Oh, by the way, last night in the condo because it was so warm, I slept in the nude."

"You did?" he asked interestedly.

"On top of my duvet," she whispered and blowing in his ear.

"No, you didn't, you're just teasing me," he said unsure. "You did?"

"And in the middle of the night, I was thirsty, so I got up and slowly walked to the kitchen for a glass of water. I drank it too fast, and some spilled on my breasts, and ran down my body in between my thighs. I put the glass down, went into your room, and kissed you on the cheek goodnight. If you had woken up, you would have caught me, naked and wet. I went back to my bed and lay down with the door wide open. If you would gotten up first and came into my room, you would have found me completely naked."

"Really?" asked Thomas getting turned.

"No," said Olivia laughing at him and running out the room.

Thomas chased after her and caught up to her in the den.

Kate was sitting on the chair behind the desk. "Oh, to be in love," she said.

Thomas noticed the clock. "You only have ninety minutes to shop for something to wear tonight. Is that enough time?"

Olivia quickly looked at Kate and they both chuckled. "Is that enough time? Men!" she said.

Kate stood up and went toward him. "You're always thinking about us," she said kissing him on the cheek. "Thanks, for getting me this place." She put her arm around him. "So, when can I move in?"

"I'll go talk to Jack while you guys' shop. Do you have any other questions?"

"No, but if we can drop off the signed documents at Jack's before we leave tonight, I could thank him.," said Kate.

"All right," he replied.

They went to the elevators, and Thomas said goodbye as the doors closed and took Oliva and Kate down, he waited, then took the elevator up to Jack's.

Chapter 35

"How do I look?" asked Kate coming into the living room.

Thomas looked away from the television and at Kate in beige pants and white blouse.

"Sexy!" said Thomas turning it off.

"Wait till you see your fiancée," she said grinning. "Want a beer?"

"Sure."

Kate went into the kitchen as Olivia strolled into the living room. She was wearing fitted brown suede pants that hung on her hips, and a cream cropped shirt that seductively revealed her navel.

"He never gawked at me like that," said Kate joining them. "Thomas, close your mouth!"

"You're only my sister, this woman here," he said going towards Olivia and putting his arms around, "is my goddess."

"Kate, please pour that cold beer over his head and cool him down, he's getting out of control."

"And embarrassing," added Kate.

"You two are just lucky I'm not sporting my leather pants, otherwise I would have to fight the girls off at the bar tonight," said Thomas turning around and wiggling his butt as he sauntered back to the sofa.

They both laughed.

"You don't even have leather pants," stated Kate.

"And if I did!" stated Thomas.

"If you did, would you wear them?" asked Olivia.

"You know I would."

"So, if I go out tomorrow and buy you a pair, you will wear them for me when we went out?" she asked curiously.

"Definitely!" he replied.

Kate glanced over at Olivia shaking her head. "There's no way would he wear them."

"Ladies beware, I warned you about fighting the girls off tonight," he said going into his makeshift bedroom, the den, to get ready.

They were drinking their beer and talking when Thomas walked in wearing a pair of black leather pants and a white cotton shirt.

"No way!" said Kate.

"Wow, Thomas, you look sexy!" said Olivia.

"Thomas, I hate to admit it, but you do look good in them," confessed Kate.

"Please ladies, please, you're embarrassing yourselves," he said placing a CD into the player, locating a song, and putting it on pause. He moved the coffee table out of the way, then turned his back to the girls, and using the remote pressed play. The Doors 'L.A. Woman' started. With the drums and bass, Thomas moved his bum with the beat, as the guitar kicked in, he moved his head, and with all the instruments he moved his whole body. Then, using the remote as a microphone, he sang the first verse drowning out Jim Morrison's voice.

"Thomas, what are you doing?" asked Olivia giggling and glancing over at Kate who gave an unsure look and laughed with her.

Thomas finished the first verse with a lyrical scream then danced around, and back and forth, with the music, still with his back to them.

"Whoa!" screamed Olivia clapping.

Kate put her hand over her face.

As the tempo slowed, Thomas stopped dancing, and just moved his hips and sang the second verse.

Olivia continued to clap, and Kate joined in, then she leaned over and patted his bum.

Thomas finished the second verse with a lyrical yell, and the music went faster, and he continued his dance back and forth still with his back to them.

"Whoa!" screamed Olivia. "Turn around, Thomas!"

"Turn around," said Kate getting into it.

They continued to clap.

The tempo slowed down and Thomas faced them.

Olivia and Kate screamed.

Thomas went down on one knee, and looked at Olivia and sang, then at Kate, and sang. The tempo picked up again, and he quickly jumped up and sang the rest of the verse to them, thrusting his hips back and forth with the music.

They screamed louder.

The verse ended, the tempo slowed down, and Thomas strolled over to Olivia, took her beer, and had a drink, then put it on the table and pointed at her as he sang. They both looked at each other and giggled. He leisurely moved in front of them, glanced down, and started to repeat the words at the end of the song. "Come on girls, you know the words, get up."

They joined him and sang into the remote.

"Keep on singing," said Thomas as he continued singing and repeating the phrase over and over.

The girls suddenly stopped and stared at him. Thomas had taken off around the condo dancing to the music; they swiftly followed him. He then stopped, dropped to his knees, and sang, as Olivia danced in front of him moving her firm abdomen in front of his face. Thomas ended the verse, kissed her stomach, and got up and danced with them. They all sang the last verse together until the music faded.

"Forget about being a writer we should take you to Vegas," said Kate out of breath.

"Or my room!" whispered Olivia. "That was hot!"

"Wait till you see what I've got planned for you on our wedding night," said Thomas with a mischievous smile.

"Oh really!" said Olivia giving him a very sexy open mouth kiss then putting her arms around him. "I have to tell you, that really turned me on."

Thomas smiled. "I thought it might."

"Okay, you two, separate, or I get the hose," kidded Kate, who was glad to see her brother so happy.

Chapter 36

"I'm so delighted Penny is going to keep most of Grandma's furniture," said Kate gazing out the taxicab's window.

"Me too," agreed Thomas.

"Jack told me I have a storage unit in the underground parking garage," said Kate looking at them.

"They're a good size," confirmed Olivia.

"Good, I think I may need it," she confessed. "He also said he is going to drop off the spare keys tomorrow morning, and I was thinking about moving stuff in the afternoon."

"You should," said Thomas encouragingly.

"Just pick up the essentials," suggested Olivia, "that way you can stay start there."

"That's a good idea," she said thinking. "I'll go home tomorrow, bring some clothes and personal stuff back, and maybe one weekend we can book a small van, and you can help me move the bigger items?"

"What about next Saturday?" suggested Olivia.

"Saturday would be best, then I can go back Sunday and clean the place up, and have one final look around," she explained. "I do need to buy some new sheets and a comforter for the bed. Maybe I can do that tomorrow afternoon, then tomorrow evening I can update our contract in my new den," she said cheerfully. "Then we can review it, sign it, and on Monday I can register the company."

"Once we're registered, I'll set up a bank account in the company's name, and get each of us a bank card," said Olivia. "Then call American Express and apply for small business credit cards."

The taxi pulled up in front of 'The Cool Cat Club.' Thomas paid the cabbie and caught up with the girls, who had bypassed the line and were talking with the bouncer. He verified their names on his VIP list and let them in, once inside, they were directed upstairs to a reserved table and realized they were the first to arrive. Kate excused herself and went to the restroom while Thomas and Olivia sat and ordered drinks.

"You look very sexy tonight," he whispered in her ear.

"Thank you," she replied with a smile.

"Thomas?" questioned a voice from behind.

He turned around. "Tracy! How are you?" he asked standing and hugging her.

"Olivia!" cried Tracy. "I've missed seeing you, and talking to you, we have so much to catch up on." They hugged for a while then separated.

"You know each other?" asked Olivia pointing at them.

"We met at Rachel's birthday party," replied Tracy. "This was the guy I was talking to you about, you know, the one that got me out of work, with pay, I may add."

"I remember you telling me, but it never dawned on me that you were talking about Thomas," she said looking dumbfounded at Thomas.

"I was telling her all about you," explained Tracy.

"But you said he was Rachel's boyfriend?" asked Olivia.

"He is, they make such a good couple, and they were having such a good time," she said then noticed something in his eyes and hesitated. "You aren't Rachel's boyfriend?"

"No, Rachel and I are very good friends, I'm engaged to Olivia."

"This is the guy you were telling me about. The one you are in love with!" asked Tracy.

Olivia smiled. "Yes, the one I am in love with."

"I never thought that your Thomas was my Thomas, and that we were talking about the same person, that's too weird. I'm so sorry I jumped to the conclusion about you and Rachel."

"It's okay, don't worry about it," he said.

"Let me see the ring," she said reaching for Olivia's hand. "Oh, it's gorgeous! I'm so happy for you, and he's a great guy." Then she faced Thomas. "And you take care of her; she's one in six billion."

"I know, and I will," confirmed Thomas. "How was your anniversary night?"

Tracy gave them a naughty look. "We drank the bottle of champagne, fooled around, and didn't get to sleep till seven."

"Anniversary?" questioned Olivia.

"I forgot, you don't know, this is what I wanted to tell you at the party. Robby and I got married in Vegas last year."

"Congratulations!" screamed Olivia. "Tell me all the details."

"Well, we'd had been on the road for eight months when pulled into Vegas for a weeklong gig, so we decided right then and there to get married. It was amazing. He proposed to me on stage, and after the show, we went to the Graceland Chapel and were married by an Elvis impersonator. It was so much fun. I'll drop by one night and show you the pictures and video, and you can tell me about your wedding plans."

"I'd love to see them," said Olivia enthusiastically. "You look like you're on cloud nine."

"I am," she said glowing. "Robby's going to come up after the second set to say hello, and we have another surprise," said Tracy excitedly.

"What is it?" asked Olivia.

"You'll have to wait and see," said Tracy mysteriously.

"All right," said Olivia staring at her curiously.

"Did you get lost?" teased Thomas as Kate approached.

"I didn't know there was a comedy act here tonight as well," she snapped back, making the other two girls laugh. "But if you must know, I met someone from work and was talking to him for a few minutes."

"Kate this is Tracy, Tracy, this is my sister Kate, and Tracy's husband, Robby, is the lead singer."

"Nice to meet you," said Kate.

"Likewise," replied Tracy.

"I can't wait to hear your boyfriend sing. Thomas said he's brilliant."

"I think so, too," she said touching her arm, "but then again, I'm a little one sided."

"Tracy, before I forget, I love my leather pants."

"Thank you," she said blushing.

"You made those!" they said at the same time.

"I did."

"They look great on him," said Olivia. "I didn't know you designed clothes."

"I know, there's so much I have to tell you," she admitted. "When we were on the road, I started making Robby's clothes, you know, to give me something to do. Then I started to make them for the rest of the band. I realized I loved doing it, so I'm going to go to college part-time, and Robby's going to help me out with the tuition."

"Good for you," said Olivia proud of her. "You're very talented, and have a keen eye for fashion, I want a pair."

"Me too," said Kate. "What color can I get them in?

As Kate and Tracy talked about her designs, Olivia moved close to Thomas and whispered. "So, you're the romantic guy Tracy was talking to me about, I should have known, but she threw me off when she said you were Rachel's boyfriend. To be honest with you, I was actually relieved to hear that she had one and thought you would be left alone. I guess I was wrong," she said kissing him. "Why didn't you tell me about Tracy?"

"You didn't know she was married, or about her designing clothes, and I knew she wanted to surprise you. So, I didn't want to ruin it for her, or for you," he replied.

"Hello, everyone," said Rachel joining them. She gave Olivia a hug and a kiss then did the same to Thomas, before turning to Kate and Tracy and asking how they were."

Olivia picked up their drinks from the table, she handed the beer to Thomas, and sipped her rum and coke. She studied Rachel in her light blue dress with her perfect figure, dazzling green eyes, and long blonde hair. "She is beautiful," she said glancing over at Thomas.

"She's attractive," he agreed.

Olivia quickly looked at Rachel. "Thomas, she has beautiful features, a great body, she's intelligent, and personable," she said turning to him. "Did you ever want to be with her?" she asked nervously.

Thomas brushed his hand over Olivia's cheek and gazed deeply into her blue eyes. "I have the most beautiful and complete woman on this Earth, standing right in front of me. I fell in love with you the first time we met, and I will love you till the day I die," he said kissing her tenderly.

"Thomas, never leave me," whispered Olivia.

"I never will," replied Thomas, "and I'll always be here for you."

"Promise me?" she asked.

"I promise," he replied as Olivia gently squeezed his hand and smiled.

Frank, Greg, Blair, Miguel, Janet, and Betty arrived thirty minutes later. They congratulated Thomas and Olivia on their engagement, and then Miguel talked about Thomas lip-synching to Billy Idol. Apparently, he had been the talk of The Village and people were asking when he was coming back from New York City.

They all laughed.

The waitress brought over several bottles of champagne in ice buckets and placed them around the table. She opened a couple, filled glasses, and passed them around. Kate stood and spoke. "To Thomas, the best brother and friend a sister could have, and to his beautiful, talented fiancée, Olivia, who I am honored to call my sister-in-law. Congratulations on your engagement, and wishing you both future happiness, health, and wealth. To Thomas and Olivia!"

"Thomas and Olivia," they all echoed.

AtlasX came on to play their first set, they watched and listened to their first couple of songs few songs, before going onto the dance floor. Thomas danced with Olivia and was hypnotized as he watched her move to the beat, she looked incredibly sexy. Then they danced with Kate and thanked her for the champagne and the wonderful toast. While Thomas danced with Rachel, he noticed how many men were looking at her. Several had already come to their table to ask her up, but she politely, and oddly, refused. When women stopped her to talk to about modeling, she would gladly take the time to speak with them. Overall, Thomas was impressed by how professionally she handled everything. When they got back to the table, Kate, Olivia, and Frank left to go dance.

"Thomas, do you still want to come horseback riding?" asked Rachel.

"Of course, whenever you want to go," he replied.

"Olivia told me you quit your job and are writing full time."

"Yeah, it was time to take that chance."

"So, you don't need the guesthouse anymore?"

"Well—"

"I wanted to let you know that you are still welcome to use it, and I don't want what happened with my father to keep you away."

"Rachel, I wanted to give you and your mother space, and was planning on talking to you about it when the time was right," he said in a comforting tone. "When we go horseback riding, afterwards, we can talk about when would be a good time for me to start coming back and using the guesthouse."

"That makes me feel better. I was afraid you may not want to," she said thinking momentarily. "Olivia really opened up to me last week, and I had no idea she felt that way about you. Going forward, I hope we can become better friends."

"I know she wants that too," said Thomas reassuring her.

"Do you remember when I was telling you that I have a photo shoot?"

"I do."

"Well, it's on Palm Beach in Aruba, and it's for the last Thursday and Friday in November, which is Thanksgiving. I was planning on flying down there Wednesday afternoon and coming back Sunday night. My mother said she would speak with Jack and ask if we could use his plane. Can you and Olivia come?"

"It's okay with me but you would have to check with Olivia."

"I'll ask her when she returns, and I'm going to ask Kate and Frank, too. Veronica and Buddy have already accepted, and my mother's coming, and she was talking about asking Jack and Penny. She could really use the break, and it would do her some good to get away and relax on a beach."

"I think you're right," said Thomas. "What about Mathew?"

"He's kind and sweet, but I really need some time to myself, especially right now, so we agreed just to be friends," she explained.

"I understand," said Thomas. "How's your daycare coming along?"

"We're still pursuing it, but it's not as easy as I thought, there's a lot of red tape, and with past events, I've been preoccupied. Mathew helped us to get started and gave us an overview of what we needed to do and was extremely helpful, but he suggested that we should look into hiring a lawyer that's an expert in the field and has connections. I thought about hiring someone from one of Jack's firms, so I talked to him, and he has suggested a couple of names. Veronica is still keen, and so am I, we just have to be patient. Hopefully by this time next year, we'll have our grand opening."

"I'm sure you will," said Thomas confidently. "I'm looking forward to it."

Rachel smiled and stared at him in a way that he couldn't describe.

"What are you two talking about?" asked Kate.

"Aruba!" said Thomas.

"Aruba?" asked Olivia joining them.

"I was telling Thomas about the photo shoot being in Aruba the last week in November, and I want you guys to come down with me from Wednesday to Sunday," summarized Rachel. "Say you can make it, please?" she begged.

"Thomas?" asked Olivia.

"I'll be finished my novel and proofreading," he replied. "I wasn't sure about you?"

"Let me think, I dance the Saturday before and I believe we have the last week in November off, and I know Nutcracker rehearsals start in early December," she said. "You know what, let me check with Frank when he gets back."

"Kate?" asked Rachel.

"School is okay. Work may be a problem. So, I'll have to ask and will let you know Monday."

"Frank, do we have the last week in November off?" she asked as he approached.

"Yes, why?"

"Thomas and I are in!" she said elatedly. "I can't wait, Aruba!"

"Aruba?" queried Frank.

"The last week in November, I have a shoot, Wednesday to Sunday in Aruba. Can you make it?" asked Rachel.

"I'll be there," replied Frank without hesitation.

"There's one condition, and it's my mother's, she's picking up the tab for everything, so all expenses paid," Rachel quickly turned to Thomas. "No exceptions!"

They ordered another round of drinks and excitedly talked about Aruba.

After the second set, Robby and Tracy joined them upstairs, and Tracy made the announcement, she was pregnant.

Chapter 37

"Thomas, can we go for a walk in the park?" asked Olivia as they descended the cathedral steps. "It's a lovely Sunday morning."

"Sure," he replied glancing at his watch. "We still have a couple of hours before we have to pick up Frank."

They crossed the road, jumped into his car, and fifteen minutes later parked. As they got out, the clouds were breaking up, and the sun's rays were starting to peak through. They slowly strolled along the asphalt path, and on the way, a family on bicycles passed them and Olivia smiled at the two small children as they peddled by. Soon after, an old man and woman walking their dog approached them, they said good morning, then talked to them for several minutes about the weather before continuing on. They walked in silence for ten minutes, and Thomas sensing something was on her mind, remained quiet and waited.

Olivia eventually spoke. "Tracy looks so happy."

"Yes, I thought they both did," he replied.

"They did," she agreed. "Imagine arriving in Vegas and deciding to get married just like that!"

"That's love for you," he said. "Besides, eight months on the road is a true test of your commitment."

"I know, but now she's pregnant. What happens if he doesn't become successful? And he's on the road and she's at home, alone?" asked Olivia.

Thomas stopped and looked at her. "Olivia, Robby told me that they were going to tour for a few more months, then they were coming back to the city, and he was going to do some local bars and clubs at night and work at a music store during the day. He also said he wanted to be with her and take care of Tracy and the baby."

"Where are they going to live?"

Thomas gave her an odd look. "You heard Tracy, her mother said they could stay in her basement till his musical career took off, and while he was working and she was at college, she would babysit. So, it sounded to me like they have it all worked out." He stopped and suddenly realized something. "Olivia, this isn't about them, is it? It's about us. Are you worried about us? Or is it about me, that I won't succeed?" he asked unsure.

"Oh, no, Thomas, it's not about you at all," replied Olivia. "I know you will succeed." She put her arm through his, placed her head on his shoulder, and walked for a while.

"Let's have a seat," said Thomas motioning to the bench and sitting next to her. "Olivia, what's on your mind?"

She collected her thoughts. "When I look at Tracy, she's been married and making love for a year, and now she's pregnant and is going to have a baby," said Olivia. "She has done all that but sacrificed her ambitions." She glanced at Thomas and tears were starting to form in her eyes.

"Olivia," whispered Thomas, "people start their lives on one path and often come to forks along the way and have to make decisions. Sometimes these decisions seem to be dramatic, more like a right turn, rather than simply going to the right or left. Tracy wanted to be with Robby more than her dancing," he said Thomas. "Are you having a hard time with her decisions?"

"No, Thomas, I actually respect her decisions and her courage," confirmed Olivia.

"We'll be married in a few months, and we'll be together. Do you want to get married earlier? Is it making love?" asked Thomas searching.

"Thomas, when I marry you, it will be the happiest day of my life, and I would marry you today, but I want us to wait and plan our wedding and give our family and friends the opportunity to be a part of our celebration. I also want to go through the excitement of picking a dress, doing a guest list, and sending out the invitations," she explained then spoke quietly, "I won't lie to you, Thomas, I want to make love to you so badly it hurts, and yet, when I look at how close our wedding day is, I know I can wait. I don't know what I would do if it were later?"

"Olivia, I'm confused, is it you and your ballet?" asked Thomas realizing it was the only thing they hadn't talked about.

"Yes."

"Olivia, I would never ask you to leave ballet, I know how hard you've trained and disciplined yourself, and I can't think of a single reason why I would ever ask you to do that," questioned Thomas.

"I know you would never put me in that position," she confirmed.

"No, I wouldn't," he reiterated.

As she looked at Thomas tears came down her cheek. "Thomas, we've never talked about children."

"No," he replied wiping them away. "We can try to plan them so that you only miss a season or two. They do give you time off, right? Professional ballerinas do have children, don't they? And your position would still be there, right?" he asked wondering what the issue was.

"They do and it would."

Thomas was confused. "Then why are you tormenting yourself over this?" he asked. "Are you scared you may not be able to have any?" We could always adopt."

"It's not that!" she stated as her tears flowed. "Thomas, I was so caught up in my love for you, and what I wanted, that I overlooked something."

"What?"

"That you may want, children," she said looking at him, "Thomas, I'm so sorry, I'm not worried about not being able to have children or adopting them. I've been worried about how you will respond when I tell you I don't want to have children, ever," she said sobbing.

"Olivia, why not?"

"What are the reasons you want children?" she asked.

Thomas thought. "I want us to grow as a couple and eventually as a family. I want to see our children grow up and be little ballerinas or writers or soccer players. I want to plan their birthday parties, drop them off at school, and see them playing with their friends. Olivia, there are so many reasons why I do."

"Thomas, I love you, I want to marry you, and live with you forever," she said. "I know you want children, and I love children, I just don't want any."

"Why don't you want any?" he asked again. "I still don't understand."

"Thomas, I've been alone for so long. I have no siblings, and had no father for the last nine years, and a mother who lied to me. I don't want to put any child through what I went through."

"Olivia, it would be different for us, and you're making a decision based on other people's lives and choices."

"No, Thomas, I'm making a decision based on my life!" she said in a determined voice. "What about Frank? What about his parents? He won't confront them with the truth because he's scared, and that's their son!"

"That was Frank's choice, and don't blame his parents for something they are unaware of," said Thomas in an angry voice. "If he speaks to his parents, and they shut the door on him and tell him he is no longer their son, then you can condemn them and I would agree with you a hundred percent, but don't pass judgment until all the facts are revealed." Thomas took a moment to calm down and spoke in a quieter tone. "Olivia, I love you so much, and I see so much love in you, and you have so much love to give. You know, I always imagined you with little Livy practicing ballet movements in our living room and me playing with little Tommy." He hesitated and spoke slowly. "Yes, I do want children, because there are a lot more good parents out there than there are bad ones, and there are so many children who live and have happy lives."

"What about your life?" she asked.

Thomas thought she was being unfair, but she was terribly upset. "You don't think I despised my parents or blamed them or was mad at them for leaving me and Kate alone? Well, I was for a long time," he confessed. "But looking back, I had a wonderful relationship with my grandmother, I have a great sister, and it made me who I am today." He tenderly held her hand. "Olivia, I also got to meet you."

"Thomas, you told me you didn't believe in fate," said Olivia.

"Olivia, I don't. I had the choice to be angry with my parents, be bitter all my life, and walk around with a big chip on my shoulder, or I could do something positive with my life. It wasn't my parents' decision to leave us, and I know that in my heart that before they died, Kate and I were the last thoughts they had on this Earth and that they would be worried for us."

"Thomas, I don't want to lose you because of the way I'm talking. I like children, I really do, and I like being around them. I just don't know if I'd be a good mother. I just don't know. I don't know what I want. Before I met you, I definitely didn't want to have children, but I don't want to say I do now because I don't know if I'm saying that because I'm scared of losing you."

Thomas held her closely and kissed the top of her head. "Olivia, I love you with all my heart, and I will always love you, and I can't wait to marry you on January 16. Let's just take it one step at a time. We've told each other how we feel, and I promise you, I will never pressure you into having children or hold that against you if you decide not to. You're confused, and I understand that, but the right answer will come to you one day. Maybe not today or tomorrow, but one day, and whatever that answer is, I'll respect and honor it."

"Thomas, will you stay with me no matter what I decide?"

"Of course, I will," he replied wiping the tears from her face. "Olivia, how long has this been on your mind?"

"I never gave it too much thought until last night when I saw how happy you were for Tracy and Robby, and hearing you talk about how much you loved kids and wanting your own. Then Rachel joined in and started talking about children and how she couldn't wait to have them. I sat there and said nothing, Kate noticed, and I think she could tell by my silence what I was thinking. Thomas, I don't want you to marry me under false pretenses?"

"Olivia, make me a promise?

"Okay," she replied.

"For the next three months, you will concentrate on us, your dancing, and planning our wedding, nothing else, promise me?"

"I promise," she said with a smile then put her head on his shoulder. "I was so worried."

"You shouldn't have been, we can get through anything," he said stroking her hair, "and I never want you to worry about talking to me."

"I'm not, that's another quality I love about you," she said glancing up at him." But I was scared you wouldn't want to marry me."

"Never think that," he said, then lightened up the conversation. "Oh, I see, you're trying to get out of it marrying me, are you? Well, it's not going to be that easy, missy!" he said tickling her.

She knew what he was doing. "Oh Thomas," she said giggling then kissing him.

"How about we take next weekend just to ourselves?"

"I would like that."

"Friday, I'll take you to The Duke, we can talk about the wedding, and decide on where we are going to have the ceremony and reception."

"Then on Saturday we can look for invitations and put together a list of who we are inviting and what we have to do," she said enthusiastically.

"Saturday night, we can go for a swim and watch some old movies."

"And I'll make lasagna."

"Then Sunday after Mass we can come here again for a walk."

"That sounds wonderful."

They kissed and sauntered back to the car, on the way, the same family on bicycles passed them, Olivia smiled at the two youngsters as they went by.

"Mommy, that pretty lady smiled at me again," said the youngest.

Chapter 38

Frank sat nervously in the back of the car. Thomas tried to make conversation with him, but he was getting little response. Twenty minutes later, they pulled into the driveway of a pretty two-story home in the suburbs.

"I'm going to tell them after dinner," said Frank ringing the doorbell.

"Frank, we're both here for you," said Olivia supportively.

The front door opened, and Frank's mother, Eileen, and sister, Stephanie, greeted them. Frank introduced them to Thomas as they entered. As he closed the door behind them, Frank's father was coming down the stairs.

"Olivia, how are you?" he said warmly.

"I'm fine John," she replied.

He shook Frank's hand. "Frank."

"Hi, Dad, this is my friend Thomas."

"Hello, Thomas."

"Hello," he replied shaking his hand.

"Come in and have a seat," said Eileen.

They followed her into the living room. Frank sat on one end of the sofa, Thomas on the other, and Olivia sat in the middle. John sat opposite them in his recliner, and Stephanie carried in a chair from the dining room for her mother, then sat on the floor. Eileen asked what they would like to drink then went to the kitchen.

"Thomas, are you a ballet dancer?" asked Stephanie.

Thomas grinned. "No, I'm not."

"What do you do?"

"I write."

"For a newspaper?"

"No, I write novels."

"That's amazing," she said impressed. "Are any published?"

"No, not yet. In fact, I just sent my first novel out to publishers," he replied, "and I'm just finishing my second."

"How exciting! I love reading," said Stephanie.

"His first novel is amazing," said Olivia, "and you'll cry at the end, guaranteed."

"Can I read it?" she asked. "It would be so incredible to read a potential best seller."

"Stephanie," said Frank disapprovingly. "Don't put him on the spot!"

"I don't mind," said Thomas. "Write down your address and I'll forward a copy."

"Make sure you don't make copies and pass them around," warned Frank.

"I won't, I promise."

"Here are the coffees," said Eileen putting the tray on the table. "I haven't added milk or sugar, so just help yourself." She sat down on the chair and looked at Thomas. "So, how do you know Frank and Olivia?"

"My grandmother used to teach Olivia when she was younger, and Olivia's current teacher, Penelope Daily, and my grandmother were old friends, so we were introduced. And I met Frank through Olivia, and we've gotten to know each other over these last few weeks and become good friends."

"Don't you think they make such a good couple?" she asked.

"Yes, they dance well together," replied Thomas avoiding her real question, and was surprised at how well he was answering without faulting, and by the look on Olivia's face, she was too. Frank on the other hand, just looked pale and extremely nervous.

"So Frank, you said you had something to tell us," queried Eileen.

"Well," said Frank anxiously then went quiet and just sat there.

"He wanted to ask you to come to my opening night a week Wednesday, it's my debut as a principal dancer, and he thought you may want to come and watch us," explained Olivia redirecting the conversation.

"Oh, that would be wonderful!" said Eileen.

"Me too?" asked Stephanie.

"Of course! John and Ted, also," offered Olivia. "After the show, we've booked a hall for a private party, and family, friends, fellow dancers, and special patrons, are invited to attend."

"Oh, it sounds delightful! Olivia, what should I wear?" asked Stephanie.

"I would suggest something elegant."

"Like?" she asked searching for suggestions.

"Something you would wear if you were going on a date to an expensive restaurant and wanted to make an impression," replied Olivia.

"I know just the dress," said Stephanie animatedly.

John sat there and said nothing.

The door opened and Ted walked in, he was six foot two and at least two hundred and thirty pounds, and his dad swiftly stood up and proudly introduced him to Thomas.

"How did your training go, son?" asked John.

"Good," replied Ted.

"He's going to be the MVP this year, Thomas, fifteen quarter back sacks, six fumble recoveries, and four interceptions, two for touchdowns," gloated John. "This year we should be hearing from all the top colleges."

"Dad," said Ted embarrassed.

"We've been waiting for you," said Eileen. "Please, let's all sit around the dining room table and I'll put dinner out."

As they sat, Stephanie told Ted about the opening night and reception.

"That sounds great Frank, I'm looking forward to it. Congratulations Olivia," said Ted.

"I thought you had practice Wednesday night?" asked John.

"I do, but I'll miss it,"

"If you miss practices, you'll be letting the team down," stated John.

"Dad, it's not as if I don't have a good reason," "he said glancing over at his older brother.

"You should really go to practice," pushed John.

"Ted, it's okay if you have practice, I understand. Your football is important," said Frank.

"You see Ted, even your brother understands," said John glaring at him.

The table went silent, and Stephanie broke it with a question to Olivia. "Maybe after dinner, we could go upstairs, and I could show you the dress?"

"I would like that," she replied.

They ate dinner and everyone spoke except John. Thomas suddenly realized he wasn't looking forward to the after-dinner conversation with him. The table was cleared, and coffees were to be served in the living room. Olivia went upstairs with Stephanie, and Ted spoke with Thomas and Frank. Eileen brought in the coffees, and called to the girls, who joined them moments later. Ted stood up to excuse himself.

"Ted, can you have a seat for a few minutes, I have an announcement to make and it's for the whole family?" asked Frank.

"Sure Frank. Is everything okay? You look a little pale," noted Ted.

"I'm fine," Frank replied but he wasn't.

"Frank don't be nervous, Stephanie and I already know," acknowledged Eileen.

"You do," said Frank confused.

"It's obvious, you and Olivia are engaged, she's wearing a ring," said Eileen.

Olivia stared down in horror at her finger; she had meant to take it off outside. Thomas looked on as well; he had forgotten to remind her.

"No, mother, it's not that," he faltered, "I'm not engaged to Olivia."

"Someone else is engaged to your girlfriend?" asked Stephanie.

"If you stop asking questions, I can explain," he said loudly and getting their attention. "Olivia and I are only friends; she was going along with being my girlfriend to help and protect me."

"Help and protect you from what?" asked Eileen.

"Mom, Dad, Stephanie, Ted," he said looking at each of them as he said their names. "I'm gay and have been for the last ten years."

The room was silent, and they all stared at Frank.

"Do you have a boyfriend?" asked Stephanie.

Frank let out a slight smile but before he could answer.

"Of course, he does, he's sitting right there," said John pointing at Thomas. "It's the faggot poet. He said they had been going out and had become good friends."

"Frank, you brought your boyfriend here into our house, to tell us?" asked Eileen.

"Mom, Thomas is not gay, he's engaged to Olivia," explained Frank.

"Oh, so now he's going out with her, that's convenient!" said John in a loud and sarcastic tone. "I want you two love birds out of my house, you too missy," said John standing, "and don't bother coming here again." He looked at his wife. "Eileen, I told you that ballet was going to turn him into a fruitcake."

Frank spoke up. "I'm sorry, I don't want to cause a problem but there are some things I would like you to hear, and all I'm asking for is ten minutes of your time. After I finish, I will leave, and you don't ever have to see me again. Please, I'm begging you!"

"I don't want to hear what you have to say," said John going into the kitchen.

The other three remained.

"I'm not here wanting you to condemn me, only to accept me," he said looking at his mother, "as your son," then at Ted and Stephanie, "and as your brother." They sat and listened intently as Frank talked for fifteen minutes about him and Olivia, Olivia and Thomas, and the media.

Eileen glanced at Thomas. "So, you're not gay?"

"No, I'm not," he replied.

"And you and Olivia are engaged?" asked Stephanie.

"Our wedding is January 16," replied Olivia.

"So Frank, these are your friends?" asked Ted.

"Yes, my good friends," he said proudly. "I told them what I needed to do, and was afraid to face you alone, they said they would come with me and offer their support."

"Thomas, if you're not gay, it must be weird being with him and his friends?" asked Ted.

"Ted, since we are all being honest, I'm not a hundred percent comfortable around gay men but that's because I'm heterosexual. A gay man probably feels the same way around a group of heterosexuals. But at the end of the day, to me, it all comes down to respecting and accepting one another. I would go out with his friends again because I enjoyed their company and they enjoyed mine, and to be truthfully, I don't even look at them as being gay only as my friends. And I know Frank wouldn't invite me to something he thought I might find offensive," said Thomas quickly glancing at Frank, hoping his response helped, and judging by his reaction it did.

Frank continued. "Ted, when you play college football, you will have gay men playing on your team. Are you going to look beyond that and evaluate them on their talents as a football player?"

"I don't know," replied Ted. "I hope I would."

"I'm not here to wave the rainbow flag, all I want is for my family to accept me for who I am, stand by me, and support me. And I want you all to see me for what I am in here," said Frank pointing to his heart. "I love you all, please, don't push me away." Frank stopped speaking and stood. "Thanks for listening," he said then glanced toward the kitchen. "Dad, I know you've been listening, all I've ever wanted was for you to be as proud of me as you are of Ted." He looked back at Ted and whispered, "sorry Ted."

Ted had a sad look on his face; he knew Frank was right.

"Ted," Frank said noticing his expression. "I'm very proud of you, and I never stop talking about my younger brother who's going to college on a football scholarship, and one day going to play in the NFL, and you know I'll be there for your finals." He turned to Stephanie. "Or my kind, gentle, loving sister, who will one day be the greatest veterinarian this city has ever known." He strolled over and crouched in front of his mother. "I would miss not seeing you walk in at lunch times with sandwiches for everyone," he said softly then kissed her on the cheek.

Olivia and Thomas followed Frank to the front door, went outside, and started down the driveway to the car. The front door opened, and they turned around.

"Frank, wait," said Stephanie followed by Eileen who closed the door behind her.

"Stephanie, Mom?" asked Frank.

Stephanie and Eileen quickly walked to Frank and hugged him. Frank started to cry.

Thomas continued with Olivia to the sidewalk. "Come on, let's go for a stroll and give them some time alone."

As they sauntered down the street, they could hear them tell Frank how much they loved him. Thomas held Olivia's hand as they slowly walked around the block. Thirty minutes later, they arrived at the driveway, and they were all laughing.

"I told them to go inside but they wanted to see you both," said Frank in good spirits.

"We just wanted to say goodbye," said Eileen.

They said their goodbyes, then Eileen grabbed Olivia and Thomas and pulled them in for a big squeeze. "Thank you for being there for my Frank," said before pulling away and turning to Frank. "I'll see you Tuesday for lunch."

"I'm looking forward to it."

Stephanie hugged and kissed Frank. "Maybe I can come down one night this week, and we can go for a drink with your friends, somewhere local."

"I would like that," replied Frank.

"I'll call you," she promised.

Eileen and Stephanie went back to the house arm in arm while Frank pulled Olivia and Thomas towards him and hugged them. "I love you two," he said kissing them on the top of their heads. "You can't believe what a weight this is off my shoulders, I wasn't expecting any of them to ever want to see me again, and now I have my mom and sister visiting me this week. All I can say is thank you."

They dropped Frank off at home, a different man, he had a wonderful smile on his face, and they laughed as he sang 'It's My Life' as they drove away.

The phone was ringing when they opened the door, and Olivia caught it in time. Thomas continued to his room, sat on the bed to take off his shoes, and looked at himself in the mirror.

Olivia ambled in. "Here you are?"

"Do I look gay?" he asked.

"I had to stop myself from laughing when he said that you were his boyfriend," she said giggling.

Thomas laughed with her. "I know it caught me completely off guard," he confessed looking at her. "You didn't answer my question?"

"No one looks gay," she replied, "but maybe I should find out for sure." Olivia strolled over to him, pushed him onto the bed, and straddled him. She then leaned down, kissed him, and caressed him. "Definitely not," she answered as she felt his rising response.

They kissed for a while and stopped when the doorbell rang.

"That's Kate," said Olivia rolling off. "She's the one who called before and wants us to sign the contract."

"Hello, Kate, come in," said Olivia holding the door.

"Hello," she said entering.

"Would you like a tea?"

"Please. Where's my brother?"

"In the bedroom,"

"Hey, lazy bones," she said going over to him and lying next to him on the bed. "What's up?"

Thomas chuckled and didn't answer.

"I had a lot of fun last night."

"It was a good time."

Kate quickly glanced toward the door, heard Olivia in the kitchen, then turned to Thomas. "There's something we need to talk about."

Thomas over exaggerated Kate's look toward the door and listening for Olivia.

She punched him in the arm. "Ha, ha, very funny!"

"Is it about Olivia's expression when I was talking about having children?"

"How did you know?" she asked.

"Olivia caught you last night staring at her when everyone, except her, was going on about having children."

"Was I that obvious?"

"I guess so," replied Thomas copying her look to the door and listening.

"Stop it you!" she said shaking her head. "She doesn't want children?"

"No."

"You said you would never marry anyone that didn't want children."

"I know I did."

"She must very special."

"She is," he said turning on his side. "What have you been up to?"

"I went to the house today and got a lot of my clothes. One, maybe two more trips, and I'll have it all over here. Are you going there tomorrow night?"

"Yes, we both are. Are you coming with us?"

"Not tomorrow, I can't," she replied. "I have three boxes on my bedroom floor; can you bring those back with you? Then I'll only have one more trip."

"No problem."

"By the way, I booked the van for Saturday at seven. I need to be at work by twelve. Is that okay?"

"That's fine."

"Should I bring the tea in here or are we having it out there?" asked Olivia standing in the doorway.

"Let's have it in the solarium," suggested Thomas.

They drank the tea and signed the copies of the contract.

"I'll have one of the senior lawyers quickly review it tomorrow, and if he says it's okay, I'll go ahead and register the company," explained Kate.

She quickly finished her tea and said she had to go upstairs to unpack some clothes and prepare for her first night in her new place.

"Did you get the sheets and duvet?" asked Olivia.

"I made it to the store thirty minutes before closing. Do you want to come up and have a look at them?"

"Of course, we do," she said standing with Thomas.

Chapter 39

"Okay, Thomas, you can ride Thunder, she's a timid horse and easy to control.

Thomas watched as Rachel, dressed in a tight-fitting long sleeve shirt, breeches, and riding boots, opened the stall and saddled Thunder. She went to the next stall and saddled up her horse. Thomas looked up and read its name out loud, "Lightning."

"That's her, she's my horse, and she's fast," acknowledged Rachel.

"You do remember I'm not very good," reminded Thomas.

"Don't worry. Thunder will take care of you. You just go at the pace you feel most comfortable," she explained. "We'll be following the trail through forests and open fields. If I gallop ahead of you through a field, you take your time, and I'll wait for you on the other side. Okay?"

"All right," said Thomas a little more at ease.

They pulled the horses out of the stable, mounted them, and walked to the grass. Then followed the trail through the trees till they came to the first open field, Lightening galloped out of sight and Thunder slowly trotted. When Rachel returned to join him, Thomas was only halfway across the field.

"Thomas, if you want to make her run faster, say trot or gallop in a soft, gentle voice, and at the same time move your hands forward and over her wither and squeeze your legs gently into her body. If you want her to slow down, just say whoa and she will go into a trot or walk," explained Rachel. "Don't worry she's not a fast horse."

Thomas did what she said, and the horse started to gallop. Before he got to the other side of the field, he said "whoa" and the horse slowed down into a trot, then a walk.

"That's it," said Rachel encouraging him. She led him through the trail in the dense woods and out into another field and galloped away. Thomas got thunder to gallop, and this time could see Rachel in the distance. They rode for an hour through woods and fields until they came to a clearing. Rachel dismounted, walked over to Thomas, and helped him off. She tied the horses to a tree then led Thomas by the hand down a steep incline. At the bottom, there was a folded blanket and a picnic basket. She let go of his hand, unfolded it, and laid it on the grass. Then sat and motioned for Thomas to join her. As he did, he looked down at the valley below and could see a small river running through it.

"This is the most peaceful place on Earth. I come here a lot on my own," she said staring down at the valley then glancing over at him. "You are the first person I've ever brought here. Isn't it amazing?'

"It is," he agreed.

"With the sun setting, it's even more beautiful."

When Thomas looked over at her, she had her eyes closed, and the sun was on her face, and he could see the freckles on her nose. Her blonde hair was blowing in the light breeze, and she was leaning back on her hands with her back arched, and her breasts were accentuated. "So, what really happened between you and Mathew?"

She opened her eyes and glanced at Thomas. "It's like I said at the club, I like him as a friend, nothing more, but he wanted more." She didn't want to tell him the truth and quickly changed the topic. "It's too bad Olivia and Kate couldn't come. You said Tracy was having dinner with Olivia?"

"Yeah, Tracy's leaving this weekend, and she wanted to see Olivia before she left. She's bringing over pictures and a video of her wedding, and the tour. Olivia's is going to make dinner, and Tracy is staying the night. Kate is working tonight, and she's been busy moving her stuff into the condo along with a hundred other things she has on the go and told me she was heading straight to bed when she gets home."

"She must be excited moving into her own place?"

"She is, and she loves it."

Rachel sat up. "Are you hungry?"

"I am."

She grabbed the picnic basket, brought it over, and opened it up. She gave him a sandwich, a coke, and opened up a bag of potato chips. "You're probably wondering, how I got these here?"

"It crossed my mind."

Rachel pointed past Thomas. "Behind those trees is a path that goes west, down to the valley below, and if you go in the other direction, east, it leads back to our house. I came out here before you arrived and dropped it off."

"Do you own all this land?"

"Yeah, just add another mile on the other side of the valley and think of it as a big rectangle. I've seen deer, foxes, rabbits, and eagles on the property."

"Wow, I wouldn't mind seeing those," he said surveying the land. "It's breathtaking."

"It is," she said taking a bite of her sandwich. "Have you made any wedding plans yet?"

"No, this weekend."

"January 16," she stated. "The engagement was so sudden, and the and wedding is so soon."

"I guess."

"Have you talked about children?"

"We have," he replied.

"When I get married, I want to be completely selfish and spend the first three years with my husband, then I want to have children."

"How many do you want?"

"I was thinking three or four."

"Really!"

"Why? What about you?"

"I guess three or four."

"What about Olivia?"

"She's not sure?"

"About how many?"

Thomas was uncomfortable with the conversation. So, he answered, "Yes," and thought zero is a number.

"I can't wait to have children and take them pony riding, swimming, to school, and having their birthday parties." She hesitated and let out a nervous giggle. "All I have to do is get the right man."

"Don't you mean find the right man?"

She smiled at him. "Thomas, I've already found him, I just haven't had enough courage to walk up to him and tell him. Unfortunately, I may have missed my opportunity."

"Do I know him?"

"I believe you've met him?"

"Was he at your party?"

"He was."

"He was?" asked Thomas and wondered who it could be.

Rachel interrupted his train of thought. "No more hints, and I'm not going to tell you who he is anyway. I am allowed to have some secrets you know, but I will tell you he's a lot like you."

"Then you have good taste," he said taking another bite of his sandwich. "I must admit, you do make the best sandwiches."

"Thank you," she said. "Wait till you taste my dessert."

Thomas ate another sandwich, then watched the sunset with her. "You said this is your special place."

"One of them, but it's my favorite," she revealed. "In the summer, I can sunbathe here in private, and in the fall, I can ride out here and watch the sunset and look up at the stars."

"What about the winter?"

"For the winter I have another place."

"Do I get to see that?"

"Maybe I'll show you in the winter," she replied.

"Is this the place you were going to bring me to that Sunday afternoon after your party?"

"It is."

"I can't believe this is the first time we've been able to go riding since then."

"I know, so much has happened," she said as the sun slowly sank out of sight. "Did you want to head back to the house?"

"I thought we were going to watch the stars?"

"Really? Do you want to?"

"Do you?"

"I do," she said getting up. "Let me clean up, so we can lie down, and see who spots the first one."

"What about your dessert?"

"That's at the guesthouse; we can have that when we get back."

As they lay on the blanket, Thomas tried his best to locate the first star while Rachel looked deep into her heart for answers on how to get him back.

Chapter 40

"Thomas, not one of your better rounds," said Jack as they stood by the bar and picked up their drinks. "Did you let me win?"

"No, Jack, I'm a little preoccupied."

"Why don't we sit in our usual spot and watch the people screw up on eighteen," said Jack leading him to the table. "Is there anything I can help you with?"

"I don't think so."

"Do you want me to listen? I'm good at that," he replied sipping his Crown Royal.

"I'd appreciate that," said Thomas collecting his thoughts. "It's very easy to summarize but difficult to resolve."

"Okay, shoot."

"Olivia doesn't want to have children and I do. When she told me, I said I loved her, and would marry her no matter what she decided. I trust my instincts, and they tell myself as time passes, she will change her mind."

"You're worried that she may never change her mind?"

"Right now, that's a great possibility."

"Why do you say that?"

"Her friend Tracy is pregnant, and Kate and Rachel have both said they want to have children. None of them thought twice about it and they all said they want more than one. Olivia seems so detached from it all."

"Would you have gotten engaged to her if she had told you this beforehand?"

"Yes, I love her more than anything."

"Do you want to be with her forever?"

"I do."

"Well, forever is enough time for someone to change their mind," said Jack. "The question is, are you willing to wait that long for the woman you love?"

"I am"

"Then I think you're on the right track," he said encouragingly. "Just trust your instincts on this one, and let nature sort this one out, it's out of your hands."

Thomas agreed with a nod. "Thanks, Jack."

Jack thought briefly. "I always wanted children, and looking back, I probably could have done some things differently. Not that I have regrets, I'm happy with what I've done with my life, but sometimes I think about what it would have been like. As you already know, Penny and I wished we had children together."

"Jack, you're never too old to have children," commented Thomas.

He stared at him doubtfully.

"I meant adopt."

"Adopt?"

"Jack, there are so many children living in foster homes and orphanages, here, in this country, and in low-income and least developed countries around the world; you and Penny could give them a better life."

"I've never thought about it like that," he said studying Thomas. "This may sound crazy, but you're the closest I have to a son. I know I haven't known you that long, that's why it's sounds crazy. I guess it's because you're everything I ever wanted in a son. Your parents would be immensely proud of you."

"Thanks, Jack," replied Thomas. "You know there was no one else I would have talked to about this except you."

Chapter 41

"How do I look?" asked Olivia strolling into the living room.

"You look absolutely stunning," replied Thomas.

"So do you," she said putting her arm around him. "The only problem, is that I don't know what jacket to wear, most of mine are a bit too dressy."

"One second," said Thomas leaving and coming back with a box. "This is for you."

"What's this?"

"I've had it under my bed for a couple of weeks and was waiting for the right opportunity to give it you."

Olivia opened the box and pulled out a black leather biker's jacket, "You got this for me? Oh, Thomas, it's beautiful!" She put it on and went to the mirror in the hallway. "I love it, and it fits perfect." She ran back, put her arms around him, and kissed him. "I love it."

"I'm glad you like it," he said holding her. "Frank's friend Miguel makes leather jackets and made it especially for you. He said that it's one of a kind, and there's no two the same, just like you."

"You are so sweet," she said happily. "I've been in his store, and he has beautiful clothes, especially his jackets and dresses, and I've been meaning to buy one from him. This is incredibly special, thank you."

"You look great in it," complimented Thomas as they headed for the front door.

When they arrived, they sat in a secluded booth at The Duke. Thomas ordered himself a Carlsberg, and Olivia a white wine, then they both ordered fish and chips.

"You seem to know a lot of people here," stated Olivia.

"Yeah, well I used to come here a lot."

"Not so much anymore?" she asked.

"I didn't come at all when my grandmother took ill, and I've been here a few times since her funeral. I tried to stay home with Kate and keep her company, unfortunately, I didn't realize I was driving her crazy. She finally told me to go out, or she was going to either throw me out or move out."

Olivia chuckled then casually looked around. "I like it here, it has a nice atmosphere, and the people are friendly. I also like all the pictures of John Wayne."

"The guy that owns this place, is a John Wayne fanatic, that's why he called it The Duke." Thomas couldn't resist. "He also makes the best fish and chips in the city."

Olivia snickered at his attempt. "We will have to see about that!" she challenged.

"How was dinner with Tracy?"

"Great. The video of them getting married by Elvis is fantastic. He sings to them, and they joined in; they had a lot of fun. We will have to do that one year for our anniversary."

"Without a doubt. I'd love to sing with the King and do my hip-swiveling and leg-shaking moves, then end it with the infamous fist-pumping, karate-stance move."

"I can totally see you doing that," she said giggling. "They'd probably hire you!"

"Yeah," he said leaning back and taking it all in.

"I never got a chance to ask. How's Rachel doing?"

"She's doing well and wanted to know if you would like to go shopping with her for clothes for Aruba."

"Did she say when?"

"She said she would call you."

"I heard they booked Jack's plane and a beautiful hotel on Palm Beach," revealed Olivia, "and everyone is going: Rachel, Jessica, Veronica, Buddy, Kate, Frank, Jack and Penny."

"I can't wait. You, the beach, the waves, and the sunsets."

"Me either," said Olivia, "I'll have to buy some new sexy bikinis and dresses."

"Any excuse to shop!"

"Thomas, you're catching on," she said sipping her wine. "When I was spending time together with Tracy, and don't get me wrong I like her, she's great company and we had a ton of fun, but I kind of wished you were there. It's a different type of fun when you're around and I missed you. I know, we need to have some time on our own, and with different people, but I still missed you. I was wondering if you felt the same?"

"Olivia, we spend enough time apart during the day, I don't think we need to spend more time away at night. At Rachel's, I kept turning around to ask you what you thought or to say something that you would find funny, and I realized you weren't there to answer. It was like a part of me was missing. I love having you with me, and I had wanted to say something to you, but I didn't want you to feel as if I was crowding you."

"I want you to," she said reaching for his hand. "I would like to go shopping with Rachel, but I know it won't be as much fun as going with you. Well, maybe I shouldn't say it quite like that, that's a little unfair to her, it's just different kind of fun. I guess what I'm saying is that I would like to go shopping with you first, and buy some things together, as a couple. Then go with Rachel and buy some surprise bikinis and dresses."

"I understand, we'll go first, and you can help me pick out some clothes."

"I would love that, and I love you," she said leaning over and kissing him. "Tomorrow, we'll go shopping for invitations then clothes for Aruba."

They started to kiss again until a polite clearing of the throat from the waitress got their attention. She dropped off their food, and they quietly ate.

Olivia put her knife and fork on her empty plate. "Okay, can we talk about the wedding?"

"Hold on, first things first," said Thomas leaning forward. "What did you think about The Duke's fish and chips?"

"I thought they were equivalent to the Hidden Cove pub, and therefore, I conclude, they are both as good as the others. So, a tie."

"In that case, I have the winning vote, and I pick The Duke."

"No, that's unfair, wait, I want to vote for the Hidden Cove."

"Sorry, too late!"

Olivia gave him a frown and a playful pout, then leaned over close to him and whispered, "if you change your vote, I'll let you undress me and take your time putting on my nightshirt, if you know what I mean."

Thomas looked away and yawned as if he was bored.

"In fact, why do I even need to put on a nightshirt."

He gave her a somewhat uninterested glance.

"I'll even let you take advantage of me," she purred licking her lips.

"Okay, okay, you can change it."

"Too late! You had your chance, and you blew it, buddy!"

"Buddy, really?" queried Thomas. "Actually, pal! I think you blew it!"

"What do you mean I blew it, buddy?" she said emphasizing the word buddy and giggling.

Thomas gave her an impish grin. "Tonight, I was going to pick you up, lay you on your bed, and start by kissing your ear," he whispered tenderly touching it. "Then your cheek," he said seductively moving his finger down to her cheek. "Then your lips," he said softly placing his finger on them, after she provocatively kissed it, he moved it to her neck. "As I'm kissing you here, I would undo the top button of your blouse, and then proceed to kiss and unbutton my way down to your navel. I would stop, open up your shirt and undo your bra, then lick and suck on your hard nipples as you moan lightly. I would continue licking and sucking as I slowly move my hand down your jeans to your knee, and then lightly run it up the inside of your leg, stopping between your thighs and caressing gently as you let out a moan. I would undo your jeans teasingly, then slide my hand down underneath your panties, and rub softly as you moan louder. As I insert my finger deep inside you, you let out a light scream, and move your pelvis in rhythm with my finger, slowly at first, then faster and faster. I suddenly stop, and as I start kissing my way to your navel, I remove your jeans and underwear. I continue past your pelvis, down your legs, to your feet. As you open your legs invitingly, I would place my tongue on the inside of your ankle and lick my way up past your calf to your thighs. You would respond by spreading your legs widely, then patiently wait, wanting me to lick your..." Thomas got the waitress's attention. "Another round please," he said then innocently glanced at Olivia. "What's up, pal?"

"That was...cruel...mean...unfair!" she said sitting up and crossing her arms.

"Well, it gives you something to think about till our wedding night."

"But you never finished," she sighed dejectedly.

"To be continued," he said mischievously, "on our wedding night."

"Thomas, I'll get you for this, you wait and see."

"Promises, promises," he replied as the waitress put down their drinks. "Now, about our wedding?"

Olivia took a deep breath, got the image of Thomas between her legs out of her mind, then thought about his question as she sipped her wine. "I'm back and forth, one part of me thinks we should have it here and book the cathedral and the restaurant. Another part of me says, go to a beautiful island and get married outdoors with the sea, sun, and sand. I don't know, what do you think?"

"I like them both," replied Thomas unsure, "it's whatever you want."

"I like them, too, but we need to decide tonight and get the invitations out next week," she said anxiously.

"Why don't we talk about getting married on an island first?" suggested Thomas. "Which ones did you like?"

"I still like Antigua, Anguilla, St. Lucia, and Virgin Gorda; they all have beautiful resorts on them. We could fly to one for a long weekend, similar to what we are doing with Aruba," she stopped and repeated, "similar to Aruba. Thomas, if we go to one of these islands, we're going to have everyone there all the time."

"Not necessarily, guests will fly out on the Sunday or Monday, and we will have the week to ourselves."

"True, but we're also going to Aruba, and that's so close to our wedding," she said realizing it wouldn't feel as special. "If we have our wedding and reception here, we can stay in a beautiful suite at an airport hotel, then fly out on Sunday to an exotic island for our honeymoon. That would be so romantic. In fact, the more I think about it, the more I like this idea best. What do you think?"

"I agree," replied Thomas with a smile. "Tomorrow, why don't we get some brochures and magazines, then check on the internet to find out what suites the resorts offer and pick the one we like best and book it."

"Perfect," she said happily. "I love you."

"I love you."

"Thomas, I like this one best," said Olivia holding up the white invitation with the pink highlights. "It has the rings, the cross, and the flowers. It's gorgeous."

"Once I have all the details, I can have them ready within twenty-four hours," indicated the salesman.

"That would be great," said Olivia.

The salesman took down their personal information, and Olivia told him she would call him Monday with the location of the wedding and reception.

"Tomorrow we can talk to the priest and confirm the date," she said as they walked out the store. "We still need to go to the restaurant and book that."

"We can do that after we finish shopping," suggested Thomas.

"I'm so excited," she replied.

They went into a travel agent, picked up brochures, and then into a bookstore, and bought some travel magazines and books.

"There are so many thoughts going through my mind: dresses, tuxedos, flowers, limousines. We're making that list tonight, right?"

"Yes, we are," confirmed Thomas.

They stopped at Bikini Village, Olivia picked out several and tried each of them on for Thomas.

"I like them all," he replied.

"I'm taking a total of four, so I need you to pick two today, and when I go with Rachel, I'll pick the other two."

"This isn't easy, I like all four," said Thomas studying them. "The dark blue one, and the floral."

She bent down. "If you're a good boy, I might give you a private showing later on," she whispered then licked his earlobe. Olivia then tried on three dresses and bought them all.

On the way home, they stopped in La Petite Maison and booked the restaurant, then dropped off the bags at the condominium, and went for a swim.

"I'm glad we got the invitations and booked the restaurant this afternoon," said Olivia excitedly, "and it didn't take us long to move Kate this morning,"

"No, it didn't. It was kind of sad leaving the house, but I'm glad Penny bought it, at least we can go by once in a while," said Thomas looking on as Olivia prepared the lasagna then put it in the oven.

"While it cooks, let's make our wedding guest list," she said leading him to the living room, getting a pen and paper, and writing down the names. "Twenty-six," she confirmed.

"What about a maid of honor?"

"I'm going to ask Penny and have Kate and Rachel as bridesmaids. What about a best man?"

"I was thinking about Jack and having Frank as an usher."

"I think they would both like that" she said cheerfully. "This all sounds so nice."

"When should we ask them?"

"Let's wait till we have all the particulars finalized, then we can ask them, and send off the invitations," suggested Olivia.

"That's a great idea."

After dinner, they looked through the holiday brochures, the travel magazines, and books, then went online. They agreed on the resort and the suite, and booked it, then their flights.

"Hermitage Bay in Antigua, the clear turquoise water and white sand, it's so romantic," sighed Olivia staring at the pictures. "I'm so glad we chose the Hillside Pool Suite, look at it, nestled in lush, tropical gardens with a panoramic view of the Caribbean Sea and beach. And we have our very own private plunge pool, that has a deck with loungers, a double day bed, and an outdoor shower. I can imagine us lying out there listening to the waves during the day, and at night stargazing, then going inside to make love on our four-poster bed. It's perfect, and when we are there, I'll be Mrs. Olivia Carlyle," she said glancing over at Thomas. "I wish it were tomorrow."

"It will be here soon," he said watching her throw the magazine on the table then place her head on his chest. "Are you nervous about Wednesday?" he asked putting his arm around her.

"No, I've been practicing for this day all my life, and I was ready months ago," she said confidently. "Are you are coming to my dress rehearsal on Tuesday?"

"I am."

"You know I also dance on Friday evening," she said apprehensively.

"You do?" asked Thomas trying to act surprised.

"It's okay, you don't have to come," she said understandingly.

"Good, because I have something important to do," he replied picking up a magazine.

"You do? What?" she asked.

"I'll show you," he said putting down the magazine, going to his room, and coming back with an envelope. "Here," he said sitting down.

"What's this?" she asked taking it from him, taking out its contents, and screaming with joy. "You bought tickets to all my performances!"

"I wouldn't miss one for the world," he replied.

"But I'm in the Nutcracker five times!" she cried.

"And I have tickets for all five," he reconfirmed with a grin, "and all front row seats."

"Oh, Thomas, I love you for this," she sighed cuddling into him.

After Mass, they went into the rectory, spoke the priest, and booked their wedding date. Then drove to the park, went for a walk, before stopping at their favorite bench.

Olivia took her wedding checklist out of her handbag. "We've booked the church and the reception, and I'll call the store tomorrow morning with the information for the invitations. We need to reserve some rooms at the hotel across the street from the restaurant, and a couple of limousines…We have to ask Penny, Kate, Rachel, Jack, and Frank, to be in our bridal party, we'll do that Wednesday after the ballet at the private party. Dresses, tuxedos, and flowers we still have to do, but that can wait till after we get back, as well as picking the meal, wine, and champagne for the reception. And finally, we need to decide on the music and the wedding cake," she said glancing up at Thomas. "I'm so excited."

"I can tell," he said pulling her close.

After she put her list away, the same family passed by on their bicycles. "Hello, pretty lady," said the youngest grinning and waving.

"Hello," replied Olivia smiling and waving back, then watched them peddle away.

Chapter 42

Thomas sat in the front row, to his left was Henry who had arrived from New York City only an hour earlier, and to his right was Kate. Next to Kate was Rachel, Jessica, and Jack, and next to Henry was Eileen, Stephanie, Ted, and John's empty seat.

"Did she look nervous?" asked Kate.

"No, she looked very comfortable," replied Thomas, who had stopped by earlier to see how she was doing. "I think I'm more nervous."

"She will be wonderful," said Henry confidently.

The lights dimmed, the conductor appeared, and the music started, then the curtain slowly rose, and the ballet began. Olivia danced like an angel, and her routines were graceful and flawless; it was like being in a dream. Thomas smiled as he watched her move effortlessly across the floor, and after a couple of minutes his nerves settled, and he enjoyed the performance. At the end of the first act, the audience applauded loudly.

"Thomas she is dancing on air," said Kate standing.

"She dances with so much passion and energy, and her routine has been perfect," added Jessica then turned to Eileen. "Frank lifts and carries her without any strain whatsoever, and they complement each other magnificently."

"They dance divinely, and I'm so proud of both of them," said Eileen.

They went out to the lounge, and Jack and Rachel came back with a tray of glasses filled with champagne. They all took a glass, and Ted moved next to Thomas.

"I wanted to thank you for standing up for Frank and being there for him, and also to let you know, I went with Stephanie to see him last Wednesday, and I'm glad I did. You know he's coming to my championship game Sunday, and I was hoping you and Olivia may want to come by and watch, but I understand if you are busy."

"What time?"

"It's a two o'clock kick off."

"We'll be there, Ted, thanks for asking."

He looked at his glass nervously. "There was something Frank said at the house that stuck in my mind, about my father always gloating about me, and ignoring him. To be honest with you, I used to love all that attention, and look at Frank and think, I have something he would never have, my father's respect. When I think about it now, I'm so ashamed of my father, and more so of myself for thinking that way. Frank has always been there for me and never let me down. Did you know he's never missed any of my games?"

"No, I didn't."

"This is the first time I've watched him dance," confessed Ted. "I'm not one for ballet, but I should have been there for him. Even when he used to come over and visit, we always talked about me and football, never about him and his dancing. I know he always brags about me to everyone, but I never talk about him to anyone, I was too embarrassed to say that my brother was a ballet dancer." He glanced over at Thomas. "My father never wants to see Frank again. I tried talking to him, but he doesn't want to listen to me." He looked down sadly at his glass. "What do you think?"

"Unfortunately, Ted, everything that can be said to your father has been. Maybe your father just needs time to come to terms with it, and it could be a couple of weeks, months, or years, or it may never come at all."

"Do you think it will be never?"

"No, I think your father will come around one day soon. You just need to be patient and let him figure it out on his own. The worst thing you can do is to push him into a corner. But Ted, don't be so hard on yourself, Frank will be overjoyed when he finds out you're here."

"I know," he said feeling better,

"Thomas," interrupted Stephanie.

"Thanks, I'll see you later," said Ted leaving to talk with his mother.

"I wanted to tell you I finished reading your novel," she said patiently waiting for him to ask.

"Okay, Stephanie," said Thomas, "I'll take the bait. What did you think?"

"I loved it! I cried and cried and cried," she said animatedly. "Have you heard back from any publishers yet?"

"Not yet, hopefully before Christmas."

"Trust me, you will,"

"Thanks."

She looked at him awkwardly. "Can I…?"

"Can you read my next novel?"

She shyly nodded yes.

"I'll send you a copy once it's ready to be mailed out," he replied. "Probably be in a few weeks."

"I look forward to it," she replied.

The bell rang to remind the patrons that the intermission was ending in five minutes, Stephanie excused herself, and went to the restroom.

"And to think I used to have you all to myself."

"Hello, Rachel, come here," he said grabbing her hand and pulling her towards him. "You look amazing, and that dress really brings out your eyes."

"You always know the right things to say," she said blushing. "When will I get a man like you?"

"I thought you had one in mind."

Rachel just smiled and sipped her champagne.

"I'm looking forward to Aruba."

"Me too, it's going to be great."

"Hi, Thomas," said Jessica joining them. "Rachel, I'll meet you back at the seats, I'm heading back with Jack and Henry."

"Okay, I'll be along in a minute." She watched her mother leave then turned to Thomas. "I know the itinerary for my shoot, maybe next intermission I can tell you about it?"

"I'd like that," he said enthusiastically.

They finished their champagne, and she put her arm through Thomas's as they sauntered back to their seats. In the second act, Olivia danced magnificently, and the crowd clapped appreciatively as the curtain fell.

"Thomas, I have never been so proud in all my life," said Henry accompanying him to the lounge before turning to him. "I'll be leaving around lunch time tomorrow, and was hoping you and Olivia would join me for breakfast and let me know about your wedding plans, say around nine o'clock."

"Of course," he replied.

"I'm hoping you will both come and visit me soon, perhaps in December?"

"I would like that and I'm sure Olivia would too, maybe tomorrow we can come up with a date," suggested Thomas. "Will we be seeing you over Christmas?"

"I'm surprising Olivia tomorrow," he said quietly and putting his finger on his lips. "I booked my tickets for the twenty-third till the twenty-seventh."

"Henry, she will be thrilled."

"I can't wait to tell her," he said grinning. "Oh, please excuse me, I would like to buy the next round of drinks and see Jack heading to the bar."

Thomas was talking to Eileen and Kate when Henry and Jack returned with the tray of drinks.

"Thomas, would you like to step outside and get some fresh air?" asked Rachel.

"That's a good idea," said Thomas escorting her out to the patio.

"Being outside reminds me of the first night we met. Do you remember the hotel's gazebo in the garden?"

"I do, I said I liked your freckles, and you got all embarrassed."

"I know," she said staring out in the distance and thinking hard about something.

"Is everything all right?"

"Uh-huh," she lied and faced him.

"Tell me about Aruba?"

"We're all flying out on Wednesday at one thirty and we'll get there around dinner time, and we fly back Sunday evening and arrive at around eleven. The photoshoots will take place on Thursday and Friday, so I'll have quite a bit of free time to spend with you and the others."

"What happens during the shoots?"

"Well, on Thursday, they're going to be taking pictures around the hotel pool, on Palm Beach, and some sunset shots on. Friday, they want some more on the beach with the sunrise and in the water."

"They keep you busy?"

"It's a lot of work," she admitted, "the worst part is the waiting around, you know, for the sun to come from behind the clouds or for a rain shower to pass. Then there's hair, make-up, and the heat, but it's a lot of fun."

"And you love it?"

"I do," replied Rachel, her eyes lighting up, then she hesitated and spoke quietly as if she didn't want anyone else to hear her. "I was hoping you would come and watch, you don't have to, but you can if you want?"

"Is it okay?"

"Yes, of course, it's okay. The hotel will set up a refreshment tent, put loungers and umbrellas inside a roped off perimeter, and you can watch from there. I'm going to ask the others as well, but I really want you to be there."

"I'd love to go, I think that would be great to watch you, and I'm interested to see what goes on behind the scenes."

"They'll take over a hundred pictures, but they're only choosing five, that's one for each bikini," explained Rachel. "The team that they have going are excellent, and I've worked with each of them on a few different shoots, and they're very professional."

Thomas tried to imagine what it would be like having three or four people fussing over you.

"It's not easy having someone matching your hair and makeup with a bathing suit, and a photographer hurrying you up before the sun goes behind the clouds."

"I was just thinking about that," said Thomas. "It sounds exciting and I'm looking forward to it." As he sipped his champagne, he studied her, and felt like there was something else on her mind. "Rachel, are you sure you're okay?"

"Thomas," she said staring into his eyes, thought about it, then changed her mind. "I'm fine, really, we should go back with the others."

He wasn't convinced as he took her arm and strolled back inside with her. After joining them, he excused himself, and walked in the direction of the restroom. On the way, he thought he recognized someone in the distance, he followed them and waited to see if they would turn around. As the person stood at the back of the theater, waiting for the last act to start, they looked around and over in his direction. Thomas realized he was right, left, and went to the restroom then back to his seat.

The curtain fell to end the ballet. The audience was on their feet, and the applause was deafening. There were shouts of 'Bravo!' from all around the theater, and the curtain rose and fell eight times. Each time Olivia glanced over at Thomas and smiled. After the eighth, Olivia and Frank appeared from behind the curtain. Olivia looked over at Thomas and blew him a kiss, then Henry, Eileen, Jack, and Jessica went to the right side of the stage and threw her bouquets of roses. Frank picked them up and passed them to her. Thomas was right behind them and was about to throw his roses and a small pink ballerina teddy bear onto the stage when Olivia whispered to Frank who signaled him to the side. Frank escorted Olivia, who then handed Frank the flowers, and met Thomas at the stairs. She put her arms around him and kissed him on the cheek. She was crying.

"I love you," she whispered, "and tonight was for you."

"I love you," he said giving her the flowers and the teddy bear.

She took a rose out, kissed its petals, and handed it back to him.

The servers walked around with trays of champagne and hors d'oeuvres. Suddenly, there was a commotion at the doorway, and the low applause increased in volume and cries of 'Bravo!' as the hundred guests realized Olivia had arrived with Frank, Alfie, and Penny. They slowly made their way through the crowd to an area where a microphone had been set up. The crowd stood around the quartet, while Thomas was with the rest of the group at the back of the room and could barely see her face. Olivia was desperately looking around for him.

"Ladies and gentlemen, please," said Alfie signaling with his hands for to them to be quiet. "Thank you. Can I please have a server bring up four glasses of champagne?" He waited for him to arrive, hand them out, and leave. "This evening, you've witnessed one of our youngest and brightest stars to ever adorn our stage tonight. Her grace, elegance, style, and techniques can only be compared to that of the late, great, and sensational Margaret Carlyle. And I think you will all agree with me, that tonight, she kept her audience captive from start to finish."

The crowd cheered and clapped.

Alfie waited patiently till they stopped. "Never have I heard eight curtain calls at that theater before, and I believe if we had not turned on the lights, we may have been there all night."

The crowd laughed.

"Please, let me hear your loud applause once more for a ballerina who is destined for greatness, and to one of the future stars, not only of the First National Ballet, but the world, Ms. Olivia Taylor."

Alfie turned and motioned her to the microphone. The applause continued for ten minutes. Eventually, Alfie had to come back up and ask them to stop.

"Ladies, gentlemen, friends, and family, thank you for being a part of this very special evening. There are several people I would like to thank so please bear with me." Olivia paused and composed herself. "I would like to thank my first teacher and mentor Mrs. Margaret Carlyle, not only were her technique and style second to none, but also her patience, passion, and devotion. She was without fault, and is sadly missed, and I know she was looking down on me tonight. I would like to thank my second teacher and mentor, and my very dear friend, Ms. Penelope Daily. She showed me how to take everything I had learned and become the complete dancer I am today." She turned to her, and gave her a kiss and a hug, then came back to the microphone. "The third person I would like to thank is our artistic director, Alfie Smythe, whose vision, focus, and interpretation is second-to-none," she turned to him and kissed him on the cheek. "The fourth person is my dance partner, Frank Gray, whose strength, technique, and timing, make my routine seem effortless, and he is an accomplished dancer whom I respect dearly. His knowledge and experience have made my rehearsing and performing a joy, I could not ask for a better partner. I am also extremely fortunate to be able to call him my friend," she said grabbing his hand tenderly then kissing him on the cheek before facing the audience. "I would like to thank all of you tonight, and for supporting me over the years, and I applaud you," said Olivia clapping her hands. "There are two additional people I would like to thank. The first is my father, Henry, who took me to the Nutcracker when I was very young, and it was then and there that I fell in love with ballet. And upon my request, enrolled me in ballet classes, and then the First National Ballet School. I thank him for his love, kindness, and ongoing support. Where is my father?" she asked looking for him. Henry made his way up to the front. Olivia kissed him and hugged him tightly. "The last person I would like to thank is an incredibly special man in my life. Outside of ballet, he has shown me how to trust, believe, care, and most importantly, love. He has helped me grow into the person you see standing before you, and mature emotionally as a ballerina. Those of you who know whom I am talking about, have been touched by him one way or another, and know the kind of person he is. To me, he is my best friend, my life, my world, my love, and my soulmate, and my fiancée. He is the type of man who will stand in the back and give me the spotlight, and allow you, my friends, this time with me. But I now ask him to come up here and share this incredibly special moment with me. Thomas, please, come join me," said Olivia searching the room.

Thomas was close to tears.

"Olivia, he's over here," shouted Jack pointing.

The crowd turned as Thomas started walking toward Olivia, who strolled quickly toward him, and met him in the middle.

"I love you," she whispered.

"I love you," he replied softly.

She kissed him tenderly on the lips and hugged him tightly. She then let go, grabbed his hand, and led him back to the microphone. The crowd watched in silence.

"Ladies and gentlemen, friends and family, I would like to thank you all once again., and I will try my best, to come by and meet each of you before the end of the evening, thank you." The crowd applauded, and Thomas tried to let go of her hand, but she held on tightly. When he took one step back, Olivia stood back next to him. Alfie came to the microphone and asked the guests to enjoy themselves then signaled to the trio in the corner to start playing. The crowd quickly broke into smaller groups and talked amongst themselves.

Olivia was radiant. "Why didn't you come backstage after the show? I was waiting for you."

"I don't belong back there."

"We'll see about that," she said playfully making a serious face.

"You look beautiful, and you danced angelically."

"You are too kind, sir," she jested with a curtesy.

"Thanks for what you said, you almost had me in tears."

"I meant every word," she said squeezing his hand and smiling.

"I know you did."

"Well, when you win your literary awards, you can praise me."

"I'm not so sure about that," he teased.

"Why you?" she said lightheartedly poking him in the stomach.

"There's a lot of people waiting to see you, so give me a kiss, and I'll see you later," he said. "You know I'll be the last one here."

"I know you will," she said kissing him. "I love you more than dancing, in fact, more than anything else in this world."

Chapter 43

"Olivia, I have a surprise," said Henry after the waitress poured their coffees and left.

"What?" she asked leaning forward curiously.

"I've booked a trip to come here on December twenty-third to the twenty-seventh."

"You have!" cried Olivia. "I thought you said you couldn't get the time off."

"I moved some things around and made the time," he replied.

"Dad, that's fantastic, you've made me extremely happy," said Olivia squeezing his hand. "It means so much to me having you here for Christmas."

"I know, and it means a lot to me, too," he replied. "Tell me, how are the wedding plans coming along?"

"Good," she replied merrily. "As you know, last night we asked Penny, Kate, Rachel, Jack, and Frank, to be in our bridal party, and they all said yes. So, I'm going with Kate, Rachel, and Penny to pick out my wedding dress, the maid of honor dress, and bridesmaids dresses a week Sunday." She then went through her memorized list. "We've booked the church, the restaurant, the limousines, the disc jockey, and reserved hotel rooms. We've picked out the wedding cake, the invitations have been mailed, and we still have to pick out the meal, wine, and champagne for the reception, and the flowers, which we are doing next week."

"Seems like you have everything under control."

"We do," she said glancing at Thomas. "Did I miss anything?"

"No, but I was I was thinking that on the twenty-fourth or the twenty-seventh we could get fitted for the tuxedos" suggested Thomas. "I thought it would look smart if you, Jack, Frank, and I, all had on the same style and color. If that's okay?"

"Not a problem, whatever you want, just let me know which day," he said looking at them both. "You're still letting me pay for all this?"

"Yes," replied Olivia, "and we have an itemized list and have been putting down the costs next to each item. After the dresses, restaurant, and flowers, we'll have an approximate figure."

"Thomas, are you still okay with me paying?"

"Henry, I think it's very decent of you to do this for Olivia. Hopefully, I will be able to do it for Kate one day. I know my father would have wanted it that way."

"I'm glad," said Henry smiling, "I would hate to be looked upon as someone who was interfering."

"Dad, you're not," said Olivia reassuringly.

"You must make me one promise then, that is, that you spare no expense when it comes to making your wedding plans. I would be terribly upset if they are not serving the best wine and champagne."

"I promise," said Olivia.

Henry put his hand into his pocket and pulled out two hand-size gift-wrapped boxes. "This one is for you Olivia and this if for you Thomas."

"What are these?" she Olivia.

"An engagement present," he replied.

Olivia and Thomas opened their gifts and looked at matching gold watches.

"Just reminders to make sure that you always have time for one another," he said then pointed. "If you look at the back, I had them inscribed."

Olivia read hers out loud, "Time is Love" and underneath it had their wedding date. "Dad, these are beautiful."

"They are," agreed Thomas.

"Try them on for me?" he asked watching them. "They look good on you. Now, Olivia, I have something else for." He went into one of his bags and pulled out a small shoebox.

Olivia opened it. "These are my first pair of ballet slippers; you kept them all this time."

"I have all of them," he smiled. "I left the other ones on your bed."

"So that's why you had to go into my room," she said giving him a playful look. "You've been hanging around this one too long," she suggested motioning her thumb at Thomas.

"I thought you might want to keep them for sentimental reasons, maybe show your children, or have a daughter who might want to wear them. Most of them look brand new," he explained. "I also have all your old costumes, and I thought you could take them back with you next time you come to visit."

"These are great," she said admiring them, "and I can't believe you kept all my ballet stuff, I can't wait to see the rest. Thomas and I talked last night about New York City, and we were thinking about the first weekend in December, Friday to Sunday. Is that okay?"

"I'll book the tickets," he said happily. "I also have Super 8mm films and camcorder tapes of Olivia, and copied them onto DVDs, and I've been waiting for an excuse to watch them again."

"Oh, I can't wait to see those!" she said eagerly.

"Me too," said Thomas.

"Dad, maybe I should watch them first and edit them," she joked lightly pushing Thomas then noticing her dad searching through his bag.

"Before I forget, this is for you, Thomas, and Kate," he said handing her an envelope.

Olivia opened it and pulled out an engagement card. "It says, 'Love, Happiness, and Health' on the front page," she said then showed them. She removed a folded piece of paper, then continued to read the card. "To Olivia and Thomas, Congratulations on your engagement, all our love the New Baptist Church of Harlem Choir." Olivia passed the card to Thomas then unfolded the note and read it:

"Dear Thomas, Olivia, and Kate,
The children are putting on a Christmas Show on Sunday, December 6. They will be reenacting the Nativity, as well as singing Christmas hymns and songs. There will be food and beverages after the show and a visit from Santa Claus. If you could be here, it would make the children's day, please say you will. If not, we understand. Thank you, Ms. Brown."

"The Opera House has purchased gifts for the children, which Santa will give out, and they know about me, and Rufus are attending, but are unaware additional opera singers which will be joining us."

"Oh, they will be so surprised," said Olivia turning to Thomas. "We should stop off at the store, pick up a card, and write a note letting let them know we will be happy to attend."

"You will be making their Christmas," said Henry.

Chapter 44

Thomas and Olivia stood with Frank on the sidelines. At half time, Eileen and Stephanie came from the other side to say hello, then went back for the second half to sit with John who refused to come over. They watched Ted's team win the championship, and Ted was presented with the game's MVP trophy for leading the team to victory with five sacks, one fumble recovery, and one interception for a touchdown. After the presentation, Ted came over and invited Frank back to the bar for the celebration party, which he accepted. He thanked Thomas and Olivia for coming and extended the invitation to them.

"Thanks, Ted, but I promised Kate we would go to her new place for dinner tonight," replied Thomas.

"Thanks for the invite," said Olivia.

"I understand," he replied staring over at his dad. "I wish he would snap out of this, it's not right him ignoring you, Frank."

"I think he's going to be like this for the rest of his life," stated Frank. "We might as well get used to it."

"I'm starting to believe that myself, he can be as stubborn as a mule, and I don't think any amount of time is going to change his mind."

"I wouldn't say that," said Thomas.

"You wouldn't?" asked Frank.

"I wasn't going to say anything but maybe I should."

"Say what?" asked Frank and Ted.

Olivia looked on.

"Last Wednesday, at the ballet, I saw your father standing at the back of the theater."

"That's impossible," stated Ted. "He said he was going over to his friends to play poker."

"I was going to the restroom after the second intermission, I thought I recognized him, but he was quite a distance away. So, I followed him and saw him standing at the back of the theater. He looked in my direction, and I don't think he saw me, but it was definitely him."

Frank and Ted quickly glanced at each other.

"I guess he doesn't want anyone to know, and the reason I'm telling you two, is so you don't fly off the handle and say something you might regret later. Besides, if you tell him that someone saw him, what would he say?"

"That he wasn't him, he wasn't there," replied Frank.

"Maybe we should give him some more time," suggested Ted.

"We should," said Frank nodding his head.

Chapter 45

"How's the manuscript?" asked Olivia standing in the doorway.

"I'll be finished tomorrow," he replied, "and you can read it then."

"Do you still have to do more?"

"No, I'm finished. How was shopping?"

"Come into the kitchen, I made some coffee, and I'll tell you," she said as he followed her. "Well, I've picked out my wedding dress, the maid of honor dress, and bridesmaids dresses."

"Tell me about your wedding dress?"

"Nice try, Thomas, you will have to wait till the wedding day."

"Anything else?" he asked.

"Actually, yes, I picked up a couple more bikinis, another dress, and a few other odds and ends for Aruba. They're all very sexy but you will have to wait till we're there to see them," she teased.

"All right," said Thomas playfully frowning.

She tenderly kissed his forehead.

"Did you have a good time shopping?"

"I had a lot of fun, especially with Rachel, she was joking and laughing all the time, and was really enjoying herself," she said sitting down. "You know, Kate and Penny tell me loads of personal things, but not Rachel she keeps those things to herself."

"She has a lot going on."

"I know," she said sipping her coffee. "When are you going shopping? I thought you wanted to get a few more things."

"I was thinking about going tomorrow. Do you want to come with me?"

"Oh, you just reminded me of something that I found odd. Penny and Jack are leaving for Aruba tomorrow. Penny said her and Jack wanted some time alone before everyone got there."

"What's wrong with that?"

"Two things: first, Penny and Jack would have wanted to travel with all of us, that's the type of people they are; second, Penny has asked me to teach her classes Monday and Tuesday, and she has never left last minute like that, ever, she always plans everything well in advance especially her classes."

"Really!" said Thomas, "I guess that is strange. What classes are you teaching?"

"Children between the ages of six and eleven; one class for each age group, and I have two private lessons. I've never instructed children, so at first, I said no. Then Penny showed me the outline and what I needed to do and said she didn't feel comfortable asking anyone else on such short notice, and if I didn't do it, she would have to cancel and leave Wednesday."

"What is she doing for Wednesday, Thursday, and Friday?" asked Thomas.

"She has someone to fill in, apparently she asked this person a while ago, but they're unavailable Monday and Tuesday," replied Olivia. "The more I think about it, the more I don't mind, and I'm actually looking forward to it. Why don't you come by and watch? Actually, come tomorrow, and then we can go shopping after."

Chapter 46

Thomas looked through the viewing room window and watched Olivia instruct the seven-year-old girls. She was on the bar, and showing the five positions, as eight sets of eager eyes watched on attentively.

"Good morning," he said sitting down.

"Morning," replied the two mothers.

"Okay, girls, why don't you find a place at the bar," said Olivia making sure they were at a safe distance behind one another before walking to the end and facing them. "Here we go. Watch me now. Position one and two and three and four and five, don't forget to extend your free hand. That's it. Good. Keep on going on your own." Olivia walked up and down the line helping them with their posture and positioning. Fifteen minutes later a buzzer signaled the final two minutes of the lesson. "Girls in a straight line behind me and let's float around the room like butterflies." She took the line of girls around the floor several times, weaving back and forth, then suddenly stopped, and turned, as they then ran into her open arms screaming and hugging her.

"The girl with the red hair is mine. Which little girl is your one?" asked one of the women.

Thomas glanced over at her and realized she was asking him. "Oh, none, I'm Olivia's fiancée," he replied.

"She's very good with the children, they all took to her straight away, and I think it's because she makes the lessons a fun, learning experience."

"She loves being around children," said Thomas.

"Let her know I'll be putting in a good word with Penny," she said, "and they should have her back."

"Maybe you could tell her," suggested Thomas.

"You're right, I will."

The door opened and two of the girls ran to their mothers. Two fathers, and four other mothers showed up, and left with their daughters. Olivia noticed Thomas through the doorway and called him over.

"When did you get here?" asked Olivia.

"Fifteen minutes ago," he replied.

"I'm glad you came early. I have the eight-year-olds next. Do you want a juice?"

"I wouldn't mind one," he replied taking off his coat and placing it on a bench.

"They're in the refrigerator, follow me," she said. "I only have a couple of minutes before the next class."

"Ms. Taylor."

Olivia turned around to look at the lady with the young girl with red hair.

"You go over, I'll meet you in the kitchen," said Thomas. He grabbed two juice boxes, placed them on the table, and watched as Olivia listened to the lady. She glanced at Thomas briefly then turned back to face the woman. They said goodbye and Olivia came into the kitchen.

"What did she say?"

Olivia smiled. "She thought that I was excellent with the children, and I should consider instructing them more often."

"That was nice of her," said Thomas. "You seem to be enjoying it."

"I really am, it reminds me of when I was young."

"You look very sexy in your leotard and tights."

"I do, do I? Well maybe I should wear these around the condo more often if it turns you on," she said impishly and taking a drink of her juice. "Don't read too much into this, but I love it, the children have so much energy and excitement. They want to learn and have fun. They're like little sponges. Do you know what they call me?"

Thomas shook his head.

"Ms. Olivia! Isn't that adorable," she said animatedly. "I have to get back out there and meet the children as they're getting dropped off."

Thomas went to the viewing room and sat alone as he watched the eight-year-olds. The six-year-olds were next, and a mother with a four-month-old in a baby seat sat down next to him.

"I hope she sleeps through this," she said. "She's not due for another feed till about twelve-thirty."

"She's beautiful. What's her name?"

"Victoria, we call her Vicky."

"What about your other daughter?"

"Her name is Christine, and we call her Chrissie. She's the one with the dark hair and ponytail. I also have a boy three and a half, he's with his grandmother."

"Busy," stated Thomas.

"Busy, but enjoyable, I wouldn't trade it in for the world. Do you have a little girl out there?" she asked.

"Actually, I do. The tallest one in the black leotard with her brown hair in a ponytail."

"Which one?" she asked noticing the tallest girl had black hair in a bun.

"The teacher is my fiancée," said Thomas.

"Oh, I see," she said with a chuckle, "and you came out to watch her, how thoughtful."

They talked about children as they watched Olivia teach the class. Ten minutes before the end, the baby woke and started to fuss. The lady, whose name was Joyce, started to worry about her crying disrupting the class, so Thomas helped her to the kitchen where she closed the door.

After the class, Olivia took Chrissie to her mom, and Thomas followed them. As Olivia was getting her a juice, Thomas turned to ask Joyce something and suddenly realized she was breastfeeding the baby under the blanket.

"I'm so sorry," said Thomas, "I'll come back in a few minutes."

"Don't get all embarrassed. She's just fallen asleep. Turn around for a minute and I'll sort myself out," she said and waited till he did. "Here Olivia, take hold of Vicky for me while I do this up…almost done…done. Thomas, I'm decent, you can turn back around."

When he did, Joyce was sitting in the chair, and Olivia was standing holding the baby. "I guess Penelope never told you that she lets me feed in the kitchen at lunch time?" asked Joyce.

Olivia shook her head.

"Usually, Penny comes in and has a talk with me while I feed, she's a lovely lady."

"She is," replied Olivia.

"You both know her?" asked Joyce.

"We do," she replied.

"You don't mind holding little Vicky for a while? My arm is a little sore," revealed Joyce. "Chrissie, bring that seat around for Olivia to sit on."

Olivia sat down and looked at the baby while Thomas made a cup of coffee for Joyce. He passed it to her and sat down.

"I almost lost her," said Joyce motioning to Chrissie who was busy reading a book. "The umbilical cord was caught around her neck while I was delivering. The doctor said a few more minutes and she may not have made it. Look at her now."

"How many are you planning for?" queried Olivia.

"Six."

"Did you come from a big family?" asked Thomas.

"Actually, the opposite, I had no sisters and brothers. I always wish I had at least one, you know, someone to play with at night when you were called into the house before dark, or watch movies with, or talk to. I never liked being alone and I said that the man I marry better be prepared to have a big family. I met Phil and we are halfway there. I look back now, and I can't remember a life without the children. I mean at your age, I was the same, you want to spend some time together and experience each other." The baby started to cry. "She's got some wind. Here let me help you out." Joyce put a cloth over Olivia's shoulder and helped her put the baby over it. "Now just pat and rub her back gently. A slight rocking motion sometimes helps."

Thomas watched Olivia who glanced over him as the baby cried louder.

"Keep on patting," instructed Joyce.

The baby let out a big burp and a little bit of milk came up and onto the cloth. Olivia continued to pat and rock the baby till she fell back asleep, then moved her, and cradled her in her lap.

"It's as easy as that," said Joyce. "You're a natural."

Olivia looked at Thomas and smiled proudly.

Chapter 47

Olivia and Kate sat next to a window, opposite each other, and Thomas sat next to Olivia in the aisle seat. The next row over was Frank and Stephanie, and opposite them, Rachel and Jessica, and sitting behind them was Veronica and Buddy. Thomas remembered the comfortable plush seats and stretched out his legs as the plane taxied then took off into the cool November afternoon. Once in the air, they had full meal service, drinks, and music.

Three hours into the flight, they flew towards the Antillas Mayores, Olivia, Thomas, and Kate, could see small islands to the west with white sandy beaches and palm trees, most looked uninhabited, but the bigger ones had roads, houses, and hotels, and the larger ones had cities. Kate told them they were all part of The Bahamas, and before reaching the blue Caribbean Sea, she pointed out the Turks and Caicos Islands, Haiti, and Dominic Republic.

An hour later, the captain came over the intercom. "Ladies and Gentlemen, we will be landing in Aruba in approximately twenty minutes. I have asked for permission to circle the island before our approach and will let you know once I receive the okay. In the meantime, please finish all drinks and food, and make sure your seat belt is buckled. Several minutes later, the flight attendant came around, cleaned off the tables and checked seat belts, then cleaned up the cabin and took her seat.

Five minutes later the captain came over the intercom. "Ladies and Gentlemen, due to low air traffic in the area, we have had the tower's approval to circle the island," he confirmed. "We will be flying to the northwestern tip of Aruba passing over Palm Beach and Eagle Beach, which are considered to be in the top ten most beautiful beaches in the world. We will then continue southeast, and follow Aruba's eastern coastline, which is known for its ruggedness and large waves. We will then come around the most southern tip of the island and pass over San Nicolas before heading out to the Caribbean Sea and turning to make our final approach. When we come in for our landing, you will notice the city of Oranjestad to the northeast, and Surfside Beach to our left. Enjoy the sights."

Thomas and Olivia held hands, gazed out the window, and took in the aerial tour; it was paradise. As the plane made its approach, Olivia turned to Thomas and smiled. "It's our first trip together, and we're going to have so much fun, I can't wait," she said excitedly, then whispered in his ear. "And just think, on our next flight to the Caribbean, we will be on our own, and I will be Mrs. Olivia Carlyle."

After the plane landed, they picked up their luggage, and went through customs. While walking through the airport, Stephanie noticed two men holding up signs reading 'Rachel's Party' and they followed them to the minibuses waiting outside. The drivers separated the group into the two air-conditioned vehicles then loaded their bags. As they drove, the men pointed out the local sights before pulling up to the front of the resort. The groups disembarked, went into the lobby, and immediately noticed in its center, an island with palm trees, chirping exotic birds, a pond, and a waterfall. As Jessica and Rachel headed to the reception desk the rest of the group went over to see the birds.

"This is something," said Kate sauntering around the island.

"It's lovely," added Stephanie joining her with Olivia and Thomas in tow.

"So, girls, what are we going to do first?" asked Thomas.

"Pool!" they answered immediately.

"You guys can register now," explained Rachel coming from behind. "The receptionist just needs to check your ID's, then she'll have you sign in, and give you your room keys. This will give you signing privileges throughout the hotel and casino."

After they did, they were taken up to the tenth floor by the hotel staff. The suites for Olivia, Thomas, Kate, and Rachel were to the right of the elevator, and the rest of the group, to the left. The attendants took each of them to their rooms, opened their doors, and proceeded to show them around.

"We only have suites on the tenth floor, and with the exception of our penthouse suite, these are the best the hotel has to offer," he stated leading the way. "In here, you will find your bedroom with a king-sized bed, a walk-in closet, a television with satellite channels, an en suite with a large oval tub and spacious shower, and through here a balcony with chairs and a table," he said opening the doors. "At night, you will find the trade winds will keep you cool, and the sounds of the waves relaxing." He closed them and they left the room. "This is the main living area, as you can see it has several sofas, recliners, an entertainment system, and there are French doors opening to another balcony that is much larger and has loungers, chairs, and table. Over here, is your wet bar and refrigerator, which is fully stocked with our finest beer, liquor, wine, and champagne. The room has fresh flowers throughout, and the fruit will be replaced as needed," he said motioning to a fruit-filled bowl on the dining room table. "If you require anything to make your stay more pleasant, please do not hesitate to call the front desk. Welcome to Aruba and enjoy your stay."

Thomas pulled out his wallet to give him a tip.

"Sorry, sir, but all gratuities have been covered already by Mrs. Carter, thank you," he said before departing.

The phone rang, Thomas walked over, and answered it. "Hello," he said listening. "Okay, come to my room as soon as you are ready." He listened again. "All right, I'll see you then, love you, bye." He hung up the phone, went into the bedroom, and as he was changing into his bathing suit there was a knock on the door. That was fast, he thought. He finished getting ready and answered it.

"I'm right across the hall," acknowledged Rachel wearing a yellow bikini, and a wrap that covered her waist and thighs.

"Wow!" said Thomas. "You look great."

"Thank you," she said entering. "Aren't these gorgeous?"

"They are," he replied following her.

"Have you seen the view?"

"Not yet," he answered.

"Come on, I'll show you," she said grabbing his hand, crossing the living room, and opening the balcony doors.

They went outside, looked out at the blue water and sandy white beaches, then down at the large pool surrounded by lush palm trees and loungers. They could see people lying on them and hear children laughing and playing in the water. There was a knock on the door and Thomas left to open it.

"For you sir," said a hotel employee handing him an envelope then watched him go across the hall.

"Rachel Carter?" asked Thomas.

"Yes, sir," he replied.

"She's in here on the balcony. Would you like me to get her?"

"That won't be necessary, if you could hand this to her, I would appreciate it. Thank you."

"Have you read the note yet?" asked Olivia coming towards him wearing a bright yellow and light blue floral bikini, and a matching wrap, it was short and revealed her long shapely legs.

"No, I've just got it," he replied admiring her. "You look good enough to eat."

"I'll take that as a compliment," she said happily.

"Then I'll be more direct," he said placing his hands on her waist. "You look beautiful and sexy."

"That's more like it," she said putting her arms around him.

They kissed, then joined Rachel on the balcony.

"Here you go," said Thomas handing her the envelope.

"What's this?" she asked looking at them "Did you get one?"

"I read mine back in my suite," replied Olivia.

"I just got mine," said Thomas opening his. "Dinner at the penthouse suite tonight at eight. Any ideas?"

"It must be Jack and Penny hosting a welcome party," suggested Olivia.

"That sounds like Jack all right," said Rachel.

They went down to the lobby and out to the pool area. It had waterfalls and several swim-up bars. They walked around till Olivia spotted Kate, Jessica, and Stephanie, and headed in their direction.

"We've just got our drinks," said Jessica, "I'm drinking a pina colada, Kate's drinking a banana daiquiri, and Stephanie's drinking a strawberry margarita. We've been trying each other's, and they're all delicious. What are you three going to have?"

"I want one of those drinks that comes in a coconut," said Rachel.

"Me too," said Olivia.

"Make it three," confirmed Thomas going into the shade and sitting in a chair next to Jessica. Olivia lay next to him on a chaise lounge, and Rachel, the next one over. They each took off their wraps, revealing high cut bikini bottoms. As they put suntan lotion over the front of their bodies, Thomas noticed the men gawking at them as they went by. "Kate, you're not sunbathing?"

"Tomorrow," she replied. "Stephanie and I want to go swimming."

"Frank's already in the pool."

"Where?" he asked.

Stephanie pointed him out and they both waved.

"Buddy and Veronica did go in with him, but they've ended up at the swim-up bar," said Jessica.

The waiter brought their coconut rum cocktails and placed them on the table.

"Okay," said Thomas. "I'm going to pass this around tell me what you think, Jessica first."

She took a couple of sips. "Um, that's good."

Kate sipped. "Wow, strong."

"It's good and strong," said Stephanie passing it back to him then getting up and going to the pool with Kate.

Thomas took a long sip. "Perfect."

Jessica and Thomas had a couple of drinks, and talked as they watched Kate, Stephanie, and Frank swimming, then decided to join them.

"Olivia, Rachel, are you coming in?" asked Thomas.

"In a few," replied Olivia, "the sun will be setting in a little while, and I want to take full advantage of the sunshine."

"Me too," agreed Rachel.

"I guess it's just you and me," said Thomas to Jessica.

Olivia and Rachel discreetly watched him remove his shirt and stroll to the pool. Olivia loved his broad shoulders, muscular build, and tight butt.

"What are you two up to?" asked Jessica.

"We're checking out the sights," replied Kate tactfully.

"What she's really saying, Jessica, is that they're checking out the guys around the pool," clarified Thomas.

"And there are lots of them," confirmed Kate. "We figure this corner is the best place. See those four over there? Well-tanned, well-built, and cute."

"Yes, I do," said Jessica glancing over.

Thomas quietly went behind Kate, lifted up her arm, and yelled in a girlish voice, "Over here!" Then let go of her hand, went underwater, and swam away out of sight. What the four men witnessed was Kate waving over to them and saying, "Over here!"

He resurfaced at the pool bar, ordered a drink, then sat and talked with Buddy, Veronica, and Frank for a while. After he finished, he swam around the bar, and out of the corner of his eye he saw a figure frantically waving to him, it was Jack calling him over.

"Hello, Thomas, get out of the pool and come with me for a minute."

"Hi, to you, too, Jack," he said lifting himself out of the water and onto the deck.

"Quick, follow me," he said, and as he walked by a pool assistant grabbed a couple of towels from her and threw them to Thomas, then led him to the poolside bar and sat in the shade out of sight.

"Two."

"Sure, Jack," said the bartender.

"What's up?"

"What do you mean?"

"Well, you look nervous," stated Thomas, "and you brought me to the most secluded area of the bar. Which tells me, either you don't want us to be seen talking together or you don't want to be seen?"

"Easy Sherlock Holmes, I'm nervous," confided Jack, hesitating. "I brought you over here so I could talk to you in private, if I went out there and called you to one side, they would think I was up to something."

"Are you?" asked Thomas slyly.

"Of course, I am," he said grinning. "I've been trying to wave you down for the last ten minutes and looked like a bird flapping its wings. Everyone must think I'm mad."

"Jack, with that red and yellow Hawaiian shirt, that straw hat, those sandals and dress socks, I don't think anyone thinks it."

"Okay, okay, enough with the jokes, I haven't been myself lately, and I need your help?"

"Sure Jack," said Thomas in a more sincere tone.

"Did everyone make it?"

"Everyone," he repeated.

"Good," he said pulling out a small bag with something inside it. "I need you to hold on to this for me and bring it tonight. It's a small gift for Penny and I don't want her to find it."

"Not a problem."

"You have to promise me that you won't look at it or let anyone know you have it. If Jessica sees you with it, she'll hound you till you open it."

"Don't worry about it, Jack, no one will see it," he said staring at him. "I've never seen you this unsettled before."

"I know, I know, I have a special night planned for Penny tonight and I want to make sure everything goes right."

"I understand," said Thomas nodding his head. "There's just one problem, where am I supposed to hide this?"

Jack glanced down at his surfer shorts and laughed as the bartender dropped off the drinks.

"I have to drink this quickly and get back or Penny will get suspicious."

Thomas looked at the two glasses. "Whiskey, Jack? We're in Aruba."

"What did you expect me to order?" he asked with a puzzled look.

"True," he replied.

As they drank, Jack thought about how Thomas was going to conceal the gift. "Come with me?" he asked. "Actually no, you wait here while I go inside, you can't go in without a T-shirt and shoes. Order two more drinks and I'll be back in a minute."

Thomas ordered two whiskies and was halfway done by the time Jack returned.

"Here you go, put this on, and put the gift in the pocket. They won't notice it if you leave the shirt unbuttoned."

Thomas stared at the bright yellow Hawaiian shirt with green pineapples. "Jack, you have to be kidding?"

"What?"

"They had nothing more stylish."

"This is style, and it cost me eighty dollars, so put it on," he said picking up his drink and downing it. "I have to go."

"What am I supposed to say when I go back wearing this?"

"You'll think of something, Sherlock," he said patting him on the back and leaving.

Thomas sauntered back sporting his new shirt believing it couldn't get any worse, but he was wrong, everyone was there and laughed.

"Where have you been? And what are you wearing? Did you go shopping?" asked Olivia going toward him.

Thomas looked at them. "Nobody ask, it's a long story, I'll tell you all later."

"I can't wait to hear this one," said Kate.

"I like it, I think it suits you!" said Jessica then turned to the group. "Did you hear what he did to Kate in the pool?"

"What happened?" asked those who didn't.

Jessica told them and they all chuckled.

"I was so embarrassed, I'm going to get you for this," said Kate forewarning him. "So, be on your best guard."

"Well, I'll be wearing this shirt so don't get me confused with another tourist."

"Oh, I won't!" replied Kate.

"Want to go for that swim?" asked Olivia.

"Let me have a drink first."

"I ordered one for you a few minutes ago, it's by your chair," she said reaching over and passing it to him. "I'll wait for you."

Rachel stood up. "I'm going in. Who's coming?"

Everyone left except Olivia and Thomas.

"What's going on? I went in the water five minutes later looking for you, and even walked around the pool. Where have you been? I was worried."

Thomas pulled out the gift. "Put this in your beach bag."

"What's that?" she asked.

Thomas told her about Jack.

"Did you look at it?"

"I promised him I wouldn't," he said taking off his Hawaiian shirt and having some of his drink. "Let's go for that swim."

They swam together in the water, kissing once in a while. Olivia put her arms around his shoulders and wrapped her legs around his waist. "I love this, and I love you," she said beaming.

Thomas put on a pair of cotton pants, a white shirt, and was about to leave, when he noticed a door by the dining room table. He opened it, and behind it there was another that was locked. He thought momentarily, left, and tapped on Olivia's door. She opened it in a sky-blue spandex dress that stopped above the knee and clung to her shapely body, her hair was in a French braid, and she was wearing velvet pink lipstick.

"You look incredible!"

"Thank you," she replied pulling him in and kissing him. "Give me a minute, I need to get my shoes and bag."

She headed towards the bedroom while Thomas strolled over to the side door, opened it, and looked into his suite. With his foot, he pushed down on the doorstop, then went and sat down on the sofa.

Olivia came out of the room holding her handbag and with a white cotton cardigan draped over her arm. "You know there is only one problem with these suites, the front doors, at the condo we have no locked doors between us."

"I was thinking the same thing," replied Thomas. "How about I knock down the wall?"

"Very funny," she said giggling. "If you can get me access to your suite, and vice a versa, I will give you..."

"Give me what?"

"Whatever you want."

"Anything?" he asked.

"Anything! I promise."

Thomas walked her over to the adjoining room doors.

"This is awesome," she said excitedly then realized he had tricked her. "You knew all along, that's unfair, the bet's off," she said pushing him.

"A bet is a bet, I'll let you know."

"Oh, you will, will you," she said curiously.

They walked to the elevators, and a staff member was standing next to one that he had been reserved and informed them he was waiting for two more people. Minutes later, Kate and Stephanie arrived, and they all got in. The doors closed, he put in the elevator card, and pressed the penthouse button. On the way up, he informed them that there was only one penthouse suite and that it took up the floor and had its own swimming pool and patio. As they exited, Jack and Penny greeted them and showed them into the living room. A bartender made cocktails and two waitresses served hot hors d'oeuvres.

"Did you bring the gift?" whispered Jack.

"I did," replied Thomas.

"Do me a favor and hold onto it till I need it."

"Sure thing, Jack."

They talked for a while, then were invited into the dining room for a five-course meal accompanied with white and red wine, champagne, liqueurs, and coffee. After they finished, they were led onto the large patio by the swimming pool. The bartender opened bottles of champagne, poured them into flutes, and the waitresses passed them around.

Jack spoke. "I want you to know that this is an incredibly special evening for Penny and me, and I am glad you are all here to share it with us. As you all know, Penny and I have known each other for many years, but what most of you may not know, is that we have been in a relationship for the last several." Jack stopped, asked Thomas for the bag, then pulled out a small burgundy box, opened it, and went down on one knee and held her hand. "Make me the happiest man in the world and say you will marry me this Saturday?"

Penny looked down at him with a delighted smile then placed her free hand over her mouth and in a quivering voice said, "I will," and cried. Jack placed the ring on her finger. "My mother's ring. Oh, Jack!" she said as tears of joy rolled down her face.

"My only regret," said Jack standing," is that I didn't ask you sooner."

They kissed and everyone clapped.

"I would like you to raise your glasses and join me in a toast to Penny and Jack," said Jessica. "To Penny and Jack."

"To Penny and Jack," everyone repeated then drank.

"Penny needs to finalize a few arrangements with the wedding coordinator tomorrow morning," said Jack. "So, the wedding plans will be made available tomorrow night."

Penny pulled Jack close and whispered in his ear. Jack nodded in agreement.

"Thomas and Olivia, can you please join us up here?" asked Jack, and waited for them to stand in between him and Penny. "Go ahead, Penny."

"Olivia, would you please be my maid of honor?" she asked.

"It would be my pleasure," answered Olivia embracing her.

"Thomas," said Jack, "will you be my best man?"

"Yes, Jack, I'm flattered," he said shaking his hand.

Everyone gathered around and congratulated the happy couple.

Chapter 48

The following morning Thomas woke up early, went into Olivia's room, and lay next to her. He then put his arm around her, kissed the back of her head, and waited for her to respond "Olivia," he sang, "Olivia."

She turned around and smiled. "Hold me."

He put his arms around her, and she put her head on his chest. "Are you coming down to watch Rachel?"

"What time is it?"

"Six."

"Six! We only got to bed at two," she said reminding him.

"If you want to sleep for a little longer, I can come back later and get you?"

"No, I'll come with you."

They got dressed, went down to the lobby, and picked up two coffees.

"That was a surprise last night."

"It was," replied Olivia. "Penny told me that last week she said to him she wanted to get married."

"They've been so careful about their relationship. Did she say why?"

"She loves him, and I think it was when he surprised her with the house and…" Olivia's voice faded.

"And?" asked Thomas.

"Jack, asked her about adopting children."

"Really? Why not? I think they should."

"Which is what she thought, too, but she wanted to get married first," she said moving closer to Thomas.

"Good for them."

They went out to the pool and strolled around it to the canvas tent. Rachel noticed them and waved them over.

"Good morning," she said cheerfully. She was sitting in a chair, with her blonde hair curled, and wearing one of the hotel's robes.

"Morning," they replied groggily.

"They're just finishing my makeup, and then they'll be taking pictures of me around the pool and by the waterfalls. I had them set up some chairs over there in the shade for you so you can watch," she said motioning to them.

"You're full of life this morning," said Olivia.

"That's because you two didn't see me leave at ten last night, and in bed by ten thirty, and it will be the same tonight. But tomorrow and Saturday, party, party, party!" she said elatedly. "You two look pretty beat. You can go back to bed if you like?"

"No," said Olivia. "We'll be fine once we get these coffees down us."

"There's lots of food in the refreshment tent, help yourself."

The makeup lady came back with another shade of lipstick.

"We'll let you get ready," said Thomas, "good luck." He was going to kiss her on the cheek but caught the makeup woman's displeased look and opted for her hand.

"Thomas, Olivia," said Rachel. "Thanks for being here."

They sat in the shade and for four hours watched Rachel posing in front of the camera. The photographer took photos of her around the pool area, using the pool, palm trees, and the beach as background. She posed standing, lying on her side, on her back, and on her stomach. They had her go in the water and stand on the ladder then lie on the pool steps. Then took pictures of her standing in front of the waterfalls, sitting on the rocks by the waterfall, and underneath the waterfall. She changed four times into different bikinis and for each change they applied a different shade of make-up and hairstyle but followed the exact same sequence of shots for each bikini.

The shooting stopped at eleven, and they had brunch with her inside the tent. They started shooting again at two at the north end of the beach. This time they shot her on the sand, standing and sitting on rocks, walking into the water, and walking out. They finished at six and were reconvening at eight for the sunset pictures and had dinner on the beach. Throughout the day Olivia and Thomas had slipped away several times to cool off in the pool and the sea, but the majority of time was spent watching her. Most of the others, with the exception of Jessica, spent their time at the pool and periodically came over to watch her. At eight, everyone showed up, and observed her posing for her final pictures. The majority of the shots were of her walking on the beach with the sun setting and waves crashing in the background. At nine, they wrapped up.

Penny and Jack told them about the wedding plans, then departed with Jessica for the lounge, and shortly after, Kate, Frank, Stephanie, Veronica, and Buddy left to go to a nightclub. Rachel, Thomas, and Olivia refused their invites and told them they were going to have a stroll along the beach and then have an early night.

"I didn't realize modeling swimsuits was so much work, I was exhausted just watching you," declared Olivia.

"It can be repetitive at times," admitted Rachel. "But I love it!"

"You have a lot of patience," praised Olivia.

"I couldn't have all those people fussing over me, and then all those people watching me," said Thomas.

"You get used to it," acknowledged Rachel. "I can't believe you guys stuck around all day, that was so sweet, and it means a lot to me, thank you."

"And we'll be there tomorrow," confirmed Olivia.

"The good news is, it's only for a few hours tomorrow morning, and I'll be finished by nine. They want to take some pictures on the east coast with the sun rising. They have a minibus picking us up at six, so you two can come with us or take a taxi, its only fifteen minutes away."

They walked down the beach and talked about how beautiful Aruba was, about the wedding, and some of the activities that they wanted to do before they left, then headed back to the hotel. When they got to their floor, Rachel went into her suite, and Olivia followed Thomas into his.

"I could do with a bath."

"Go and get undressed, put on your robe, and get a nightgown, and I'll run a bubble bath for you. After, can we sit on the balcony, listen to the waves, and the sounds of the island."

"That sounds wonderful!" she cooed. "Can we order some room service?"

"Of course," he said holding her. "What would you like?"

"Surprise me," she said cuddling into him. "You always take care of me."

Thomas ran the bath, ordered the food, then went outside and gazed over the balcony at the beach below. He listened to the waves lapping, the hum of people talking, and the distant beat of the nightclub.

After her bath, Olivia came out onto the balcony wearing a short silk nightgown, and walked up behind him, put her arms around him, and rested her head on his back. Thomas could feel her hard nipples pressing up against him as her soft hands caressed his chest.

"I am so in love with you," she said squeezing him, "and I'm so glad you're in my life."

"And I will be for as long as I live," he promised.

"Thomas, I will only ever love you," she whispered. "You are my soulmate."

"And you are mine," he said turning around and lifting her up. She wrapped her legs around his waist, and he gently placed her on the chaise lounge, then lay on top of her and kissed her. When he stopped, he tenderly touched her cheek with his fingers. "I am the luckiest man in the world."

She smiled and kissed him.

There was a knock at the door.

"Hope you're hungry?" he asked.

"I'm famished."

"Wait here and I'll bring the food out."

"Thomas, you are definitely the last of the romantics!"

He came back, put the food on the table, and sat on the patio chair next to her. As they ate, they talked about the photo shoot, Aruba, and their wedding.

"Thomas the food was perfect, and everything tasted so good," she said sitting back and glancing over at him. "Is there anything you want to do while we are here?"

"I thought it might be nice to rent some jeeps and tour the island tomorrow. Maybe stop off at some beaches, have some lunch, and visit some of the towns."

"That's a great idea, I think it'll be a lot of fun," she said heading toward the doors, the balcony light caught her silhouette, and he noticed she wasn't wearing anything underneath. She returned a few minutes later. "I talked to the assistant manager, and he is going to take care of it."

They sat on the balcony for another hour, stared up at the stars, and picked out the constellations.

Olivia was starting to fall asleep. "I think I'm ready for bed."

Thomas helped her up, and they went inside, and she started for her suite.

"Olivia," he whispered. "Why don't you sleep with me tonight?"

"I thought you would never ask," she said heading for his bed and getting under the sheets.

Thomas changed into boxers, lifted up the covers, and lay next to her. As he put his arm around her, she placed her head on his chest, and he affectionately kissed the top of it.

"The breeze is lovely, and the sound of the waves is so relaxing," sighed Olivia falling off to sleep.

Chapter 49

"That was an adventurous day," said Kate.

"It was a lot of fun," replied Stephanie.

"Except the bats in the caves," said Rachel shuddering.

"What did they call those caves?" asked Thomas.

"I marked them on the map," said Olivia opening it out, "The Quadiriki Caves! And we also went to the California Lighthouse, De Olde Molen, Bushiribana, and Hooiberg."

"I like the De Olde Molen," said Thomas. "I've never seen a Dutch windmill before."

"No, no. Lunch in San Nicolas was the highlight," said Jack.

"Men! Shopping in Oranjestad," said Jessica knocking Jack's hat off. "That was the best!"

Jack fixed his hat then sipped on his whiskey. "What should we do tonight?"

"Let's go for dinner at a local restaurant," suggested Penny.

"And after that?"

"Well, Jack," said Thomas, "since it's yours and Penny's last night being single, I suggest we all go out and have some fun."

"I say we go for that meal, hit the casinos, and then a dance floor," stated Rachel. "Penny?"

"I don't like the casinos that much," replied Penny with a disapproving look.

Jack laughed. "Don't you believe her for one second. She loves them. In Vegas, I went to bed before her. I'm actually surprised she still wants to go for the meal."

"I do love them," said Penny with a chuckle. "Let's meet in the lobby for seven and go for an early dinner, that way we can hit the tables by nine, just when they're getting hot!"

"I already have my shirt picked out," said Thomas.

"You're not?" asked Olivia shaking her head.

Thomas smiled and nodded his head.

"Me too," said Jack.

They both laughed, touched glasses, and said, "Cheers!" then drank.

"Penny, what are we going to do with them?" asked Olivia.

Thomas put Jack's elevator card into the slot then Olivia pressed the button for the penthouse suite.

"Did he say why he wanted us to drop by?" she asked.

"No, he just gave me his card and said come up at six thirty. I'm guessing they probably want to talk to us about the wedding."

"Probably."

"I like your outfit," he said tickling her bare mid-section.

"Hands off pal or I'll give you one of these," she said lightheartedly clenching her fist at him, then opening it up, caressing his clean-shaven face, and kissing it. "My little Pineapple Boy," she said looking at his shirt.

"If you look closely at this pineapple," he said pointing, "you can see SpongeBob SquarePants coming out of it."

She giggled. "Very Funny!"

The door opened and Jack was standing there with his Hawaiian shirt on.

Olivia laughed. "You two have to be kidding!"

"Aloha, Thomas!" said Jack.

"Book'em, Jacko!" replied Thomas and they both chuckled.

"You two are as bad as each other," she said then noticed Penny walking toward her. "Finally, someone sane to talk to, hello, Penny."

"Hello, dear," she said taking her hand and leading her into the living room as Jack and Thomas followed behind. "Olivia, I was wondering if I could ask a favor?"

"Anything."

"Can I stay with you tonight?"

"Of course, you can," she replied.

"It may sound foolish, but a part of me would like Jack to see me for the first time tomorrow at the ceremony walking down the aisle," explained Penny.

"Penny, that's not foolish at all, that's the way it should be."

"Thomas, maybe you could stay up here tonight there's extra bedrooms, and tomorrow we could leave together," he suggested.

"Definitely, Jack," he said enthusiastically.

"This is a small token of our appreciation," said Penny giving them each a gift.

Thomas watched Olivia open up a small box containing a pair of waterfall drop earrings and Penny put them on her.

"They're gorgeous," she said looking in the mirror. "You shouldn't have."

"I wanted to," said Penny. "There are five carats in each one, and they look beautiful on you, and will go lovely with your dress."

"My dress?"

"It's in the spare room closet next to mine, we'll take them down with us when we leave," replied Penny.

"Go ahead, Thomas," said Jack.

Thomas opened his box and inside were a pair of gold cufflinks and a gold money clip, and each had a setting of diamonds in the shape of the letter T.

"Jack, Penny, these are beautiful, thank you," replied Thomas.

"Our pleasure," said Jack turning to Penny and Olivia. "You two should go drop off your clothes and we'll meet you downstairs in the lobby."

Penny went to the room with Olivia, and they came out with the garment bags, two shoe boxes, and Penny's overnight bag.

"I should come down with you and grab my stuff," said Thomas and started to follow them.

Jack grabbed his arm. "No need, you're all set, come with me."

Thomas followed him into the spare room and hanging in the closet was his outfit.

"It's all Armani: suit, shirt, shoes, and boxers, and you can wear your cufflinks with it," commented Jack. "There's also an outfit over here for golfing tomorrow morning."

"This is great, Jack."

"I'm glad," he said with a grin. "Now, let's go meet the girls, have dinner, and hit the tables."

They went to a restaurant and ordered Aruban specialties such as Scavechi, sopi di pampuna, Keshi yena, and for dessert, Pan Bollo. It was delicious, and the local band added to the energetic atmosphere. After the meal, they hit the casinos and played blackjack and roulette, and then went to the nightclub. Olivia, Penny, and Jessica left before twelve, while Thomas and Jack made it to bed just before one. The rest stayed out till three.

Chapter 50

Early the next morning, Jack got Thomas out of bed and took him to the golf course for nine holes while Olivia and Penny went to the spa and got their nails, hair, and makeup done.

At two thirty, Jack and Thomas arrived at a quaint church in the countryside and waited in a small room off to the side of the altar. Thomas pulled out a flask of whiskey and passed it to Jack, who smiled and took a long shot, then passed it back to Thomas who took a gulp. Jack handed Thomas the ring, then they talked for twenty-five minutes before going inside and standing in front of the altar. Five minutes later, the music started, and Olivia walked down the aisle holding a bouquet of bright colorful flowers and wearing a pretty knee-length lilac dress; she looked beautiful. Behind her was Penny, who was being walked down the aisle by Frank, she was in a white dress, similar in style to Olivia's, except hers was calf length, and the bridal bouquet was white lilies. She let go of Frank's arm and stood next to Jack. Throughout the thirty-minute ceremony, Olivia and Thomas occasionally glanced at each other, both wishing it was their day.

Jack and Penny went off in a horse-drawn carriage and at a distance the group followed behind in a minivan. They took a long, windy road and eventually arrived at a small, charming restaurant that overlooked the sea. After a delectable meal, drinks, speeches, and the catching of the bouquet by Rachel, they followed the carriage to the harbor and boarded a yacht. Once the yacht left port, the music began, and everyone danced. As the sun started to set, the disc jockey put on some background music and the group watched the sun fade. As Thomas put his arm around Olivia, they looked into each other's eyes, and kissed lovingly. That night, Thomas would sleep in Olivia's bed, but they would wait until their wedding night to make love.

The next day, they spent on the beach. Olivia and Thomas made sandcastles with several children, played volleyball, swam, and went for a walk. At five o'clock, they headed for the airport and boarded the plane.

By eleven, Olivia, Thomas, and Kate were back in their condos. Olivia went into her room, collapsed on the bed, and Thomas joined her.

She suddenly sat up and looked at him. "I've just realized that I never read your manuscript."

"I never brought it with me," revealed Thomas. "I figured we would just relax and take it easy."

They both chuckled at the word relax.

"I need a week to recover," said Olivia.

"More like two," suggested Thomas. "I thought it was nice of Stephanie to come with Frank."

"I thought so, too," she replied.

"I meant to ask. How were Jack and Penny able to get married in a church in Aruba? I overheard a couple saying they were getting married in a civil ceremony first, and then doing a ceremony on the beach."

"I'm not sure of the particulars, but Penny is Aruban, so I'm guessing that's why."

"She is?"

"Her great-grandparents were from the Netherlands and moved to Aruba. Her mother was born there, and her father was with the British government, and was stationed there for several years. Her parents met, married, and had her there. They moved when she was two or three to England, then here. That's why her name is very British, Penelope Daily."

"I never knew, that's interesting."

They both stared silently at the ceiling.

"Thomas, I can't wait till we're married."

"How many more weeks?"

"Seven, yesterday."

"Well, we have five days together before we leave for New York City, Christmas, New Year's Eve, our wedding, and then the rest of our lives together," he said glancing over at Olivia's sad face. "It will go quickly."

"I know," she replied a little gloomy.

"Come on, I'll run you a bath and when you get out, I'll have a nice cup of tea waiting for you. I'm sure that'll make you feel better." He got up, went into the bathroom, and ran the water. On the way back, he kissed her then headed to his room, got a copy of his manuscript, and placed it on her bed. He heard her in the bathtub singing 'You're the Best Thing' and listened for a couple of minutes, smiled, then left for the kitchen.

Chapter 51

They arrived in New York City, changed, then went straight to the Opera House and watched Henry perform Scarpia in 'Tosca.' After the show, they went backstage and waited for him.

"Olivia, Thomas," said Henry hugging and kissing them. "How are you both?"

"We're doing fine," she replied.

"You must be hungry? I have reservations at a lovely Italian restaurant, this way," he said directing them.

As they went through the stage doors and into the night air, there was a crowd of people waiting outside, and after noticing him, they called out his name. Henry waved to them as they strolled over to the limousine. After Olivia and Thomas jumped in, Henry stuck his head inside and asked if it was okay for him to spend a few minutes signing autographs. Olivia told him to go ahead and to take his time.

She looked at Thomas and smiled. "Six weeks tomorrow."

"Do you have to remind me?" he joked.

"Why you rotten scoundr—"

Before she could finish, he kissed her. "The more I see you the more I realize how beautiful you are" he said admiring her, "and nothing you wear looks bad on you. Everything fits you perfectly; especially this black gown."

She gave him a naughty look and sensually whispered, "you should see the black underwear set I have on underneath," then gently nibbled his earlobe.

The door opened, and Henry waved to the crowd one last time, before getting in and instructing the chauffeur to drive to the restaurant. On the way, Olivia and Thomas talked about Aruba, and Henry told them that he had been invited, but unfortunately had commitments that he couldn't break. After the meal, they went to Henry's place, and as they sipped their wine, gazed out of his window at the lights in Central Park.

"This is an amazing view," said Thomas mesmerized.

"It is," he agreed walking up and standing beside them. "Olivia, tomorrow I have a full day planned for the three of us, but before I go ahead with them, is there anything you want to do in particular?"

"No, whatever you have decided is great."

"Good, then makes sure you wear comfortable shoes and dress warm; these December mornings are cool."

Henry took them on a tour of New York City. In the morning, they took the ferry to Ellis Island and went up the Statue of Liberty. In the afternoon they went to the Empire State Building, and before crossing the road, Thomas grabbed Olivia's hand and asked her to hold on tightly and reminded her of what happened to Terry in *An Affair to Remember*. She happily smiled and squeezed it. After eating lunch in Times Square, they took a ride in a horse drawn carriage through Central Park then finished off with a walk down Broadway and a coffee in a small diner. Afterwards, they went back to Henry's apartment, and they all helped make dinner and drink a couple bottles of wine.

"Dad, that was a great day and a fantastic meal," said Olivia.

"It was incredible, thank you, Henry," added Thomas.

"It was my pleasure," he replied lifting his glass and taking a sip. "Olivia, let me get the suitcase for you." When he returned, he placed it on the table, and opened it. "I did have these in a box, but I bought this suitcase for you to make it easier for you to take them back home. There's your old ballet slippers, leotards, and dance costumes in her," he said then started to pull them out. "Here's your fairy costume, the princess one, the kitten, the lioness…they're all in here."

She kneeled down and continued to go through them. "These bring back fond memories," she said joyfully.

"You know your mother made all these," stated Henry. "Well up until you were eight."

Olivia looked up at him surprised.

"She was exceptionally good with her hands, and I remember her being up to the early hours in the morning cutting and sewing. I recall the embroidery being painstaking and taking her a lot of time, but she was incredibly happy doing it, and I never heard her complain once. You made her so proud when she watched you dance in them."

"I never knew or maybe I'd just forgotten," said Olivia unsure.

"Your mother wasn't one to brag, she was always quietly content and very humble about it, and she just loved being involved with you, and your dancing, and your friends."

"Why did you only have me then?" she queried.

The question took Henry by surprise but realized there was no better time to answer than now. "Your mother and I tried to have more children, in fact, she miscarried once before you and twice after. During your pregnancy, the doctors had to watch her constantly, and they had her stay in the hospital for her last trimester. After she had you, I remember how we cried with joy, we knew God had blessed us. We would have kept on trying, but the doctors told her that after her second miscarriage not to, for health reasons." Henry stared at her and continued. "Olivia, you can't blame your mother for everything that happened between us. I was on the road all the time, and when I was in town, I was working late. I know many people saw me walking you to your classes, and watching you, but what they didn't realize was that your mother was up late at night making your costumes and going to work early the next morning. It was easy for me; I worked at night and was off in the daytime. Don't get me wrong, I loved taking you to your classes, watching you, and being part of your life, but your mother was just as involved as I was, just in a different way. And she never missed any of your competitions," confessed Henry. "As you got older, she wasn't allowed to make you dresses anymore, because we had to buy them through a costume designer, so she stopped. This left her with a void in her life, and I wasn't around as much as I should have been to help fill it. So, she felt empty, and quickly grew lonely, and I was somewhat to blame for that." He slowly sipped his red wine then gave her a smile. "Olivia, just remember that your mother loves you. You may not see her or talk to her as much as you used to, and I'm not too sure why not, maybe you remind her too much of the life she, we, once had. Or maybe it's just too much pain. But whenever I speak to her, she always asks after you. I don't know if this helps you, or makes much sense," he said glancing at his glass. "This wine has loosened my lips but the words that come out are true."

She stood up, put her arms around him, and held him. "I love you," she said softly and contemplated what he had told her. "Daddy, why did you keep on trying to have children after the first miscarriage, the one before me?"

"We loved each other, and we wanted to have a family," he said candidly before pulling away. "Look at you, you've grown into a fine young woman and an angelic dancer, and I couldn't be any prouder. When you have children of your own, as a parent, you will understand what that means." He thought momentarily. "Come on, let me show you the good times," he said leading her to the sofa. "You sit here, next to me, and I'll put on the home movies. Thomas, join us, you'll get a laugh out of these."

Henry put on the DVDs. "They're mostly of Olivia, me, and her mother, and were taken from the time she was born up until she was sixteen."

They looked on at the footage of Olivia just being born at the hospital, playing in the backyard, walking in the park with her parents, having birthday parties, dancing in competitions. Thomas had never seen her mother before, and because they were taken when she was younger, her resemblance to Olivia was uncanny. So much so, that it could have been Olivia he was watching on the television. Then there were several shots of her mother up till two and three in the morning making Olivia's costumes and then asleep in the chair. Henry looked a lot younger, and he had long hairy sideburns, and Thomas smiled to himself when he saw them. Her parents looked extremely happy, and Thomas assumed that the separation must have been devastating. The scene ended and the television went black. Suddenly, a scene of Olivia's mother showing her pregnant stomach came on, and she looked different to the way she did in the earlier footage when she was carrying Olivia, she looked older. Henry scrambled to turn it off.

"Dad, what was that?" asked Olivia pointing.

"Nothing" replied Henry turning off the set, and not realizing that was on there.

"Dad?"

Henry sadly sat down next to Olivia. "The first and second miscarriages had been within the first trimester, the third, was in the second. It was a terrible shock, and exceedingly difficult for us both," he explained trying to keep his composure. "I had filmed your mother up until that last week, just a few days before the miscarriage, and I didn't realize I had copied it onto the DVD."

"Why didn't you tell me about the miscarriages before? Why did you wait until now?"

Henry held her hand. "That miscarriage in particular hit us both awfully hard. We had seen the baby on the ultrasound a week earlier, everything was normal, and the baby seemed healthy, and we were devastated when we lost her at such a late stage," he said stopping, fighting back his tears, and collecting his thoughts. "When you become husband and wife, you are starting a new life together, a life in which you share everything with one another and grow. All decisions you make as a couple, and the reasons for making them, are based on what you believe are in your best interests. If you decide to keep some of them a secret, that's because you have both agreed that it's your own personal business, and no one else's. So, your mother and I discussed it, and agreed not to tell you the particulars of the miscarriages. The main reason at the time was that the memory was too painful for us. Later on, because of the divorce, neither of us wanted to talk about and be the one to tell you," he said as tears rolled down his cheeks. "We always wanted you to have brothers and sisters."

Olivia pulled his head toward her and he cried. Thomas left, went into the kitchen, and made coffee. As he did, he gazed out the window and thought about Olivia and her not wanting to have children. Fifteen minutes later, she joined him.

"He's gone to bed, he's upset," she said unhappily. "I shouldn't have pushed him."

"Don't feel bad," he said comforting her. "You had questions that you needed answers to."

Henry suddenly came into the kitchen. "Olivia, I don't want you to be upset, I'm relieved we talked about it, and that you know. I'll see you in the morning," he said kissing her and ruffling Thomas's hair. "Goodnight." He turned, stopped, and looked back. "Olivia, Thomas, no matter how painful it was going through the miscarriages with Margot, if the doctors would have let us, we would have kept on trying." He gave them a half-smile then looked at Olivia. "Imagine having two or three delicate creatures like my angel, Olivia," he said softly, smiled, and left.

Olivia held Thomas closely, closed her eyes, and wept.

Early the next morning, Thomas felt Olivia get under his covers and hold him. He fell back asleep and woke a few hours later, and she was awake and watching him.

"Good morning," she said caressing his hair.

"Did you sleep okay?"

"No," she whispered.

"Are you okay?"

"I'm fine, but I was up most of the night thinking."

"Do you want to talk about it?" he asked.

"Not now," she replied, kissed him, and then smiled. "Maybe later."

The afternoon was spent watching the boys and girls of the New Baptist Church of Harlem Choir perform. Thomas and Olivia were their special guests, and were given the best seats, and the audience consisted of parents, family, friends, and several members of the opera company. They performed the Nativity, and when they finished, members of the opera company were invited up to sing Christmas hymns and songs with the children. After the show, they had a sit-down lunch of sandwiches, coffee, and Christmas cake, and Thomas and Olivia got to meet the children's parents and were thanked for giving them the opportunity to see the operas. After the meal, Rufus made a speech, and Santa joined him on stage and handed out the children's Christmas gifts.

Olivia, Thomas, and Henry stayed as late as they could, then left in time to catch their flight. At the airport, they said goodbye to a jovial Henry, who looked as if a big weight had been lifted off his shoulders.

On the plane, Olivia continued reading Thomas's manuscript, when it started its descent, she turned to him and told him she only had another fifty pages left and would be finished in a few days.

Chapter 52

"It's been so nice this week, just the two of us," said Olivia nestling into him.

"When did you jump in bed with me?"

"Very early this morning," she replied. "Your body is life a furnace, and as soon as you cuddled me, I was out like a light."

"You do know that's every morning this week?"

"I do, and you're right, I'm being selfish. So, starting tonight till next Sunday morning, you can sleep with me in my bed. That way I don't have to bother waking up early in the morning and jumping in your bed, okay?" she asked innocently.

"And then?"

"Then we swap, and I sleep in here with you for the next seven nights."

"Back and forth till we're married?"

"Oh Thomas, if that's what you want, I accept," she said squeezing him.

"Olivia, you know that was a question."

"Huh? What?" she said playfully ignoring him and getting up.

"What happens if I decide to sleep in the nude?"

"Oh, no!" she exclaimed pretending to act shocked, then giggled. "I'll just have to join you, silly." She leaned over and kissed him. "I'll put the coffee on."

Thomas slowly walked into the solarium and sat, moments later Olivia brought in their coffees and the wall calendar from the kitchen and joined him. She sat down pretending to be studying it, Thomas bit.

"All right, how many weeks till the big day?" he asked.

Olivia gave him a disapproving look. "It's thirty-four days."

"Days now," said Thomas grinning and shaking his head.

"Of course," she said. "I think they should make a wedding chocolate calendar that you open every morning till your wedding day, and inside, there's a wedding-themed chocolate."

"Like the Christmas ones?"

"Exactly!" she said sipping her coffee, looking serious, then breaking into a laughter.

Thomas joined her. "I actually liked the idea," he admitted, "and if they made them, I would have definitely bought you one."

"I know," she said reaching for his hand.

"So, how are we with your checklist?"

"We're just waiting for invitations to come back, and you guys to get fitted for your tuxedos. Then after Christmas, we'll work out the finer details, like where you guys are staying the night before the wedding, me having the bridesmaid here, and what time the photographer is coming."

"Olivia, I know we did everything together, and we made all the decisions, but you did a fantastic job putting it all together," he said tenderly squeezing her hand.

"Aw, thank you," she said sitting on his lap and kissing him. "But I'll be honest with you, I'm glad we got it all done before Christmas, because now we can just concentrate on each other."

"I like the sounds of that," he said kissing her passionately.

Olivia immediately responded and wrapped her legs around him. Thomas stood and carried her towards the living room.

"The sofa or my bed?" she asked breathing heavily.

Thomas carried her around the sofa then gently placed her down and lay on top of her. Their hands slowly explored each other's bodies, and as their breathing increased, so did their hands. Olivia didn't want him to stop; she was all his. Thomas kissed her neck, and knew if he continued down, he wouldn't stop. He slowly glanced up at Olivia, her eyes were shut, and she wasn't going to stop him. Olivia realized he had paused and slowly looked down at him; he was waiting for her to close her eyes again and give herself to him. They stared deep into each other's eyes, then smiled, and it was at that very moment they knew they had decided to wait. Neither of them had to say the words, instead, they kissed, then held each other for a while, before getting off the sofa and going into the kitchen. As they made breakfast, they talked, joked, and laughed, all the while knowing they would never forget that very moment when their hearts spoke, and they became one.

Chapter 53

Present Day: Sunday, December 20

Thomas hung up the phone and put on his jacket before returning to the kitchen to pick up the piece of paper that he had written the information on. He glanced at his watch; it was almost twelve. He could catch Olivia for lunch and tell her the exciting news, he thought, as he closed the door behind him.

Outside the wind was brisk, so he did up his jacket then looked up at the cloudy sky. They were calling for snow over the next few days, and he smiled at the likelihood of there being a white Christmas, before sauntering down the path to the sidewalk.

As he strolled down the street, he recalled how much fun they had putting up the Christmas tree and decorating the room, and how excited they were when they talked about going shopping for presents this afternoon. While Thomas contemplated their holiday plans, he smiled happily at the people passing by with their bags filled with gifts. There was definitely a feeling of Christmas in the air and Thomas was looking forward to spending his first with Olivia.

"My little girl!" screamed a woman standing to Thomas's far left. He turned to watch her drop her bags, point over his shoulder, and start in his direction. Thomas turned around to see a young girl on the road picking something off the ground. He looked at the approaching car, and at the driver talking on his cell phone, not paying attention to the road. Thomas realized he wouldn't see the girl till it was too late. Maybe he could shove her out of the way, but he would be pushing her into on-coming traffic from the other direction, and they would both be hit. He could grab her, throw her off the road onto the sidewalk, but there was no guarantee she would make it. Definitely not, if the car tried to swerve out of the way. As these options ran through his head, Thomas was already moving toward the girl and picking her up. He wrapped himself around her, pulled her close to his body and protected her head with his hands, then waited for the impact. The driver slammed on the brakes, but it was too late, he hit Thomas with the full force of the car.

Thomas felt a tremendous pain in his legs as he was lifted off the ground and into the air. He held the girl tightly as his right shoulder and right side of his back hit the windshield, and along with the sound of the glass shattering, he heard the distinct cracking of his bones. He bounced off the windshield, turned in the air, then landed on the trunk on his back with a loud thump, it was followed by his head whiplashing off the metal with a sickening thud. He rolled off the car and onto the road still cradling the girl's head and body as blood poured out onto the street. Thomas saw a bright light, then everything went black.

Chapter 54

Thomas was in darkness but not in total obscurity, for there was a small bright light very far off in the distance, and it looked like a star in the evening sky. He knew he wasn't of body, and couldn't speak, taste or touch, and he wasn't even sure if he was seeing through his eyes or hearing through his ears. Was he in his subconscious or in his soul? He didn't know, but he knew that the light was life, he didn't know how, he just did. He also knew he was in hospital and had been in an accident, but how did he know that? Someone had told him. Unexpectedly, he experienced a great sensation, Olivia, and he suddenly realized he wasn't alone.

"Oh no, no, no, no, no, Thomas!" she cried running to his side as tears streamed down her distraught face.

"I'll get the doctor," said the nurse leaving.

"Olivia?" asked Kate slowly coming behind her then noticing her brother's state. "Thomas!" screamed Kate running to the other side and holding his hand. "Oh no, I didn't realize it was this bad."

The doctor walked into the room, and noticing the two girls sobbing, wasn't looking forward to what he had to tell them. "Hello, my name is Dr. Moore. May I ask who you are?"

"I'm his sister, Kate, and this is his fiancée, Olivia," she said between sobs.

Olivia was too emotional to acknowledge him.

"Are your parents coming?" asked the doctor.

"My parents have passed, and I'm the only living relative," replied Kate, and upon realizing this, cried even more.

"Please, I understand this is a very difficult time for you both, but I would like to speak to you about his condition," he said to the hysterical girls. "Perhaps, I will come back later," he suggested heading for the door.

"No!" said Olivia staring at him and wiping away her tears. "Is he going to die?"

"Please, if you could both have a seat over here?" asked Dr. Moore pointing to the chairs by the window.

They walked over and sat.

"Unfortunately, your question is not that easy to answer," he replied, "but before I get to that, let me explain something first. Typically, when an individual gets hit by a car, they are not expecting it, and their bodies are somewhat relaxed and go with the impact. From what I understand, Thomas was quite aware he was going to get hit, so when he took on the force of the car, his body was very rigid, and even more so, as he protected the little girl."

"Little girl?" queried Olivia with a puzzled look.

"You don't know what happened?" he asked.

"The police said that he had been hit by a car and was in hospital, and I phoned Olivia," answered Kate.

"I guess they were waiting for me to tell you," he said taking a deep breath before telling them what he had heard from the mother and the police.

Olivia and Kate looked at each other, then the doctor.

"You're telling me that Thomas jumped out onto the street, picked up the little girl, and took the full force of a car to protect her?" asked Olivia.

"Yes," he replied.

There was a momentary silence.

"And the little girl?" asked Kate.

"She has scrapes and bruises on her legs, a broken arm, a couple of bruised ribs, and a bruised jaw. We are keeping her overnight in the ICU just as a precaution, and tomorrow we will be moving her to the children's ward, and the following day she will probably be released. Right now, her condition is stable, she's sedated, and sleeping," he explained then paused briefly. "Without a doubt, Thomas saved that little girl's life. If he hadn't done what he did, she would have been killed. Her mother has been asking me about him all afternoon, she's very upset."

Olivia stood, strolled over to Thomas, and stared at him. "Doctor, I don't want him to die, and I want you to promise me you will do everything you can to save his life, just like he did for that little girl."

The doctor stood next to Olivia and promised he would do all he could, then asked her to come back to her chair. "I need to tell you about Thomas's condition."

Olivia followed him, and after she sat, Kate reached over and held her hand.

"From what was reported, after Thomas picked up the young girl, he leaned in with his left side to protect her. The car hit him, making contact with his legs, mostly his left which is broken, his right is bruised. Thomas then went up in the air and landed heavily on his upper left region against the windshield, resulting in a broken collarbone, arm, three ribs, and a badly bruised hip. Thomas was bounced into the air again, before landing flat on his back on the trunk, thankfully, there are no spinal injuries.

Unfortunately, because of the way he landed, it caused his head to whiplash back against the metal trunk with tremendous force." He sadly looked at them both. "This injury was very serious, and the impact to his head has caused severe bruising and swelling of the brain." The doctor waited momentarily to let them absorb what he had just told them. "When he rolled off the trunk, he landed on the road, and has a cut on the right side of his head above the ear, a badly bruised jaw, and scrapes and bruises over his face and body." He glanced over at Thomas. "I have to be honest with you, he's very lucky to be alive."

"Is he going to be okay?" asked Kate.

"Thomas hasn't regained consciousness and is still in a coma," he said slowly. "We had to operate to remove the blood trapped between his brain and skull, it's called a craniectomy. Before the operation, we gave him less than a twenty percent chance of pulling through, after the operation, it went up to fifty percent. As each day goes by, the odds improve in his favor and that percentage will increase, but after a while, staying in the coma for too long will soon become a concern."

"Meaning, he could die?" asked Kate.

"I have to be honest with you, Thomas is in a fight for his life, and needs to come out of his coma sooner than later. If his condition remains unchanged, over time there is a high probability that he may never regain consciousness."

Kate and Olivia stared distantly at the doctor as his words slowly sank in.

"I'm sorry," he said snapping them back to reality.

Olivia and Kate held each other and cried.

The doctor left, and shortly after, the nurse came in and comforted the two crying girls until a hospital volunteer took over.

Jack and Penny walked into the room expecting the worst, but nothing they imagined would come close to what they witnessed. Penny cried in Jack's arms as he looked away in pain. Kate explained to them what the doctor had told them, prompting Jack to leave the room insisting on talking to the head nurse and the doctor. He could be heard in the hallway yelling and demanding that Thomas get the best treatment and care possible, to which they responded that he was. Jack came back into the room and told Penny he was off to find Mackenzie the director of the hospital.

"To think I donated a wing to this place," he said shaking his head as he left.

Kate, Olivia, and Penny stood in silence and stared at Thomas. Kate and Olivia broke down and cried, and Penny comforted them.

Jessica arrived an hour later. "How is he?" she asked strolling in unaware. When she saw Thomas's condition, she almost fainted, and they had to help her into a chair and give her some water. "Poor Thomas, what happened?"

Penny told her.

Rachel was next. She looked at her mother, then Penny, Kate, and Olivia. "He's, okay? Tell me he's, okay?"

"He's not, honey," replied Jessica sadly and going towards her.

Rachel quickly moved around her and looked at Thomas. She left the room with her hand over her mouth bawling. Jessica left to comfort her, and told her what had happened, before coming back in with her thirty minutes later.

They stood around the room and said nothing. One would start crying, then another, and then they all would, then all would be silent again.

A nurse came in and glanced around the room at the distant faces. As she checked Thomas's vitals, she started to talk to him. "Hello, Thomas, I'm your nurse, Sarah. How are you doing this evening? Okay! Good. I'm the night nurse and I'll be here in case you need me. Well, everything looks fine. Now, you get yourself all better and wake up soon. You have a lot of visitors here tonight," she said looking over. "There's a pretty young girl with blonde hair, her name is?"

"Rachel."

"Rachel," repeated the nurse to Thomas, and there is a beautiful girl behind me who hasn't left your side since I've been here, and her name is?"

"Olivia."

"Olivia," said the nurse. "There's another attractive lady at the end of the bed?"

"Kate."

"Named Kate, and sitting in the chairs are?" she asked.

"Penny."

"Jessica."

"Penny and Jessica. There's also a big man standing at the door who is?" she asked in his direction.

"Jack."

"Jack," she said fixing his sheets. "Thomas, all these people are here because they care about you, and I wanted to let you know that you have company while you're sleeping, and that you're not alone." She quickly surveyed the room then went back to Thomas. "They are terribly upset right now, but once they've gotten over that, they'll start talking to you, I promise. So, you hang on dear, okay? Good. I'll be back in a couple of hours." Sarah walked toward the door then turned to them. "You know Thomas can hear you, so talk to him, he's listening, and he'll feel so much better knowing that you're at his side," she said with a kind smile then left.

They were silent for a few minutes.

She couldn't wait any longer. "Thomas, it's me Olivia, I want you to know I love you, and I'm going to be here day and night," she said holding his hand. "And I need you to get better because Christmas Eve is in four days, and we still have to do our shopping." She became too emotional to continue and cried.

"Thomas, it's Kate, I'm here too, and I want you to know that I love you, and to let you know that the little girl is fine and that you saved her life. We are all very proud of you but it's time to come back to us now, please." Kate couldn't stop herself and wept.

One by one, they told Thomas they loved him and wanted him back, although they all broke down afterwards, each of them felt better.

It was getting late, and Olivia and Kate thanked Jack, who had arranged for them to stay for as long as they wanted, and the rest of the group for coming, who, in turn, said they would be back in the morning.

Chapter 55

Monday, 21st

The small bright light in the distance had increased to the size of a quarter. Thomas didn't know if he was moving toward it, or it was moving toward him. He heard vibrations coming and going and they were soothing.

"Thomas, it's me, Olivia, it's almost three and I wanted to let you know that I was still here. Kate and I had been talking to you, but I left to get some water and when I came back, she had fallen asleep. So, I thought I would spend some time and talk to you alone," she said cradling his hand. "I've been thinking about this, and I was wondering why you were out, you said to me that you weren't going anywhere…Maybe you were going to surprise me and meet me for lunch or were going out to buy me a secret present? I guess when you wake up, you can tell me all about it," she said smiling at him. "Thomas, I know what you did and why you did it, and I love you for that, but a little piece inside me wishes you hadn't. Actually, more than a little. I know I shouldn't talk this way, but I can't help it. All I know is that today her mother has her and I don't have you," she whispered sadly. "Thomas, you must have known when you picked her up that the car was going to hurt you, and possibly kill you, and yet you still did it. I'm so angry, not with you, but with that little girl and her mother. I really want to tell them what you are going through and what I'm going through. I know you wouldn't want me to do that, so I won't, but that's how I feel. I love you; I miss you, and I'm very scared."

"Thomas, if you are feeling something next to your left thigh that's Olivia's head lying on the bed next to you, she's fallen asleep. I slept for a couple of hours and just woke up. How are you?" she asked trying to be strong and fussing with his sheets. "You have a lot of people hoping and praying for you to get better. So, you take your time, but not too much, because I don't want you to stay away for too long," she said fighting off the tears. "Remember, Thomas, you promised you would always be here for me, and I know you never break your promises. So, I'm begging you, please keep this one, I don't want to be left here on my own, alone."

As they sipped their coffees, Kate noticed Olivia's sad, distant look, and realized them sitting in silence was making it worse. "What's it like, to know that Thomas is the person you want to spend the rest of your life with and no one else?"

"It's difficult to explain," she said thinking. "It's like Thomas is the piece of me that was missing, and him being in my life, makes me whole." She looked over at Kate. "I remember the first time I met him, I thought he was the handsomest man I had ever seen, and I fell in love with him straight away. And the more I was with him, the deeper in love I fell, and I just knew there was no one else," she said with a smile. "Thomas is my soulmate."

"So, how did you feel when he saw you with Frank that time?"

"I was so upset. I thought that was it, he was gone forever, and it was all my fault," she said animatedly. "In retrospect, I should have told him about Frank before that, but I wasn't going to give up until he knew the truth, and when he didn't want to talk to me, I thought maybe he didn't care for me the same way that I did for him. It was only after what he did for me and my father that I knew that he did and that I had a chance," she said gazing at him.

"Thomas can be too proud at times, and I told him to talk to you and clear the air, but he felt like you had deceived him. I guess you had, but not in the way that he had perceived it," said Kate following her eyes. "Do you know I actually talked him into going to the fundraiser?"

Olivia shook her head.

"I was hoping he might meet someone who was in the publishing business, or maybe talk about his novel and make some contacts, and it would open a window of opportunity for him. I guess it did," she said as Olivia looked at her." He met you, fell in love, and you pushed him to send off his novel, and I am so grateful he did," she said reaching over and squeezing her hand.

"Thank you," replied Olivia managing a smile then remembering back to the day they sent off his manuscript. "I feel so bad that he hasn't heard back from anyone yet, we had set Christmas as the deadline, and were going to follow up in the new year. His story was excellent, and I can't believe none of them were interested."

"Don't worry, there's still time," reassured Kate.

"There is," said Olivia nodding her head in agreement. "Have you read his second?"

"I started it this week."

"It's better than the first, and he was going to send it out in the new year." Oliva realized what she had said and corrected herself. "He is going to send it out in the new year."

"Good morning," said the nurse walking in. "How are you doing?"

"Okay," they both replied then watched as she took his vitals.

"He's doing better today."

"Really?" asked Olivia enthusiastically.

"Slightly, and believe me, that's a milestone in the right direction," she said opening the blinds. "The doctor will be making his rounds within the hour and giving Thomas a full examination. You won't be allowed to stay, and it will take him about thirty minutes, enough time to get some breakfast, a wash, and change of clothes," she thoughtfully suggested before departing.

When the doctor arrived, they told him they were going to pick up some breakfast and would be back in half an hour. He said he would wait for them to return so he could let them know how Thomas was doing. As he examined him, he talked him through it, then finished by telling him he was doing fine. He pulled the curtain back, noticed the girls standing in the hallway, and called them in.

"How is he?" asked Olivia.

"Thomas is doing better, better than I expected," he confessed. "This afternoon Dr. Peterson will be in to take a look at him. He's the doctor who performed the operation and is the expert in head traumas. If he confirms what I believe, that Thomas is stable, then tomorrow we will move him from the ICU upstairs to a private room. Up there, he will be listed as critical but stable, and from that point on, all we can do is wait and see how he reacts to his injuries."

They thanked the doctor and watched him leave, then sat down and started to eat. Kate called over to Thomas. "We're back, we went and got some juices, muffins, bagels and cream cheese, and a cup of tea." Then she glanced at Olivia. "You look tired?"

"I didn't sleep very well last night. I kept thinking about us putting up the Christmas tree and decorations a couple of days ago, and how we should have been shopping on Sunday, and how this should be a happy time of the year," she said trying not to get upset but failing and crying.

Kate held her.

"I'm sorry, I'll be okay in a minute," she said composing herself. "I just want him to be okay, that's all."

"I do, too…come on, try eat some more," she said waiting for Olivia to finish her bagel before getting up and going over to see Thomas. "How are you doing today?" she asked expecting him to wake up and answer her.

"How is he, Kate?" questioned Rachel coming toward her holding a gym bag.

"The doctor said he's doing better, and that the specialist who performed the operation will be coming in this afternoon to check on him, and make sure everything is okay," she replied anxiously. "Then they're probably going to move him into a private room upstairs."

Rachel comforted her before leaning over and kissing him on the cheek. "Good morning, Thomas, it's Rachel," she said, then sat next to Olivia, held her hand, and looked at her. "How are you holding up?"

"Fine," she replied putting on a brave face.

"I brought shirts and track pants for you both, and some toiletries, I thought you might like a change of clothes," she said motioning to the bag on the floor. "Just help yourself."

"Thanks, Rachel," said Olivia.

"I think I'll take you up on that offer, I need to get out of this work blouse and skirt," said Kate picking it up and leaving.

"Why don't we put these two chairs closer? You can put your feet up, close your eyes, and I'll watch Thomas for a while," said Rachel pulling them together, helping her lift her feet up, and getting her a pillow. Olivia closed her eyes and was asleep in minutes.

She walked over to Thomas and stared at him. "Thomas, it's Rachel again, you're looking better, and the doctor says you're going to continue to get better," she said smiling at him, her face crumbled, and she started to cry but quickly regained her composure. "Thomas, remember the last time you were in hospital and you told that nurse that your eyesight was okay," she said laughing. "That was pretty funny…and I still have to get you back for that by the way!"

Penny came into the room, noticed Olivia sleeping in the chair, and joined Rachel. "How is he?"

Rachel repeated what Kate had told her.

"Good," said Penny. "Jack is talking with Mackenzie and setting Thomas's room up. Where's Kate?"

"She's getting changed. I brought them some clothes."

"Good girl," replied Penny. "And your mother?"

"She'll be here soon; she wanted to get some flowers to brighten up the room and didn't like the ones they had in the gift shop."

"I know, me neither, I bought mine at the florist."

Jack sauntered in with a bouquet in a vase and placed them on the side table next to Thomas, then looked down at him and asked how he was doing before turning to Rachel. "How are you?"

"Okay, Jack."

"The snow's starting to fall."

"Is it?" asked Kate joining them.

"It's going to fall all day," continued Jack. "They reckon ten inches today, and then it's going to fall on and off over the next five days."

"A white Christmas," said Rachel. "Thomas was wishing for a white Christmas."

They all stared at him.

"It's really coming down out there," said Jessica coming into the room. "How is everyone? Kate, you look tired."

"I'm okay," she replied.

"Olivia?"

"She's sleeping," said Kate pointing behind Jack and Penny.

"Poor girl," said Jessica. "I brought some flowers, fruit, doughnuts, juices, chocolates, and music magazines for Thomas to read," she said placing them on the end table. "Music magazines for Thomas to read, for God's sake, where's my head at?" she asked breaking down "I'm a mess, I just want him to wake up and read them that's all," she said sobbing, Rachel comforted her, and she began to cry, then they all did.

"Can I come in?"

"Frank," said Olivia. "Of course, come on over."

He strolled over, stared at Thomas and his heart went out to him. "How's he doing?"

"He's stable," replied Kate.

"How are you doing, Kate?"

"I keep waiting for him to open his eyes, and sit up in that bed, and say something."

"He will soon," reassured Frank. "Olivia, how about you?"

"I'm okay," she replied. "If I only knew he was going to be all right, I'd feel much better, this waiting is eating me up inside."

"He'll be fine," comforted Frank. "I brought a portable CD player and some CDs that I think he might like. The nurse said music would be good for him but to keep it low. I also bought a few books and magazines that you may want to read to him," he said putting them down.

"Thanks," said Kate.

They all sat around and talked to Thomas as if he were involved in the conversation, and once in a while, one of them would answer on his behalf.

Dr. Peterson came to check on Thomas, and he told them he had recovered as well as could be expected from the surgery but was still very concerned about his comatose state and that they would have to take it one day at a time. Before he left, he said that he would be back tomorrow morning with Dr. Moore, and if everything remained stable, they would move him upstairs.

Jack came in and informed them that Thomas had an extra-large private room waiting for him, and that they were going to put in a couple of cots, extra chairs, and a television with a DVD player. Also, that a private nurse had also been hired to take care of him full-time, and Mackenzie had assured him she was one of the best.

"Hi, Thomas, it's Rachel, everyone has gone downstairs for dinner, and I said I would stay with you. I've wanted to talk to you for a while about something, and I've been quiet up until now, but it's time I told you," she said taking a deep breath. "Remember the night of my party, we were in the hot tub looking at the stars, and I asked you if we could be friends? You said yes, and I said I was glad, well that was a lie. I really wanted to hear you tell me that you liked me more than that and kiss me. Thinking back, I should have just told you I found you interesting, attractive, and sexy, and that I wanted us to be more than friends, and asked you how you felt about me," she said holding his hand. "I also have a confession to make, I only dated Mathew to get a response from you, something, some sign that you liked me or were at least jealous. What a fool I have been! I should have just told you how I felt, at least you would have known, and maybe things may have worked out differently between us," she said slowly sitting. "I always looked forward to you coming over, and I'll never forget the afternoon we went riding and had the picnic. I often lie in bed and think about us that day, and I even fantasize about us making love, right there on the side of the valley. Do you remember us staring at the evening sky to see who could spot the first star? Well, I was thinking about how I could get you back, and then when we saw the shooting star, and you said make a wish. Do you know what I wished for? You to be with me," she said then thought momentarily. "I know if we had gone horseback riding the afternoon after my party, I would have told you then how I felt about you, but we never did. Then there was the first Tuesday you came to the guesthouse, on the way there, I should have just kissed you. And that time when I messed up my hair and was peeking at you through the strands, and you came over, I should have just pulled you on top of me. I had so many opportunities," she said wiping the tears from her eyes. "Aruba! I was so happy when you watched me at my photo shoot, and you were there the whole time, and both days," she said with a smile. "I brought the pictures with me, I haven't seen them yet, and I'll show them later when everyone is here, and I'll describe them to you." She paused and gently caressed his hair. "It was then and there I realized you and Olivia were my best friends, and it was at that point, I decided I would never come between you two, or let you know how I felt." She leaned over and kissed him tenderly on the lips then whispered, "Thomas, I'm in love you, and I've been in love with you since the night we met at the fundraiser, and I will always love you, but you will never hear me tell you this again, it will be my secret."

When they returned from dinner, Jessica gave Rachel a sandwich and a salad, and she sat quietly in the corner and ate. The redness in her eyes gave away the fact that she had been crying hard, and they decided to leave her alone and give her some space. As they sat around Thomas, they talked about the weather, celebrities, and sports. Then Jack read out loud a gossip magazine in which everyone gave their input as to whether the story was true or not.

Rachel opened the envelope and took the pictures out one by one as Kate and Olivia looked on over her shoulder. She described them out loud for Thomas, then put them in front of his face before passing them on. "Here we are all sitting on the plane waiting to take off for Aruba…This is the four of us in the van going to the hotel…These are pictures of the pool, beach, and sea, from my room. Here's one of my mom, Thomas and Olivia, Me, Olivia and Kate, Buddy and Veronica, Kate, Stephanie, and my mom in the pool."

"Remember when Thomas called out to those guys and he went under the water and they thought it was Kate," said Jessica.

"That was so funny I'll have to get him back for that," said Kate trying her best not to get upset.

"Kate, tell them about the time in New York City with my father, you know, the singing," said Olivia.

"Oh, okay," she said, then told them about her singing to Olivia's father in front of the people at the lounge. "Here I was singing a song to Henry Taylor, one of the greatest opera singers in the world, right after he'd just finished singing to me. I was so embarrassed, and your father was looking at me a little confused, but that's Thomas for you," she said chuckling and feeling a little better.

Rachel continued going through the photographs.

Olivia liked the one of her in her dress and Thomas in his suit outside the church, and remembered thinking at the time that it wouldn't be long before they would be getting their wedding pictures taken. There was another picture of her talking with Jack, and in the background, Thomas was looking at her unaware he was being photographed. She could tell he was thinking about something and wondered what it was and would have to ask him. She smiled at the pictures of her, and Thomas making sandcastles with the children and loved the one of them coming back from their sunset walk on the beach.

They all laughed at the picture with Thomas and Jack in their Hawaiian shirts, then talked about them at great length as Jack fought back the tears.

"You know he has that shirt hanging in his closet and told me he was going to wear it to his bachelor party," said Olivia, then corrected herself again. "Is going to wear it."

"Thomas it's me, Olivia, Kate has gone downstairs to walk Rachel, Jessica, Penny, and Jack out, and to get some fresh air," she said tenderly caressing his cheek. She stared at him and had never felt so alone in all her life, and quietly sang 'You're the Best Thing' then cried with all her heart and soul.

Chapter 56

Tuesday, 22nd

The light had now grown into the size of a basketball, it was brighter than any light he had ever seen, but it didn't hurt, and it wasn't warm, and he suddenly realized he was moving closer to it. The vibrating had changed to a hum, and it made him feel better.

Dr. Peterson and Dr. Moore examined Thomas then told Olivia and Kate they were moving him upstairs and re-emphasized their concern about his unconscious state. As promised by Jack, he was moved into a large private room, where Olivia and Kate met the hired nurse, Anne, who was very well spoken, gentle, and kind. She explained her qualifications, talked about her husband and children, and they took an immediate liking to her.

"Hello, may I come in?" asked a woman in her early thirties wearing an overcoat.

No one knew her.

"I was there when Thomas was struck by the car," she explained.

"Come in and have my seat," said Jack standing.

"No, thank you, I prefer to stand," she said anxiously. "Are you all family?"

"The girl on this side of the bed is Thomas's sister, Kate, and on the other side is his fiancée, Olivia. I'm Jessica, my daughter, Rachel, Jack, and Penny, and we are very close friends."

They all stared at the nervous woman.

"My name is Elizabeth Robinson," she said wondering where to begin and how to explain it. "I am the reason Thomas was hit by the car," she said as the group looked at each other confused. "My little girl, Jenny, had received a letter from Santa Claus, and she wanted to let him know she had gotten it and to show him, so I took her to the mall. She had been holding onto this letter all day, and I told her it was windy outside, and it would blow away, and she should put it in her pocket. But you know how seven-year-old children are, she wanted to hold it all the way there and back. After we left the mall, she was walking next to me and I was carrying these heavy bags, so I put them down for just a moment. As I rested, the wind blew the letter out of her hand, and it was right there next to her, so I told her to pick it up. I leaned down, picked up the bags, looked over, and she was gone. The letter had blown onto the road, and she had chased after it and was trying to pick it up. I shouted, dropped my bags, and pointed. Thomas heard me, looked over, and saw her. He ran and picked Jenny up…and then…then, the car hit him hard…and his body and his head hit the car so hard…and that sound and the blood." She began to shake and cry. "I'm having a tough time sleeping and I've been waking up screaming, and I wanted to come sooner, but I knew you would need some time alone and I was scared to come. It's all my fault, and I'm so sorry, and ask you to forgive me, please," she said falling to the ground in a heap.

Olivia ran over with Kate and helped her up.

"Elizabeth, it's not your fault, it's nobody's fault," said Olivia comforting her.

"You can't blame yourself," said Kate helping her to a chair. "It was an accident."

"I just want him to be okay," she said wiping her eyes as they sat next to her.

"We all do," said Olivia feeling sorry for her.

"I have something I want to read to you," she said pulling an envelope out of her pocket, opening it, and removing a letter written in red crayon.

Dear Santa Claus,

I wrote you a letter asking you what to bring me. I changed my mind. I don't want toys. I don't want dollies. I don't want teddies. I don't want any candy. None of them. I want you to make my Christmas Angel better for Christmas Day. He's very sick in hospital and his name is Thomas.

Thank you,

Love Jenny.

"She wrote it last night and asked me to take it to Santa straight away, and I told her I would. You see she wants Santa to sign it and make her a promise he'll be okay," explained Elizabeth.

"How is she?" asked Kate.

"She's fine, and they're releasing her tomorrow," she replied. "Her father is in the army, and he'll be home Christmas Eve, she doesn't know yet, and he doesn't know about this."

"Why don't you bring her in tomorrow before you leave?" asked Olivia.

"Are you sure?"

"Yes," said Olivia smiling, "I'd like to meet her."

"Me too," said Kate.

"Thank you for your kindness," she said slowly standing. "I've been praying for Thomas's recovery and will continue to do so until he wakes." She started for the door then came back. "I almost forgot, Thomas had this in his jacket, and it almost blew away, but I picked it up and wanted to give it to one of you," she said opening her bag, taking out a folded piece of paper, and giving it to Olivia.

"Thank you," she said taking it from her, then watched Elizabeth leave before unfolding it and reading it aloud:

Elliott & Davis
Janice Jacobs
Wants me to meet with her first week in January at Manhattan Office.
Will email information.
Extremely interested in manuscript and want to discuss publishing it.

Olivia glanced up at them. "Elliott and Davis had called and told him they were interested in his novel and wanted to meet him in Manhattan."

"That's where their head office is," confirmed Jack.

"This is why he was on his way over to see me, to tell me that they wanted to publish his novel," she said tearing up, "he must have been so excited."

Frank dropped in that evening and read magazine articles to Thomas as Kate, Olivia, and Rachel listened on, then stopped when the Village Choir came in at seven.

"Okay, Thomas," said Greg, "we got the CD and printed the lyrics, and practiced this song because we were told how much you like it, so here goes." They harmonized Genesis' 'Dancing with the Moonlit Knight' and were incredible. When they finished, Kate, Olivia, Rachel, and Frank clapped and asked for an encore. They graciously accepted and sang Billy Idol's 'Rebel Yell.' Then one by one, they stood over Thomas and wished him well.

"Thomas recited John Donne's poem 'The Good Morrow' for me and Greg at our anniversary. It was so beautiful and meant so much to us that I typed it out, framed it, and hung it on our wall," explained Blair. "So, I made one for you, Olivia, because I believe it applies to you and Thomas, also."

"Thank you," said Olivia taking it from him and cuddling it.

"For when he wakes up, it's a present from us all," said Miguel placing a leather coat at the end of the bed.

"Thank you," said Kate wiping the tears away from her cheeks.

"We'll stop by on Christmas Eve and sing some carols," said Greg.

"Thanks, guys, that would be nice," said Frank following them out.

Olivia looked at the framed poem and read what Blair had written on it, 'To Olivia and Thomas, for Love that is Perfectly Mixed' then read the poem out loud and imagined Thomas reading it to her.

Alfie stopped by and dropped off flowers, chocolates and a get-well card signed by the First National Ballet, then told Olivia that under Penny's request, she had been excused from any further classes and performances of the Nutcracker. "Me, and the First National Ballet are praying for you both, and please take whatever time is needed," he said holding her hand.

"Thank you, and please thank my fellow dancers for their kindness and understanding," she said gratefully.

"I will," he replied kissing her on the cheek then going to Thomas and holding his hand. "I'll keep him in my prayers."

As Alfie was leaving, Eileen, Stephanie, and Ted walked in. Stephanie cried hysterically, and Eileen put her shocked hand over her face as tears welled up in her eyes. Frank went over and comforted them.

Is he going to be, okay?" asked Ted.

Kate explained everything. "We just have to wait and see."

"Why does this always happen to the nice guys?" he asked.

"Why does it?" said a voice from behind, it was John.

"I thought you were going to wait in the car?" asked a surprised Eileen.

"I changed my mind," he said joining them in front of Thomas, and as he spoke, he stared down at him, but what he had to say was for Frank and Olivia too. "After the three of you left my house that evening, I despised you telling me how I act differently towards Frank and that I should change and accept him. Then my wife and daughter return from the driveway and they're against me. Then Ted goes with Stephanie and has a drink with Frank and his friends and the next day he turns on me. You know what Ted said to me, Thomas, I'm sure you will all get a kick out of this, he said I was a bastard. Actually, a self-pitying, loveless, homophobic bastard who didn't know what he had. I suddenly realized I was being pointed out as the bad guy and that they were all ganging up on me. So, I started to think about what Ted said, and what happened that Sunday afternoon, and about Frank," He looked directly at Frank. "You know Frank, when you guys were younger, I never wanted you to be bigots. I always said to love and treat everyone with the utmost respect no matter what their race, color, sex, or religion was, and you did, you all did. I took a long, hard look at myself in the mirror and wondered why I had changed. Then I quickly realized I hadn't changed toward the people at work, with my neighbors, or people I meet on the street; I accepted them for who they were. Yet my own son, my own flesh and blood asks me to accept him, not for being gay or for being a ballet dancer, but just as my son, and be happy for him and be proud of him." He glanced over. "Eileen, I realized that our children have all turned out pretty good. They don't do drugs, they aren't criminals, and they've always respected us and our house." He then turned to face his family. "I knew I was wrong, I was just too pigheaded to admit it, so I went and stood in the back of the theater and watched Frank dance. The next day at work, I spoke to the mechanics at my shop, my neighbors, my friends, and told them that I went to watch Frank dance in a ballet and that he is one hell of a dancer!" He looked down at Thomas. "Do you know on Christmas Eve, my wife, my daughter, my son, are going out and leaving me alone in the house and meeting Frank for a drink at the pub." He stopped momentarily and collected his thoughts. "You see Thomas, I was going to surprise them and show up that night, and have a drink with them, and tell them what I just told you. Then I heard about your accident, and I felt this pang in my chest because I thought to myself what if this was Frank that was in hospital? He would never have known how sorry I was, or how proud of him I am, or how much I love him." John broke down, wept, and slowly walked to Frank and put his arms around him. "I'm so sorry my son, please forgive me."

"I love you Dad, there's nothing to forgive," he said then went with him outside with his family in tow.

Olivia leaned over. "You're right, Thomas, I should have had more faith in families," she whispered in his ear then kissed his cheek.

"Olivia and Kate, I'm terribly sorry for what's happened to Thomas, and I hope he recovers quickly. If there is anything you need or we can do, please let us know," said John standing with his family, then he glanced down at Thomas. "Get well soon and thank you for being Frank's friend."

"Thomas, it's me, Olivia, Kate just left to get some coffee, and I while she is away, I wanted to remind you that we only have twenty-six days until our wedding, so you need hurry up, and wake up," she whispered. "I've been wondering about the special dance you are going to do for me on our wedding night, and I can't wait to see it. I remember you dancing around my living room in your leather pants, that was so hot and turned me on, if it's anything like that then I'm in for a treat," she said with a grin. "Do you remember at The Duke? When you described what you were going to do to me, then stopped, and said I would have to wait for our wedding night for the ending. Well, since that time, I've imagined several different steamy scenarios, and they all end with us making love all night. So, don't you deny me my ending Thomas. Do you hear me?" She started to cry. "I sometimes wish we had made love and were married already, but we decided to wait, and I don't want to ever regret that. So, please, don't let me regret it, Thomas. I would give up dancing forever to have you wake up and be with me. Do you hear me?" Olivia sobbed. "Thomas, if you can hear me, please, come back to me. I love you so much and I can't go on without you, and I can't go on like this, I'm a mess. I don't know how much longer I can last before I go out of my mind," she said throwing her head on the bed and crying herself to sleep.

"I was gone a while so Olivia could have some time alone with you. I have a cup of coffee for her, but she's fallen asleep," said Kate sipping hers. "I wanted to let you know that I'm really proud of what you did for that little girl, Jenny, that's her name, but I miss you and want you to know that if you leave, I'll be here all alone, and I don't think I will be able to handle that. So, I need you to wake up and be with us," she said getting upset. "You've been the best brother a little sister could have, and you've always taken care of me, put me first, and helped me have a normal teenage life." She suddenly recalled something. "Do you remember when Mom and Dad were away, and I got my period for the first time, and you explained what it was? Then you went out and bought me tampons but also came back with fifty dollars' worth of other items from the drugstore because you were embarrassed to buy them on their own. You had toothpaste, toothbrushes, soap, chips, chocolates, and magazines," she said chuckling. "It wasn't till I got older that I realized how much courage that must have taken, and how much you loved me…Since then, you've helped me through school, got me a part-time job that I love, bought me a new car instead of one for yourself, and got me the condo so I could be close to you, and you never complained once. But Thomas, you still have to come see me graduate, start my new job as a lawyer, fall in love, and walk me down the aisle, you know nothing would make me prouder, big brother." Kate started crying, wiped her eyes, and decided to talk about something else. "We had a fun time in New York City, and I still laugh when I think about you getting me up to sing, that was one of your best practical jokes ever. Then having them put my picture on the wall, that was pretty good too, but I got you back for that! We also had a lot of fun in Aruba," she said glancing down at Olivia, "and it was nice seeing you two so happy and so in love. You know I really like her, and if I could have picked out someone for you to marry, it would have been Olivia. Rachel's amazing too, and she would have been a close second, and I think it's great you guys all became best friends." Kate moved Olivia's hair from her eyes then stood and leaned over Thomas. "Olivia really loves you, and misses you, and so do I. So, Thomas, please hurry up and get well, and wake up," she whispered then kissed him on his forehead, and as her tears fell onto his cheek, she wiped them away, but they were falling faster than she could dry them.

Chapter 57

Wednesday, 23rd

The light had taken up half the space and was quickly replacing the darkness, and as it did Thomas could feel pain, and he soon realized as the light grew so did his level of pain. The hum had now changed to a murmur, and it made him feel happy.

"Hello, Thomas, it's Henry. I brought coffees and doughnuts for Olivia and Kate, but they are sleeping. Kate is on the cot and I'm going to put Olivia on the other one," he said picking her up, laying her down, and throwing a blanket over each of them. He then came back and sat in a chair next to Thomas. "I talked to Anne outside, she told me about your condition and that everyone has been talking to you, and that you can hear them. So, I will sit here, drink my coffee, eat my doughnut, and talk with you. First, the choir have been renovating their practice hall, and they said to say hello and Merry Christmas, that was last week and didn't know about your accident, but Rufus is going to call them today and let them know. I have some pictures of them fixing up the place, painting, and such, and will show them to you later. I was looking forward to us getting fitted for the tuxedos so that we could spend some time together. I wanted to tell you how fond I am of you, and that Olivia couldn't have met a finer man." Henry was finding it difficult to speak, he kept trying, but when he looked at Thomas his heart was in his mouth and ended up putting his head in his hands and weeping.

"Daddy?" whispered Olivia. "Daddy!" she said jumping out of bed and holding him. "I'm so glad you are here."

There was a knock on the door and a young girl with auburn hair and big blue eyes came in. She had a cast on her arm, and the right side of her jaw was yellow and purplish. "May I come in?" she asked.

"You must be Jenny?" asked Olivia going over to her.

"Yes, miss."

"My name is Olivia."

"Hello, Olivia."

"My name is Kate."

"Hello, Kate."

"Come on in," said Olivia leading the way. "This is Jessica, Rachel, Penny, Jack, and Henry."

"Hello," she said.

"Hello, Jenny," they replied.

"Does your arm hurt?" asked Penny.

"Not too much but it gets itchy," she replied.

"Where's you mom?" asked Kate.

"She'll be here in a minute."

"I'm right behind you, honey," said Elizabeth joining her.

"I brought some candies for Thomas," she said showing them.

"Do you want to put them on the table next to his bed?" suggested Kate.

"Okay," she said walking over, reaching up, and placing them down, then struggling to look at Thomas.

"Dad, why don't you put her on the bed?"

Henry placed the little girl at the bottom of the bed as Olivia stood next to her.

"Is he sleeping?"

"Yes, he is Jenny," she replied.

"Can we wake him up?"

"Not now honey, he needs his rest."

"Soon?"

"A day or so."

"He looks sore."

"He's a little sore, but he'll get better, just like your arm and chin. See, he has a cast on his leg and a bruise on his face too."

Jenny examined him then looked at Olivia. "I made this for Thomas, it's a Christmas card," she said handing it to her.

"Kate, come over and have a look," said Olivia waiting for her to join them.

They gazed down at the round head with hair, eyes, and a smile, wearing a triangular gown with two stick arms, hands, legs, and feet protruding out of it, and a halo hovering above it.

"That's Thomas, he's my Christmas Angel, and he's floating over the earth and taking care of me," said Jenny. She took the card from Olivia and opened it up. "I wrote something inside. Would you like to hear it?"

"Yes," they replied happily.

"My mommy helped me," she clarified, then read it:

"Dear Thomas,
My Christmas Angel,
I told Santa that I didn't want any toys for Christmas.
Instead, all I wanted was for him to make you all better,
and I know he will.
Merry Christmas,
Love Jenny."

"That's beautiful," said Olivia.

"Would you like me to put it on the table next to his candy?" asked Kate.

"Yes, please," she said watching her. "I'm going home today."

"You are?" said Olivia. "Just in time for Christmas Eve and Santa."

"Uh-huh," she replied. "Can we come here tomorrow evening before I go to sleep?"

"Do you like singing Christmas carols?" asked Olivia.

"Yes, I do."

"Good, because we have some singers coming in around dinner time and you can sing with them."

"I would love that."

"Maybe we should ask your mommy first, what do you think?"

"Mommy, can we?" she asked turning to her.

"As long as it's…" started Elizabeth, then quickly noticed Olivia and Kate smiling and nodding. "Of course, we can."

"Yay!" she said joyfully before facing Olivia and Kate. "I'm sorry I was a naughty girl and got Thomas hurt."

Olivia and Kate's eyes filled with tears.

"It's not your fault, honey, and don't you ever worry about that," said Kate. "Okay?"

"Okay," she repeated then hugged them. "Can I give Thomas a kiss goodbye?"

"I think Thomas would like that," said Kate moving her up the bed.

Jenny leaned over and kissed Thomas on the cheek then Kate helped her down and they watched her skip over to her mother. "Bye, I'll be back tomorrow," she said waving.

"We'll see you then," they replied.

"Bye, and thank you," said Elizabeth then held Jenny's hand as they left the room.

A few minutes later, a priest came in and asked how everyone was doing. He said a quick Mass, blessed Thomas, and gave out communion to those that wanted it. "I'm here Wednesdays and Fridays, and will be in

Christmas Day afternoon, so I'll drop in and see you then. I'll also mention Thomas at the Masses, and offer him our prayers," he said pleasantly before departing.

Olivia glanced over at Henry snoring then turned her attention to Kate who was staring out the window.

"It's still snowing," she said moving away from it and joining her.

"A white Christmas," said Olivia holding Thomas's hand and watching Kate as she sat next to her. "He was so excited about us spending our first Christmas together and we had everything organized. On Sunday and Monday, we were going to go shopping for gifts, and on Tuesday evening, I was performing in the Nutcracker, and afterwards, we were going to The Duke for something to eat and a drink; Thomas loves those fish and chips," she said with a grin. "Today, he was supposed to be going with my dad and Frank to get fitted for the tuxedos and I was going to slip out and pick up his gift." She tried desperately to hold back the tears. "This evening, Thomas, my dad, you, and I were going out to buy the turkey, the groceries, the beer, and wine, and when we got back, we were going to have some eggnog, watch the fireplace, and listen to Christmas music. Christmas Eve, Penny, Jack, Jessica, and Rachel were going to meet us in the afternoon at the outdoor ice rink, and we were going to skate to the festive music and drink hot chocolate with marshmallows. Afterwards, we would drop in and have a drink with Frank, then the four of us would go back to our place, put on the fireplace, and watch Christmas movies." The tears started to roll down her cheeks. "On Christmas morning, I would watch Thomas open his gift and see the surprised look on his face, and I would smile because he would be so happy. Then he would give me mine, but first make me guess at what he had bought me," she said with a giggle and wiping her eyes. "Everyone would come by in the afternoon, and we would have a wonderful dinner, play silly games, have fun, and laugh. On Boxing Day, we would all go up to Jack's cabin, take a sleigh ride, go skiing, and tobogganing. A couple days later, we would go to Manhattan and visit my dad, and go for a horse drawn carriage ride through Central Park. On New Year's Eve, we would watch the ball fall at Times Square, and I would turn to Thomas, kiss him, and tell him I loved him, then remind him in sixteen days we would be married, before singing 'Auld Lang Syne' with him." Olivia paused and stared at Thomas with a distant look in her eyes. "Kate, I want him to come back to me," she said breaking down and sobbing. Kate held her, and they sobbed together.

Chapter 58

Christmas Eve

Thomas was surrounded by light, and the darkness was a basketball shape off in the distance, and it was shrinking at a much greater rate than the light had expanded. He knew once the darkness disappeared something bad would happen because the pain was becoming unbearable. The murmur had now become familiar fragmented sounds.

"Hello, Thomas, the girls have gone to get a shower and change their clothes, and Penny and I wanted to take this time and let you know that we are both hoping that you get better soon, and also to tell you we got you a membership at my golf club as your Christmas gift. I know you probably would have objected, but it was something we wanted to do. Besides, I would feel a lot better you beating me there as a member," said Jack chuckling a little. "You've been more than a good friend to me, and when I look at you, I think of the son I never had but would have wanted. So, you have your rest, get better, and when you're ready, you come back to us soon." Jack had so much more to say but the tears streamed down his face, and he had to walk away.

"We all miss you, Thomas, and we're looking forward to you and Olivia getting married, seeing you grow as a couple, and having a family," said Penny reaching out and touching his arm. "Your grandmother liked Olivia immensely, and she would have been overjoyed knowing that you two were tying the knot. In fact, when you two were younger, we always hoped you might end up together, so don't disappoint us now. We all love you, Thomas, and we're all praying for you, and it would be the best Christmas gift if you were to open those eyes and smile." Penny began to weep and sauntered over to Jack who held her. When Rachel came in, they left to give her some time alone with him.

"Thomas, I have your Christmas present under the tree. Now, I'm not going to tell you what it is because that will ruin the surprise, besides, I know you'll be waking up soon and I'll be able to give it to you in person and see your reaction. You're going to love it!" Rachel thought she was going to handle this a lot better but was already crying uncontrollably. "Oh, Thomas, why did this have to happen to you? We love you, and miss you, and we need you here with us now. Wake up, Thomas, wake up! Heaven can wait!"

Olivia, Kate, Henry, Rachel, Jessica, Penny, Jack, and Frank played Christmas music and decorated the room, then they sat and talked about Christmas, the snow outside, and skiing. At five o'clock, Jenny, Elizabeth, and Jenny's dad, Chet, joined them. Dressed in his sergeant's uniform, he thanked Thomas for saving his little girl's life and saluted him before placing a rosary in his hand. He then told Thomas that Elizabeth had given him that rosary to make sure that he came back safe from the Middle East, and now they wanted him to have it to ensure his safe return back to his family and friends.

At six, Frank, his family, and the Village Choir arrived. They sang Christmas carols and told Christmas stories while Eileen served homemade sandwiches and Penny poured apple cider and eggnog. At eight, Chet, at his daughter's request, recited *'Twas the Night Before Christmas,* then at ten, everyone except Olivia, Kate, and Henry, left. They sat next to Thomas and talked about how nice it was having everyone around and how special the day had been, during which, Olivia would periodically glance over at him wishing he would open his eyes.

"Thomas, I'm going to put on some Christmas movies, the first is, *It's a Wonderful Life* with James Stewart, I know that's one of your favorites, and the second is, *A Christmas Carol* with Alastair Sim." Olivia pressed play, sat next to Thomas, and held his hand. Henry fell asleep in the chair before the first movie ended, and Kate, lying on the cot, fell asleep halfway through the second. Olivia watched them both, and made comments throughout them to Thomas, then turned off the television and there was an unsettling silence.

She turned to him, played with his hair, and thought. "Thomas, we have so many wonderful memories and I remember every single one of them," she said half-smiling. "There was that time we met in May during the intermission of Giselle, then there was the fundraiser, the cathedral the next day, and afterwards we went for a long walk, talked and laughed," she said starting to feel better. "Remember when you came to my house for dinner, we danced to our song and watched those old romantic movies, then the following day we went shopping. That was so much fun. Then at Jack's cabin, where we confessed our love for one another and had a romantic dinner. The next day we went on the picnic, and I danced for you, and you read poetry to me." She contemplated momentarily. "I love singing and dancing for you. Do you remember when I sang with the saxophonist in the park and afterwards danced on the stage for you? And then you watched me dance at my debut and I got to kiss you right after my performance. Did you know I got in trouble for that? I told them I didn't care, and if they wanted to fire me, go ahead, fire me! They just asked me not to do it again, but I will if I want to," she said giggling and smiling at him. "You've made me so happy, in fact, I've never been happier in all my life. And I'm so in love with you, and knowing that you love me just as much, makes it so special and so perfect," she said before admiring her engagement ring. "I'm looking forward to being Mrs. Olivia Carlyle, and married to the world-famous writer, Thomas Carlyle. By the way, you still have to read me your first novel, you promised, and now you have to read me your second." She was starting to get upset and paused briefly. "Thomas, we still have so much life to live, so many memories to create, and love to make," she whispered, then leaned over and kissed him on the mouth before returning to her seat. She noticed the time and gently caressed his face. "Since it's 3 a.m. and Christmas Day, I guess I can tell you what your gifts are. Now there are three, so if you wake up today and you remember them, pretend you don't and act surprised, okay? Promise me? Good. The first one, well, I was supposed to go to the store yesterday and pick it up, but as you know I was here. I really wanted to show you and see your reaction, but thinking about it now, it would've have been more fun me telling you anyway…Ready? Here goes. I've booked us on a trip in August for three weeks. Guess where? Okay, I'll tell you. The first stop is in London. I thought we could spend three days visiting Buckingham Palace, Trafalgar Square, and Piccadilly Circus, see some shows, and have fish and chips in a cozy English pub. On the fourth day, we leave London via train through the Chunnel to Paris and stay there for three nights. They say Paris is for lovers and is very romantic, which suits us to a T. While we are there, I thought we could take a boat ride on the Seine, visit the Eiffel Tower, and have a glass of wine at some quaint sidewalk café. After Paris, we fly to Cannes, and have fun in the sun for two whole weeks; I know how much you wanted to go there. In the evening, we can eat delectable meals, go to the casinos, and dance the night away. In the day, we can lie on the beach, and go for a swim in the Mediterranean. Oh! Guess what hotel I booked? That's right! The Carlton! The one John Robie and Frances Stevens stayed at, in *To Catch a Thief,* you said you always wanted to stay there. Doesn't that sound so wonderful and exciting?" she asked staring anxiously at him, waiting, hoping for a response, but none came. It was too much for her, and she cried for a while, then eventually stopped, and wiped her eyes. "The second gift is more personal," she whispered caressing his hair. "You don't know this, but in my spare time I choreographed a routine for the Genesis' song 'Firth of Fifth.' Do you remember I borrowed your CD to stretch to? Well, I know how much you like them, and you know how much I love that song, so I choreographed a special ballet for you. I was going to take you to the theater on Christmas morning and dance for you on the stage." Olivia suddenly realized that would have been later on this morning and tears rolled down her cheeks. "But we can wait till you're better and I can perform it for you then, okay? I know you will love it," she said quickly wiping them away. "My last gift is something very personal and incredibly special…I want to have children, not immediately, but sooner rather than later. I knew you would be ecstatic about that," she said smiling "Remember when we were in Manhattan, that morning in bed, I was going to tell you then, but I changed my mind and decided I would surprise you on Christmas Day instead." She suddenly became upset. "If only I knew then what I know now, I would have told you that morning, but how was I to know," she said fighting back her tears. "You're probably wondering why I changed my mind? Was it the little girl on the bicycle in the park? Perhaps it was me teaching the children ballet? Or when I was holding the baby in the kitchen? Maybe when we were making sandcastles with the kids in Aruba? Or was it what my father told me? Maybe all those events contributed, but the main reason is that I love you, and I want us to share our love with one another, have children, and share our love with them. And I want to see our children grow, have children of their own and be grandparents, and have everyone over for Christmas dinner. I want a family, a family of our own, and I want us to grow old together," she said and began to sob. "Thomas, I love you, I miss you, and I need you. Please, come back to me!" She put her head on the bed and wept, then slowly dried her eyes, looked at him, and softly sang 'You're the Best Thing.' "Thomas, that's our song, so if you can hear me, please, come back to me…come back to me…come back to me," she whispered, then cried herself to sleep.

Chapter 59

4 A.M. Christmas Day

The darkness was quickly fading in the distance, and the faster it faded, the more excruciating the pain. When it had completely disappeared, Thomas was surrounded by a bright light, and the pain was killing him. The vague fragments of sound had now become words, and Thomas could hear Olivia's voice saying, "come back to me." She had found him, and Thomas knew she needed him. He had to go to her and slowly started moving towards her voice. When her talking stopped, so did he, and when she started to sing, he recognized their song and started moving swiftly through the white light towards it. As her singing became louder, the bright light around him started to shatter and break up, and he felt as if he was falling at an incredible speed. Olivia's singing became clearer, and he could distinctly hear the words. The light disappeared and he stopped suddenly, and everything became blue. The blue light slowly dissipated, and objects gradually came into view. He was in a hospital room, hovering high above and looking down at himself. He could hear Olivia repeating, "come back to me," and see her crying at his side before falling asleep. Unexpectedly, he was turned around and thrown with great force toward the bed and back into his body. The pain was agonizing, and he fought desperately to open his eyes, but his eyelids were too heavy. He needed to see Olivia, he needed to be with her, he needed her. Thomas realized he was fighting for his life…Suddenly, everything went dark.

At 4 a.m., Thomas slowly opened his eyes. The room was out of focus, and he waited till his eyes adjusted before glancing over at Olivia asleep on the bed; she looked so beautiful. Her head was resting on his hand and with all his strength he slowly moved his fingers. She started to stir. He moved them again. She quickly realized what was happening and looked up at him.

"Thomas?" she whispered.

"Olivia," he replied softly.

She moved closer and kissed him gently. "I thought I had lost you."

"No," he said. "You found me."

"I did?" she asked as tears of joy ran down her smiling face.

About the Author

Kevin McGann lives in

the small, friendly town of Aurora,

Ontario, Canada.

You can contact him on his website:

www.kevinmcgannauthor.com

Or on Facebook:

Kevin McGann – Author